Daughters
of the Labyrinth

By the Same Author

Daughters
of the Labyrinth

RUTH PADEL

corsair

CORSAIR

First published in the UK in 2021 by Corsair

1 3 5 7 9 10 8 6 4 2

A CIP catalogue record for this book
is available from the British Library.

HB ISBN: 978-1-4721-5639-6
TPB ISBN: 978-1-4721-5640-2

Typeset in Caslon by M Rules
Printed and bound in Great Britain by
Clays Ltd, Elcograf S.p.A.

Papers used by Corsair are from well-managed forests
and other responsible sources.

Corsair
An imprint of
Little, Brown Book Group
Carmelite House
50 Victoria Embankment
London EC4Y 0DZ

An Hachette UK Company
www.hachette.co.uk

www.littlebrown.co.uk

In memory of Nikos Stavroulakis
artist and scholar
who rescued Crete's last surviving synagogue
and made it a place of prayer, recollection and reconciliation

Look how a single candle can both defy and define the dark

ANNE FRANK

I was gazing at the sea, trying to make out
a ship sunk here years ago ... The broken masts
rolled to and fro at an angle to the deep
like tentacles, or the memory of dreams ...
I'm not talking to you about the past
I'm talking about love.

GEORGE SEFERIS, 'Thrush'

CONTENTS

Nikos Stavroulakis

The World Can Fall to Pieces Any Moment

1

Yellow bananas. Custard yellow, in a blue plastic crate the colour of evening sky. Each skin has its own pattern of black streaks and dots but in this dim light they all have a mysterious blush, a kind of inner gold.

Black, gold and blue on the floor of the Afghan grocers in the high street and tears in my eyes. Everything reminds me of David. Three years without him is nothing. You get on with it, the pain becomes an everyday white noise, then some stupid thing like bananas hits out of the blue.

They're not really bananas anyway. I know now, they are plantains disguised as bananas, reminding me how David and I brought them back here with apologies, they were bought by mistake, could we exchange them for bananas? The Afghan owner, who was so kind to me later when David died, roared with laughter. We all laughed. Right here.

I blink away the tears, buy coffee and gingernut biscuits, get out on the street, go down the alley into the park. Wet green grass, pure white sky, a few boys kicking a ball and a line of bare trees at the far edge of the playing field. I like English trees in winter, when you can see the forms and they are not cluttered up with leaves.

The phone buzzes in my bag.

'Good luck tonight, *chryso mou!*' My brother is speaking Greek because that's our language. He doesn't speak English except when selling CDs to tourists or taking them out in his boat.

'Nikos. Is Mama OK?'

She's over ninety. She had a fall last week. They say once an old person starts falling they fall again.

'She's fine. Will you bring a catalogue at Easter? We're dying to see it.'

'Mama too? I don't believe it.'

He laughs. Mama was always prickly about me painting at home. They run a B&B, still do in their nineties, she always said paint made a smell, guests hated it, and we had big rows when I was young. But when David died I thought, dammit, I'll go back to my roots, *paint* my roots – the town, the mountains, the family. Mama said just come and relax but the others leaned on her. I even did a portrait of her, which may be the best thing I've done. She'd never allowed me to even draw her before.

'She's suspicious,' says Nikos, laughing. 'But curious. You know how she is. Vasilis is longing to show off the catalogue in his hotel. *My sister, the famous artist. Here's one she did of me.*'

We laugh, we love our brother Vasilis really, we chat on and I don't notice those boys have stopped kicking their ball until I'm surrounded.

'Speak *English*! You're in fucking England!'

'Shut the fuck up!'

'Go back to your own country.'

Three of them. Shaved heads. Only about sixteen, but big. I've heard of people getting punched in the face for speaking Spanish, Polish and French. I can see a few people the other side of the park but over here I'm on my own.

'Can I help you?' I pack my voice with forty years of English husband, English daughter, English colleagues and students. 'Come on, guys, let me pass, I've a sick kid at home. I need to get back.'

'You were speaking foreign.'

'Speak English, you're in England,' repeats the shortest. His face is white as the sky. A scalp of dark fur, hand on his belt.

4

Four stabbings in Camden last week.

'I *am* speaking English. Look, let me through, I've got to get home.' I start walking forward. The tallest leans back just enough to let me by, as if he isn't really doing it. When I get out of the park I phone Nikos back. I'm fine, send everyone my love.

Nashita is on the doorstep. An elegant Indian woman of sixty, well, she must be sixty-two as we're exactly the same age, in a smart green coat and skirt.

'Ri! At last!'

We have only seen each other twice these forty years, when she passed through London. She's never come here to the house. Short curly hair, that's new. But same heart-shaped face, high cheeks, mischievous eyes and glowing skin like the moon is alive beneath. My sparky slangy friend. My closest friend, when the two of us were the only foreign students at Camberwell School of Art.

I knew her before I knew David. She was there when I met him.

We hug. By sixty-two, you've got a hundred selves buried inside you. I don't know all hers now, and she doesn't know mine. We did know, at twenty.

'You've cut your hair,' I say. 'So glamorous.'

Over her shoulder, in the hall mirror, I catch a glimpse of the me she is seeing. Small and dark, like a feral pony. Greek tragedy eyes with shadows under. Polo-necked sweater, a helmet of black hair and dark eyebrows, one higher than the other, feathery at the inner ends, flicking up to little points. Lucky not to be getting wrinkles, good. Deep furrows round my mouth, not so good. Cheeks sunk as if I was biting them inside. When David died, I got out of the habit of eating. My daughter Katerina made me eat but now I'm on my own I don't, much.

The kitchen is full of fuzzy morning light. Nashita smiles. 'Where to start, yaar?'

I got an email from her after David died, saying how sorry,

how sorry. And last week another, saying she was passing through London, saw my show was opening, could she see it with me? Now here she is, in my kitchen, waving a gingernut in the air before we take the bus to the gallery. She prowls around lifting photos and drawings as she used to do in my bedsit. Each of her black curls is outlined in a strand of white like a night portrait in oils.

When we first met, we were both between cultures. She made sense to me when the English did not. It was the Seventies. We bonded over our shock at English winters, English food.

That's why they had to colonize us, Nashita said. To get a decent meal. That's why they scorch themselves in our sun, I said. To get warm.

We had both pictured a safe clean country full of polite people and were surprised to find this was not true. But the English had politenesses of their own. I once stepped on a woman's toe in the bus and *she* apologized. I tried to imagine a Cretan doing that.

Nashita had it worse because of her skin. She was called names in the street.

Why did you come to London? I asked once after a horrible encounter on the Tube.

For paintings, man.

Of course. That's what England meant. Pictures we had studied in reproduction we could now see for real, free. We didn't want a famous teacher to tell us how to be a successful artist, we wanted to discover what painting could be, what *we* could do. Our tutors didn't take us seriously, we were foreigners and, worse, we were women. They never mentioned any women painters, they didn't take even the Bloomsbury painters seriously. Their greatest compliment was to treat us like men.

The male students saw us as oddities. We didn't jump flirtatiously at any chance to model for them or the professors, or any of the big male artists who blew through, we just wrapped ourselves in our foreignness, ignored the rivalries, and worked. We also talked for hours about subject, content and form, especially a painter I'd never heard of whom Nashita revered. India's pioneer modernist, she said proudly, and showed me colour Xeroxes, dark glowing paintings, women carrying water, women whispering together. Earth tones, flat blue shadows, rust red, blazing orange, lizard green. They excited me, they made me want to paint like that. Dark, mysterious, powerful – and by a woman.

Amrita Sher-Gil, said Nashita.

Amrita died at twenty-eight. She was a girl, like us. Before she died, she blazed new paths for all Indian painters. But, like me, she began in Europe. She was only half Indian, the other half was Hungarian-Jewish.

One of her paintings, *Two Girls*, seemed miraculously to be about us, but also about her own half-and-halfness. A European girl with no eyeballs, as if she was blind, as if Amrita's European self couldn't really see. And an Indian girl in shadow, like a dark part of herself she did not yet understand.

She had to migrate to India to find it, said Nashita. That's when she took off.

I was fascinated. I too wanted to migrate to paint. By now I had a Jewish boyfriend, had met David and his family, and loved their warm English-Jewish life. So that was another link to Amrita. I also felt a silly private claim. When I learned to talk as a baby, I could only say one syllable in any word and called myself Ri, short for Arianna. The name stuck. At eighteen, my name being part of Amrita's felt like a sign.

Nashita and I began calling ourselves the two Amritas. Like her we felt divided, between *I have a world inside which these people know nothing about* and *I'm lost in this snooty place I don't understand*. But the worlds we had left, and the role the English played in them, were very different. Nashita told me stories passed down in her family about the British in India that horrified me. Racism, injustices, all the exclusions. Then partition, when many of her family, whom she had never met, went to Pakistan.

Filthy Brits, she said, laughing but not. How to repair the damage is one thing. How to move on is another. And who you are. As an artist, a person.

She looked at people walking down a grey cold rainy English street. There's a lot to exorcise, she said.

But for me the English were a force for good. The history I knew was Cretan resistance to the Germans in the war, which my dad played a small part in as a teenager. The British were our allies, the people who helped. Yes, they could be patronizing, but English archaeologists discovered the palace of Knossos, which was now boosting tourism, and my English godfather got my dad a job and paid for me to come to London to study. Nashita was at the heart of the empire that exploited her country for centuries, but the empire that exploited Crete for centuries, the people we fought against and got massacred by, were the Ottomans, the Turks.

So here we both were, in London. Did the two Amritas want to stay, in this country of watery light and even more watery food? No, said Nashita, and went back to India. But, despite the cold, and the food, I did want England as my country. It had David in it now, and his family saw England as safety, as generosity. He was born here, he was passionate about making documentaries, he had discovered what he wanted to do, and so had I. We wanted to do our work side by side, together. So we did.

Nashita looks at a robin on the birdfeeder.

'That's nice. We have flowers on our balcony in Mumbai but I'd love a real garden.'

'This one's gone wild. I've hardly touched it since David died. The bushes have turned into trees.'

'So sorry, Ri. Awful. Awful.'

8

'He was just crossing a road. The truck driver did his best to avoid him.'

It happened on the way to the corner shop. I was out, I was teaching, he must have been taking a five-minute break to get milk for his coffee. I know exactly what he was doing – planning his documentary on homeless hostels and people who work in them. He'd worked on it for years, we talked about it, I went with him to hostels in Camden on winter nights and did drawings. He was concentrating. That's why he walked out without looking.

'He was so gentle,' Nashita says, looking at the robin.

'Do you mind no milk? I forgot to get any. David liked white but I drink it black.'

'Black's fine.' She wraps her hands round the mug.

'Do you ever get any Amritas in your gallery?' I want to move on. 'There was a show at the Tate. So exciting, seeing her actual paintings.'

'We get small ones sometimes. I advised on that exhibition but I couldn't come, my mum fell ill.'

'Oh – is she . . . '

'Yes. She passed. Both my parents are dead now.'

'So sorry, Nashita. I should have written.' How lucky I am my parents are still around. In their nineties, but still here.

I know practically nothing about Nashita's life in India. I know she has two sons, and a husband I met once at a party. She won't know much about mine either, she has never met Katerina. We have to pick up with each other, really, from how we were as students.

'We so should have kept in touch.'

'We were so far away, man. Different worlds. Do you paint here, at home?'

'Come and see.'

We take our coffee across the hall. Our voices echo up the stairs. I'm used to being alone here now but it seems wrong, a whole house to myself.

9

'We've been here thirty years. It was falling down when we got it. Peeling wallpaper, gas mantles poking through walls.'

I open the door. The room used to have a blue carpet, which David knelt on to spread out his papers. Now there are bare boards, canvasses against the wall, paint tubes scattered about.

'Still the bad habits! You left paints on the floor even as a student.'

'I must need chaos, mustn't I? I draw all the time, but I can't do it in a sketchbook, so there are loose sheets all over the house.'

I pick up two tubes, check the tops are straight and drop them on my paint-carrier, the trolley David and Katerina gave me for Christmas when Katerina was ten. I remember her giggling. *A hostess trolley.* Hilarious. Choosing it with Daddy in John Lewis had been an adventure. Now it's covered in jars of brushes, fossilized dabs of colour. In one corner is a tower of hard pigments piled on each other like coins. Old friends like Naples Yellow, Alizarin Crimson, Burnt Sienna and Chrome Green.

'This used to be David's study. When he died, I did a painting of it.'

'*Paint!*' says Nashita in a growly voice. '*There lies salvation.*'

'Good old Cézanne.'

We laugh, remembering the men who taught us at Camberwell. They were scarred by awful things they had seen in the war, and were desperate for certainty – which they found in Cézanne. Cézanne was God. Every word he wrote, every word he said that someone randomly remembered, was dinned into us along with the paintings.

We loved Cézanne too. But we wanted the opposite, we revelled in his uncertainty. We loved the way Cézanne mixed perspectives, painted from several points of view at once, spread out an apple so you saw its other side.

'Where's that painting now, Ri?'

'New York. There's a gallery there that takes my work now, which is nice. But I kept some sketches.'

I find one. It flops in my hands and feels furry and helpless. I lean it against a wall.

'I borrowed from Matisse, painting his studio red. Mine's blue.'

Blue for grief. Blue for David's carpet and the blues David loved. No shadows, just floating biros, books, video boxes, his chair and laptop, the printer that kept breaking, and his mobile. All adrift. Like me when I painted it.

I stand awkwardly while Nashita looks at it. Always nerve-racking, showing your work to someone whose opinion you care about.

'Lost in the blue,' she murmurs. I'd forgotten how quick she is to see the point of things, how she gets what you are doing and takes it further.

'*That's* what I should have called the big painting, *Study in Blue*. When I painted it, I felt like a ship sailing out of my own life. Then we cleared this place. You can't live with a closed door, can you?'

'So you went back to your roots, isn't it? Crete. Your new show. That's what the gallery website said.'

'Yup. Katerina went to New York, everything turned nasty here with Brexit talk, and I scuttled back home. My old safe place.'

My last show was very dark. David was doing his project on homelessness and I shared that with him. The hostile environment was getting to both of us, I found myself painting city streets at night, rough sleepers under flyovers. Ironically, now he's dead, the new show is all light and colour. I was desperate to get back the brightness I grew up with. A bit of joy.

'You were a happy child, yaar?'

'Sure. My parents struggled, after the war, but things were easier by the time I came along.'

11

2

'What's really going on in this country?' Nashita stares at passengers on the bus to Shoreditch. 'What are all these people thinking? Everyone in Mumbai says, *Why are the Brits tearing themselves apart?*'

'I'm not the one to ask. I've thought of myself as British, on and off, for forty years, but I'm more and more not. Everyone here now is fed up. They don't know if Brexit is happening, should they sell a house, get a job? I don't have a UK passport, I have to apply for something called Settled Status, which they say you can only do on an Android phone. It's a mess, families and friends divided, everyone furious. You can't know what anyone's thinking except they're angry and upset.'

We get off in the rain and walk through cool London, designer London. Noodle bars, pop-up boutiques and vegan cafés.

'Last week someone scrawled swastikas and *Hail Boris!* on Oddbins in Hampstead. *Hampstead!* All four of David's grandparents migrated here from Kiev to be safe. But hatred has happened so quickly.'

'Happened?' says Nashita, ducking an umbrella. 'Or emerged? You're not telling me it wasn't there in the first place.'

'Well . . .'

'We have it too. A friend from Bangalore showed me messages from the WhatsApp group in her apartment block. *Kill them! Rape their women! Get Hindu seed inside those Muslim bellies!* She's the only Muslim there.'

'Are you safe?'
'Oh, Mumbai's OK. For the moment.'

We reach the gallery, stand on a rainy pavement beside a craft beer shop, and Nashita looks at the painting we picked for the window. *White Mountains*. A hundred grey pinnacles. Hazy shadows below, a thistle-blue sky above.

'They're the heart of Crete, those mountains.' I sound like a tour guide, exactly what I don't want. 'That heap of stones in the foreground used to be a cottage. Put in my name when I was born. For my dowry, imagine. Sort of thing that happens in Crete. Maybe that's where I'll go if Brexit kicks me out.'

'You never said much about living there, back in the day.'

'I was eighteen, wasn't I, obsessed with getting out. When I was little, I was wildly proud of Crete. Still am.'

She looks at me as if she is going to say something, and doesn't. I take her inside and introduce her to Josh and Marcus.

Josh is Publicity. He has a shaved skull and a neat brown beard. Katerina calls it a Hoxton Hipster. Marcus owns the gallery, selects the artists and shows, is quiet and fair and savvy with a dusting of acne scars over his cheeks like rosy gravel, and beautiful grey shirts he somehow makes look raffish. He has money behind him but also a real love of contemporary art. Under a gentle, old-fashioned courtesy he is very determined.

Also brave. I'm not cool by today's standards. I was, twenty years ago. But after shows everywhere, Rome, New York, Sydney, Hong Kong, and paintings in the Imperial War Museum and National Portrait Gallery, my career began slipping a bit. Then David and I met Marcus by chance on Crete. Marcus was at Christie's then and we got on. He loved Crete, it started as a holiday friendship but he got interested in my work. When he opened his own gallery, he offered me a show and when David died he encouraged me to paint at home, in Chania. He has the

13

confidence to back me, he makes me feel wanted and understood. What more can an artist ask?

'Nashita and I were at art school together,' I tell them. 'She runs a gallery in Mumbai.'

Josh makes coffee from his new toy, the espresso machine, and Nashita reads words stencilled on the wall that were not there last night, when I left.

Vibrant new work from Ri Gold. We know her as a British artist, celebrated for her expressionist landscapes, poignant figuration and social themes, generating uncertainty over questions of identity, violence and power. But after the tragic death of her husband, prize-winning documentary-maker David Gold, she turned to her Greek roots, experimenting with looser brushwork and heightened colour. Here are cities, mountains, myths from her native island of Crete, land of the labyrinth and Minotaur, and intimate portraits of her Cretan family.

In front of Nashita, I'm embarrassed. I can't bear to think of all the people coming tonight for the opening, reading this the moment they walk in.

'We said we wouldn't mention David.'

'Darling, they like a personal angle.' Josh's hands make unapologetic circles in the air. I can tell Marcus wasn't sure about the David bit, but most of those words are his.

Nashita walks into the first of three white rooms. I follow, letting the paintings take hold, and feel a lift of lightness. Maybe those words are OK. Maybe there'll be something new for me after this.

The first room is Cretan dazzle. Bright strong colours, big canvasses. Nashita laughs and puts a hand over her eyes. I grin. What people say about your work, especially at this moment when

14

it's unchangeable, can really go through you. Even the most well-meaning friend can make you feel raw. But I'm not apologizing for the colour.

'I was getting back the sun in my heart.'

The first is *Glass-Bottomed Boat*. Broken shapes, looming through diamonds and swirls.

'My brother's tourist boat. It has a glass hull. You look down and see the ocean floor. If you're lucky there's an octopus or turtle. But also the wreck of a plane from the war. Always in the same place, unlike the turtles.'

Nashita laughs again. There are too many pictures to take in and she picks the brightest, all ochre and gold.

'*Rooms Karderini?*'

'That's the house where I grew up. My parents let rooms to tourists. *Karderini* is a thorn-bird, a goldfinch, no idea why they called it that. I think they had more fruit trees once, so maybe there were more birds. The place used to be a market garden. My dad jokes that first they grew vegetables, now they grow tourists.'

'What are those shadows round the door?'

'Just – shadow. You have to have the dark. Otherwise it'd be chocolate-box Crete, tourist Crete. Cretan light is dry and very sharp. You're as close to North Africa as Europe. Very black shadow. The contrast's really violent. Isn't India like that too?'

I think of painting for hours in that unrelenting sun, with such loud screaming from the cicadas you forget to hear them. Like you forget you are sheathed in an envelope of sweat.

'Well, you painted those shadows,' Nashita says. 'But I see menace in them.'

'Funny things happen in that light.' Funny things also happen when people ask about your paintings. You start to think you're hiding some deep truth. I'm really not. For a second I'm furious with Nashita. And with everyone coming tonight who might see things that aren't there.

Opening nerves. You arm yourself and go on.

Nashita moves on to the only dark painting in this room. *Shelter.* A winter painting. Hooded figures standing, leaning, immersed in mobile phones.

'That was the first I did.'

I was all over the place when I got there, nothing worked, I thought at least I could be useful. Crete doesn't have refugee camps, like the islands near Turkey, but a lot of families have been settled there and the system's really groaning. There's a wonderful humanity in Greece, always, but the refugee thing is a real crisis, everywhere. This centre, the Lemon Tree, gives clothes, food, help with the system, and Greek lessons. All sorts of lessons. I did drawing workshops. Some of the girls were brilliant. Finally I painted this. Not their faces, but they felt OK with me painting them like this.

'Lot of despair.'

'Yup. People covered in shrapnel scars. People who lost children and husbands. Kids who've gone mute, who saw their parents die. I didn't want to make art out of their suffering, I wanted to say something like, your stories are our stories. You are part of us.'

'So what's all this about being a British artist?'

Damn Josh. I laugh uncomfortably. 'What *is* a British artist?'

She smiles, walks on to the middle room and stops by my big experiment, a hanging of waxed cloth. At first, you think you are looking at a globe floating in blue sea like Earth in space. Close up, you see it is a labyrinth of interlocking figures, with a bull's head at the centre.

'This must have taken ages.'

'It did! And research. I put Minoan figurines from Knossos alongside the old Cretan myths. There's Europa, look, and the bull that took her to Crete. That's the beginning of Europe, Nashita – a kidnapped girl.'

Nashita laughs the boisterous laugh she always had, and peers at the bull's head.

'Europe is also the monster under the palace,' I say, rather self-conscious now. 'Crete has so many earthquakes some people say that's what the Minotaur was. When the ground shook, the Minotaur was stirring. Others say it's the beast at the heart of civilization, the monster in the human psyche.'

I remember the winter I spent working on this, in Knossos. Making connections, looking at statues, reading the myths. Trying to sort out the stories inside us – inside me, anyway – from what archaeologists found in the earth. Wondering if it was all a muddle of interpretation. Archaeologists dug that palace up while Freud was digging up the unconscious. Can anyone be sure about any of it?

'They build labyrinths in ashrams today,' says Nashita. 'Walking a labyrinth is big business. It's fashionable, man. The route to enlightenment. They say it promotes healing.'

'Not with a Minotaur in it.'

Museum Courtyard took ages too, for different reasons. Personal, not mythical. Or maybe those are the same. I look critically at the sunlit garden and broken statues. Two distant figures by a table and a blood-red poppy in the foreground, rising like a resurrected spirit.

'That small guy's my dad. The other's my English godfather.'

'Your benefactor, isn't it? The one I never saw. He was always going to come and take you out to dinner and never did. I was so disappointed. I dreamed he'd benefact me too.'

'When I was growing up, he was with us every summer. We called him Mr Michael, he was a kind of summer uncle. He gave me my first real watercolour paint-box. It had a metal lid that doubled as a palette. I used it for years.'

Nashita looks closely at the figures.

'Handsome guy, what I can see. Giving nothing away, though.'

'He was with my dad in the resistance, but really he was an archaeologist. I became obsessed with archaeology. It was glamorous on Crete then. Anyway, I thought so. I called it the dark trade of the earth.'

We both burst out laughing.

'It sounds better in Greek. Funny ten-year-old I was. He introduced me to the museum and I started sketching bits and pieces there. Someone told me Minoan Crete was the lost world of Atlantis, I loved the idea of objects from a lost world. Then I started painting. Mr Michael encouraged me to apply for a grant, he paid for me to come to London. I owe him my whole career.'

The last room is portraits. That was Marcus's idea. First the town, then myths, then faces. Mama's eyes stare from the back wall.

'Do you paint your family a lot?'

'David and Katerina, yes. Here. In Crete, I sometimes drew Papa, my brothers and their families but I'd never painted them before. See, London was where I worked. Crete was holiday-time. That changed when David died.'

Nashita glances at her watch, passes by my brothers, and pauses at my self-portrait. I look rather fierce, with circles under my eyes. Gazing at it with her, I suddenly feel something is missing, some inwardness. Nashita says nothing and goes on to my parents.

'What are their names? How odd I've never known.'

'Andonis. And Sophia.'

We stare at them. One light portrait, one dark. First Papa, sitting in sunlight in front of a yellow wall. He was eighty-nine when I painted it. His long beaky nose. The broken veins, the wrinkles everywhere. I called it *Papa with His Broken Pots*. His hands rest among scraps of clay that have lain apart three thousand years. You feel his fingers itching to search out edges that might join up. You also want to smile, or I do. I feel that warmth of his shining out into the gallery.

'You adore him, isn't it? He's an archaeologist?'

'Oh no! I don't think he even went to school. He worked for archaeologists, mending ancient pots.'

18

Now Mama. Her forehead criss-crossed with wrinkles, like linen wrung out and hung up to dry. The slug veins of her hands. *Mama, you're so beautiful but you've never let me paint you. Can I, now? Well . . . You'll have to sit very still. I know.*

'Portrait of the Artist's Mother,' Nashita says. 'So formal, man. Do you get on better with your dad?'

'It's a different sort of portrait. His is outdoors, natural light. Hers is more – traditional.'

'What's that saucer she's holding?'

'Her hairpin-holder.'

Her fingers are too clumsy for embroidery now, but they were always busy when I was young. I tipped the hairpins out and asked her to hold it. Even so she couldn't keep her hands still, she kept stroking chase-lines in the bowl.

'You've got her cheekbones, isn't it? And eyebrows. But hers are symmetrical. She must have been stunning when she was young. Have you any photos?'

'No.'

'What's that empty birdcage?'

'Always been in their room. I liked the shape.'

'What's she scared of?'

'That's just how she looks, sometimes. She's in her bedroom, nothing to be afraid of. But she'd never let me paint her before. She really didn't want to sit.'

When my dad saw his portrait, he laughed and said, *I look like my grandfather.* When my mother saw hers, she said nothing.

'Got to catch that train,' says Nashita.

At the front desk Josh is nudging wine glasses into line and Marcus is piling catalogues. He gives one to Nashita.

'What are these amber spirals on the cover? We didn't see that.'

'A small painting in the myth room. A snail shell on a thread. The labyrinth in miniature.'

Josh wanted my mum's portrait on the cover, but that might

cause difficulties at home and anyway I wanted this. Daedalus, the artist who built the labyrinth for King Minos and also a dancing floor for my namesake Ariadne, was asked to thread a snail shell. He did it by tying cotton round an ant and smearing honey at the mouth of the shell. The ant crawled through and got the honey and Daedalus got his thread through the shell. I love that story. It seems to me to sum up everything. The quest. The problems we have to solve when we start a painting. I often feel like that ant.

Out in the rain, Nashita says, 'Marvellous show, Ri. Wish I had more time. The colours – the shadows! Very Amrita.'

She pauses. I know what's coming. The *but* every artist dreads, even with their closest friend. Especially with a friend. And Nashita is a gallerist, she judges paintings all the time. I might learn from whatever's coming but I don't want to hear it just now.

'They're beautiful. Vivid *and* subtle. Very powerful.'

'But.'

'Something's missing, isn't it? Disruption. The darker edge. Something cutting through familiar stuff. I don't think Crete's done with you. There's more in the shadows than you've said. And surely more sea, in Crete? Not just through the bottom of a boat.'

'You think you've done something, then your oldest friend says you've missed the point.'

She laughs. 'Not missed, man. They're gorgeous! The light, the rhythms. The colours and patterns. You know that. But there's something – I don't know – withheld.' She is silent a moment. Rain drums on her umbrella. 'What are you going to do now, Ri?'

'No idea. Amazed I've got this far, to be honest. Withheld or not.'

'Come and paint in Mumbai. See what we're doing there. We've got wonderful painters, doing all sorts of new things. Let's hatch a plan, yaar?'

20

'What an idea! I'd love that.'

'I'll have a think about studios.'

I suddenly remember how hope feels. Fruit on every branch. We hug again. The two Amritas.

3

Tonight's the opening. Alone in the house, the March evening dark outside, I bat away first-night nerves, try to do up a necklace David used to fasten on me, and worry about *withheld*. Did Nashita think the work was facile?

The clasp won't click. I swing the thing round, peer in the mirror, flick back the little hook and look myself in the eye. My face in a frame. The same oval shape as my mum's, but hers is classic beautiful. As Nashita said, mine is not symmetrical. My eyes are hers, brown with light flecks, but seem to challenge rather than offer mystery. Plus I carry my chin too high, I know that from press photos. And I have my dad's eagle nose.

The phone rings. Nikos again, but anxious and urgent.

'Mama's had another fall. She's in hospital, unconscious. Can you come?'

One call, and the person you are falls apart. I start breathing very fast, I feel like a smashed lightbulb. 'Nikos look, look Nikos, I'll ditch the opening, I'll come now, get a night flight, did she hurt herself, what's wrong . . .'

'No, darling, go to your opening. Tomorrow's fine. I'll be with her all night, they say she's stable, nothing's broken.'

'How's Papa?' My voice sounds weird. Something in me, maybe my brain, is suddenly raw and flinching. Terrified.

'Exhausted. But he won't go home. I'm in the corridor, he's

sitting by her with his *komboloi*. The doctor was good, but he's gone. There aren't any nurses.'

'Can you find a private one?' Everyone does this, if they can afford it. There never seem to be enough public nurses. 'I'll pay. I'll stay there with Mama from tomorrow night.'

No direct flights till Easter. I'll have to wait for hours at Athens. With the time change, it'll take all day. I'm due to go at Easter anyway, this is only a month early. My hands are trembling, the internet is maddening, but I manage to book a flight to Athens at nine, then another to Crete in the afternoon. That means airport at seven, leave here five-thirty.

In the Uber to Shoreditch, I WhatsApp Katerina. *Granny ill, going Chania tomorrow, talk later if you're free?* Then I'm standing in yellow light spilling onto a pavement crowded with smokers, and people getting out of the crush. The gallery window is like an aquarium. My reflection, black dress, necklace, black hair round a very white face, overlays the White Mountains. And behind them everyone drinking and talking.

Inside it is so full I can't see the paintings. Who can? What the hell's the point? Marcus puts an arm round me, Josh ushers up seriously rich collectors, I smile, I can't hear what any of them are saying, and old friends hug me, people who bought my work early on and now show up to give support. I spot critics in the crowd, some who like my work, some who don't, and exchange smiles with artists who know what this moment is like.

I also hear a lot of people talking Greek. Josh has organized Greek canapes, *dolmades*, mini cheese pies. Some people – not Greeks – are drinking retsina, where did Josh get that? There's a girl from the Embassy. A tall silver-haired man from Mykonos expects me to know who he is, though I don't, and invites me on his yacht. I escape and hug ex-pupils, chat to art students in black leather with silver chains and emerald lipstick, art students in cherry velvet, bowler hats, mauve hair and peacock feathers, students who actually go close to the work and look at it. I love them, I feel at home with them. But while I whizz round in a defensive daze, Mama is unconscious on a hospital bed and Papa is beside her with nothing to hold onto but his *komboloi*. I leave early, soon as I can.

'Mum, what happened, how's Granny, shall I come?' Katerina's voice is high, almost accusing. She lost her dad so suddenly, now Granny's in hospital and she is far away. We are both due there for Easter in a few weeks anyway, she is making a documentary on refugees, she wants to sort out filming access for Chania's ref-ugee shelter.

'Tell you tomorrow, love. I'll see how she is. If you have to come now, I'll pay your flights. But let me get there and see.'

'Oh Mum.' A little sob. 'How was the opening?'

'All right. I left early, to pack.'

'You OK?'

'Yep. Bit of a shock. Goodnight, honey.'

I'd better pack for some time, who knows how long I'll be stay-ing, I'm finding it hard to think straight. Passport. Euros. Warm clothes, cool clothes. Crete changes so violently this time of year, it can be freezing or boiling. Pencils, graphite, oil paints, sheaves of paper. I can get materials in Chania but I'll be stuck in the hospital and I panic without paper. My normal drawing-diary is loose leaves but I unearth a spiral notebook just in case. Not sure about charcoal, it's difficult to fix in a sketchbook, but I pack some anyway. Then I set the alarm on my phone and turn off the lamp, wondering if Mama will be alive when I wake. The glow of the bulb dissolves in the dark.

At Heathrow next morning, the sky still black, I settle into the limbo of transition. As a student, I used to see myself as Persephone, travelling between English dark and Cretan light.

24

Even now, the journey still has the romance of the in-between. People lining up at Gate 25 are souls waiting to cross the Styx.

I ring Nikos. 'How's Mama?'

'Still breathing.'

'I'll be there by eight.'

'Room thirty-one, sixth floor. We'll have food for you.'

I buy a pack of Cadbury's Flakes. It's not summer, they won't melt. Papa loves them and you can't get Cadbury's in Crete.

In the first plane I see cracks of watery sunrise through streaked plastic. David would be getting out the Greek phrasebook now, and peeling a tangerine. He always brought tangerines on planes, he said they were very refreshing. At Athens, I walk from International to Domestic, gaze at hills wreathed in pollution haze and spend hours drawing at a café table. A Greek newscaster on a TV screen says Earth has reversed its magnetic field. What it is like, to reverse your magnetic field?

I ring Vasilis.

'I'm waiting for the Chania plane. Did you find a nurse?'

'I'm collecting one today. Bulgarian.'

'Do they know what happened to Mama?'

'A heart event.'

The plane bumps, judders, drops a little. Seat belt signs come on. We're going through grey cloud, solid as packed snow. Then we're flying through last tassels of sunlight and I look down at a wrinkled sea like ripples etched in lead, and papery frills of foam round a rocky coast.

A line from the *Odyssey*, dinned into me patriotically in the Chania classroom, pops into my head. *The island looked like a shield laid on the misty sea.* Crete turns beneath us like a jewel, speckled with mossy light. For a second we seem to be plunging into that misty sea, then we are lolloping over tarmac at Daskalogiannis

Airport, named for a Cretan resistance hero who was flayed alive by Turks in the 1770s. We have long memories in Crete.

On top of the aircraft steps, in the swift twilight that comes down on your skin like a shawl, I stop to look at darkening hills. In the taxi I see pale spikes of asphodel in the fields, roll down the window and let in the night. Black hills flow by and then it is all bare rock, tumbling ravines, the smell of new grass on the wind.

The hospital, built in a gentle valley outside Chania at a moment when Greece was doing well, is surrounded by these hills. I get out of the cab and breathe smells of earth. The white glow of the entrance shines through olive leaves. Inside, the corridors are dark with many missing bulbs. We're lucky a generator is still going.

There are two wings to this building, I don't see which to choose and there's no one to ask. A friend who works in a Heraklion hospital sometimes gets a *negative* pay packet. A month's work, then a slip saying she owes the state her insurance. After ten years of economic crisis, pensions slashed, salaries on hold, the hospitals are struggling. But I find the right floor finally, and track down a small dim room with dark figures, silhouetted against a faint loom of light from an outside lamp, who resolve into my family.

Nikos kisses me and takes my bag. I hug Papa, his gnarled hands, his face chilly even in this sickroom warmth. Nikos introduces the nurse they have hired. A bulky woman, Bulgarian, with a wide pale face and hair in a brown frizz round it like the lion in *The Wizard of Oz*.

'Kyria Bisera knows the hospital. She's found a mattress for you.'

'Thank you, Kyria.'

Bisera smiles, and answers in Russian-flavoured Greek. 'Pleased I helping your mother.'

'How does she look to you?'

'Very well. She will waking soon.'

'There, Papa.'

26

'The doctor came,' he says hopefully.

'He said high blood pressure has damaged her heart muscle,' says Nikos, looking at Bisera. 'And she may have – a diseased valve?'

'Heart muscle it is thickening,' she says. 'Tomorrow, they will testing.'

'She's going to be OK?' I hear my voice go up like Katerina's.

'The doctor says yes,' says Nikos.

Something has happened to my knees. Nikos propels me to the chair. I see Mama on her back hung about with instruments and wires, and put my cheek against hers.

'Mama? It's Ri, I'm here.'

We all listen to her jagged breathing. Her lips purse in a thin O. From those famous beautiful cheekbones, her skin sags inward like soggy parchment.

'Ri, dear Ri, welcome,' whispers Vasilis's wife Irene. She is small, solid, kind, and a brilliant cook, and shows me three foil-covered dishes as if the whole point of this gathering is my supper. 'Chicken, rice, *horta*.' She spoons food onto a plate. 'Salt. Lemon.'

One of the differences between my two countries. Hospitals don't really provide food. That's what families do. Heaven help you if you haven't got one.

'You've thought of everything, Irene.'

'It's easy for me. I take food to the refugee shelter every day. In the hotel kitchen, we have the dishes, it's easy.'

I love her. She and Vasilis run a hotel, of course she takes food to refugees. I just hadn't realized.

'Papa, I'll be staying here now, with Kyria Bisera. Nikos will take you home. If anything happens, I'll call. We don't want you getting ill too.'

'You'll bring me back in the morning?' Papa asks Nikos. Father and son look at each other through these chiffon shadows. They are so alike. Both abnormally slender, though Papa has a little pot belly now. Both have bright hazel eyes. Nikos's nose, like Papa's,

27

looks like someone pulled down on it when it was still soft from the mould. Their laughing is one of the best things ever.

Papa keeps his arm round me as if he has to hold onto something, anything, female. Nikos steers him to the door. 'I'm staying with him,' Nikos whispers, meaning he'll sleep over at home. Papa can't look after Rooms Karderini on his own. Even if Mama lives, we'll have to make changes now. Nikos's daughter Leila works there during the day, but maybe Nikos and his wife Loukia should move in. Or me. Could that be my answer to Brexit?

My brothers live the life I would have lived if Mr Michael's bounty hadn't swept me off to Camberwell. Vasilis, oldest of us, is deep embedded in the tourism Chania depends on and runs his own hotel. Nikos's music shop and radio job don't make much, so a few years ago David and I gave him money for a boat. Nikos made a fuss about taking it but loves the boat. He has a gift for enjoying, he takes tourists out from Easter to October. Occasionally, after a lot of raki, he'll say Crete should split from Greece and be independent, as it was for a while after the Turks left. It even had a parliament. Then he plays his lute and calms down.

I picture him taking Papa home, trying to raise a smile, and Papa gallantly responding. They are alike in the way they face things, and joke their way through if they can.

When everyone leaves, I spread my mattress, Bisera closes her eyes in the armchair and I hear an owl call outside. Mama and I are alone, as if in the heart of a snow-globe.

4

I don't want to sleep. This time alone with Mama won't come again. Her hands hold each other slackly on her chest. One has a cannula in the back. A mottled knuckle catches the violet-yellow glow from a lamp outside. I imagine painting her like this, then rest my head beside hers on the pillow and try to face something I've spent my life not facing.

Nashita was right, I did always get on better with my dad. The divide was deeper and earlier than those teenage rows over painting. She got on fine with my brothers, but with me there was always something missing. I could never do anything right, I thought it was my fault. When David died, missing him opened it up again – how she seemed to resent what I became.

One thing I became was a Daddy's girl. Mr Michael was with us in the summers, working in the museum and I hung out with him and Papa. I told myself I didn't need Mama. It was a sadness I buried in some deep trench in my soul. The afternoon before I left for England, I sat sorting paints at a patio table. I was eighteen, nervous about a new country. The gate squeaked, I squinted though my fringe and saw Mama walking down the slope. I thought she would stop and talk. She did hesitate a moment, but then disappeared in the house. We didn't have another moment alone before I left.

After that, I made my life in a language she does not know. Most people meeting me for the first time in Britain think I'm

British. Mama and I grew closer when I had a daughter. We were here for summer and often Easter, the most important moment of Mama's year. Yet there's a gulf. I've never known why.

Her breathing is noisy but regular, like waves on a shore. *In. Out. In.* Her skin is the texture of wax, with an eerie glow like a candlelit turnip.

What do I know about her life before she had us? She grew up in Chania, I don't know where but a lot of the city was flattened in the war. She lived through the bombing but would never talk about it. I think that's when her parents died.

I know her father was a silversmith, Papa met her when he built her dad a shed. Her best friend Eleni lived next door and was in her class at school. I don't know her parents' names, but she called her mother Moumo. 'I had my own pet name for her,' she once said. 'My own, no one else's.'

Moumo, this unknown grandmother, was a mythical figure to me when I was growing up. I knew she was very beautiful, she kept her dowry rugs in a painted chest, and loved brushing my mum's hair. That's it, Mama would never say more, she made us feel it was wrong to even wonder. I grew, I learned the sorrows of Crete, the history of risings and massacres and the more recent history of the war, and assumed this wonderful being had died in the bombs.

Papa told us more about himself. He was born poor, in Chania. His father made musical instruments but got cancer when Papa was five. For the next five years, he lived in the mountains with his mother's family. When his dad finally died, Papa was sent back to Chania to live with his mum and crippled grandfather and ended up supporting them, aged about twelve, by manual labour and carpentry, which he taught himself with his father's tools.

He was an only child, like Mama, but had an older cousin Georgios, son of his father's older brother, who often led him into scrapes. Just before the war, Georgios worked as a labourer for the

British when they were fortifying Crete, and wangled Papa a job with them a while. Papa loved Georgios's family, loved visiting their village in the hills, but that village was massacred by the Germans and every man in that family died, except Georgios. It is one of Crete's many famous tragedies but for us, because of Papa, it was personal.

That was why Georgios and Papa joined the resistance. They were only teenagers, but Papa knew the mountains and became a messenger, while Georgios was a fighter. Papa thinks Georgios must have been killed. He doesn't know as he himself was wounded, he can't remember how, and was ill for nearly a year.

The *andartes* he worked with, the guerrilla fighters, lived in one of Crete's many caves, which seemed thrilling to us when we were small. That was where Papa first knew Mr Michael, who was an archaeologist co-opted as an agent by the British. After the war he stayed with us every summer. He taught Papa to mend pots and got him a job in the museum. Papa was lame from his wound and Mr Michael paid for an operation so it didn't hurt.

Mr Michael was a glamorous figure. He was English but worked in America, brought us presents, we looked forward to his coming. He played football with my brothers and tried to teach them cricket too, but it didn't take. He funded a hotel management course for Vasilis, bought Nikos an antique Cretan lute, and made us feel special because he knew Crete in a special way. A deeper way, I annoyed my school-friends by insisting, because he knew what lay under the earth.

When I started going to the museum where Papa worked, and drawing archaeological bits and pieces, Mr Michael was delighted. He worked in the museum all summer and he and Papa often swapped stories there about life in the mountains. Painting away in my corner, I felt proud to be part of their memories. Now, as Mama lies here unconscious, I suddenly wonder what she made of that and whether she minded.

Bisera gives little rusty snores. Her sleep makes me feel more alone with Mama. I close my eyes and wake when I hear a little snuffle from her and a whimper.

'Mama? You OK?'

'Where am I?'

'You're safe in bed. In hospital. You've been ill, but you're going to be OK. They've all been here, Papa, Nikos, Vasilis. They'll be back tomorrow. Want some water?'

'Will you say *kaddish* for me?'

'*What?*'

She's silent.

'What did you say, Mama?'

Christ. *Christ.* What was that? I feel I've been hit round the head. After a moment, her breast starts juddering up and down, her hands unclasp, and the one without the cannula crawls over the sheet towards me. I put mine down, she clutches it.

'Will you?' she whispers urgently. 'Nikos, Vasilis and you too? All of you? Say *kaddish?*'

She really said it. Is she delirious? Maybe that heart event affected her brain.

She is getting agitated.

'Of course, Mama, if that's what you want. But you'll be fine, we'll take you home, Katerina's coming for Easter.'

That seems to calm her. The clock ticks, the corridor seeps yellow light under the door, the heating whirrs, instruments buzz. Her forehead is dry and cool. But the world is exploding in little senseless pieces. I've never heard that phrase, *say kaddish*, in Greek. I heard it first in English, when David's aunt died. Then they said *kaddish* for David. But there are no Jews on Crete. I got suspicious looks when I married one. There is lots of antisemitism here under the surface. David never saw it, he had some quality of sweetness that made even people who couldn't speak his language be nice to him straight away.

32

There must have been Jews here long ago. A ruined synagogue was renovated for the tourists, and I remember a nightclub I was too young to go to, called Synagogi. We have the Ovraiki, the Jewish Quarter, but then there's a Venetian Arsenal, a Turkish Fountain, Ottoman Gardens, Minoan ruins.

But Mama said it so naturally. She's peaceful now, and I'm the one in turmoil. I can't sit down, I lean against the windowsill gazing out at the dark, at Crete in the dissolving mystery of night, until the soft grey fuzz of dawn begins. The scrubby hillsides glow, the lamp outside goes off and Bisera wakes.

'How does she look to you, Kyria Bisera? She did speak at one point, but maybe she was delirious.'

Bisera takes Mama's temperature and we change her. Bisera does all the wet stuff calmly, kindly. 'Everything working. Is being OK. She will waking. No fever. No delirious.'

Her accent feels so trustworthy, like the click of a door, I feel her good prognosis must come true.

'Do you like Crete?' I ask. 'Have you been here a long time?'

'I like. I am here three years. Having garden. Lemon tree, orange tree.'

Maybe lemons and oranges don't grow in Bulgaria. I imagine her in Cretan sunlight, picking an orange for breakfast.

At seven, Nikos's wife Loukia looks in. She works in a popular vegetarian restaurant. Vegan has hit Chania now and the place is always busy, even in March before the tourists.

Loukia has dark red curls, brown-amber eyes, a creamy high-cheeked face, and adores Nikos. They are the happiest couple with each other I know, except my parents.

'Hey, Loukia!' I hug and hug her and suddenly want to weep. She smooths my hair.

'Did you sleep, Rioula? Want anything from town?'

'Nuts or seeds, to nibble? How are you, how is Leila?'

33

'Fine.' Loukia kisses Mama's forehead.

'Mama woke, once. Asked where she was.'

When Loukia goes, I look out of the window. The sky is smoked glass above the mottled patchwork of rock, scrub and olive trees. At eight, Papa puts his head round the door, wearing a burgundy cardigan I brought him from England, carrying cappuccinos on a little fibre tray. Nikos follows. He will take Bisera home and bring her back at six. Our little world is establishing a rhythm.

'Mama woke?' Nikos says. Loukia must have texted him. 'Did she know you?'

'Not sure.' Mama's question burns in me but I'm not going to share it, even with Nikos, until I've grilled Papa.

Nikos takes Bisera away, Papa places his coffee beside Mama, looks at her anxiously and takes his favourite *komboloi* from his pocket. *Komboloi* sweeten the passage of time, he says, but what they are crucial for is crisis. His fingers push beads down the string in pairs, frantically, over and over. He probably does not realize he's doing it.

I pull up the armchair, he sits down and takes her hand. Sunlight slants across the room, drops of condensation on the window are wild with glitter. Scrunching the beads in his palm, he lifts the cup to his lips, afraid it will be hot.

I look at his crinkly wizened face in morning light. The long curved nose I used to pat when he carried me in his arms, the eyes that love laughing. Insane to think there's a dark secret behind them. He is Papa, the light that saves, my pool of clear water. I thought. Now I wonder if I know him at all. I pull a chair up, knee to knee.

'Mama said something odd last night. She asked me to say *kaddish* for her.'

Silence. Maybe he does not know the word.

'It's the Jewish prayer for the dead. They said it for David.'

'She didn't know what she was saying.'

34

'But why say *that*? I'm sure she did. She thought she was dying and knew what she wanted me to do about it.'

Papa puts his hands on his chair as if it might take off to the moon.

'What *is* this, Papa? There are no Jews in Crete.'

This feels like the silence of the pyramids. Finally he says, 'We always said we'd never tell.'

'*What*, Papa? What would you never tell?'

Papa is always straight with everybody. I thought. But he does what he's told and Mama comes first. If he was commanded not to tell, he wouldn't. But this isn't only about Mama, this is all of us. Our history. I see Mama handing out Easter candles. Kissing the fat silver padding round the ikon of the Panaghia in church. Teaching us to cross ourselves.

Papa glances at me, then drops his eyes to Mama. He is like plaster loosened by demolition, falling away from a wall. I know he feels helpless between us, but I'm here asking the questions and Mama is asleep. Or unconscious.

'She said, better they never know.'

'Know *what*?' It is like seeing a sinkhole open in your front room.

'She was, she used to be.' He swallows. 'Jewish. A long time ago. She was Jewish.'

I take a breath to ask more but a young man in a white coat looks round the door. He is pale as if he has not slept for a month. His small chin and full upper lip give him the look of a harassed monkey, but dark circles under his eyes make him more of a panda. He looks as if he has been making pronouncements on life and death all night. Papa gazes at him like a sleep-walker.

'Good *morning*! Doctor Stamatakis. How do you do? How is she today?' He looks at notes on a side-table, takes Mama's pulse.

'I'm her daughter, Doctor. They said she had a *heart event*?' He is holding Mama's wrist as if listening to a bulletin from outer space. 'Is she going to recover?'

35

He feels her forehead, inspects tubes. 'She has stabilized. But we must reduce the likelihood of blood clots. The heart's a busy organ, it's got to keep pumping. We ran basic tests when she came in. Today we'll do more tests, and refine her medication.'

'She didn't recognize us,' says Papa suspiciously.

'We're putting many drugs in her, sir. They make her sleepy.' I like this doctor. He's not brushing Papa off, he's taking him seriously. 'Our drugs are conserving her energy for getting better. Her body is trying to recover. That's more important than recognizing people just now. They'll take her for tests at 11.30. I think we can be hopeful.'

He goes out. We sit and look at each other. Thank goodness Papa came clean about Mama before the doctor mentioned drugs. She will get better. But who is she? It's only just beginning to sink in that, all our lives, she has kept an enormous secret from us. And so has he.

The real pain is not that the world has fallen into little pieces, but that it is still here, whole and real and mysterious. And different from what I thought.

I watch Papa take Mama's hand and cradle it in his. We smile because the doctor said there's hope but there's a gulf between us and we can't stop here. I sip my cooling coffee.

'Papa?' He feels I'm accusing him. Maybe I am. 'What happened to her family?'

He looks at me. I feel exasperated and terrified, as if he and Mama are floating out to sea and I'll never know who they really are. I must calm down. Papa hates questions, he has to do things his way and his way is usually a story.

'Can you tell me about them? How did you meet Mama, can you say again, now I know she was Jewish? Everything you know about her family, from the beginning?'

'It was a difficult time.' The *komboloi* slip frantically through his withered fingers. 'English soldiers all over town, Italian planes

36

dropping bombs at Suda, food scarce. Then Kyrios Mois stopped me in the street.'

'Kyrios who?'

'Mois. Your mother's father.'

'What sort of name is that? Mois who?'

'A Jewish name. Mois Trevezas.'

My grandfather. 'When was that, Papa?'

'Before the Germans came. Before Easter.'

'Spring '41. You were fourteen.'

'If you say so.' He sounds creaky and mutinous, like a toy that might wind down. I'll get more out of him if I shut up and let him talk. 'I lived under the old fort in the Ovraiki. Your mum was called Sara, then.'

'*What?* You mean – not Sophia?'

I feel stupid and weak now. When David first met me, he thought I was Jewish. He must have seen in me, straight away, something I didn't know myself.

'Her Jewish name was Sara.'

I feel dizzy. The air in this little room seems suddenly full of dark wings. 'And she – Sara, Mama – and you, both of you, lived in the Jewish Quarter?'

He's often mentioned the shack he lived in with his mum, but I assumed it was on the outskirts. If we asked where either of them lived when they were children, we got fobbed off. *It was bombed. Everything disappeared.*

'Everyone was friendly in the Ovraiki,' he says dreamily, pushing beads with his thumb as if telling stages of a fairy tale. Maybe the *komboloi* help him remember. 'Christian kids, Jewish kids, all went to the same school. Not me, I was earning from age ten. But your mother went to school with her Christian friend, Eleni. People said hello in the street, they lent each other sugar and oil. Some people, like my mum, called the Jews foreigners. I took no notice of that till I worked for Kyrios Mois, in Kondylaki.'

37

'*Kondylaki?*' You can hardly move in that street in summer. Tourist shops sell postcards, jewellery and resin penises inscribed *Love from Crete*. 'Those are huge houses. Was Mama's family rich? Which house?'

He looks at me crossly. He hates being interrupted.

'The one with a lion door-knocker. Next to the house with a balcony.'

My Dad Is a
Glass-Bottomed Boat

5

So Papa, aged fourteen. I'll call him Papa because that's what he is, even though this history of his is so new. And also so long ago. He walked along the wall of the larger synagogue, where at Easter they baked the special Jewish bread that wafted lovely smells through these streets and made your mouth water. But the small man who stopped him in the street had said to come to the other synagogue, the little one, so that was the door he knocked at. It was beautifully polished. Morning sun cast stabs of shadow into foreign letters on the stone lintel above. The door opened, and the same small man, Kyrios Mois, looked out and smiled. Glasses, a bald forehead, a back-fringe of grey curls. You would never think he was father of the girl all the boys talked about, the most beautiful girl in the Ovraiki.

Mois stood back for him politely. Papa stepped in, and then unexpectedly down, to a courtyard in front of what looked like a church. When the door closed behind him he suddenly felt a stranger in his own town. His mother's stories of Jews killing Christian babies raced through his head, but Mois smiled and gestured to the building.

Welcome to our synagogue, Andonis. Kal Kadosh, Holy Congregation. We call it the Kal but its true name is Etz Hayyim, Tree of Life. It was a church once, but when the Turks bombed

41

Chania it cracked and the Venetians abandoned it. They made these streets into a ghetto, but when they left, that was good for us because the Turks took down the ghetto walls and gave us this church for a synagogue.

Papa had never heard of Turks being good for anybody.

Inside, the building felt like a church, with a pulpit at one end, an altar cloth at the other, but no crucifix, no statues, no cross. Mois bowed to what must be the altar. Papa felt uneasy at this foreign magic but the silence and grace of the place pooled in him like wine. He looked up and saw a balcony, half-hidden by a latticed screen. Delicate work, but chipped and broken.

That's what we want to replace, said Mois, and led Papa upstairs, to benches behind that screen. The women's gallery, he said. They take part in the service from behind this. Can you copy the design?

Papa made the screen outside his shed, which stood behind his mother's house on common ground, a grass-covered citadel on the old city wall. He kept his tools there, in his one private place. He remembered his father building it, when he was five and there were only a few bushes round it. Now it was entirely hidden by trees.

A few days later, he carried the screen to the synagogue and fitted it, imagining the pretty daughter looking through it to take part in some mysterious service. Then Mois asked him to check over the wood panels, benches and doors in the big synagogue too. Every surface must be perfect for Passover, no splinters or loose hinges. He led Papa into a courtyard with a fountain, then a large building with marble pillars.

This was the first building in Chania to have electric light, Mois said. My father worshipped here. So did my grandfather, and his father. Its name is Beth Shalom, House of Peace. This is the centre of our world, Andonis. Welcome.

When Papa finished, Mois looked at him rather shyly. My wife wants my workroom for a store-room. I'm a silversmith, I need a shed to work in. Can you build one in my yard?

Yes, sir, said Papa, thinking of his own shed. He could copy that.

Could you come now, and measure?

They walked down Kondylaki. Sunlight fell in honey stripes on women scrubbing doorsteps, old men chatting, children playing. Mois stopped at a front door with a lion's head knocker. The lion had a ring in its mouth and the wood was silver with age. Mois opened the door, touched a slanting twig on the door-frame and put his fingers to his lips.

We put God's word, he said, on the doorpost to our home.

Papa followed him into a stone passage. Through a door on the left he glimpsed photos in silver frames, a polished table, a glass-fronted bookcase. Passing a wooden staircase, rising to an upper floor, Mois showed him into a room with a workbench, tools and shelves. All this, he said, must go in the shed. On the other side of the hall was a kitchen where Papa saw a sink and another big table. He had never been in a house with so many rooms. Or tables.

Then a large woman blocked the kitchen from his gaze. There were gold flecks in her brown eyes and her hair was swept in two black wings around a perfect oval face.

My wife, Kyria Simcha, said Mois. Simcha, this is the boy who will make the shed.

She nodded stiffly and closed the kitchen door. Mois led Papa outside to a yard.

૭๑๑

it is a grey day with a smell of wood-smoke on the air
    the mountains float in a haze of ash-blue, first time she has
    been downstairs in three weeks

43

fresh-cut planks of wood are leaning up around the olive
tree, curls of wood-shavings are floating through the yard like
lemon peel
father tells her to walk round the olive tree ten times to
make her strong

she limps round the tree and comes face to face with a boy, the
sun comes out and lights his black hair
his face is deep brown, his nose hooks and humps like an
eagle's beak, he is so thin that when you look from the side you
feel he might break but when he lifts things you see strings of
muscles in his arms
she would like to draw them
when you draw a thing you begin to understand it

he says hello miss will you help me build this shed?

☙

Papa carried timber through the hall and saw the beautiful daughter at the top of the stairs. She hesitated, then began gliding down
towards him. Close up, he saw her eyes too were brown with gold
flecks. Her lips had a little flick each end.

Hello, Miss, he said. He laughed, he couldn't help it, she was
so crazily beautiful. Are you real?

She frowned, a little ghost of her mother's stiffness, but looked
as if she was trying not to smile. Later she brought him a sage
tea. Then he saw her in the kitchen, helping her mother struggle
with a cupboard door. Lavender spikes hung in bunches from the
rafters, silver, mauve and violet. Their sweet smell filled the air.
He offered to fix the cupboard and the girl stayed silent while he
tightened screws in the hinge. He suggested building shelves in
the empty room once they moved the tools, and the Kyria thanked
him. Then the girl spoke up.

Moumo's always wanted a store-room, she said.

My daughter, the mother said. Sara.

Sara asked if his own mother had a store-room. Papa laughed.
Our house only *is* one room. My mother has to store me. And
my grandfather.

This made both of them smile and he felt he had broken through.

He did not see Sara again that day but after leaving her house
he locked his tools in his shed, ran up the grass mound, stared
down at the sea, and flung his arms out to the wind. He stayed
a moment, staring at the blue horizon, then ran down for supper
to his mother's yard and suddenly saw his home through what he
imagined were Sara's eyes. What would she say to their one outside
tap, small table and corrugated metal roof sloping down from bare
rock? And, inside, the dirt floor that winter rain, pouring down the
rock face, turned to sloppy mud? Or the calluses on his mother's
hands, the bitter line of her mouth?

His mother, small, thin, in the rusty black she always wore,
was washing at the tap. She did not like him working for a Jew.
Her disapproval was unspoken but visible to him like the darkness in a crescent moon. He held up the money Mois gave, his
mother nodded and went on washing while bats swooped in the
darkening air.

Hello, boy, Grandfather said, and laughed. When Grandfather
was sitting down, you didn't notice his twisted back and legs. Papa
felt a rush of pity mixed with pride. He should not be ashamed.

Next day, as he was working in the shed, Sara brought a glass
of water. For a moment, she was just a silhouette in the doorway.
Then he took the glass, their fingers touched, he sensed the warm
softness under her blouse. He knew a handsome boy lived next
door. Jewish, and older than him. But people said that boy was in
Albania with the Cretan Division.

Ever been up Kastelli, Miss?

Kastelli, the hill above the harbour, the most beautiful place

45

he knew. From there you could see both harbours and far out to sea.

No.

Her breath touched the skin of his throat. They were alone with the clean hot smell of sawdust.

Like to go? On Saturday?

That's the Sabbath. I can't go out.

Sunday?

How long would it take?

An hour? Two?

All right.

He waited for her on Sunday. The sun was hot for March, he was sweating. When she came, they stayed silent a moment looking at each other. She wore a green dress and the wind whipped her skirt round her legs. He led the way down to the harbour and every time her arm jostled his, the touch seemed to clarify what was false in him and what was true.

The harbour was full of English soldiers unloading crates, pulling trolleys, pouring concrete plinths for guns, shouting in their foreign language. They heard the thud of distant gunfire and saw plumes of smoke from Suda Bay up the coast, where Italian planes were bombing British ships. Papa led her up wide stone steps into honey-coloured colonnades, past palaces, buttresses and creamy staircases like the sweep of a priest's robe at Easter, and stopped by an arch of golden stone.

Like to see this church?

I've never been in a church.

Your Kal was a church once.

They passed through a sunlit courtyard to a dim interior, heavy with incense. He watched her gaze at the soaring dome. Help me choose a candle, he said, for my father. Five candles were alight in the sand tray. He dropped a coin in the slot, took Sara's hand and guided it to new candles in the box. Her fingers twitched and he felt roused, instantly hard. He shouldn't be in this state in a church. She slid her fingers away, leaving a candle in his.

What's it for?

My father's soul.

He lit it. They both stared at the blue triangle, nub of the flame.

Your father's dead though, isn't he?

His soul's in heaven.

Is it? What do you believe, Andonis?

He looked round, at all the religious stuff he scoffed at with friends but secretly took for granted.

I believe in good *people*. Like my grandpa. And your dad. What do *you* believe?

I don't know.

He saw the strangeness of the place to her and remembered his fear of the synagogue.

Now I'm here, she said, part of me knows I belong with the prayers Father teaches me. But something in me always wants to do the opposite of what he says.

I think God is the same. Yours and mine.

Not *that*. She looked at the cross, the naked torso, the belly wound gaping like a gutted fish. We have nothing like that. Awful!

He laughed and led her to the top of Kastelli where sea stretched away all round them, blue-green speckled with white, up to a horizon of hazy violet. Below them, sunlight slanted on red-tiled roofs.

She gazed at the harbour. Where's our house?

Behind. In the Ovraiki.

So small! She stared at her home as she'd never seen it while Papa watched a small caïque enter the harbour. Men lay exhausted in the hull, flopped like washing over the side. At the quay, they struggled out. Some fell and lay on the stone, others ran to help them.

English troops, Papa said. They've escaped from the Germans in Greece.

She hid her face in his shoulder. He put his arms round her, smelled sun on her hair, locked his fingers in the hollow of her spine and felt filled with power and mystery.

What's going to happen? she whispered.

I'll look after you.

They stood holding each other, with wind around them and the untouched palaces below.

∞

she says don't move but sara does little frowns and sucks in her cheeks with hollows like leaf-shadow coming and going under her skin

they are sitting where they always sit, on the window-ledge, their backs against the shutters

she is using her favourite pencil with hexagon sides and light showers around sara in little waves spreading flickers down her hair

sara has an angel's face, everyone says that, sara's forehead is wide and smooth, her eyebrows are like a hawk's feather downy at the inner end, her chin is a soft point like the top of an egg, the upper line of her mouth curves like two birds facing each other stretching their throats up and beaks down to meet in a bird-kiss and when sara smiles their heads slide up and down

sara's breasts are nearly as big as mother's, they move under her blouse with lives of their own, what is that like?

maybe you can't truly see someone you are jealous of as well as love, or maybe love gets in the way as much as jealousy

she shuts her eyes

even in the red dark behind her lids she sees sara

when she is thirteen she is not going to waste time on embroidery

48

she's going to be an artist

and a skylark

༄

Suddenly, thanks to his cousin Georgios, Papa landed work until Easter with the English at Suda. Big money, but three weeks without seeing Sara! Still, he had to. He finished Mois's shed without seeing her, told Mois he would come back after Easter to move the things, and waited for Georgios at the harbour. It was dawn, the sea was furred with mist, the harbour full of ghostly cranes and cement mixers. Beside the Mosque of the Janissaries four machine guns pointed at the sky.

Hey, wanker, came a whisper. An arm jerked round his throat. Try this.

Papa smelt raki.

Get off me. He turned to see his cousin's broad face and bulgy eyes. We're in Lent!

So? said Georgios. It's dark, God's asleep! Aren't we *Cretans*?

Papa took a guilty sip.

My dad gave it to me, said Georgios. He was here last night, singing for English officers.

Did you sing too?

You can't compete with a dad, can you?

Georgios never remembered, or didn't care, that Papa's father was dead. Georgios didn't have to struggle to feed others. His mother owned land, his father was alive and working.

You've been working for Jews, said Georgios. Pretty girl, I hear. He began to sing, very softly.

Turkish girl, go to the mosque to say your prayers.

White roses in your chamber—

Is Turkish the nearest you can get to Jewish? Papa said scornfully. You don't *know* any Jews. They're Cretan, like us.

Georgios ignored him and sang on.

49

White roses where you sleep alone ...

The old song poured into the mist, conjuring Sara's face and shoulders so sharply it hurt. I'm in love, Papa told himself. He tasted those words, *in love*. They made him feel huge. Life had singled him out and was rushing at him from the sea.

The sky was lightening at sea, over the peninsula. A fat dark cloud shone silver at the edge, a scarlet rim shot up behind as if someone was pushing it from below, changed to a crimson crescent, an orange disc and then a white you couldn't look at.

Come on, said Georgios. A truck is picking us up.

Walking past the cathedral, Papa felt keyed and tense. Anything could happen. Rain had fallen in the night, mud gleamed like aspic, pools of water lay in it like mirrors. When the truck came, an English truck with English soldiers in it, the driver sat on the right, which Papa had never seen. They jumped up, clung to the back and were swept between groves of orange blossom till they looked down at the long shining arm of Suda Bay and its burnt-out harbour-front.

Georgios pointed to a ship crawling in from the open sea, followed by a screaming plane. Shells exploded round it in the water, one hit the ship, flames shot up and men jumped in the sea, burning as they jumped. Anti-aircraft guns spat. Shrapnel rained on the harbour like flung stones.

The English are bringing guns, trucks and soldiers, shouted Georgios above the engine noise. Men die out there the whole fucking time.

All day, through the crack of anti-aircraft, they shifted crates and boxes. At night they slept on a friend's floor. Georgios often went out in the evening but never invited Papa, he said he was singing for English officers and came back smelling of raki. One night he said, The Germans have *invaded Greece!*

You mean Italians, said Papa.

Forget fucking Italians – *Germans!* From Yugoslavia.

Next day he said, They've captured the Cretan Division. Our

palikaria are prisoners. The English say even Greek gods can't help Greece now.

Next day they heard the Greek armies had surrendered. And then, that the Germans were closing in on Athens. Crete would be next and everyone expected an invasion from the sea.

But the English paid Papa for his work, he bought lamb for his mother, leaped on the back of a truck and found himself arrowing through grainy twilight towards Chania, towards Sara. The wind was her hair, the rushing air filled him with power. He had meat in his hand, money in his pocket. He could do anything.

After three weeks away, Chania felt like a foreign country. Smoke from Suda hung over everything. Foreign soldiers, English and Greek, walked in shadowy groups along the waterfront. No lights in the harbour, all you saw was silhouettes and the red eyes of cigarettes. In the Ovraiki, that delicious smell of Jewish baking drifted through the alleys. Unleavened bread. He had smelled it all his life, never known what it was. Now he knew a Jewish family, he felt proud of it.

Welcome, boy, said Grandfather in the yard. Back from the wars.

His mother crossed herself. Don't talk of war. People say German tanks are in Salonica. They'll be in Athens any minute.

They won't come here, said Grandfather. We'll kick them out.

Our Cretan boys aren't here to stop them, she said.

Papa handed her the lamb.

Smoke was pouring from that Jewish temple today, she said sourly.

They have their festival too, said Papa. Their bread needs a very hot oven. It mustn't rise.

Why not?

Bad luck, I think.

Is it tasty? said Grandfather.

How should I know? Smells great, doesn't it?

Grandfather laughed. Bread's hard to find but we grow fat on the smell.

51

His mother went inside to put the meat away and Grandfather cocked his eyebrow. He talked with his eyes better than anyone. When Papa was small, and Grandfather was his protector in the mountains, he saw Grandfather's eyebrow go up like that in many places. Kind, when he twisted his ankle trying to rescue a lamb. Excited, when they saw a wildcat take a hare. Now it meant asking for help. He put his arm round Grandfather and half-lifted, half-dragged him to the earth closet behind the house. Grandfather hung on his arm, the smell was all round them, Grandfather wiped himself, Papa brought water to wash, helped him indoors and settled him on his couch. Grandfather lay back with a groan. Papa reached under the bed for the pistol, one of a pair that once belonged to Papa's great-great-grandfather who won a famous battle against the Turks. Grandfather couldn't walk properly but did have his *pistoli*. He slept with it clasped to his chest.

Next day Papa went to Kondylaki. The sky was pale blue, the mountains pearly purple, the air smelled of cinnamon and drains. He loved the alleys sleepy and empty like this, knife-sharp shadows on the walls, shafts of sun lighting the upper face of each house. It was hard to believe German tanks were in Salonica, but after Suda he knew nowhere was safe. He knocked on the door and stared at that little stick on the jamb. God's word. Did it forbid Sara to like him?

The door opened. Sara was so close he saw little gold hairs on her upper lip. She gasped, as if seeing him winded her.

I've come to move your father's things, he said.

She let him in without speaking. In the workroom, he stood beside her feeling every rise and fall of her breasts.

Welcome, my boy, said Mois. I have emptied the drawers.

Papa hefted the bench into the shed and went back for the equipment – a miniature anvil, tiny toothed blades, clamps, tongs, pliers, frayed leather gloves that looked too large for such a small man, and a vice with a horizontal cog-wheel.

52

My father's filigree machine, said Mois. Papa, remembering his own father, recognized the love of a craftsman for his tools.

You pass the silver, Mois said, through these holes, look, until it flattens. You twist the flat wire to make loops, then fill them in with these florets. With your skill, Andonis, you'd be good at it. If I'd had a son, I'd have taught him.

At the word son, Papa looked up and met Sara's eyes. She was standing in the doorway and glanced hurriedly away, as if he were someone who figured in an intention of hers but she didn't want to let him know. Then she looked embarrassed, as if he had seen her thought. Mois moved around the shed unaware, tucking things away.

Have to go, Sara said, and vanished. Papa felt stricken but Mois smiled.

Lots of kitchen-work needed now. Look, I've polished her Passover gift. It belonged to my grandmother.

He held out a necklace, a stream of silver flowers. Papa imagined them round Sara's throat, remembered the soft flesh of her hand and felt a surge of longing that made him feel both powerful and helpless. He walked to the door and held the necklace to the light.

The English are our only hope now, Mois said, suddenly behind him. But their soldiers are eating all the food on Crete. Simcha had to scrape to find any at all for Passover.

෧෨

a bird of her own, a real live bird
    sara says why'd he give it to you, she says do you want it
sara you have it, sara says what would I do with a bird and goes
out leaving a hot feeling as if sara had slapped her face
    she goes up to the bedroom and puts the cage on the chest
    she is sure it is a boy, he looks like a dreamy sparrow, his
pale copper head is fluffy round the sides, his black wingtips
latch together over his back and on each wing are white marks
like hooks or tiny skeletons dancing

53

under the black is a smudge of saffron as if he was all gold
underneath but covering it up

    he darts forward and pecks the thistle with his ivory beak,
small as the nail of her little finger

    she puts her face close and he flies up hitting his head
on the roof

    sorry

    he puts his head on one side, gazes at the saucer, flutters to
the floor and drinks

    when he jerks up his head a bright drop rolls off his beak as
if he were weeping

〇〇

6

Papa shifts uncomfortably, trying to get out of his chair. He's old, shrivelled and very frail. His face is yellowy, almost transparent in this light. Talking has exhausted him. I help him up, trying to fit what he has said into the stories I have always known.

I know the war began for Crete when the Italians invaded Albania. Greek armies, including the Cretan Division, all our fighting men, rushed off there and pushed them back. Then Hitler invaded Greece from Yugoslavia and they marched off to north Greece. But they weren't enough. Hundreds of German tanks rolled down through Greece. I also know that's when our one ally came to help – the British, bringing Australian and New Zealand troops with them. But they weren't enough either. Hitler captured mainland Greece in three weeks and then looked at our island, halfway to North Africa where the British ruled Egypt but Rommel was advancing, and the Middle East where the British ruled Palestine but Hitler planned to invade.

Now I know that this little family, my family, was meanwhile about to celebrate Passover and Papa was in love with their daughter.

And here he is, seventy plus years later, standing beside her swaying like a foal.

'Two minutes,' he mutters. He hobbles off to find a toilet and I get out my spiral notebook. Drawing helps make sense of the world. I draw Mama's unconscious face, the feathery silver brows,

55

the scooped beds of her closed eyes in their home of bone. Then the rhythm of the line in these alien tubes, that dangling piping running to her wrist and her flaccid, dead-looking arm.

Rhythm is everything. It directs all the tissue of a drawing. If you find it, you enter a world apart because all this is there already, it's the world, it's what you have to try to understand. I'm not making up the flow of lines, I'm following them. Also letting Papa's story soak into me.

Under the sheet, Mama looks like a figure on a tomb but the mystery of who she is and what she has been is so intense it nearly overwhelms me. So many confusing new pictures of her. My mother who taught me to pray to the Panaghia, gazing at a crucifix for the very first time? And both my parents, young teenagers in a time of chaos, unsure of each other but drawing together, lighting a candle in the first church Mama entered.

I'd like to paint that. The untouched faces, gazing at a stem of fire on an island about to be invaded.

I will her to get stronger. And then fucking *explain*. Our grandparents, what happened to them, what were they like?

The Holocaust was in Greece, I've never heard of it happening here. How can I fit that enormous thing into what everyone knows did happen here – the Battle of Crete, fought by British, Australian and New Zealand troops? Hundreds of them died here, they come every year to commemorate. And the famous Cretan resistance, supported by the British – how can I fit the Holocaust into that?

When the British lost Crete, they evacuated some troops to Egypt and told hundreds of others to surrender. Many refused. Cretan bookshops today are full of memoirs by British, Australians and New Zealanders who took to the hills and helped the resistance. Meanwhile, all those oddball Brits who knew ancient Greek were suddenly useful to British Command. People like Mr Michael who had excavated all over the island and were friends with the fierce mountain clans that later became centres of resistance.

56

But the Jews? Papa spoke as if there was a whole Jewish community here. Why didn't I push harder to discover what lay under our lives? Maybe I knew there was something I didn't want to find.

A porter trundles Mama away for tests. A nurse walks alongside, steadying the dangling tubes hooked up to her veins. Papa returns and looks horrified at the empty bed. I tell him they've taken her for tests. He goes to the window as if he hopes to see her outside, fingering the beads in his pocket.

'What happened to her family, Papa? And the other Jews?' That word seems to go on ringing like a struck wine glass.

'Taken away.' He keeps his back turned. I stare at the grainy cloth of his jacket, his bent bony old shoulders.

'Why didn't you tell us?'

He jumbles the *komboloi* harder. 'She said, better to forget.'

'But it's our family.' He limps to the chair and sits down. I feel a rush of love, pity and exasperation. 'Go on with how you got to know Mama. What happened after you finished the shed for her dad?'

'I got lucky.' A ghost of a smile. 'Her father asked me to escort them . . .' He stops. 'Sara had to have Hebrew lessons, you see. All the Jewish children, they all learned Hebrew. The teacher lived outside the Ovraiki and Sara was not allowed to go there alone now there were all those soldiers. She hated those lessons! But it was my chance. I said I'd take her after Easter.'

57

7

Andonis, April 1941

A south wind had been blowing, the really wild hot wind that sends you mad. Along with the feelings of helpless oppression that burdened everyone when that wind got going, Papa was bursting with anxiety to see Sara. But the wind dropped, leaving red dust from Libya over every surface like powder on a butterfly's wing, and on Easter Day, neighbours came into his mother's yard through the broken arch carrying chairs, tables, babies, and dishes of lentils, *pasticia*, potatoes. All families in their alley ate the Easter meal in his mother's yard, because she was at the end, she had space.

Christ is risen, Grandfather said and everyone said it back. Christ is risen.

The babies gurgled and laughed. There were no young men, they had gone to Albania and must be prisoners if still alive. Papa had been too young to go but the two sons of Stephanos the shoemaker had and the babies belonged to their wives. One, born the day its father left, was now six months old.

Vine-buds were breaking, young leaves rippled over everyone's head like green hands. Grandfather poured wine sent by Georgios's parents from Kondomari, their village in the hills.

Fasting gets longer every year, Grandfather whispered to Papa, winking as if he knew about the raki he'd drunk with Georgios.

His mother didn't smile, when did she, but Papa saw her pride when she brought the lamb. She had no husband but she had a son, she could put meat on the table.

Eat, eat, she urged.

Sara's festival was yesterday. Today, she would be free to leave the house and after everyone went to sleep, Papa prowled the maze of alleys until he spotted Sara outside her friend Eleni's house. The street felt like moon-land, uninhabited except for them.

Hello, Miss Sara. Miss Eleni, how are you?

Eleni smiled but Sara turned her head away like a cat. Was she ashamed of him? Shy in front of her friend?

Won't you speak? he coaxed.

She met his eyes. Why? she snapped.

Why do you think? he snapped back.

Her eyes were dark pools. He felt their darkness enter him. They stared angrily at each other. Behind her was a wall of cream stone with little holes. Then Eleni opened her door and the girls disappeared.

Next day he went to Kondylaki to take Sara for her lesson. Her face looked thunderous. Her hair was piled on her head, her throat looked too slender to hold it up, she did not meet his eyes. He led the way up Kondylaki, and then his secret path up between rocks onto the grass. They passed the trees that hid his shed and came to the rampart, covered in wildflowers. Sara's blouse was blue as air. She looked away from him over the sea.

You don't want to go, do you?

No! I never do the homework. I *hate* Hebrew. I'm alive, why should I learn a dead language?

She tossed her head. Her hair whipped Papa's face and he laughed. Sara thought he was laughing at her, then saw he was laughing at her hair in his mouth, and blushed.

They came down the hill, and into a garden of fruit trees, blossom and vegetable beds. An African man came to meet them. Papa

59

had seen him in town but never spoken to him. People said he had been a Turkish slave.

Tinu, muttered Sara to introduce them.

Papa found her sullenness a mystery. This garden was one of the loveliest places he had ever seen, and she seemed affronted by everything in it.

Tinu himself smiled warmly. His skin was black, a rare sight in Chania. He looked about sixty and moved in a gentle slumberous way, leading them down to a cottage where an old man stood under a pomegranate tree. Doves flew in and out of the branches. The old man's figure threw a shadow like a slanting column.

Kyrios Rafael, said Tinu ceremoniously. Kyrios Andonis.

Welcome, said the old man. His eyes glittered like pieces of sky. Tinu will make you coffee while we work.

Papa felt honoured. Coffee was scarce, he was only a boy, Kyrios Rafael was treating him like a man. When Sara went in for the lesson, Tinu showed him the garden. He was Muslim, also rare now in Chania. He cut winter greens for Papa's mother and gave Papa a glass of pomegranate juice.

Kyrios Rafael prepares the syrup in winter, he said. He breaks his Yom Kippur fast with this drink, and gives it to his pupils.

Papa sipped. He had no idea what Yom Kippur was but the drink was delicious. A white dove flew into the tree and Tinu led Papa under the branches, pointing out a complex of nest boxes he had fitted to the branches. Papa admired the craftsmanship. White doves with rosy legs flew in and out, and a cotton-woolly cooing bubbled from the boxes.

Dove City, Tinu said, smiling. When I first came, Kyrios Rafael showed me how to prune this plant. When it grew to a tree, I made these nesting boxes. Now it has a double harvest. Fruit and eggs.

They talked about the Germans in Athens, the Prime Minister's suicide, the thousands of English and Australian soldiers trying to get out of Greece. And what might happen here.

When Sara reappeared, she was crying. Kyrios Rafael laid a hand tenderly on her shoulder and Papa couldn't believe he was harsh. But her tears were his chance. On the way back he wiped them with his sleeve.

I should be kissing them away, he whispered. I will, if I catch you crying again.

She smiled. He said he had to go outside town next day, to work among the orchards of Perivolia.

But I'll be back in a fortnight to check on you. Then we'll see if you're still crying!

When Papa got home, his mother asked where he would earn money now.

Perivolia, he said. For two weeks. A rich man wants me to raise his fences to keep out foreign soldiers camping in his orchard.

They've been defending Greece, said Grandfather. They're brave English and Australian soldiers, here to defend Crete.

This guy wants to defend his property, said Papa.

What will become of us? said his mother, scooping Tinu's greens into a pan.

8

Simcha. That's the first thing I hang onto. The grandmother I always dreamed about. Now, my Jewish grandmother. Her name is a jewel rescued from the earth.

Papa has been talking slowly, not his normal storytelling flow but hesitant, like someone picking their way barefoot over stones. He's suppressed all this for decades, I guess it takes time to dredge up, but I'm floundering with the history. Tinu – a Turkish *slave*? Really? Four hundred years of Turkish rule is what we were taught at school. In Greece, that finished in 1821, but in Crete the Turks stayed on till at least 1900. If this man had been a boy then, well, yes, he could have been sixty when Papa met him.

I'm still trying to work it out when we hear wheels in the corridor and a porter pushes Mama in, still hooked up to her tubes. The sheet has fallen off her bare feet and her toes look awful, like crooked purple roots. Her bunions gleam, two shiny balls of bone. I pull the sheet over them.

'How were the tests?'

'Someone will inform you of the results.' The nurse checks the cannula and disappears. Papa sits down and raises Mama's other hand to his lips.

'Sara?'

Nothing.

'She's breathing, Papa. We have to wait. Tell me more about

her as a girl. I had no idea she knew any other language. Why was she angry that day, what had you done?'

He strokes Mama's hand.

'Girls are changeable. They blow hot and cold.'

Nikos puts his head round the door. He's brought lunch and I fling my arms round him, press my forehead in his shoulder. My brother, whom I can rely on, whose history I'm sure of, whom I'll share all this with when I know it properly. And when Mama's safe.

After lunch Papa dozes and I draw his sleeping face. Lines, wrinkles, long nose, stringy hands loose on his thighs, fingers twined through the *komboloi*, their tassel flopping on his jeans.

I'm desperate for fresh air. Since I got here last night, I've hardly left this room. The two of them should be OK a while, so I go downstairs. No one around. The hospital must run on a shoestring. I stand at the door looking out. The air is cool and fresh, the sky pale grey shading to an apricot flush above the hills. This is my home, the landscape where my parents grew up. And so did I. These slopes of olives, the rock and scrub scored with dark ravines and dotted with black pines, are as familiar to me as my own mind.

As a teenager, I came out this way with friends to small music joints with sawdust on the floor. One of my friends drove a furniture van, we would pile in and speed out here, first beside the black sea, moonlight on the waves, then up to these hills, and dance all night to the *bouzoukia*. Dancing, singing, scents of thyme and resin, and dawn breaking over the island Homer called hospitable, fertile, beautiful. A rich and lovely land, Homer calls it, we had to memorize the lines at school. Surrounded by wine-dark sea, he says. An island of ninety cities, five tribes and several languages. And also the island Hitler invaded when my mum was a Jewish girl of thirteen and Papa was falling in love with her.

I find a canteen in the basement and ask for two teas. A girl pours hot water on tea bags in Styrofoam cups. When I take them upstairs, Papa has woken and is holding Mama's free hand. The room feels rank with his distress.

'Here, Papa. Go on with your story. Where were you when the Germans came? Where was Mama?'

'They bombed Chania. For two weeks. I saw it from Perivolia, how they broke the town to pieces. I was frantic about my mum and Sara. But they said in the village, wait, you can't do any good by going there. And that man wanted me to finish his fences.'

9

Andonis, May 1941

Papa finished off the top bar of a fence, sat on a boulder and watched an old woman with a donkey dig a terraced slope. Two boys were herding goats nearby. The older was maybe ten, the little one six or seven, but he caught a straying kid expertly and brought it back to the bleating mother.

He saw a line of planes over the sea and heard ear-splitting blasts over town as they bombed Chania. Goats ran in all directions and the boys scuttled after them. The planes circled, dropped another round of bombs and flew away towards Athens, but then another line of planes appeared, eyelash-thin against white sky. They came in low, anti-aircraft guns fired and several broke up, bodies fell with the debris but hundreds more planes came on, wave after wave, not dropping bombs but flying up towards the hills, right over him. Then they too started dropping things but not bombs – parachutes, like shoals of drifting jellyfish. They floated down over the hillside, one landed in an olive tree, others landed on the ground and men stepped out of the billowy silk. Papa heard cracks and did not realize at first that they were shooting. Shooting at the boys. The smaller boy fell, his legs cycled in agony on the earth. The other ran behind a tree and the men came after, firing. Now that boy was down too, and the little one was still.

Those men disappeared but the one in the tree was climbing

down. The old woman rushed at him with her pitchfork. He dropped on the grass, and she stabbed him in the chest, he screamed, Papa saw her jerk the prongs out and smash them down again into the man's face, head, stomach, groin.

He heard a noise behind him. Another parachute. He grabbed his hammer, ran up as it landed and smashed his hammer in the man's face. The man grunted and lashed out but Papa struck down again, with all his force. There was a crunch, spurts of blood and sludge, and the man stopped moving.

The only gun Papa had ever touched was Grandfather's pistol. But as if his body knew what to do without his even thinking, he grabbed a revolver from the messy body and raced down to the old woman. She was splashed with blood, grimly leading the donkey towards the dead boys. My brother's children, she said. Quick. We must tell the village. Papa lifted the boys onto the donkey. He saw a fresh graze on the little one's knee and imagined the boy saying, proudly, it was nothing. Blood sank into the wooden saddle as they walked.

So he joined the villagers of Perivolia, fighting the invaders. He was desperate to get back to his own family but the road to town was now packed with German soldiers. Then people said the English were fighting a battle on the coast – and then that the English had lost, surrendered, escaped into the mountains, sailed off to Egypt.

Freedom or death! said the villagers. We kicked out the Turks, we'll kick these buggers out too. But that night Papa set off for town across the fields. The sky was moonless, black as basalt. He hid among vines, in ditches, behind walls. When he reached the edge of town he could hardly breathe. It was the beginning of June, the city was hot like an oven, stinking of burn, broken sewers, rotting flesh. Bodies on the street, crunched houses, craters in the road and catch-pools of moonlight between. Little fires burned in the dark, rats poured over mashed rubble.

66

But all the houses in Kondylaki were standing. So was the arch to his yard. The vine had grown, its moon-shadows patterned the ground – and then he was in his mother's arms, while Grandfather wheezed welcome from his couch.

In the morning, German soldiers rounded him up for clearance work. They marched into his mother's yard like a machine and dragged Grandfather to his feet. But Grandfather fell so they left him there and marched Papa off. He trod over corrugated iron, broken railings, pipes, plaster lintels, ripped-off balconies. He slipped in a pool of blood where a photograph of a bride and groom was floating. Cables hung like looping snakes from the innards of bombed houses. Every now and then a mound of debris cascaded when something inside gave way.

In the harbour, a red flag hung from a balcony and a shiny black car stood outside. When did that arrive on the island? Kastelli was a heap of ruins, Splantzia was rubble, balconies dangled off façades with nothing behind. In a fallen *plateia*, an officer sat at a table and made them sign papers. A Greek interpreter, the first Papa met, said this was a contract for two months' free labour.

Dead bodies are a health hazard for German soldiers, he said. You won't get paid. But they'll put you in jail if you refuse.

Papa couldn't look at him, he was so embarrassed to see a Greek working for the enemy.

All day he removed rotting bodies from streets and wrecked houses. Afterwards, walking back through a town that was no longer his, soldiers at every corner, he saw a pinned-up notice. *Cretans are ordered, on pain of death, to declare all weapons and bring them to the bus station. Signed, The Commander of Crete.* How could a German be the Commander of Crete? Everywhere he heard whispers. *The mountains. We're fighting in the mountains. Freedom or death!*

In blue twilight, he dug a hole behind the latrine, wrapped in oilcloth the pistol he brought from Perivolia, laid it inside and asked Grandfather for his. But Grandfather, propped in the yard with a glass of raki, said, You're not putting my great-grandfather's pistol in the shit, boy! I'll spit in their bastard faces first. It's shot a thousand Turks.

He hummed the old Cretan war-song. *When will there be a starry night, so I can take my gun?*

Papa laughed. You're a tough old bird. Grandfather laughed too. Freedom or death, he said, raising his raki.

He had to see Sara. If the pigeons that roosted in trees round his shed had not been eaten, or scared away by the bombs, he could take her some food. Before dawn, he scooped crumbs from his mother's bin, climbed to the mound behind, collected fishnet from his shed and spread it over the grass. He scattered his crumbs, tied string to it and hid, clutching the other end.

The sky was mottled with cloud like blobs of solder. He heard shouts by the harbour, engines starting up. Birds twittered, so some birds were still around. The sky paled to pink, he heard clapping wings and saw pigeons fly up. Three dropped down and began pecking. Then more, treading delicately among the holes. When ten were down he jerked the string, rushed out and grabbed. Wings flapped, his hands were scratched and pecked, but he got five and slung the net over his shoulder.

He found his mother sweeping the yard. Inside, his grandfather was snoring like a pot bubbling, hands folded over his pistol. Papa wrung the necks of two birds, laid them on the side and tugged gently at the pistol. Grandfather's grip tightened. Papa looked at the whiskery face, the long nose he had inherited, and touched the moist forehead with his lips.

That gun must be hidden, he said to his mother.

When he wakes, she said. He was moaning all night, didn't you hear? Holding that thing calms him.

I left you some pigeons, he said. His mother looked at the other birds on his back in silence and went on sweeping.

Papa felt torn.

Kyrios Mois has been very kind to me, he said to her back.

The door in Kondylaki was thick with dust. He knocked. After a while the bolt went slowly back and Kyrios Mois looked out. His face was sunk and grey.

Andonis!

I have meat for you, said Papa. Alive. I think you kill your meat a special way.

Very kind, said Mois. We are not allowed to eat anything smothered or strangled. Come.

The kitchen was hot and dark, the shutters still closed – no, the window and shutters were broken, it was just rough wood blocking the light. But there, in the dim, was Sara. Their eyes met and a shock went through him like the tingle up his arm when he struck the hammer. He ached to hold her and saw she wanted it too.

Good morning, he said. How are you all?

Kyria Simcha embraced him and he saw a raw wound on her temple. He promised to find new glass for the window. As he followed Mois to the front door, he heard Sara say to her mother, Can we eat them?

Should I not have brought the pigeons, sir? he asked.

We're supposed to eat only domestic fowl, said Mois. But I can invoke the dispensations of disaster. You gave a precious gift, thank you. We have had no meat. We are all very weak.

Next afternoon, Papa left work exhausted, turned up Kondylaki, and heard wailing. In his mother's yard he saw the table and chairs overturned, Grandfather lying on the ground with a hole in his forehead, and his mother rocking back and forth, gouging her cheeks with her nails, and two neighbours wailing with her, who said Germans had come looking for weapons. Grandfather refused to give up his pistol and pointed it at them. They shot him.

He had no bullets, screeched his mother. Where would he get them? They searched me, their hands all over me, heaven strike them! They took my oil, my knives, they smashed my pots. Curse them, God, she sobbed. Strike them dead.

Through June and July, as Crete grew hotter, Papa cleared corpses and rubble and kept an eye out for panes of glass. When he found a large one he carried it to Kondylaki and Mois led him through to the yard where he saw a chair with a knife on it. A knife with a beautifully carved handle and blade like a polished moon.

I am saying goodbye to my *sakin*, said Mois. It has been in my family for many generations. The Germans have forbidden ritual slaughter. We have to hand in our ceremonial knives, even those for circumcising. Are they afraid we'll use these holy things on *them*?

Papa balanced his sheet of glass against the shed, placed the chair under the kitchen window, got up and removed the wood blocking it and saw Sara blinking at the sudden light.

Hello down there, he said. She looked so delighted to see him he nearly overbalanced. He stepped down, laid the broken shutter on the ground, and saw her beside him.

Are you all right? he asked.

I am, she said. Are you?

Being with her again, after all he had seen, was like coming into himself.

The Germans shot my grandfather, he told her. I'm going to join the resistance.

He hadn't known that until he saw her. Her presence, her being, seemed to float everything good in him to the surface. He felt her eyes looking into him and telling him what to do.

Kyria Simcha placed a cup of tea on the broken shutter.

The Germans killed his grandfather, Sara said, and burst into tears.

When he was released from clearance, Mois asked him to do another accompaniment to a Hebrew lesson. The town was

70

struggling to get back what life it could, with Germans running the public buildings, platoons on every street and all the coast out of bounds. Again, Papa led the way over the wasteland. Again, they looked down on the sea. But now, only four months later, the troops and ships they saw were German.

I have to go, he told Sara. I know the mountains, you see. And my knowledge is useful. I can avenge my grandfather's death, help get these murderers out of Crete.

But—

I'm Cretan. He gazed into her eyes. I'll come back when I can. I'll think of you all the time.

That evening, they met secretly in a ruined house. He hooped her into his arms and for the first time touched her lips with his. He didn't know what lay ahead, but she was his destiny, for ever.

10

I've never thought of Papa's hands as hands that have killed. They lie on his knees now as if they are weighing the world and finding it light as air.

When we were children, our friends had photos of uncles and fathers shot by Germans, sometimes backed up against their own walls, gazing calmly at invisible executioners. The stories we had were Papa's adventures with the *andartes*. We turned them into games and chivvied other kids to join in.

Our favourite was when he was nearly discovered carrying explosives to Chania. Everyone wanted to be Papa. Usually that was Vasilis, the oldest. Papa had to hide the explosives in a donkey's saddle under wheat and *horta*. On the outskirts of town, two soldiers saw him and shouted, Much stick, that! Papa understood the words were meant to be Greek, aimed at the donkey. No food, he said. Donkey kaput. No kaput, said the soldiers. Much stick. They hit the donkey with rifles to make it go faster. The donkey staggered, the saddle wobbled, Papa saw the wheat shift and knew if they found the explosives they'd be battering him next. They passed a fence with a rusty vine and two girls in a garden. The Germans stopped hitting the donkey. Grapes, yes? one was supposed to say to the girls. You like me? said the other. The girls smiled. No one wanted to play them. It usually fell to me, the only girl, and the youngest.

So Papa walked on, saved by the girls. When the donkey turned

a corner, he looked back and saw the Germans laughing with
them.

Papa also told us how he first met the *andartes* he lived with
for three years. A shepherd led him up to their hide-out above
Omalos, and stopped at a blade of rock between two cliffs with a
sheer drop either side.

Afraid? said the shepherd.

No! Papa set his eyes on the far side, and heard Grandfather say,
as he often had when he was small, Don't look down. He walked out
along the knife-edge into sky, with a howling wind trying to blast
him off. Then he was on solid ground facing a cave and a group of
unsmiling men, black handkerchiefs round their heads, with knives,
pistols, long boots and baggy trousers. A man stepped forward.

That was Kyriakos, Papa always said at that point. The leader.
A great man.

Kyriakos grilled Papa about mountain routes and villages, said
he was little and scraggy but a patriot, and appointed him to take
messages to other guerrilla groups, meet British plane-drops,
and escort fugitive British soldiers to the coast, to meet caïques
going to Egypt.

You'll always be in danger, he said. If they catch you they'll
torture you, to say where we are.

I'll never betray you, said Papa. Kyriakos smiled sadly and told
him to watch out for traitors. In every village, there might be
men in German pay. Already, some policemen were informing on
families hiding British soldiers.

Then Papa met Mr Michael, an Englishman who looked and
sounded completely Cretan.

In real life, Mr Michael told him, I'm an archaeologist.

Isn't this real? said Papa laughing, waving at the mountains.

Mr Michael laughed too and showed Papa a scrap of painted
clay. This tells us the Minoans were here before us, he said. It's

my little piece of hope. It says something survives, however bad things get.

All that, I knew. That was Papa's story. But now we're watching Mama fight for life and I am trying to take in that when Papa joined those fighters, he left behind a Jewish girl in a city occupied by Nazis. As we wait for Mama to wake, he retells his story once again, with Mama, her family and the whole Jewish community in their proper place.

11

Andonis, August 1941–May 1944

As Papa carried his messages through the mountains, he also carried Sara in his heart. The flick at each end of her lips, the gold flecks in her eyes. Sara made him watch where he put his feet, scan every slope before he risked an open path.

But there were more and more German patrols to hide from. Germany must be empty, someone said. Why are the English bothering to bomb it? All the Germans are here with us.

They're looking for the British, said Mr Michael. Crete is paying a high price for having us.

One British agent was caught drinking at a village well. The Germans thought he was Cretan but an informer said he wasn't, so they took him away; and the family who had been feeding him.

Where to? Papa asked.

Aghias, said Kyriakos. The prison outside Chania, where Charon has his black kingdom. No one leaves it alive.

Papa's wages would be paid by the British. Another agent, whom they called Kapetanios Kat, would bring the money from Cairo.

You may have seen him at Suda, said Kyriakos.

Next time Papa returned to camp, he saw a kid turning on a spit and a young man with a chestnut moustache singing Georgios's Turkish-girl song. His eyes were dark blue with a frosty sparkle,

75

like winter sky. For a moment Papa couldn't breathe, as if the stranger beamed a torch into his heart.

Here, pal, said the stranger. Have a drink. He patted the rock beside him.

Thank you, sir, Papa said. In a minute. He stowed his pack in the cave and wondered why he'd taken against the man.

Mr Michael only arrived when the meal was over.

You missed all the fun, said Kapetanios Kat.

Mr Michael said nothing. As days went by, Papa heard in the two Englishmen's voices, when they spoke their own language, how one kept trying to charm and provoke, the other fended off.

Kapetanios Kat asked how he knew the mountains so well. Papa explained he grew up here. How about mountain girls, how many did he have stashed away? Papa laughed and said nothing. One day, Papa was coming back along the knife-edge – he was used to it now, the trick was to not think what would happen if he stumbled – and saw Kapetanios Kat on the other side, smoking a cigarette. The Englishman came to the edge and reached out his hand.

I'm all right, sir, Papa said. Better without.

But one step from the edge he slipped. An arm was under his elbow at once, another round his waist. The Englishman pulled him to his feet.

They shouldn't let you out alone, he said lightly, holding him till he recovered.

Thank you, Papa said, embarrassed. He wouldn't have stumbled if Kapetanios Kat hadn't been in the way.

One night, Papa walked up a ravine on the south coast with Mr Michael to meet a plane-drop. In the black V of sky between blacker cliffs either side, the moon kept appearing then vanishing in cloud. They heard wind in the leaves, the rustle of small animals and then the crescendo of a plane. Mr Michael flashed a torch, the plane circled, packages thumped through trees and the plane sped away. They gathered boxes of boot soles, wireless crystals, batteries, explosives, then Mr Michael brought out a flask and they sat with their backs against a rock. The sky had cleared and was crammed with stars. The Milky Way was a spray of white on black. Made bold by the raki, Papa asked about Kapetanios Kat.

A nickname, said Mr Michael. He's no *kapetanios*. His real name's Robin Cathcart. I knew him at Cambridge. Don't trust him too much.

One autumn day, Papa's first autumn in the mountains, a continuous steely downpour forced him to stay in the cave. Mr Michael was the only other man there. Smoking, looking out at rain like glass bullets, he asked about Papa's family. Papa talked about his grandfather, then about the house in Kondylaki.

Jews? said Mr Michael, surprised. I've never met any Jews on Crete.

Papa described the synagogue, the house, the beautiful daughter.

You like her, Mr Michael said after a moment.

Yes, Papa said. But Jews don't marry non-Jews, and my mum doesn't like them. And I'm poor and no good at letters while they have books. They even read Hebrew.

Stranger things have happened, said Mr Michael, and Papa felt suddenly hopeful. Stranger things have happened, he told himself as he lay down to sleep.

His only chances to go to Chania came when he had to deliver explosives, or messages to saboteurs there. The first time, he saw a notice over the Besantzis printing-shop. *JEWISH BUSINESS, FORBIDDEN TO GERMANS.* And others over Solomon Milcho's wine shop, and Markos Kohen the tailor. Why? He hurried on to his mother's, gave her a dead hare and saw a flash of pleasure on her face. Two women whose homes had been destroyed, and were sharing hers, looked delighted too. He was glad she had people with her, but gave her the bag of gold from the English in secret, ready to smile proudly. She put it away without speaking. She was more familiar with food than bags of gold.

77

Next day he took another hare to Kondylaki. Kyria Simcha let him in and he was shocked – six months since he'd seen her and her hair hung in jagged frizzles, her cheeks were hollow, her hands twitched, her mouth trembled, there was saliva at the corners and she kept fingering the scar on her temple. Suddenly Sara was there too, putting an arm round her mother. She looked like a skeleton, her bones stood out as if stripped of flesh, but her joy at seeing him was naked. They couldn't be alone but they knew, they knew.

∽

she is standing on the old city rampart, she has loved this place since the first time he brought them here, before the germans came, thistles wave in the wind, the sea below is white lace over satin blue, the air smells of flowers and thyme, the grass is emerald, scarlet poppies tickle her ankles

she sees a lizard motionless on a rock and hears a song like needles embroidering the air, a skylark is above her, quivering its wings

her feet look exactly the same but the left ankle thinner than the right

the teacher says she might dance this year but not if she limps because the syrtos chaniotikos is a dance for crete and for freedom, it has to be perfect, she mustn't spoil the line

an ant is carrying a speck of white through grass blades

the grass must look to it like trees

but the lizard is watching, a tongue flicks out like hair, the ant is gone

once upon a time these stones were walls of the city, maybe long ago another little girl stood here looking at the sea

three planes roar over, the lizard doesn't move

one day those planes will be ruins like these walls, the germans won't be here for ever, conquerors come and go,

barba rafael said, but they all leave in the end, we shall be
free again
    then she will fly across this sea like the wild birds and
be an artist
    the wind hisses yessssss in her hair

⟨∿⟩

Georgios joined the *andartes* and Kapetanios Kat embraced
him as a long-lost friend. They had known each other at Suda
and Georgios had taught him his songs. Soon Papa was feeling
uncomfortable because Georgios kept teasing him about Sara and
Kapetanios Kat joined in, singing love songs everyone laughed at.
He hated them *all*.

In June, though, he went on a mission to Chania and scrounged
thistle-root and oil to take both families. Mois opened the door
this time, and smiled. Smoke-coloured wattles of skin hung under
his jaw and his eyes were bloodshot. Papa hoped to be invited in,
but Kyria Simcha appeared, snatched the food and vanished.

I have money, sir, said Papa, which I don't need in the mountains. Can you use it?

Mois looked stricken.

Please, said Papa. To buy food, or medicine. Keep everyone strong.

He put coins in Mois's hand and left. When he got back
to the mountains, Mr Michael looked gently in his face.
Disappointing? he said.

It was good to be understood without words.

By Papa's second Easter with the *andartes*, Georgios hardly
spoke to him and he felt he had lost part of himself. On Easter
Sunday, with the cave wrapped in mist like icy wool, they sat
around a roasting kid.

Sing, Georgaki, said Kyriakos. Georgios looked out across the
mountains and flung back his head. As his voice floated into the
mist, Papa saw a purple mark on his neck like a bruise.

79

On the edge of a cliff stands an eagle
asking the sun
to melt the snow on his damp back . . .

Even as a boy, Papa knew that eagle was the rebel heart of Crete, the Cretan warrior longing for spring when he could go down to the valley, kill the Turks and shout *Crete is free!* Georgios's voice carried all Crete in it, the wounds, the knives, the reckless courage. It was Grandfather waving his pistol, everything Papa had ever known and loved, before Sara. He saw tears in everyone's eyes, and raised his glass. Georgios looked at him and raised his own like a reflection in a mirror. Then Kapetanios Kat clapped Georgios's shoulder and Georgios looked away.

Something lost and irreplaceable swept through Papa. He saw Kyriakos looking at Georgios and suddenly realised Kyriakos thought Kapetanios Kat was fucking him. And – and maybe he was.

He flushed hot, then cold. Georgios was always *lively.* That time he fucked a chicken and it died . . . But wait, did Kyriakos think *he* was . . . Did everyone here believe he and Mr Michael . . .

What about Sara? Two years now he'd been away, walking all over west Crete evading German patrols, but hardly ever able to get to Chania. Two years. Sara was with boys all the time at school, she must have forgotten him. And was he a real man anyway? Maybe everything he felt was a useless dream.

☙

she is standing in the half-moon of dancers at the end of the
spring term between myrto and yasemi
  she is holding their hands and her two feet in white
stockings are even on the ground
    mother and father are watching, a bony old man with
moustaches is tuning a lyra, there are german patrols outside
the wall but at last she is wearing the red headscarf like all

the other girls, and the long red skirt, white apron and jacket embroidered with gold

round her neck are the gold chains kyria myrtakis keeps in her cupboard, kyria myrtakis is skinny now, she gives her food to children whose parents have nothing

the lyra starts playing, she copies yasemi's feet moving hers exactly the same, in – back – out – back – cross over – and one step on, every muscle feels like hot wire, her leg aches, the lyra plays faster, now yasemi is leading, yasemi dances to the back and it is her turn to lead

she twirls in liquid circles, dancing the dance of freedom

she releases myrto and dances to the back of the line, looks up and meets sara's eyes

sara's lips move silently saying bravo

∽◌

In spring, after a long, third, murderous winter with many men lost, they heard *andartes* from Heraklion and British agents had kidnapped a German general.

They walked him right over Mount Ida, Georgios gloated. They took him down the Amari Valley, and ferried him to Egypt! The whole world knows we've stolen their general.

Kapetanios Kat shot Georgios a furious glance and Papa realized he'd have loved to be part of that exploit himself. He also saw Kyriakos was worrying what the Germans might do in return. But nothing happened and soon Papa had another chance to go to Chania. His joy was followed by dread. Was he really a man? What would Sara think?

In town, the last year had turned everyone to wraiths. People moved slowly, many had rashes. Papa found someone new living with his mother, a Kyria Pelagia from another part of town. He was glad someone was with her, but soon disliked the woman intensely. Everyone gossiped, but Pelagia did it spitefully.

They're going to send the Jews away, said Kyria Pelagia that night.

Good riddance, said his mother, looking defiantly at Papa. They don't belong.

Papa looked at Kyria Pelagia. She stared back, stony and blank.

You mustn't say I work for *andartes*, he whispered to his mother next morning.

I haven't told *anyone*, she said.

He was not sure he believed her. They said in the mountains you could tell an informer by their eyes.

Next day, he took a dead squirrel to Kondylaki. Mois left it in the kitchen, led him to the front room where Kyrios Rafael was reading a newspaper, urged him to sit, and placed water beside him on a mat embroidered with flowers. Papa wanted to ask if Sara had sewn it but did not dare. Everything in this house said Sara to him anyway. The glasses in the cabinet, the rugs, the photos in silver frames of babies in white frocks, women in high-throated dresses, wedding couples. Generations, this family had lived here.

His own family had a single photo, great-great-grandfather Vasilis in his mother's uncle's house, in the mountain village where he grew up. These comparisons between their lives and his were not simple. But after three years in the mountains he was aware of a great love for this house. Not only for Sara but for the people, the gentleness, that made her.

Kyrios Rafael too looked skeletal, but smiled and asked how Papa was.

We've been talking about the massacres, he said. People are sending a delegation to the Germans, to ask them to be more lenient. They kill too many people.

Mois said the rabbi was a friend of the old German consul, who loved Crete so much he had converted to Greek Orthodox. When he retired, he stayed in Chania, and now was sad that his country-men were behaving so cruelly. Mois gestured to the paper and said there was talk of sending the Jews away to a land of their own.

But Crete is your land, said Papa. He felt proud sitting with them in this gracious room where men like these had talked calmly for hundreds of years. No one believes that newspaper anyway, he said. Everyone knows the Germans pay for it.

He said goodbye, agonized to have missed Sara yet again, walked round a corner and came face to face with her. The shock hit like an axe. Three years he had carried the image of her and now here she was, flesh and dream. Bone-thin, like everyone, and her lips were cracked, but she was even more beautiful. He tried to feel for any sign his body thought so too. Nothing. No arousal. What had three years of Kapetanios Kat, Georgios and Mr Michael done to him? Sara gazed at him and said nothing.

I couldn't come before, he whispered, and heard footsteps behind. Can you break curfew and meet tonight in the Zafirakou alley?

They met in a bombed house. Stars glittered through empty windows. Broken walls towered above. It was a hot May night, he held out his arms, she clung to him and buried her face in his neck.

I shall love you till I die, he said.

Don't talk of dying. She put her face up in the moonlight. He kissed her lips, slipped his tongue in her mouth, felt himself hardening, tightened his arms and she moaned.

Did I hurt you?

No. She laid her head on his shoulder, he kissed her again and she put her hands on his cheeks, holding him off, holding him close. They heard a rustle in the rubble and she jumped.

A rat, he said with a silent laugh and felt her tremble. It had better watch out. People are catching and roasting them. Or frying ...

Don't.

He ran his hand down along her collar-bone, then down. She shuddered but didn't stop him till he held her heavy breast in his hand.

They met again. Again. Every evening. One night he said, Come to my shed with me tomorrow night. Just for a short time. I'll get you back safe.

83

12

Papa closes his eyes. I think dizzily how old he is, how much he went through, how much I didn't know. He must be exhausted. But there's a change in Mama, each breath sounds like she's climbing a mountain. After each breath comes a terrifying pause, longer and longer, as if there might not be another. I run out to the corridor.

'Hello? Anyone here?' She *can't* die. I'm desperate. I'm only just beginning to learn who she is.

A white coat appears. The same young doctor.

'Doctor Stamatakis! She's worse, please come.'

Papa looks fiercely at him. 'What's happening to her?' Even though he's feeble and ancient, the Cretan warrior in him, the *palikari*, is still fiery underneath.

'I was coming to see you, Kyrie. We have the results, we need to change her medication. There is a danger of blood clots. The hospital does have this medicine, but it's a question of money.'

'Now?' I ask. Medicines are expensive, hard to find. We're lucky they've got it.

'Can you sign for it?'

I sign, a nurse comes, installs a new bag of liquid and gives Mama an injection. Her breathing begins to calm. I feel I see the medicine working.

'She'll be out for the rest of the night,' the doctor says. 'I can't promise, but I think she will make it.'

Papa is pale as vellum. *Click click* go the *komboloi*. I settle him in the armchair and think of one of Goya's *Disasters of War*. A crowd of starving refugees, a man struggling to reach a woman with a child, and a soldier holding him back. Goya wrote on it, *Yo lo vi*. 'I saw it.' War marks you, our tutor said at Camberwell. Those etchings made him cry and we felt for his trauma. Why did I never think of Papa like that, and what he had been through?

And Mama, what were those years like for her? Her mum going mad, everyone starving, soldiers on the streets, and the boy she'd given her heart to in danger, far away. I *have* to know her story from inside. What about those notices on Jewish businesses? Were they the only sign? No yellow star?

'Didn't *anyone* know what was going on, Papa? Thousands of Jews were taken elsewhere in Greece, especially Salonica. Didn't Jews here have any idea? Mr Michael was in contact with Brits in Cairo, didn't they know?'

He looks at me helplessly. I feel a kind of burning pity mixed with awe. He went through all that so young. Now he is rickety and ninety-two.

'Later, people knew. Not then. Salonica is far away. No one I knew had a radio. The Germans were killing people here! They tortured people, there were firing squads. I saw, we all saw. No one thought about the Jews. Not till newspapers talked of sending them away.'

13

Andonis, May 1944

Papa woke in his shed with Sara's head on his chest and thought he was dreaming. But no, she was here, with him, both of them hot under a sheet he had found in a bombed house and carefully washed for this very occasion.

Then he saw a sparkle of light on the wall. Dawn was coming, he hadn't meant to fall asleep, he must get her back. He stroked the tangled hair. After years not daring to touch it, now he had to clear it from his mouth.

Don't move, she murmured.

It's nearly sunrise.

Her eyes flew open. How will I get in without anyone seeing?

She slithered out and stood in front of him, hair over her shoulders, breasts round as pomegranates. She was all songs he ever heard, all dreams he ever dreamed. She began to dress. Pale stripes fell through cracks in the wall over her round thighs. Often, afterwards, he thought, if only we could stay for ever in that moment.

No one was around when they stole out, but when they reached the top of Kondylaki they stopped and gasped. There were piles of furniture outside the houses. Many doors hung open, but not all. Old Kyria Antigone was sweeping her steps.

Run, girl, she said. Or they'll take you too.

What's happened? said Papa. Sara began to tremble.

Antigone told her the German soldiers had taken her people.

My people? said Sara.

The Jews, said Antigone. And they're coming back for the furniture.

In the growing light, Papa saw the street was littered with scraps of cloth, straps, pretzels, even a child's shoe.

Come away, he told Sara, before anyone sees.

He hustled her back to the shed and told her to stay put, he'd go and find out where her parents were. Did she want anything from the house? Food? Her embroidery? He told her to lock the door and raced back to Kondylaki.

A large truck, with its engine running, now stood at the bottom of the street. Every now and then it rolled forward and stopped again for soldiers to carry furniture from another house and load it on. To his disgust, Papa saw some of Sara's neighbours smiling and chatting to the soldiers. Many people now knew words of German. Outside Sara's house a soldier guarded the glass-fronted cabinet and chest painted with red doves.

He saw Eleni outside her own house, terrified, and asked what had happened to Sara's family.

The Germans banged on doors, whispered Eleni, and dragged people out into the street. Old people, some in their night-clothes. Sara's father fell down, they kicked him and *laughed*. Where's Sara?

I'm going into her house to get food, said Papa. He was not going to tell Eleni any more. Her cousin Thodoros was a policeman and the police worked with the Germans.

Come with me. Help me find her embroidery.

The truck rolled one house nearer. Papa looked at the guard.

You ask, they like girls. He's more likely to say yes to you.

Eleni looked petrified so Papa pulled her forward. *Bitte*, he said to the soldier. *Bitte?* He pointed into the hall and then at his mouth. *Essen. Yah?*

The soldier looked at him with cold grey eyes. A face that

87

was hard and young but with watermelon lips, full and oddly pink. Papa wanted to knife him. Instead, he looked sorrowfully at Eleni.

Schwester, he said, trying to remember other words. *Hungrig . . . Sehr hungrig. Bitte?*

The soldier glanced down the street. *Zwei minuten*, he said, jerking his head for them to enter.

Quick, said Papa. The hall was strewn with paper. In the store-room he found a cotton bag, rusks, a jar of lentils. Eleni found Sara's embroidery in her bedroom. Papa thought of the tools, Mois would hate to lose those, but there was no time. He darted to the empty front room, saw one book left on the floor, stuffed it under the rusks, grabbed Eleni's hand and approached the soldier.

Danke, he muttered, longing to poke a gun in that tailored belly.

The soldier nodded them through, Papa hurried Eleni up the street, looked back and saw the truck outside Sara's house. Soldiers carried out a wooden bed.

Sara's *parents'* bed, said Eleni, horrified. Sara told me it belonged to her father's grandmother.

More soldiers carted out the workbench, on its back. The tools must be jumbled up inside. Then another bed, the sheet still on. Papa gave Eleni the lentils and told her to say nothing to anyone about him or Sara.

Her round face was blotchy with tears. I've got to go to school, she said. All my life I've gone to school with Sara. How can I tell them what's happened?

In the next alley he met little Dimitri who sold pistachios. Dimitri's monkey face stared in bewilderment.

They took the Jews out of their homes, he said. In ten minutes, they lost *everything*.

Where did they take them? Papa asked.

They put them in trucks, said Dimitri. People say they took them to Aghias Prison.

Papa told Sara where they were. Why prison? she asked, shaking with fear.

No one knows – I'll find out what's happening, then take you to the mountains.

Mountains? she said. She made it sound like the moon.

Papa pictured the cave. Mr Michael would help, but he was often not around. And there was Kapetanios Kat and Georgios, Ionides, Christos ... All busy, all covered with lice, and all men. He must take her further, up to the village where his mother's uncle and aunt lived, where he lived when he was little. He looked at her shoes. Good strong leather.

Can't I stay here? she said.

They'd find you. People will talk. Already people know I'm asking about the Jews.

The road to Aghias was the part of town the Germans entered first, three years before. Now it was full of tanks and barbed wire. By the turn to Vathypetro, three women sat sewing outside a wrecked cottage. Toddlers played and a hot wind blew grit into little dust devils. Across the road were soldiers, trucks, iron gates and a long low pale building.

Is that the prison? Papa asked. Why so many soldiers?

They locked up the Jews, one woman said.

Why? he asked.

They're not ours. They don't belong.

Did you see them? Papa said. How many people? He thought of Mois and poor confused Simcha, all his neighbours from the Ovraiki. Were they really all there in that silent building?

Hundreds, said the old woman.

They came in those trucks, said a little boy. Soldiers took them out of the trucks and pushed them in through the gates.

Behind the iron gates, Papa saw mulberry trees in an empty yard. There was nothing he could do.

Back in town, Sara's neighbours were joking with the soldiers, wheedling, hoping to enter the empty houses. Kyria Antigone staggered out of Kyria Esther's house carrying a spinning wheel. Children, women, old men, spilled out of houses brandishing what they'd found. One old man clutched a doll, a woman yelled with glee as she swung a bucket.

Aus! said an officer, as if he'd stopped finding it funny. Soldiers pushed everyone out of the street, smiling to see them laden. Someone started singing as if they were leaving a party. Soon all that was left on the street were crumpled photos. People must have taken the frames and tossed these away. Which came from Sara's house? There was no time to look, the soldiers were clearing the street.

He woke Sara before dawn. She barely understood where she was. When he led her out to the dark, her hand felt as if it had no bones.

This will be hard for you, he whispered, but we can rest on the way. He took her through blossoming orchards of almond and apricot, and heavy-scented orange trees.

I used to be scared walking here because of the dogs. I used to pray they wouldn't attack.

She looked round nervously.

Don't worry, there aren't any now.

Why? The first word she had uttered.

They've been eaten.

On a rocky path, she said her feet hurt. He sat her down and took off her shoes and socks.

Well done, he said. No blisters.

What do you mean? They're agony!

That indignation sounded more like her.

The skin's not broken. He massaged her toes. They're the most important part of you, in the mountains.

Hours passed. The sun blazed and sank, shadows lengthened. They trudged over roan-coloured slopes along sheep tracks, across dry riverbeds, up through thorn scrub. Sara sank down, he coaxed her on, made her drink water, nibble a rusk. They slept under the sheet. Next day the same. They hid from the road, saw no patrols. Tomorrow we'll eat properly, he said.

She fell asleep sobbing. He looked at white stars pasted across black sky and saw a shooting star sailing across them. Next morning, he poured a drop of water on the last rusk and gave it to her. Below, above and all round were loose grey stones and ginger earth showing through like a wound. Beyond were peaks threaded with shafts of light. A ravine, luminous blue at the edges, fell away to the left. This was the world he'd shared with his grandfather. To him it was home and freedom. To her, it must be savage wilderness.

He watched her chew as if every movement hurt. Her eyes were blank as if they couldn't let anything in. Step after step, hour after hour, he urged her on. At the foot of a cliff they saw a fallen sheep, neck twisted, legs folded under a slur of dirty fleece. The pecked-out eyes were crusted maroon and she burst into tears. When they reached the knife-edge she stopped in horror.

We can't cross that.

I've done it hundreds of times. Pretend you're just walking through your hall. A straight line, five steps and we're there. Don't look down.

I can't! She looked round and saw only flinty mountainside, sheets of loose scree, a thousand peaks.

Look up and follow me.

He took her hand. *One.* He put his foot on the rock. *Two.* Her foot must be on the rock. *Three.* She dragged, he felt a thrill of horror and moved faster. *Four.* He felt a violent tug and leaped over, pulling her on top of him. She burst into wild sobs.

Who's there?

91

Papa looked up. His cousin Georgios was staring at them, holding a revolver.

Well, well! said Georgios.

Papa helped Sara up and saw envy, lust and curiosity chase each other through his cousin's eyes. Georgios leered into Sara's face and she flinched, then fainted. Papa caught her as she fell.

Help me carry her.

He put his hands under Sara's arms, Georgios took her knees and they carried her up the path. Georgios grinned as they went.

Good fuck?

Shut up, said Papa. To his relief he saw Mr Michael outside the cave, doing something to a transmitter.

Put her in the middle, said Georgios. We'll take turns.

But Mr Michael stood up and Papa relaxed.

Is she hurt? Mr Michael said.

Fainted, said Papa. She needs rest.

Put her in the shade. I'll get water.

Georgios stalked off to pee. Mr Michael said everyone had gone to ambush a patrol that had burned a village and killed five hundred men. He had stayed back to fix a transmitter, for Georgios to take to Rethymno tonight.

If all that is happening here, thought Papa, the arrest of a few hundred people in town won't seem that important.

Is this your Jewish girl? said Mr Michael.

Georgios returned, ostentatiously buttoning his flies. Papa covered Sara with the sheet. She lay on her back under the pine tree.

I've got a stew going, Mr Michael said. She can have that when she wakes.

They ate looking out at the peaks. The slopes looked empty but every fold might hide a hundred Germans. They heard a burst of distant gunfire.

Charos has his sword ready, said Georgios. He tossed back more wine and went into the cave to sleep.

Where will you take her? said Mr Michael.

My mother's relations. Further up.

Tomorrow. You sleep too now, you must be exhausted. I'll guard her.

In the cave, Papa felt how weary he was. Georgios was fast asleep, fingers curled as if asking for communion. Papa stretched beside him as he used to do when they slept on the floor as boys in Georgios's village at Easter. He shifted his spine to a smooth patch and closed his eyes.

When he woke, Georgios had gone. He looked out, recognized the butter-yellow moment of late afternoon before colours thickened into twilight, and walked to the cave entrance. Sara was sitting, with a plate, on the very rock where he had sat for years, thinking of her. He walked out of the cave and Mr Michael laughed.

You look so surprised.

You slept *ages*, said Sara. Kyrios Michael gave me food.

As she ate, light dwindled, and the mottled green and orange colours of the mountains were filmed with misty purple. Papa took her into the cave and made a nest for her.

No one's here but us. You're safe. I'll be beside you.

She closed her eyes like a child. When he came out, Mr Michael gave him a bag of coins.

For your relations, so they can feed her.

Mr Michael knew Crete all too well. Of course it would be easier to ask Stavros and Aspasia to look after Sara if he brought money. But he didn't like to take it.

Call it a loan, said Mr Michael.

They left next morning in the dark.

I'm not going over that precipice, Sara said, and Papa was glad to hear a familiar spark of challenge.

We're going the other way. On, not back.

It's terribly cold, she said.

Walking will keep you warm, said Mr Michael. Safe journey. Good luck, both.

Dawn grew around them, peaks flushed red. They trudged over loose stones, and every step could break an ankle. Down one slope, up another, hotter and hotter, down again then a long way up till they were above all trees. Shreds of gold cloud littered the sky like bird tracks.

Papa avoided villages and chose invisible paths through broken highlands. The sun burned, their lips parched, he saw grief and terror going through her like a pulse. They slept that night in a stone cheese-hut full of sheep droppings. He found an unsheepy patch and tucked the sheet around them.

They were near the snowline now. At dawn, Sara stared up at white peaks.

Are we going into *snow?*

No, no. Askordalos has snow in winter, not in June.

He began to see home crags.

Black Head, look! And Donkey's Nose – Grandfather used to say it opened its mouth at night to bray. Another hour and we'll be there. But you'll need a new name.

He hadn't thought of this before.

Why?

Sara's not a Cretan name. Mountain people don't know any Jews. They say the Jews killed Christ. I'll say you're a cousin of mine, from my father's family in Rethymno. How about Sophia?

OK, she said dully, as if it was nothing to do with her.

The first houses of the village came in sight, grey stone walls rising from grey stony ground facing a steep drop, and more grey mountains rising to enormous blue sky. His mother must have walked here often as a girl, looking over these same mountains and wondering, like them, what the future held. Her own mother

94

died giving birth to her and she grew up here, with her father, her father's older brother Stavros, and Stavros's wife Aspasia.

But Stavros and Aspasia were a disappointed pair. They lost their own son Nikos when he was nineteen, when Papa's mother Maria was a little girl of six. These days, Nikos was the secret sadness of the house. When Stavros looked at Papa, he saw the grandson of his younger brother, not his own. Papa, last male descendant of Vasilis Manoudakis who won a battle against the Turks, carried the ghost of that ancient brother-rivalry on his shoulders like thorn-rash.

He couldn't explain all that to Sara and had no idea what they would think of her.

Askordalos was a handful of small houses. Papa heard moaning in the half-ruin where Mad Pipina lived with her idiot son Achillea. He hoped Sara had not heard and explained that the husband of the woman in that house had been a *vrikolax* – someone who had died and come back, was both alive and dead, who escaped from his grave and slept with his wife. She had Achillea long after he died.

The son's not dangerous, he said. Just not quite right in the head.

Sara looked blank and terrified. Maybe this was not the best introduction to the village.

In Stavros's yard, he sat Sara at the millwheel Aspasia used as a table and thought of the gracious house Sara grew up in – and then as he'd last seen it. This house was little and rough, but safe. Through its open door, he saw a space on the wall where the pistol, twin to his grandfather's, used to hang beside the sepia photo of his great-great-grandfather who owned both pistols long ago.

Aspasia hobbled round the corner with one hand holding her back, and welcomed him. Her whiskery face was even more furrowed than he had last seen it. He introduced Sara as Sophia, his father's cousin from Rethymno, and said the Germans had taken her family.

95

Aspasia's eyes flicked over Mama. Welcome, girl.

Something wrong with your back? said Papa. Aches and pains?

Not as young as I was, Aspasia said.

You need someone younger to help you.

Aspasia shot him a glance. She was onto him. Come in the house, she ordered. I need your help. They left Sara sitting dazed outside.

You want us to hide her, don't you? said Aspasia.

She can work for you, Papa said.

Doesn't look strong. You want to marry her?

Yes.

What does Maria say?

She doesn't know. I have money for you, Aunt. You can buy chickens and oil.

People don't use money much now. We trade with villages below. But – but the messenger could buy me rabbits.

Aspasia ladled a lump of walnut preserve onto a saucer. From her precious stock, she was giving Sara a formal welcome. Papa carried the dish and four small spoons outside, Aspasia followed with glasses of water. Sara drank thirstily and replaced her glass on the millstone where sunlight played through it in a sudden rainbow. Stavros came round the house with his rolling mountain gait and Papa introduced Sara – Sophia, now – again.

Take some sweet, urged Aspasia.

You need building up after that little walk of yours, teased Stavros. While Sara took a spoonful of preserve, and gazed numbly at Stavros's grey tangle of whiskers and moustache, they agreed she would help with the house and land.

Papa felt uneasy. He had brought Sara to safety but what would she do now? They had scarcely spoken to each other since they arrived. Well, it was up to her.

I'll find out what's happening to your family, he said, and come back.

It was a horribly public goodbye. Stavros and Aspasia stood each side of Sara as if they had already taken charge. At the gate Papa turned to wave but Sara was talking to Aspasia and didn't see.

Two days later, he walked into his mother's yard with a bag of snails. He saw their neighbour Barba Andreas sitting at the table talking to Kyria Pelagia, who was polishing a copper lamp. Papa recognized those brass flowers on its side. Pelagia must have taken it from Sara's house. He pictured her ferrety face in those rooms, and longed for a genie to rise out of the lamp and tear her to shreds. But he mustn't show he knew where it came from, or that he minded. Pelagia would not hesitate to betray him as Jew-sympathizer, as well as *andartes*, if she could get anything out of it.

He embraced his mother and gave her the snails. Andreas and Pelagia were arguing about the Jews.

They're our neighbours, Andreas said. The *Germans* are our enemies. Why should they take people out of their beds like criminals and drag them away with nothing? Then *you* take their hard-earned things! Is that something for Crete to be proud of?

Aren't *we* poor? said Pelagia. Aren't *we* starving and suffering? Good they have gone. Maybe they were why the Germans came in the first place.

Papa saw his mother agreed. She was glad the Jews had gone. She might not know Sara was not taken. But she might. Kyria Antigone knew. Eleni knew. Every shadow in these streets had eyes. And everybody talked.

That night he stared at the moon and listened to Pelagia snore. In the morning, in sunlight brilliant and clear as crystal, he watched a crowd gather at the synagogue as soldiers attacked its door with pickaxes. They stumbled on the unexpected step down, then came sounds of banging and splintering and they carried out benches, hangings, lamps, the carved doors, a chalice. He saw the screen he made bobbing away to a truck.

97

Treasures of the Jews, someone said.

When they've gone, said another, we'll dig the floor and find gold.

He walked out of town on the Aghias road again, past tanks and barbed wire. Opposite the prison, he saw the three women sitting like the Fates among fallen window-frames, with children playing round them.

Children play anywhere, he thought. Thank God.

Are the Jews still there? he asked.

The women looked at the building. Soldiers patrolled the fence. Seagulls swooped in raw blue sky.

Who knows, one said.

They turned back to their sewing.

My Mum
Is a Labyrinth

14

Papa passes a hand over his eyes like someone waking from sleep. I hold Mama's hand, stroking the familiar knobbles and wrinkles.

Sophia. Her name was Sophia. The mother we grew up with. But really some other unknown person. A Sara.

Nikos looks round the door. He has brought the nurse but also his daughter Leila, to say hello. Leila works for my parents in their B&B. She has huge blue eyes and dark red hair heaped on top of her head. She's a year older than Katerina, they played together as toddlers and hung out as teenagers. Now she has two children and an out-of-work husband, but her mouth is still set in a permanent smile as if she looks at everyone from a great distance and is delighted by what she sees. She hugs me and I rock her in my arms. I miss being hugged.

Nikos puts a hand on Papa's shoulder. 'All right?'

In my portrait of Nikos, I painted him playing his lute. His eyes are dreamy, lifting into space, but his narrow face is alive as if he welcomes life and will run with whatever it brings. When I was little, he often sang that Turkish-girl song, and I joined in the funny chorus not knowing Papa's cousin sang it to tease him about being in love with a Jew. Papa has carried all this hidden in the shelter of himself. I feel strange hugging my brother and niece, because now I'm carrying that secret too.

'Mama not woken?' says Nikos.

'They changed the medication. She should wake tomorrow.'

Nikos and Leila take Papa away and the nurse settles into the armchair. I go out to the echoey corridor. It feels as if we're the only people in the building. Everything silent, except my feet squeaking on the floor. I look through a window at the end. In England, twilight is a gradual thing. Here it happens in a heartbeat, the world turns dark before your eyes. I stare at the sleeping hills and a cluster of lights high up in inky night. I keep picturing those torn photos in the street. I'd love to see what my grandparents looked like.

Papa left so much out. Why go to the house when it was being looted? Just to get food and Mama's embroidery? Really? As for the neighbours, plundering those houses . . .

Katerina never liked History much but when she did the Holocaust, at GSCE, David talked about his grandparents from Minsk, who escaped it, and other relatives in Ukraine who didn't. Katerina was awed and devastated. But it still was History, something one lot of human beings did to others, once. Now History is coming at us out of the long grass. The past is not dead. It is not even past.

I can't imagine Mama walking all the way up the fiercest mountains in Europe. When I decided to paint them, I rented a car. Papa said he'd show me the house he lived in as a child and we bumped for hours up rocky tracks above appalling drops. I'd never been so high. I wondered if I'd ever manage to turn round.

Askordalos was a ghost village, abandoned, over six thousand feet up, silent as a famine village in Ireland and bare as pictures of the Andes. Scorching grey rock and naked pinnacles as far as you could see. I did sketches, took photos and was very glad Papa was with me. All the buildings were roofless except the little church. The one he'd lived in was a heap of wall-stumps like the exoskeleton of a beetle.

What he did not say was that he'd brought Mama there in the war. That those walls I put in my painting were her asylum.

Sara to Sophia, what was that like? A soft Jewish girl from the city, alone in mountain Crete, changing identity from one moment to the next. And, long after, what did she feel when her daughter brought a Jewish boyfriend home?

Even worse than marrying a Turk, some Greek parents might say. I was ready to be defiant. But David's curiosity and gentleness shone through the language barrier. I thought that was what won Mama over, but did she feel a secret kinship, which David might have felt too but did not recognize for what it was?

It was a Friday evening when we came. Mama lit two candles. I hadn't yet met David's mother, who also lit two candles on Friday nights. I didn't know about that, I thought Mama was just being welcoming. But it must have been the first time she sat down with a Jewish man, with any Jew at all, since she last saw her father.

I remember her looking at David as she passed the bread. I thought she was wondering what sort of man I was joining my life to, but maybe she thought he might say a blessing. As David's father did on Friday nights, I later discovered. The last thing David would have dreamed of doing.

Before we married, in Crouch End register office, David and I discussed living a partly Jewish life. Neither of us was religious, but we cared about where we came from. I said I wouldn't change my passport, we were all part of the EU, thousands of Greeks live abroad and return for summer. David always went to his parents for the Seder so I did too, I wanted to be a good daughter-in-law, I read up on Judaism, did my best to understand.

But what will Katerina feel? She adored both her grannies. She helped Yasmin prepare the Seder and did Easter with Mama. She carries the difference between them in her bones. What is she going to think, this fierce girl of mine who inherits David's passion for truth? I wish I could think this through with David. But David only exists inside me now, along with the sadness and mystery of the self.

I rest my forehead on the chill glass of the window, watch olive leaves stir in the wind outside and suddenly feel I must withdraw my self-portrait from that show. Self-portraits are dangerous things. Mondrian fired a pistol at one of his. I know what's wrong with mine now, it's the face of someone in denial. Something in me must have known I was not what I thought. How do you paint that?

I go softly back to the room. Bisera is still asleep. I lean over Mama. Hanging between us are two childhoods, hers and mine.

'Mama?'

Nothing. At the window, I see night cloud drifting. I breathe moonlight in my lungs. I am only just beginning to let myself imagine what she went through.

In the morning, with that wrinkly bag of fluid hanging over her like an empty purse, she opens her eyes. 'Where am I?'

Same words as last night. But then she sounded lost. Now she sounds determined to rejoin the world. She's conscious, she knows me. But do I know her?

I take her hand. 'You're in bed, Mama. You've been ill. I'm staying in hospital with you. We'll soon take you home.'

The last word rings between us like an unanswered bell. She smiles, and watches me stack my mattress in the washroom. Bisera has managed to find chicken and lemon soup and she drinks it in a plastic beaker with a pursed spout like a whistling bird. By the time Nikos brings Papa she's asleep again but Papa sits down eagerly beside her as if reclaiming his true place in life.

I walk the six floors down to the canteen. The lift isn't working. Lifts aren't working all over Greece, either to save electricity or because no one has paid the bill. The canteen is empty except for the girl behind the counter, scrolling her phone. No windows, only one light above the coffee machine. The place looks designed to the Rembrandt Lighting formula Nashita and I learned when we studied Photography. We turned it into a chant.

104

The subject turns away / from a single light/
    high to the side. / The reflector / illuminates /
    the far side of the face. / Chiaroscuro /
    does its work on the other.

What about the far side of Mama's face, the side she's never let us see?

I get out my mobile and WhatsApp Katerina. *Mama better. Drank soup. You don't need to come till Easter.*

Josh has sent reviews from the gallery. I look at one headlined, 'Cretan Gold', and decide not to read them.

Sales brilliant, he texts. *Swiss collector bought Labyrinth. Hope yr mum's OK.*

Better, thanks, but can we withdraw the self-portrait?

Nope. It's sold. That guy from Mykonos.

Can't you call it back?

No. The guy loves it.

He's a creep. Offer him another.

Ri, he BOUGHT that painting! Paid good money.

It's false.

Josh doesn't answer. I picture his hipster beard bristling. An email comes from Marcus.

What's all this about?

I want to withdraw the self-portrait.

It's a good painting, Ri. If you feel there's something unresolved there, great, it means new ideas are stirring. Do another. Rembrandt kept doing them.

Fuck off, Marcus. Rembrandt's self-portraits are genius. Each brushstroke another lash of memory. He's painting all the hurt he's ever known.

We've had great reviews, by good people. This show is a big new step for you. Three collectors are after your mum's portrait. How is she?

I don't answer. I'm being childish. I need someone to be childish with.

I look crossly round the canteen. Blue plastic chairs, empty tables, dusty floor, all lit on only one side. It reminds me of a Rembrandt painting of two old men arguing about the Bible with a shaft of light between them, which lights the side of one face, the old man pointing to an open page. The other guy has his finger in a different page. Just scholars arguing, but Rembrandt turns it into a quarrel between radiance and the dark.

I think of Mama's father and teacher arguing about the rumour – here, in Chania, I still can't take it in – of sending Jews to 'a home of their own'. While Nazi propaganda, in a shamefully collaborative Cretan newspaper, lay beside them on a table that would end up as Nazi loot. They had no idea, apparently, what was happening to Jews elsewhere in Greece. Difficult to imagine how cut off they were. No internet, no WhatsApp, few radios, hardly even any phones.

I get out my sketchbook and draw the fall of light and shade over chairs, the coffee machine, the girl with her phone. When you shade, you have to decide exactly where the light is coming from. There are no accidental shadows. Shadow is a result.

Marcus is right, as usual. Something is stirring. I am starting to process all this in terms of paint.

When I finish, I find an email from Nashita.

Edinburgh's freezing, man! Can't believe how wet it is. Your catalogue's great. Really rich work. How about coming to Mumbai?

I'd love to come. Really.

I buy a baklava and a Greek coffee with lots of sugar, and carry them up to the sixth floor for Papa with a little bubble of joy, imagining living and painting in Mumbai. We have only one lifetime. We're made by the one we have, we are what we have thought and done. Whatever that unknown city is like, I can now think and do new things.

When I get back, Mama's eyes are open and Papa is telling her about the current guests at their B&B. It occurs to me, as something I have always known, that my mother is a very strong person. But they are both so old and wonky. How long can they last?

'An American family,' Papa is saying. 'Two children. No trouble at all. Quality tourists.'

Mama smiles at me and fine seams above her top lip fan out like a child's drawing of sunrise. I kiss her, cling to her, prop her higher on the pillow. Papa tucks into his *baklava*. He has finished his Cadbury Flakes.

Next day the *sorokos* arrives, the scorching south wind that villagers call Big Tongue. You see it hurtling through the mountains at hurricane speed, a lick of haze that fishermen know for the devil it is and make for port. Now it hits in a rush, howling round the hospital, churning the distant sea to angry foam, blowing spray up from the rocks like a geyser, raising little twisters of dust on the white roads. The air is clogged with yellow-red dust. Historians say it was blowing when Knossos burned. And when the worst massacres happened, when Turks slaughtered Christians, when murderous new risings began against them and they hung Cretan bishops on a plane tree.

This is Crete too. Headaches all day. The first day of a *sorokos* is bad, the second worse. By the third, with all that violence inside and out, you're ready to murder someone yourself. Then, as suddenly as it began, it drops. Mama, with true Cretan stoicism, has been getting stronger all through and I get her ready to go home. Papa watches me brush her hair into a soft white cloud, innocent as mist.

'You'll turn everyone's head,' he teases. 'You always did, always do.'

The most beautiful girl in the Ovraiki, I think. Mama has no idea Papa has told me this.

'You'll have to watch out,' she tells him. Delighted, not by the compliment but because teasing means life is ordinary again.

We walk her downstairs, floor by floor. I prop her up, Papa limps behind with the bags, Nikos has the car at the door. Only a gentle west wind is blowing now and the sky is egg-blue, with clouds like flecks of candyfloss. As we drive, Mama gazes at the spring we thought she wouldn't live to see. Blossom everywhere. Emerald grass, yellow daisies, sunlight pouring on tarmac like grain on a threshing floor. On one side, the sea sparkles like amethyst. On the other are green hills that will soon be lion-tawny, dry as bone. Climate change is making our summers hotter than ever. Sometimes Crete goes six months without a drop of rain.

Now the dusty clutter of the suburbs. Nikos skirts the Old Town and cuts down to the sea beside the restored Venetian wall, built to protect Chania against the Turks. Sixty feet of blond fortification, angled away from the vertical so cannonballs fired from the sea would bounce back. But no use against German planes, or parachutes. Picturing my home town crushed by bombs and invaded by enemy soldiers is like trying to imagine Muswell Hill and Crouch End under military occupation.

I conjure up barbed wire over these rocks and my teenage Papa, not yet wounded, hurrying past it to find where the Germans had taken Mama's parents. Aghias, which means Holy, is further up this road. I suppose the prison's still there. I've never seen it.

We turn left, away from the sea. Nobody is going to invade today. We are bringing my mother home. She is making conversation as if we haven't been immured in one room together for over a week.

'How is London, *agape mou*? How was the show?' Conversation makes her feel safe. But now I know that all my life she has kept something enormous away from me and I don't feel safe at all. How upsetting it is, that the moon has a dark side, always turned away from Earth.

15

I open the gate beside Papa's sign. *Rooms Karderini.* The folk-art lettering and the goldfinch's smiley face say 'home'. It's like a sugar rush. The world is not meaningless. Making sense of it began here, in this garden.

This is a suburban road now, but our house must have been pretty isolated when Chania was smaller. For so close to the centre, we have a lot of land. A flat patch here by the gate, at the top, then a gentle slope down to apricot trees at the bottom, where Mr Michael built a small bungalow, on the understanding he could use it every summer. The rest of the time it was ours, to rent out as we wanted.

Our own house is halfway down the garden. Half-hidden, from up here, by two old trees, an olive and a pomegranate whose scarlet buds are just beginning to show. We make tea and salad from its leaves. On New Year's Eve, Papa used to smash a pomegranate on the doorstep for good luck. We cheered as the red seeds burst like jewels on the earth.

It was originally a one-storey cottage. Papa added an upper floor, whose rooms are reached by an outside staircase. This is now whitewashed every year, but started out the pale khaki of naked cement. I remember the mixer sloshing round, my brothers gazing at it in masculine enchantment.

On the patio, Leila is taking breakfast to a young couple with two girls who look about thirteen and nine. Behind them, the White

Mountains are veined with folds of mauve shadow. We smile at the guests and trundle Mama into the house. She looks around Reception, relieved to be home but checking how well it has been looked after without her.

She is very proud of Reception. It is full of light, because in the Sixties Papa knocked out the front wall and put glass in. The furnishings have barely changed since. A vending machine offers Cola and Sprite, there is a vase of plastic roses on a coffee table, and a spindly sofa covered in gold brocade worn to fuzz at the edge where generations of tourists with sunburnt thighs have scuffed up whiskers of thread. On the walls are a TV, a red Cretan woollen bag, and a poster with a bull's head saying *LABYRINTH! Visit Knossos*.

Knossos is far away, but that bull is an ikon of Cretan tourism and Mama likes its crystal stare. As a teenager, I meanly pointed out that, close up, his eyes have red pupils and rims so his gaze is really bloodshot and dangerous. Mama ignored me. From a distance, he seems wise and calm.

Reception is for guests, like front of house in a theatre. We do our private living in the kitchen behind, but someone is always here at the desk to keep an eye. Long ago, that was Papa's mother, Kyria Maria. Now I know more about her, I try to remember her better but all I can dredge up is a thin black ghost. I don't even remember when she died.

'I'd like to lie down,' says Mama. We help her to their bedroom, she collapses on the bed and I ease off her shoes. On the lampshade beside her, a small white moth is spreading out black-edged wings as if guarding the bulb within.

They've always slept here, next to the kitchen. We've done things to the kitchen, a freezer, dishwasher, but she never let us touch the bedroom. On the chest of drawers, under one of her embroideries, is the saucer she keeps hairpins in and that pointless birdcage.

Papa plants himself in the armchair. Leila and I put away Mama's things.

110

'This room's too small for five,' says Nikos. 'Coffee?'

I get out three catalogues. One for here, one for each of the other families. Nikos and Leila study them over coffee in Reception. Leila flicks through places and people she knows, and looks up with a smile.

'OK?'

'Lovely.'

Nikos stops at Mama's portrait. He knows the paintings, but they look different in a catalogue. Will he see it now, the menace of the shadows, the fear Nashita saw on Mama's face? No. He smiles at me. He sees what he knows. That look of hers is so familiar.

I introduce myself to the guests. They are Californian, they backpack in the Rockies, they are showing their daughters Europe.

'Trip of a lifetime,' says Doug, the craggy young dad. Kelly, the mother, is slim and blonde with a smooth tanned face. She is used to the sun. No burning for her. She looks flexible, fluid as a cat. The younger child, a glossy brunette like her father, is eyeing the pomegranate tree as if planning her route up into the branches. The older girl is blonde like Kelly, and rolls her eyes when her sister darts off to swing on the gate.

Kelly laughs but Doug looks anxious.

'Don't go near the road, Bonnie.' Bonnie ignores him. 'Can you tell us a walk to burn off all this energy? It's too cold for the beach.'

'How about the Minoan ruins on Kastelli Hill?'

'I thought the ruins were Knossos,' says Kelly.

'That's a palace. What's here is only a few Minoan streets. But that hill was the ancient acropolis, and you get a great view.'

'How do we get there?'

'Past the Mosque of the Janissaries, that's an exhibition centre now, might be interesting. Then past the horse-carriages and the Turkish Fountain and up the Street of Knives. Come back by the Ottoman Gardens and a wonderful ice-cream shop.'

111

Doug smiles. 'OK, girls, get your things.'

The girls run off. The parents finish their coffee.

'It's lovely here,' says Kelly. Doug puts his arm round her. Their heads, close together in front of the mountains, look like a god and goddess stamped on an ancient coin.

'Is Sophia OK now?'

Kelly is good at names. I tell them she is and take my bag up the outside stairs to the top front room, where I slept and worked while I did the paintings. Two beds, a chair, a little table, a chest of drawers. All you need. My easel and painting stool are still on top of the wardrobe. This is also the room where all three of us kids slept when we were little, though when the place was full we slept on the roof. I loved sleeping up there under the stars, safe between my brothers.

Mama sleeps all afternoon. When I take her to the bathroom, she staggers dangerously and flops back on the bed like a wounded hen.

'I'll stay with her tonight, Papa. Can you sleep upstairs?' He is shaky himself. If she needs to get up in the night, that moth on the lampshade would be about as much use.

'I'm sleeping here,' he says. 'Our rivers flow from the same sea.'

I can't argue when he goes all Cretan and flowery.

In the late afternoon, at the window of my room. I take in the familiar evening smells of burning *souvlaki*, cinnamon and petrol fumes. You can't deny your past, but what if you never knew it? I'm Jewish but don't know how to be. Like the Indian girl in Amrita's *Two Girls*, I am a self in shadow, dark to itself. A self I don't understand. Yet here is the same old evening star coming out to greet me through leaves of the tree that guarded us as we grew, as if still communing with the child who slept and dreamed here, argued with her brothers, and felt safe.

Underneath the grinding sadness for my mother, I realize I'm thinking of my Jewish identity, an identity I never knew I had, as lost treasure. Is there some ritual, some ceremony of possession, that can call it back? I've lost other identities too, selves I've grown like rings of bark and took for granted. The English painter with a Cretan soul. The Cretan who never thought about church but celebrated Easter anyway. Now I'm the woman who married a Jew, and took part in his family festivals, not knowing they should have been hers.

The pomegranate tree rustles. Sound of my childhood.

I look at the mountains beyond. Cézanne poured his loneliness into his native landscape. He said there was sadness in it. When he paints divisions in the road, or knots in a tree where branches divide, I see him searching for a pain that spoke to him. He said the real discoveries come from chaos, from going to the place that looks wrong.

We embark on Holy Week, sharing Christ's last days as a human being. Loukia and Irene do the cooking this involves while I sit with Mama. Every now and then she wakes, asks what's happening and drifts back to sleep, but she's awake a little longer each day. Papa comes in and out. We are co-conspirators now. No one else knows the history swirling round Mama. The word Holocaust is in my head all the time but I can't say it to anyone.

I sense Papa feels bad all round. To Mama, for having told me. To me, and all of us, for not having told us before. But I'm in danger of doing the same thing myself. Already I feel bad not telling Nikos and Leila. And not telling Katerina is unthinkable.

Katerina bounds in one afternoon like a dark gazelle, waving her taxi goodbye. She always chats to cab drivers, she loves practising her Greek at once when she's been away. She's wearing a pale blue sweatshirt saying *New York*, has had her hair cut in a feathery cap, and looks so like David it catches me in the throat.

113

'*Mum!*'

'Sweetheart! You look beautiful.'

She lays her head on my shoulder, then rushes off to Granny. When I go in, she's sitting beside Mama, her back against the pillow. They look up with the same smile, same downy eyebrows, same deep-rilled top lip and I suddenly feel – no, not David – I am looking at the woman we all three came from. Kyria Simcha, the granny I always longed to know.

'We must plan for Easter,' Mama announces happily. Life is getting back to normal. She has always said it with food. When we were little, if something upsetting happened, a bad quarrel, or someone hurt, the house would fill with smells of garlic and cinnamon that said, This house loves you, whatever.

Now she's worrying about *lambropsomi*, Shining Bread. Katerina has always helped her with the Easter brioche. So did I, when I was little. Stretch the dough into strands, braid the strands around red eggs. It is ancient family lore, part of Katerina's childhood, and mine.

But surely not Mama's. When did *she* first make *lambropsomi*? Her mum must have made *matsah*, for Passover.

'It's all in hand, Mama. Irene's doing the bread.'

Katerina hugs her. 'Goodnight, Granny. Sweet dreams.'

We are fasting for Lent so no oil, no wine. I make lentils and *horta* for Katerina and Papa. That's fine with Katerina, who is going vegan.

'Where's the catalogue of your show, Mum? How did you like your picture, Grandpa?'

'Very nice,' says Papa. 'But she made my hands too big.'

After supper, Katerina comes to my bedroom. She's in the room next door, we have the top floor to ourselves. We've been through a lot together since David died. She put her life on hold then to help me, now she's doing a Film Studies PhD and living in Bushwick. She's sent me photos of a tiny shared apartment under the J train.

114

'How's it going in that wild city? How's your room?'

'I don't think the stairs are ever cleaned! *Totally* thick with dust. Each flat is just a corridor, with rooms off. I'm next to a young black guy from Florida who lives in a cupboard. Really a cupboard, Mum. He goes out every evening covered in silver paint, even his clothes, and earns his living dancing in 14th Street subway. Real New York.'

She sits on my bed leafing through the catalogue, and smiles at the figures in my labyrinth.

'I remember these! How old was I when we went to Knossos?'

'Seven. That was such a lovely day.'

David and I rented a car to take my parents to Knossos, which they had never seen. Tourist attractions didn't exist when they were young. And the Villa Ariadne, the house British archaeologists built above the Palace, became the German headquarters. That was where the German general was going when he was kidnapped.

In the palace, Katerina raced ahead along stone corridors said to be the origin of the labyrinth, then scuttled back to hold David's hand in case there really was a monster round the corner. David had been telling her Greek myths at bedtime. Mama admired the Throne Room, the frescoes reconstructed on the walls. I could see her wondering how a griffin might look in Reception. Papa was fascinated by the earth, the walls of trenches cut by archaeologists, the layers of living he could see in them. Especially the burnt levels, that moment when the palace was destroyed, and the jumbled layers above when squatters camped in the palace ruins.

I had a pamphlet about Edward Lear in Crete. He came when Crete was still Turkish but the rest of Greece was free, just before an uprising and an awful massacre. But he had a fine time painting landscapes, and did one of Knossos with no idea that, fifty years later, paintings from a whole civilization that would change

115

the history of art would be dug up from earth where he settled his easel.

I imagined him painting the gentle lines of Knossos valley and thought of what you fail to see, even when you think you're looking. What you could have seen, but didn't.

Then we went back to Chania, and Mama looked after Katerina while David and I went to dinner alone. We walked into town under a throbbing sky of dark blue with corkscrews of pink cloud, and ate courgette balls with white wine. Harbour lamps joggled in the wind and a yacht came in like a fairy ship, cutting a wake of light in black water. I don't remember what we talked about. Only the yacht, and David's face, and laughing. And the moon.

Katerina looks closely at my refugee painting. 'I must go to that centre. I've got funding now. In the summer, I'm going to film a refugee project with a Lebanese guy in my cohort. Someone called Dora has emailed the security protocols.'

'Wonderful, darling. Dora's the centre's director. Maybe you can interview my friend Ayla who cooks there and teaches hairdressing. She was a hairdresser in Damascus. ISIS beheaded her husband. She brought their three daughters out of Syria alone. She's a wonderful person. Let's go tomorrow.'

'Cool.'

Next day, walking to town, I wonder how to tell her. We skirt the men resurfacing the Old Harbour with marble like jagged pieces of thin icing. Resurfacing has to be done every spring, because the winter seas surge over here right up to the Venetian houses of the waterfront. These houses are now boutique hotels in the upper floors and souvenir shops, or restaurants, below. Waiters are putting cushions on chairs, shopkeepers set out racks of jewellery and postcards, foreigners drink coffee.

All so familiar. Katerina automatically slows down at the

necklace shop that fascinated her when she was little. I spent hours with her as a toddler here, in full summer heat when she refused to sleep through siesta, watching her finger the beads. Now, with Papa's story in my head, I picture swastikas hanging from these balconies and a black Mercedes waiting here, for a Kommandant who has just ordered the massacre of a village and the arrest of all Cretan Jews. I knew all that, though not the Jews. But somehow never really pictured my parents living through it.

At the Turkish Fountain, we watch pearly water falling in clustering dribbles. When I was little, the marble was dirty grey. Now it is milk white.

'I've got something to tell you, darling. It's going to be a shock.'

'You're getting married.'

Where did that come from? 'Christ, no. Nothing like that.'

'Good. Spit it out.'

As I tell her Mama's story, her eyes go shadowy as though something dark has spilt in her.

'So that's it, honey. Granny was Jewish. Is Jewish. The Nazis took her parents. Here, in Chania where no one's *heard* of any Jews, the Church controls everyone's lives, and no one's ever mentioned the Holocaust.'

The relief of sharing it with Katerina starts me crying. She steers me to Starbucks, sits us in the wicker chairs outside, and orders cappuccino. Then she explodes. I didn't expect this. Her first reaction is not shock at the tragedy, but fury.

'All that Christianity's a fucking lie. Shining Bread – piss off! Aren't *you* angry, Mum? If I found out you hadn't told me something like that, I'd be livid. Why haven't you asked her?'

'She nearly died, Katerina. Think what horror she's lived with all her life. I can't ask her till she's stronger. Let's get Easter over first.'

'You're too passive, Mum. It was your right to know. And mine. I'm nearly *all* Jewish. Granny and Grandpa Gold would so totally have loved to know that.'

117

David's parents died ten years ago, before he did. I loved his mother Yasmin, she welcomed me so warmly, she must have felt some loss about David marrying out but never let me feel it. Yes, she'd have loved to know. She and Katerina talked a lot about being Jewish. Katerina often said she wished she was a full Jew.

'And *Dad*,' says Katerina, bursting into tears herself. 'Your life with him was a lie. Our life was a lie.'

'It bloody wasn't. Of course he'd have liked to know, I wish he had, but he wouldn't have cared that much. What mattered to Dad was who people were, not what.'

'God, Mum, I can't believe it – her own neighbours taking things. And her parents . . . *Poor* Granny.' Tears stream down her face and the waiter bringing our cappuccinos looks embarrassed. I dry both our cheeks with a Starbucks napkin.

After a while I say, 'The signal's such crap here. I never know when the wifi will work. If you have time in New York, might you research the people we come from? Cretan Jews?'

'I've got a lot of work.'

'Just – if you have time. Someone must know who they were, what happened.'

I take her to the refugee centre. On the outside wall hangs a line of orange life-jackets painted with letters spelling the Greek word for welcome.

'Everyone working here is cheerful and hopeful,' I tell Katerina, 'but be prepared for a lot of trauma. People whose homes were bombed to pieces, who lost children and parents, who were gassed and spent years in camps. In my art workshop, the pictures the children drew were all about bombing and killing.'

'It's my world,' she says as if she thinks I am warning her off. 'I have to live in it.'

In the courtyard, I introduce her to the director. Dora is a tired young woman in jeans with honey-brown plaits round her head.

'Hi, Katerina,' she says and Katerina is instantly at home.

Someone her age. Someone who gets things done. 'I printed out your security permissions, for filming,' she says.

'Great, let's look them over in the office.'

'Is Ayla around?' I ask.

'Sorry, Ri, she's taken her kids to Athens. She thinks there'll be better schools there.'

I stare at a blackboard where lesson times are chalked in Greek, English and Arabic. After all the details Papa has given me, what he saw here, what happened to him and Mama, walking through town with Katerina has really thrown me. I feel as if, all my life, I've just been flicking pebbles, far away from the centre of myself, across the surface of a pool.

16

All week, while we are supposed to be thinking of Christ approaching Jerusalem, I draw small things using as few lines as possible. A glass with wildflowers, Mama's pans in the kitchen, the moth on her lampshade. While you draw, you follow the shapes and structure of something else, something not you, and can let your thoughts drift. Underneath, I am trying to figure out how to tackle Mama. Everything that happened to her, losing her parents, that lonely covering up of who she was, seems to have made her untouchable. A taboo creature, dedicated to the god of anguish.

Drawing helps. Drawing is like planting seeds in bare earth. Shoots appear, then a stalk, a leaf. Painting is different, I am not up to that yet. To make a painting, like making a life, you have to scrub out things that don't work. Scrape away, rebuild, scrape again. You lose some possibilities to let in others. Sometimes painting itself feels like a language of loss.

When I first met David's parents, I thought being Jewish was about writing and reading. They really were people of the book. Then I went to their Seder and suddenly 'Jewish' meant being together in the wilderness, love in the face of loss. Maybe having left my own country at eighteen made me think that. Or maybe I carried Mama's sense of loss in my genes like haemophilia and didn't know.

Katerina runs every morning, then sits with Mama. I still feel a deep anger in her. She is angry with everybody, and angry she has to hide it. Mama doesn't pick this up. She sleeps half the day and spends the other half enjoying her escape from mortality.

'I've told Katerina,' I tell Papa. 'She won't say anything till I talk to Mama. Have you told Mama you told me?' Papa looks as if I'm pointing a pistol at him and shakes his head.

'I wish you hadn't told me,' Katerina says one night, painting her toenails on my bed. The varnish is swirly, like syrup on frappuccino. In my bare room, her sprawl of smooth limbs and spiky hair are like exotic plants in a desert. If I painted her like this, focused on her toes, the brightest points of light would be the domes of her nearly closed eyelids. I'm used to having mixed feelings about Mama, I'm her daughter, but for Katerina Mama is the one person she never fought with. Now she is someone who lied to her, to us, but is also armoured in unthinkable pain.

'It's not fair to tell me and say I can't talk to her.'

'Would you really rather not know? She's got to recover before we ask her. Her heart has damaged muscle or something. A damaged valve.'

She wiggles her toes like a row of bright red beans. 'Mum, you're too thin, and you're not getting proper exercise. I'm going to write out some exercises for you.' She replaces the little brush in its bottle and disappears.

On Great Friday, church bells toll all day for the death of Christ. We stay in with Mama and don't join the Epitaphios procession, nor Saturday's midnight service. But Mama gets up for the first time and when Papa, Nikos and Leila come back from midnight Mass laughing, guarding their candle flames, she is there to greet them and say *Christ is risen*.

We eat Holy Saturday soup. Katerina watches her and says nothing.

121

'These flames come all the way from Jerusalem,' says Leila. 'From a fire in the Church of the Holy Sepulchre. Imagine.'

Nikos smiles at her, looks at the candle flames and sings a *mantinada*.

'Why does your mother say, she'll light the lamp at night,
'When she has living in her house, the sun and moon
so bright?'

Papa laughs. Lent is over, he has a glass of wine. He answers Nikos with another, raising his glass to Mama.

'I try escaping fire but I am burning in its flame.
'My destiny has ordered this, there's no one else to blame.'

We all laugh. *Mantinades* are a Cretan institution, a traditional contest of quick male wit, men sing rhyming couplets at each other to the tune of an ancient Cretan epic. Katerina says it's like battle rap without being vicious. It's supposed to be extempore, but many old men remember thousands of verses. I hear cigarettes in Papa's voice. He's allowed one a day but I bet he's sneaking more.

Leila gets up. She's having a tough time, husbands without work are not always nice to working wives, but tonight her husband is babysitting and she's enjoying her evening out. She waves her candle against the wall to make the smoke cross that protects you from the Evil Eye. Usually you make it on the doorpost, but since our private lives are lived here, in the kitchen, Papa has always drawn them on the kitchen chimney breast. There's a whole forest of soot crosses up there, marking Easters we've celebrated.

Mama smiles with satisfaction at the house getting its annual dose of protection. Katerina draws her brows together in two small lines like a huffy emoji and I suddenly wonder who lived here before, and what protection they found from the evil I am now so conscious of.

Next morning, church bells ring for hours and everyone says *Christ is risen* again. Leila puts red eggs on the guests' breakfast table, and I take Mama over to say Happy Easter. She's walking easier now. She shows the American girls the game of cracking eggs, how to hold yours so it stays uncracked while smashing your opponent's egg.

They instantly crack all the red eggs on their table. Bonnie shows me a toy wild goat from one of the souvenir shops.

'He's a *kri kri*,' I say. 'A wild mountain goat, special to Crete. There are real ones living on that island you see from the harbour.'

'How do we get there?'

'My brother could take you in his boat. It's got a glass bottom so you also see the sea beneath.'

'Cool.' Bonnie gallops her goat behind her sister Ruby's chair. Ruby shifts irritably.

'Quit that!'

'It's a *mountain* goat,' says Bonnie, making it gallop harder. 'It jumps from rock to rock.'

'It's *annoying*.'

Mama looks at Ruby sympathetically, and smiles.

The father has booked Easter lunch in a village. When they drive away, we set up our own lunch on the patio. Vasilis and Irene arrive in an SUV and unpack a whole lamb, golden-brown, steaming with *rigani* and glowing with oil, roasted at their hotel on a posh portable spit. Nikos runs to help them carry it down to the patio.

'Ri! At last, *paidi mou*! Christ is risen.' Vasilis folds me in a big hug. He is head of the family really, now Papa is so ancient. His suspiciously black hair and moustache are very glossy. With my nose in his crisp new Calvin Klein shirt, patriotic black for a

Cretan Easter, I am drenched in his aftershave. I catch Irene's eye and smile. She's the one responsible for the lamb and the perfect ironing. She smiles back, delighted.

Katerina carries out the salad we made and Vasilis fetches a crate of Cretan wine from his car.

'Bravo,' says Nikos, embracing him too. 'Christ is risen.' He unzips his lute and plays a few bars of a Syrtos, whooshing me back to teenage dances, the smouldering electricity of a boy's eyes meeting yours across the circle, clutching people's hot shoulders, your feet following scurrying notes in a haze of sexuality.

Vasilis spreads his arms like a cross and dances a few steps. They have done this ever since they were small – two brothers, one playing, one dancing. Then Vasilis knocks back a tumbler of wine and attacks the lamb. Nikos goes on strumming. The lute's sides shimmer, its metal clasps wink in the sun. I try to fix in my memory the shimmer of light across the sandalwood rose. I am not a British artist. Or maybe *British* is so many things it does not matter.

Nikos croons under his breath the old summons before a *man-tinada*. *Ela, ela, ela, aman, aman.* Listen, listen, listen. Leila hands round plates, Irene distributes potatoes. Nikos winks at me and sings louder.

'If you go to Aghia Tapho, and don't get drunk out there,
'It's like visiting the Panaghia, without saying a prayer!'

Everyone laughs. Vasilis straightens up from his carving and sings back.

'For chestnuts you need wine. Walnuts need honey, right?
'And a beautiful girl needs kissing hard, morning, noon and night!'

Papa laughs, and turns to Mama in mock melancholy.

124

'What good to me is one heart? I want another too.
'I'll love you hard with both of them, but that still – won't – do!'

Mama smiles. Loukia looks up, and starts singing herself.

'I'll break into your hard drive, I'll hack your heart,
'And keep you on a CD Rom, so we're never apart.'

Mantinades always used to be male, but what do I know of young Cretans these days? I am never here long enough. 'Loukia! Did you make that up?'

'Someone sang it in the restaurant. Lots of new ones like that going the rounds.'

Katerina crackles away in rough Cretan to Leila's kids, helping them take selfies on her phone. She doesn't have a dad any more, but however she feels about her granny just now, she does have this. Soon Nikos's fingers are racing round the strings and we are all dancing to the music of home. David should be here. This is the sort of moment I miss him most. There's a new edge to missing him now. Never mind risen Christ, I tell him in my head. I'm half-Jewish, the half that counts. I was one of you, all along.

After Easter, Mama dresses every morning. Katerina says she has to learn Granny's vegetable recipes so she can cook vegan in Bushwick. She sits in the kitchen chopping to Mama's direction, slipping in casual questions about Mama's childhood, and Mama blocks her every time. As delicious smells rise through the house, I'm shocked at how expertly Mama stonewalls. The past is inaccessible but no way is this her fault. Nothing to do with her. 'Everything was lost, child.' 'I can't remember.' I feel the tree of knowledge rotting before my eyes.

'I hate this,' Katerina says one night, walking in from the corridor holding an electric toothbrush against her teeth. The

125

toothpaste dribbles down her chin like tribal markings. 'Not saying, *Granny, tell me about it.* I'm going to ask her every bloody detail in the summer.'

On her last night, I go into her room when she is packing. 'Where are you with Dora now, love? Can I do anything?'

'Fine, Mum. Don't interfere. We're filming at the centre in July.' She empties her rucksack on the bed and an envelope flips to the floor. 'Oh yes. I forgot. Your New York gallery asked me to pick this up. Some guy left it for you.'

'*Your New York gallery* sounds so grand.'

'It *is* grand. Don't undersell yourself.'

I put the envelope away unopened but when I'm going to sleep Katerina comes to my room in the dark and gets in beside me, as she did in the weeks we were comforting each other after we lost David.

'It's so *awful* what happened. It must be horrid for you too.' I put my arms round her and stroke her mossy hair. 'Good luck,' she whispers. 'Tell me what she says.'

Early next morning I kiss her goodbye and stand a long time waving at the cab.

Mama is drinking coffee on the sofa in Reception. Above her, the Knossos bull gazes into space from his red-rimmed eyes. I picture Mama's heart, the damaged muscle, the medicine keeping it beating, the layers of loss. If I were a stethoscope, I could hear what she has hidden inside.

Now's the time. I feel like an ant at the mouth of the labyrinth. I sit beside her and take a breath but Papa limps in from nowhere and sits the other side of the coffee table, fingering a pack of Karelia Blue. He is not allowed to smoke in the house but he is nervous, he has to finger something. He must have been lying in wait for this moment. OK, I'll ask Mama with him here.

Mama looks suspiciously at both of us.

'How are you feeling, Mama?'

'Fine.'

'When you were in hospital, you said something in your sleep. You asked me to say *kaddish* for you.'

Mama stares straight ahead as if she hasn't heard.

'Papa said you were Jewish. He said your name wasn't Sophia when you were little but Sara. Why didn't you tell us?'

Mama stares at Papa across the plastic roses. There are things any of us might say now that could feel like a knife in the heart. I'm sixty-two, Nikos sixty-eight, Vasilis seventy. They've kept this from us all our lives. It isn't being Jewish and not saying, which might not mean much in England or America, though here it's huge. It is something that has had no place in the Cretan story. Or our family.

'He said the Germans took your parents to Aghias Prison. What happened to them? Why didn't you tell me you were Jewish when I married a Jew myself?'

I'm suddenly shivering. This barely seems real. Maybe we all three feel a bit like that. Staring at the roses, Mama mutters, 'For you, it made no difference. For me, better to forget.'

'That's not true. It would have made all the difference.' I surprise myself by starting to cry, great hot fat tears running down my cheeks. I don't know if I am crying for her or me. 'What happened to your parents?'

This is the silence of earth. Dug into, suddenly exposed.

'We didn't know,' she finally says. Still her eyes on Papa, waiting for a cue. 'Not for years.'

'I told her you lived in Kondylaki,' Papa says suddenly. He has come to her help all his life. 'I told her you came to Hebrew lessons here.'

'*Here?*' This is a whole new unexpected thing and throws me completely. 'You didn't say that, Papa! This house? *Our* house? Is *this* where her Hebrew teacher lived?'

Neither of them says a word. Every minute feels battled for.

'What happened to *him*?'

Mama closes her eyes. Her face looks grey.

'She has to lie down,' Papa says. He takes her arm. I heave her up. We half-walk, half-drag her across the floor but Papa is the one she leans on. She detaches herself from me, shuffles with him into the bedroom, and they close the door.

I feel as if I'd been flung against a wall. I hear her voice, then his, very low. No sounds of panic, she must be all right. I look up at the Knossos bull. OK. OK. I'll walk to town, look in on Nikos and the museum, catch up on emails in Starbucks, find the house Mama grew up in. And that synagogue.

Outside, I pick a pomegranate leaf. How long do pomegranate trees last, how old is this one? I try to remember what Papa said about the garden. Fruit trees, he said. Vegetables. White doves. How clever of him to deflect me like this, knock my questioning away onto the house. I do remember more trees when I was little. But the man who'd been a Turkish slave, and the silver-haired teacher – what happened to them?

I pass through the gate feeling like a child sent away from home to an unknown destination, seeing everything with new eyes. The sandy pavement, mulberry trees in the *plateia*, the kiosk where Papa buys Karelia Blue. How did all this look when he brought Mama here to Hebrew lessons? And how did they get to live in this house?

17

The harbour water is dull pewter under a heavy sky. I walk up the central street, past jewellery shops, leather-workers, the Orthodox cathedral and Catholic church, a new ice-cream parlour, and a foot-spa where tourists get skin nibbled off their feet by fish. At the top the Judas trees are in bloom. Their black stems, frosted with purple blossom, creak in the wind like masts.

Nikos sells CDs and electronics in a space squeezed between one shop selling sandals and another selling watches. In his window are posters of Cretan musicians in black shirts. He would love to be among them. Instead he sells other people's CDs and DJs on a Cretan music radio station. In summer, his group does an occasional gig in outdoor restaurants. I was so lucky that what Mr Michael's bounty did for me was whisk me off to London.

'Nikolaki! When are you starting your boat trips? Can you take our guests?'

'Sure. I start tomorrow. I've lined up a boy to run this place.'

The shop is empty. The boy won't need to do much. 'Listen.' He puts on a song. 'Doesn't this remind you of Papa?'

> *My love for you was deep and true.*
> *Never would I part from you,*
> *my lovely little komboloi!*
> *When my woman left, there was a cost –*
> *but it's worse now you have gone! My life is lost!*

We listen and laugh and for a moment I think I might tell him, but two foreign girls come in asking about nightclubs and I leave him to it.

In Starbucks, I catch up on emails.

Nashita is back in Mumbai. *Hey lady I've got you a studio! An old friend, Sanjiv, an archaeologist, he's usually away digging up a temple somewhere but he's a sweetie, you'll like him, his wife died a few years ago – his dad's studio might be free. Not far from us and the Gateway of India. How's that?*

Fantastic! Yes please. But hey, no matchmaking.

No? I'll put you in contact anyway. When are you coming?

I don't know how long I'll have to stay here. I'm teaching in the autumn. February?

I'll work to that. Everyone here wants to meet you!

I feel as I do when starting a painting, searching for a space to trust.

I wander numbly a while. Everyone is getting ready for the season, whitewashing, setting out window displays. Thinking of Mumbai, and gateways to India, I buy a few small canvasses, stretched and primed, in the art supplies shop.

Normally I love walking through the Old Town. The shades of stone, butterscotch, ginger, saffron. Complicated arches, court-yards, iron grilles, balconies. Always something unexpected. Today I keep noticing the way we need protection. The church of San Rocco protected the town from plague. The mosque used to contain a sword of healing. I look up the barrel of its minaret, gold against a cornflower sky. They all met here – churches, mosques and synagogues, Muslims, Christians, Jews. The architecture, at least, is harmonious.

I picture the bombers Papa saw, and smoke spiralling up from the town. How did anything survive? Lots didn't. There are roofless houses here too, mustard-coloured walls now smothered in deep blue

130

morning glory. I'd love to be able to drop in on Ayla in the refugee centre. She was a lesson in endurance, always kind and hopeful.

Be good to her and her kids, ferocious Athens. All these lives, blown through Crete like leaves stripped from their tree in a storm.

I'm in the Street of Knives now. On one side, shops with the black-handled knives that sum up Cretan pride. Well, male pride. On the other, an ochre stone wall, a wall of all our history, Greek, Roman, Byzantine, Venetian and Ottoman masonry on top of each other like a golden sandwich. Crete has so many layers. You walk from one epoch to another in a second. And here are the earliest ruins of all, in an excavation railed off from the road. The only Minoan ruins we have are domestic streets. A whole unexplored palace may lurk under the modern town too, but no one will let you get at it. The roof and fence fling diagonal shadows over gold cobbles. These little streets are Chania's oldest memory. A flash of the unconscious, the labyrinth beneath us all.

I tighten my fingers round the railings and think how light still shines on us from stars that no longer exist.

The museum was originally a Venetian basilica. Since then it has been a mosque, a cinema and an arms store. In the Sixties it became a museum. I linger by a new clay seal-stone, found in a bombed church on Kastelli. The museum has given it a glass case all to itself and put beside it a drawing of the picture carved on it, a tiny Minoan landscape, seemingly the very hill the stone was found on, with a building on top. On the roof is a half-naked male figure gazing out to sea. The museum calls him Master of the Harbour.

I draw him, and let the peace of this place, the dark soaring arches, take me over.

Now the octopus vase. I always stop here, I remember watching Papa stick it together. A two-handled thing, with a stylized octopus painted on it, black and orange. The octopus is really just a simple joyful flourish suggesting two big round eyes. They could

be two hands pressed together from the elbows, juggling pomegranates. I remember seeing Papa add all the pieces till the whole
thing stood up complete on his table. He was excited too, he didn't
often get to rebuild a whole pot.

Around the octopus are wavy black and red stripes. You can see
individual hairs where the brush flowed with paint. It was the first
thing that made me think, paint *lasts*. It gives you the touch, and
the mind, of someone else.

Out in the garden among trees and statues where Papa used to
work and I began drawing, I let myself think back to that conversation with Mama. *We didn't know what happened to them.* How
much she has always withheld.

Two Italians runs the best ice-cream shop in Chania. I choose
strawberry and pistachio for the family freezer and plunge into the
pedestrian alleys of tourist Chania. Most boutiques are still closed,
so in Kondylaki I can see the old houses uncluttered by souvenir
stands. I'm still staggered Mama grew up in one of these. Like
Katerina, I always used to try and ask about her past, but when I
tried directly Mama slapped me down.

The things we can't ask our mothers. The family freezer. Now I
see my part in that as a kind of collusion.

The house with a lion door-knocker, next to the one with a balcony, now sells Indian clothes. As I stand outside, looking in the
window, a girl wheels out a clothes rack of harem trousers. Many
boutique owners here spend half the year buying clothes in Jaipur
or Bali, and the other half selling them to foreigners.

'We're just opening,' says the girl in English. 'Can I help you?
Try anything you like.'

Inside it smells of damp and incense. Beside a rack of wrap-
round skirts, I look at an arched stone ceiling. The stairs must
be walled off, the wall between this and the old front room has

been demolished, but I should be standing on the spot where Papa first spoke to Mama. I buy a scarf and get out. Opposite me is a tiny passage to the synagogueand a small notice saying Etz Hayyim. Tree of Life, I remember Kyrios Mois explaining to Papa. Why did I never come here with David? Maybe because this is the most crowded part of a tourist town and if you have grown up in a town that grows fuller and fuller of tourists you shy away from things you think are made for them. Or maybe I'm kidding myself and some part of me was afraid of what I'd find.

I turn a corner and see a cul de sac, a wall running alongside, a stone Italianate doorway, and a grey sentry box with no one in it. Maybe Jewish places of worship need a police guard these days, but this one is off duty. Still, the door itself is open so I step in, and unexpectedly down. I find myself in a walled yard under an olive tree, beside an ancient little church.

The tree has been hard-pruned. Only the tips are in leaf, tiny grey fingertips feeling for light, but a haze of new growth runs along every branch. Roots have thrust up under the cobbles, blistering them into a mound with the broken handle of a clay amphora plastered over them. A bare vine-stem writhes round a carved stone niche containing a tap, a basin, a copper flagon. Papyrus and water lilies grow in a clay *pithos* high as my chin. There is a homely table with chairs around it, a cup of coffee, an open notebook. I was wrong. This is not for tourists. Everything here has the glow that comes from being used.

A young woman, tall and pale, comes out and smiles.

'Could I see the synagogue, please?' I speak in Greek and don't know if this is an ordinary request. They must get a lot of tourists pushing at that door.

'Certainly. Come.' She takes me into the building. I stand still, dazed. This is where my mother's parents, my grandparents, came to worship. And Mama, when she was a child. But also where Papa watched German soldiers at work, plundering.

133

It is a small peaceful hall full of silence, glinting with textiles in deep earth-colours like a rusty rainbow, amethyst, chocolate, burgundy. White arches. A sheaf of open doors through which I see a patch of garden. Light filters down from high windows onto polished benches glimmering with embroidered cushions. On the left is a wood panel hung with taffeta of smoky topaz. Rose-brown silk lies lightly over a large book open on a lectern.

'The Ehal, the Torah Shrine,' says my guide.

'It is a . . . working synagogue,' I say feebly, embarrassed.

'It is. The service is every Friday night. Everyone is welcome. The prayers are in Hebrew and English.'

She has shiny brown eyes and wide eyebrows, wears a soft green shirt, brown cardigan and flip-flops, and can see I don't really know where I am. This is unlike any synagogue I have seen. The one near David's parents in Belsize Square is brighter and much bigger. The one near us in Muswell Hill is a modern hall.

She points to an upper arch. 'Behind that screen is the women's gallery. We don't use it for that now.' She smiles. 'Everyone sits here.'

Has Papa never wanted to come and see this restoration? She leads me through to a back courtyard with bare rose stems and tombstones on which small stones have been placed.

'Whose graves are these?'

'Rabbis. Buried here around the time Greek uprisings began in mainland Greece against Ottoman rule. We think there was unrest in town and it was too dangerous to take bodies to the Jewish cemetery.'

'Is there a Jewish cemetery in Chania? I had no idea.'

'There used to be a huge one, in Nea Chora. There are apartment blocks there now. And a primary school.'

She shows me the ritual bath, a small building with a well in it, then takes me up a curly iron staircase to the library.

'Our archive. All we have left. We lost the rest in two arson attacks.'

'*Two?*'

'Our Albanian caretaker gave the alarm in the first, and whoever they were ran away. They left behind a bar of soap. You know the anti-semitic taunt, *I'll turn you into a bar of soap?* We think it might have been a reference to the Holocaust.'

'Christ.'

'Quite.' She smiles sadly. 'It still goes on. But we try and educate people here about the town's Jewish history and make friends for the synagogue. It was rededicated twenty years ago.'

'Are you Jewish? Sorry, is it OK to ask that?'

'Of course! Lots of different people come here, all faiths and none. No, I'm not Jewish. I *am* the librarian, though. And a historian. I like to get at facts. The truth of what happened. This is a very special place.'

We are standing on the roof of the next-door building. Below is the empty sentry-box. All the houses are so close together. A breeze ruffles my hair and hers. I can't tell where she's from. She has a slight accent. Somehow this place encourages you to bring it your private feelings but not bubble over with them, it is too dignified for that. I'm too overwhelmed to say who I am, why I am here, and she doesn't ask if I'm Jewish. I guess you learn here to let people ask their questions and not intrude your own.

A synagogue. In Europe. Every story is charged. What if I told her about Mama? That will come. It has to.

'We cleaned up the damage the first attack did, and held a service. But that night they got in again. The second fire was worse. We lost over two thousand books and manuscripts. And our computers.'

'Did they catch them?'

'They caught two Brits. Nightclub waiters. And one Greek, who confessed. Two Americans were involved as well, but no one came to trial. We think pressure was brought to bear. The prosecutor said the evidence was too weak.'

Then she tells me. Of course someone knew. I didn't need Katerina to go on the web. This girl is a historian, she gives me facts. Yes, the Holocaust. Yes, here, where I was born. Three hundred doctors, teachers, workmen, pistachio-sellers, civil servants. Bootblacks, merchants, barbers and lamp-makers. Ribbon-makers, dressmakers, wine-sellers, children, housewives. The last remnants of one of the oldest Jewish settlements in the world.

All gone. Except, apparently, my mum.

Walking back, I feel cold. Not just horrified and dislocated but unreal. This was home. This harbour and sea, these golden alleyways. But the town I grew up in has disappeared.

Mechanically, back in Rooms Karderini, I put the ice-cream in the freezer and help Leila make lunch. Inside me everything is seething and confused. Then the bedroom door opens and Papa helps Mama into the kitchen. They are doddery and hunched but their worn old faces are preparing to be fierce if need be, like elderly householders braving a burglar.

'Come, Mama, sit. Come, Papa. We've made *stifado*.' Leila knows nothing of what is going on so it is easy to chat. Where will Katerina be now on her way to New York, how did our American guests like their Easter lunch, will Nikos give them a discount on his boat? Then Papa takes Mama off for a sleep and I wash up with Leila, wondering what she will think when she hears.

Mama seems to me now like a door that only opens from inside. She has kept it closed all my life. And look what lay within. A whole community disappeared and I have never, ever heard anyone speak of it. And here is the Holocaust squatting silently across our island's past.

The nearest sea is a sandy civic place with a cement walkway where I used to take Leila and Katerina to make sandcastles. It is a calm day, the waves are flat and lazy, the stones are blueish grey with a

136

dull silvery glitter, heaped up like counters in a game played on this coast by some ancient god. They are veined with zig-zaggy white, pitted with chips smoothed by the sea. I sit on a big pale flat one and draw the tousle of the waves. You see each wave come in, and traces of it after as it is pulled back, but when it breaks you can't see what is happening in the splintering water. I try drawing the aftermath, the fan and trickle as each wave slides back to the ocean.

How impossible it is, to see the present as you live it. How difficult, to scrap the story you have been told about yourself. I feel like that strand of weed sliding about in the surf. How far down do you have to dig, to get beyond the silence?

When I finish drawing, I think of Katerina and do star-jumps on the sand.

At home, I find Papa chatting to our guests on the patio. They are going south tomorrow to explore the island and would love to go out with Nikos when they return.

'Mama OK?' I ask softly.

Papa nods. 'You can talk to her now.'

Mama is on the bed staring into space. The afternoon light is liquid gold and the little room is exquisitely neat, objects arranged on the chest of drawers with such care you feel there must be deep meaning behind them.

'Can I get you anything, Mama? Coffee?'

She has on her let's-get-this-over-with face. The one she takes to the dentist. 'What do you want to know?'

'Everything,' I say, lightly as I can. 'I went to your old house this morning. Next to the house with the balcony, is that right?'

She dips her head.

'It sells tourist clothes now. Have you seen it?'

'No.'

'The synagogue's been restored, have you seen that?'

'No.'

137

'They told me there, the Germans took all the Jews. Was that how your parents died?'

Another dip of the head.

'And your teacher, who lived in this house?'

'I suppose so.'

'Why didn't you *tell* me? Tell us?'

'To protect you. So you didn't carry it all your lives.'

That's not what she said before. But she's right. I'd be a different person if I'd known *My mum's family died in the Holocaust.* I'd have carried that constantly in me.

I sit beside her. Hug her. Under the softly sagging flesh, her bones are those of a bird. She rests her head on my shoulder. We have never been so close.

'Tell me about you, Mama, as a child? Your parents. School. Everything.'

18

Sara/Sophia, March 1941–May 1944

She slept, she had always slept, in a wooden bed with fruit carved on the headboard. Morning sun slipped through cracks between the shutters, lit the wooden ceiling and turned the rafters, which were full of little holes, into long gold sieves. When she opened the shutters, she saw the yard and an olive tree. The White Mountains behind were either wrapped in foggy coats, invisible, or sparkled against blue sky as if cut by Father's jewel-saw.

Coming out of the bedroom, she looked down from the landing to the hall, which was really a stone-flagged passage, running from the front door to the yard. The front door's bottom edge was carved with flowers, their petals softened by layers of white paint. The creak the door made when it opened was the sound of her father coming home, the sound of love. But also of adventuring outside to a street full of friends.

The Ovraiki, only a few streets, was the Jewish Quarter but Christians lived there too. Everyone spoke Greek, though Jews also knew Hebrew. Not to talk of course, but to pray. Eleni, her best friend, was Christian and lived next door. Eleni was plump with a round face, her left eyelid fell half over her eye so she looked as if she was winking, but she had a sweet smile and was not a winking sort of person at all.

Eleni liked her cousin Thodoros, who was in their class at

139

school. But Jews had to marry other Jews. Mama did like Amos and Immanuel who lived in the next street, but the boy she really thought about, as she sewed her dowry, was Yosif.

Yosif lived next door on the left. His voice was warm and deep, he was five years older, and his mouth went lop-sided when he smiled.

On Friday nights, Moumo lit the two Sabbath candles. *Zakhor* and *Shamor*, she would say, looking down smiling. Two is a good number, she always said. *Remember* and *Protect*.

Saturday was the annoying day when she couldn't go out and the other annoying thing was learning Hebrew. Always looking for the verb was like walking in the dark. Father taught her when she was small, then Barba Rafael took over and it was harder.

Barba Rafael taught all the Jewish children Hebrew. He lived in a little house beyond the harbour where he grew fruit and vegetables and had been a friend of Chief Rabbi Evlagon before Rabbi Osmos came. Rabbi Evlagon had lived next door in the house with a balcony, which was Eleni's house now. Papa didn't like Rabbi Osmos, but he never said so straight out. She just knew he didn't.

Moumo taught her cooking and embroidery, which were much easier than Hebrew. But Father coached her in the Questions to ask, as the youngest at the Seder, and she did like that because she knew them by heart and Father practised them with her in his workroom. He said the Seder was about finding a way out of Egypt, a way to be safe, but she always felt safe in his workroom anyway. The little boxes held painted beads, silver offcuts, tiny silver tongs and miniature hammers, whose wood handles were velvety with the years Father had used them.

What does Seder mean? he would ask.

Order, she said.

What does this order help us remember?

Escape from Egypt. How to escape what's imprisoning in our lives.

What is *matsah*?

140

The bread of affliction. Because the Jews ate it when they were slaves.

Only affliction?

No, also of going forth because they made it before they escaped, so it's the bread of freedom too. But the bread isn't free. She used to giggle at her own joke. Because it mustn't rise. The Jews had no time to let it rise.

What does the roast bone represent?

The lamb they sacrificed. They sprinkled its blood on their doors so the Angel of Death wouldn't kill their sons.

When she was twelve, her period came and afterwards she had to be purified in the *mikveh*. She had always known she would have to go down into it one day.

You plunge in over your head, Moumo said. We all do. Then we are women.

Kyria Esther, the old woman who looked after the *mikveh*, took her into the stone building behind the synagogue. It was dark like a cave.

Take off all your clothes, Kyria Esther said.

Mama's skin was goose bumps, puckering the scabbing over a graze on her arm. As she stood on the top step, feeling with her toes for the step below, under water, Kyria Esther suddenly stuck her nail under that scab and ripped it off.

Mama screamed.

Everything has to come off, said Kyria Esther. Your whole body must be clean so God can get to all of you.

Mama thought nothing would ever be so frightening again.

One afternoon in October, in the Kal, she helped Moumo decorate the tent for Sukkot, the Feast of Tabernacles, to celebrate the Israelites' camp in the wilderness. They tied fresh-picked pomegranates round the tent because Sukkot was harvest too. Then Yosif came in, ducking his head through the entrance, arms full of barley stalks.

What do we do with these? he asked with his crooked smile.

Mama showed him where to hang them, he hung the first

141

bunch upside down, she laughed and showed him the right way, their hands touched, they tied bunches like little straw dancers all round the tent. Then Father rushed in, spoiling her time with Yosif.

The Greeks have said *No*, Father said.

Moumo went on hanging a pomegranate but Yosif straightened and Mama felt him forgetting her.

We are at war, Father said, with Italy.

Foreign soldiers appeared in town. English soldiers, come to protect Crete. Tavernas cooked potatoes for them a special way, long and thin and fried, which was how the English ate potatoes. In November, Yosif went to Albania with the Cretan Division. He had new yellow boots like lion's paws, a present from the army.

The Greek army needs us, he said proudly. I'm going away like a swallow but I'll come back like a lion. We'll soon sort out those Italians.

In December, Yosif's mother read a letter from him. He said they captured hundreds of Italians. But other Italians went on dropping bombs over Suda, and the town still echoed with gunfire. At the Christian festival, Christmas, they saw English soldiers ride through streets on tanks, smiling and waving. Everyone cheered and waved back. The Bishop of Chania blessed them.

Why are they here? she asked. If the English left Crete, the Italians would go away.

Italy has allies, said Father. The Germans have invaded other countries and may try to invade Greece. But the English will stop them.

There were no more letters from Yosif.

In spring, she helped Moumo prepare festival sweets for Purim, when the Jews were saved from the wicked Haman. She moulded Haman's Ears from almonds, Haman's Fleas from sesame. At supper, Father said a Jewish lady, Kyria Sezana, had come from Heraklion to talk about art history to the Chrystostomos Society. Kyria Sezana studied art history in Berlin, but came home when

142

she saw German people smashing Jewish shops and synagogues. Smartly dressed women clapped their hands, she said, and held up their babies to watch people break Jewish windows. She said German people did not like Jews.

There was a little silence after Father said that.

Rabbi Osmos says it's not true, Father added, and Moumo suddenly said she needed a store-room. She had said this before but now she sounded urgent. The only place, she said, was Father's workroom. So next day, Father said he had asked a young carpenter to make a shed in the yard so he could work there.

That boy's not one of us, said Moumo.

He's our neighbour, said Father. He's fourteen and a good crafts-man. He supports his mother and crippled grandfather. Good deeds to anyone, Simcha, Gentile or Jew, bring you closer to God.

To her annoyance, Mama couldn't see this boy. She left for school before he came and returned after he left. She knew his name was Andonis and watched the shed he made grow in the yard, bigger every evening. She wondered what he thought while making it, whether he wondered about her.

On the last day of term, she sat next to Eleni twisting thread for their spring bracelets.

Tie them round each other's wrists, said the teacher Kyria Myrtakis, who was fat and strict but fair. She had a moustache and glasses and a mole by her mouth. Take the bracelets off, she said, when you see the first swallow. Then hang them on trees, for birds to make nests.

I'm hungry, whispered Eleni. She was wearing a little cloth badge, like a pair of miniature soldier's boots, for her father and all Cretan soldiers who had gone to Albania. Mama longed to wear one too, for Yosif.

It was the last day of winter uniform. Her blouse itched, the classroom felt like a ginger beer bottle about to explode. The boys smelt of sweat and feet, sniggering behind her, then pushed and

143

shoved when everyone filed outside to practise dancing. Thodoros, the bully, said something she couldn't hear. Other boys laughed. It was a mystery why Eleni liked him. The bigger boys had kept him down, but they had all gone to Albania.

Now boys, shouted the teacher. The Pentozali! Remember our hero Daskalogiannis danced it the night before his great last battle against the Turks.

Thodoros strode to the front. Amos and Immanuel, who looked so alike no one could tell them apart, mock-staggered to their places, other boys fooled around swapping positions, only quiet little Philippos stood calm till everyone was ready. Then Thodoros led the boys out, leaping high in the air, smacking his ankle.

Now the Syrtos Chaniotikos, said Kyria Myrtakis. A dance for Chania and for Crete. This is how we won freedom from the Turks, children. By moving *together*. It is a war dance in disguise. Thodoros is *kapetanios*, leading everyone into battle.

Freedom or death, yelled Amos. Or maybe Immanuel.

The end of the dancing was the end of the term. Everyone surged out of the yard, longing to get out of long black winter socks, long-sleeved shirts, prickly skirts and trousers. At home Mama ran upstairs, tore off her uniform, looked out of the window and saw a thin boy, carrying a plank as if it were a feather. She put on a blue blouse, went onto the upper landing and saw the boy in the hall below, looking up.

He had deep hazel eyes. When he laughed, he watched for her to laugh too. Was the rest of him as sunburnt as his arms? Each time they met she felt something happening between them. When she gave him a glass of water, her knuckle brushed his hand and she felt a shock as if something had given way within her. She found herself in a confused feeling of continuous surprise. Through all the hours she didn't see him, something kept shifting that changed the way they were together next time.

144

it is so hot at night you can't clasp your hands, each finger
makes the others hotter

when andonis looks at sara she looks away, it is like two birds
jumping back and forward, always the same distance between
    the not-looking is a kind of looking and shuts her out

she keeps her hand in the cage holding a thistle and feels light
claws on her fingers, he is standing on her hand to peck seed,
he raises his head and looks at her, next day he hops on her
finger and starts on the seed
    the afternoon is hot and still, even the floorboards seem
asleep, she takes him to the front to draw him with a different
background, she draws the cage, the street behind and sees
andonis walking round the corner
    he won't be coming to the house not now when everyone's asleep
    she sees sara coming from the opposite direction, neither
looks surprised to see the other but they don't look pleased
either which makes her glad
    they stand close to each other, sara brushes her hair off her
cheek the way she does when she's not sure what to do and
andonis put his hand up to do it for her
    sara puts her other hand up and holds his hand on her cheek

she carries on drawing and hates what she has drawn, his hand
on sara's cheek is too big and all wrong, then when she looks
up andonis has gone
    some mean part of her wants to wake father and show him
her drawing, another part says no one must see this ever
    she shouldn't have seen this
    she can't unsee it now

enchantment means wanting something and feeling on the
edge of having it
    enchantment also means something you're not really
going to get

慘

Why should I go to Hebrew? Sara said. It was hot, her skin prickled as she faced Father on the upstairs landing, and the wood of the stairs, walls and ceiling creaked around them.

To know the words, Father said. To ask God for help in these uncertain times.

How can knowing another language stop the Germans?

Father looked angrier than she had ever seen.

You need to understand the meanings of our prayers. I have asked that boy Andonis to take you.

She followed Andonis out of the house resentfully, but as she walked in the spring air through blue thistles, white daisies and red poppies she couldn't help feeling happy. Andonis had rolled up his sleeves, and there were dark patches on his back where his shirt stuck to his skin. He led the way down to a *plateia*. Under the mulberry trees it was splashy and green like being in a pond. Splinters of light slanted over the furry black hair on his forearms. He smiled and she dropped her eyes to stop herself smiling back.

In Barba Rafael's study, with books on the wall rising to the ceiling, books she could not read in front of her, in a room that felt like a cage despite the beautiful red embroidery, she felt ashamed. She had not done the work. Barba Rafael was sad not angry, which made it worse and she began to cry. He put his hand gently on hers.

Don't weep, Sara. Your mother's name, Simcha, means Happiness. Did you know that? Stay happy, my dear. You will do better next time.

On the way back, where the path was steep, almost a little cliff, Andonis suddenly stopped, turned, and wiped her face with

146

his sleeve. He smelt of earth and sun. His hazel eyes were very close to hers. Serious, but with a glint of a smile like sun behind a thundery cloud.

Like to get out of the house a while this evening?

It's Friday. The Sabbath starts tonight.

Sunday, then? The Zafirakou alley at nine?

She felt he understood her better than anyone in the world and always would.

When she got home, Father said they were all going to the synagogue that night to pray for those defending them in the north.

On Sunday night, Andonis put his arms round her, fingertips light on her hips, and pulled her to him. His lips touched her cheek. She heard his heart, *lub dub lub dub*, and felt, this is where I belong.

And the next night, and the next, every night after supper. She said she was at Eleni's house, revising for exams. Father didn't like her going out.

The Germans are in Greece now, he said. No one knows what's coming.

I'm only next door, she said, and felt guilty for lying. Then angry. It was Father's fault she lied and felt guilty.

Then Andonis went away to Perivolia. She couldn't sleep. She relived his arms round her, the touch of his hands. The lying frightened her but love took you to a new world, didn't it, where the old things did not matter.

One night it was very windy, one of those fierce winds that felt as though they would sweep away your soul. A shutter kept banging somewhere. She felt it was thumping out her guilt. *Bad girl. Thump. Bad girl.* Then the world burst around her in crashes, screams and howls. The house juddered and thrashed, she got up and ran to her parents' room. Father was helping Moumo out of bed.

Quick, Sara. Downstairs.

Is it an earthquake?

147

Bombs. Quick. Under the kitchen table.

She sat squashed under it all day, curled into Moumo's lap. Every roar grew louder and was followed by a scream, then a *crack* that shook the house. Father kept praying. *The Lord is my rock, my strength in whom I trust. The earth trembled, foundations of the hills were shaken because He was wroth.* She squeezed her eyes shut, saw God shaking the White Mountains like tambourines, her body shook, her teeth skipped and rattled, dishes jumped to the floor and smashed, the house trembled like jelly.

They didn't open the shutters all day. Blades of sun shone through and moved slowly across the floor until evening, when the bombing stopped and they sat in shocked silence.

Father crawled out on hands and knees, they all came out from under the table. Father unbolted the front door and went out. Mama sat on the stairs looking numbly at familiar edges of the flagstones until her body stopped shaking. At last Father came back, shot the bolts and leaned against the door, tears sliding down his cheeks. She ran into his arms.

Shh, little partridge. Nothing's the matter with me. It's the town. They say the Germans bombed all three cities today. Chania, Heraklion, Rethymno. Our neighbours are safe, thanks to God. But oh Sara, he caught his breath in a sob, the big synagogue has gone. It is just – rubble. So is the kindergarten next door.

At the same time next morning the bombs came again. And again, every day the same. They got used to the timing, they had breakfast before the bombs began.

That one's landed. Can't hurt us now, Father kept saying. You're brave girls.

It was very near, Moumo always replied.

◌

she huddles on father's lap in the front room, they don't use the safe place under the kitchen table any more, the planes shriek and

148

roar but she shows him her drawings, here is the ziz she says, the great bird that shuts out the sun when it spreads its wings, and here is a bad black firebird, look, its long fiery tail is spraying bombs, but here is goldie he is a good firebird he lights up the room

father presses his chin on her hair
    she says, this is *maror* isn't it, the bitterness sandwich
    father says nothing
    she says we're in the narrow place but we'll get out won't we
because bitterness and new life go together, that's what you said
    is it her trembling, or him, or the house
    no question is ever the right question, no answer goes
deep enough

wine in the seder is red for the blood of children pharaoh killed

ᦂ

A whole week of bombs. The distant whine, the *whump* of thunder. The house quaking. Plates jumping and smashing.

We'll wrap them in cloth, said Moumo, and all through the ear-splitting din they took dishes out of cupboards and wrapped them while Moumo made bread. By the time the planes left, the plates were safe and bread was baking in the oven.

God He is God, said Father, blessing it before they ate.

One morning before the bombs, they heard a tap at the front door. Their blind neighbour Kyria Anna stood outside, white hair straggling, milky eyes streaming with tears.

I don't know where my daughter is, she said.

Come, said Moumo. Sit with us.

Kyria Anna sat in the kitchen and trembled so much she seemed to melt. Moumo put her arms round her and she stayed all day while the house juddered. Afterwards Father went out and found her daughter, who was frantic not knowing where her blind mother was, and then

149

went round all the neighbours. He said Eleni was fine, so were Amos and Immanuel, though their mother complained it was noisy even when bombs weren't falling, shut in with two boys of thirteen.

Osmos does nothing, said Father. If Rabbi Evlagon were still here, he would make sure no one is hurt or in need.

The bombs went on through Sabbath into the following week. Once, when Father opened the door, Mama saw someone lying face down in the street. Later Father stumbled into the kitchen, saying Splantzia had almost gone and Kastelli was nothing but dust. He looked at Moumo like a child asking a grown-up to make it better. The harbour buildings have not been touched, he said. People say the Germans plan to use them themselves.

໑

in the middle of the crashing and shaking she follows sara to the front room, sara is crying, holding her embroidery to cracks of light in the shutters

she says can I hold the wool for you, sara says no, she says can I draw you, sara says you have enough drawings of me go away

she goes upstairs trying not to cry, she tries to think of god being with her but all she sees is sara not wanting her to hold the wool, her body jitters as if it will never stop, her teeth won't stop chattering

she holds seed in the cage, goldie is used to bombs now, he is on the seed at once, his little throat swallows, he is a messy feeder, husks fall from him in dusty arcs, she strokes his back, the top of his wings is brown then black and further down a gold bar like egg yolk, when he spreads his wings the feathers are black and gold, she wants him to fly, to soar, but not now with the world crashing and shaking

150

if only she could see what is happening outside

 she climbs up to the windowsill and opens one shutter a
little, there are black dots like hawks circling very high, she
hadn't thought they would be so high and far away

 another thud and crash, then the draining *shump shump shump*,
the house shakes, then that terrible rushing sound *whewwwwwww*,
how can there be people up there, real people driving those planes

she knows what bombs look like now

 black eggs, rushing down to blot out the world

∽

The taps stopped working. Father said pipelines had smashed. They
had to ration water, luckily Moumo had put *stamnes* of water in the
store-room. The toilet made a smell through the house. Bombs all
day, and at night so hot even one sheet felt heavy. She was slippery
with sweat, sweat between her breasts, sweat around her nose, but
her mouth dry and her lips cracking.

One day in the kitchen there came a deafening *crack*. Glass
smashed, wood smashed, a big wind blew, there was sudden light
and something huge burst the shutters. Moumo screamed, the
thing was with them in the kitchen, a thump and tinkle, then a
hole in the window, and broken glass everywhere. Moumo lay on
her back with blood on her face and a broken piece of glass beside
her like a wing. A plane roared away above, triumphant.

They carried Moumo to a couch in the front room. Her eyes
were closed. Blood everywhere.

Part of a house came off, Father said. It flew in at our window. I
think it did not hit her, I think she banged her head when she fell.

In the evening, Moumo opened her eyes. Soon her wound
began to heal and she began to speak again, but refused to go in
the kitchen. Father blocked the kitchen window with wood, which
left them all in gloomy darkness.

151

One morning, as they braced themselves, the planes did not come. Only a single plane droning overhead. Father went out. When he came back he said the Germans were in charge of everything. The Town Hall, newspaper offices, the *Lexiarcheon* where everyone's name was registered. The Germans had entered the town and set fire to it, the streets filled with people running away.

Many people died, but not in our quarter, Father said, thank the Lord. Eleni is alive. And Kyria Allegra, Kyria Anna and her daughter. The twins. But we must say *kaddish* for Philippos and his family. Their house was hit. Only the walls are left.

Mama thought of Philippos's eager face. How he wanted to be a doctor like his father, how he helped her with maths.

Father also said he saw Andonis in a work force, clearing rubble. So at least he was alive.

When she went outside, the first thing she saw were clouds of flies, then broken bits of house. There was a terrible shit-smell. The sewers had burst, there were also dead people. She saw German soldiers marching through the street in metal hats. Their eyes were not like eyes of any human she had seen.

Moumo started cooking again, but it was she who went out to shop. Queuing for flour, oil and salt took all day. Through the rubble outside, little powdery paths appeared, wayward but clear, like cloud-edges lit by the moon. There was a new word, curfew. It meant you couldn't walk in streets after dark.

Barba Rafael stayed with them a while. Soldiers had smashed his door, stolen his vegetables and doves, and Tinu was repairing the house. The night he arrived, she laid the table in the front room as she had for the Seder only two months before. It was dark then, and the shutters were closed. Now it was June and the front room swam with summer light. But the Pesach china was smashed. What about next year? How would they keep separate the dishes that needed to stay apart?

Father poured wine. Many precious objects had smashed but Father still had a few glasses.

No worries about getting you to Hebrew now, Sara, Father said. Barba Rafael said the Germans had asked Rabbi Osmos for a list of all Jewish names and addresses. Mama watched a mosquito circle his hand. Small mosquitoes were worst, they were cleverer than large ones, they hid when you tried to swat them.

Next day she sat with him in the front room.

The Third Psalm, he said. A prayer for salvation. He held a finger under the first verse.

Mama sucked the ends of her hair. The letters wriggled on the page. *Many rise against me*, she translated. *Many say there is no help in God but you Lord are a shield. I lay down*, she said slowly. *And ... and ...*

Slept, said Barba Rafael.

And slept. I ...

I woke.

I woke because the Lord ... I don't know that word.

Sustained. You've met that verb many times.

Sustained me. She took a breath. *I will not be afraid of ten thousand people that ... that ...*

Set themselves against ...

Set themselves against me. Roundabout, she added, pleased to know that word. She thought of the soldiers marching up Kondylaki.

Barba Rafael knew what she was thinking and made his voice comfortingly flat. Let's turn to grammar, he said. A bluebottle, trapped behind the shutter, buzzed against the glass.

Early one morning, Father brought Andonis into the kitchen. Andonis met her eyes and she felt herself come back to life. He brought meat, he said he would mend the window, but then did not come for two months. She was hungry all the time, so hungry she felt sick. Everyone kept falling ill, they shivered with fever, they felt weaker and weaker. Even Eleni was thinner, though her face was still round. Moumo began repeating words, over and over, it was hard to listen, hard to bear.

When Andonis did come to fit glass in the window, he told her the Germans had killed his grandfather and all his father's family. And, this was a secret she must not tell, especially not to Eleni, he was going to join the resistance. Then he went away into the mountains and for three years, three whole years, she hardly saw him. He brought food occasionally but usually when she was at school.

The Germans took over the school for their army barracks and school moved to an old leaky building where they had to sit on stones. Amos and Immanuel carried stones to it for her and Eleni. Kyria Myrtakis allowed them to wear anything to school now but clothes were hard to find and make. Mothers cut up parachutes, sacks, thin blankets, but a lot of thread was rotten and clothes came apart. Heracles's mother sewed him trousers from a sack that had P printed on it. Other boys caught him in the playground and added Rs so he had *Prrrr* on his bottom and everyone laughed.

Mama laughed with the others but kept thinking of Andonis. Maybe he'd met a girl in the mountains. Someone prettier, someone not Jewish. Maybe he was dead. Or she had only dreamed he liked her.

One spring morning, Thodoros blocked the way as they walked to school and told Eleni not to walk with foreign rubbish.

We're as Cretan as you, Mama said hotly. Afterwards Eleni said Thodoros was getting a job with the police.

He says I shouldn't come to your house.

What did you say? asked Mama.

I said, Don't be silly.

Early in August, Father said the next day was Tisha B'Av, saddest day in the calendar. They would read the Book of Lamentations and fast for twenty-five hours, to mourn the destruction of the temple in Jerusalem.

What difference does Tisha B'Av make? Mama said bitterly. We fast all the time anyway.

Father looked as though she had struck him.

In September came Rosh Hashanah, and ten days later the confessing of sins. Was it a sin to kiss someone not Jewish, love someone not Jewish and not tell your parents? Was talking back to Father a sin, knowing she was hurting him? Or feeling angry all the time? When they walked to synagogue for Yom Kippur, she saw Thodoros strutting towards them in uniform, a cudgel bumping his thigh. He shoved Father, who staggered. Mama caught his arm. Thodoros had always been a bully, but would never have pushed Father before. A door had opened and monsters of violence nobody knew about had climbed up through it onto the streets.

One evening at supper, they talked about people *marrying out*. Father said he heard from a friend in Heraklion that Kyria Sezana, who once studied art history in Germany, had married a Gentile.

Tsk, said Moumo.

Father said this lady was now hiding in a village with her husband and baby and told Father's friend she had seen what Germans did to Jews. He told her she was a stupid hysterical woman to imagine Germans don't like Jews, they would never do anything to harm us.

But the Kyria *went* to Germany, said Mama. You said.

She was cross about the marrying thing really. Why shouldn't Jews marry non-Jews? But the way she had spoken, it sounded as if she was hurling a javelin at Father.

Sara, Father said as if explaining to a five-year-old. She could hear the hurt in his voice. Rabbi Osmos says the Germans are civilized. He was a friend of the old German consul who just died. Rabbi Osmos attended the funeral. He says the German officers are very polite.

If they're so polite, what are they doing here?

Mama got up and started washing dishes. She felt like flinging

155

them on the floor. She hated everyone, especially Andonis. It was his fault she was quarreling with her dad.

You haven't eaten all your rusk, said Moumo.

Andonis came soon after, in the third spring of the Occupation. She was in the bedroom and heard his voice in the yard. Deep, with a sparkle in it like a laugh waiting to happen. She heard Moumo thank him for oil, looked out and there he was. Bigger. Still thin, but his shoulders seemed wider. Or maybe she had just forgotten how he looked.

Oil's so expensive, she heard Moumo say. Coffee and sugar are *impossible*. Wheat and barley, dearer every day. But it's oil we miss most.

You find those things in villages, Andonis said. But the Germans take them. Now their general has been stolen, there are even more patrols up there. I can't go back to the mountains, I'm staying here.

He looked up and saw her. The window was open, she felt her blood beat madly round every vein, she saw him smile but felt unable to smile back. At last a smile floated up inside her, but by then he had bent his head and she thought he didn't see.

She looked in the mirror. She was a different person now. Terribly thin. Her ribs knobbly and ugly, like a skeleton. She went out into the yard and couldn't meet his eyes. But when everyone was saying goodbye, he whispered, Nine tonight? And she breathed, Yes.

So she started seeing him again. And lying again, saying she was going to Eleni's. And feeling guilty again. But there was a new world round the corner and love running freely ahead. One night he said he had a secret shed, well hidden, really hidden, among trees. They could go there. Just for a while.

I'll get you home safe, he said. No one will know.

156

father says get dressed quick, pack a bag, hurry we have
ten minutes

can she bring goldie, no, my books my books, she throws
clothes on, puts her books and new sketchbook in her
schoolbag, goldie doesn't like being woken in the dark, she
tells him she will be back, eleni will look after him, she hears
shouting down in the hall, shoves the cage under the bed and
stumbles downstairs with her bag

the front door is open, the hall is full of giants, uniforms,
guns, noise

father says we must take food for nine days, put this bottle
of water in your bag

a soldier looks in her bag, he pulls out her books and
sketchbook and tosses them on the floor, another soldier kicks
them aside and laughs

another waves a paper and bends his face near hers, his
breath smells, his moustache is a cockroach on wet red lips

he says where's your sister, everyone looks at her, everyone
is suddenly silent

she says, she died

the soldiers drag her to the front door, father stumbles after
her, touches the mezuzah with his fingers, raises his fingers to
his lips and kisses them, a soldier knocks him to the ground

outside in the dark are more people carrying bundles, more
soldiers with cudgels and guns, they push people, they punch
people and they laugh

157

19

'Oh Mama.'

I fling my arms around her. A great desolation fills the room. I don't know if it is hers or mine. She's so old, so precarious. And her voice sounded so far away, as if on a long-distance phone.

I picture her as a child on her father's lap. I'll give him a pointed chin and spectacles, smiling as the little girl chatters about escapes from Egypt. And now a rebellious teenager, living through bombs with a secret love seething inside her.

She held all this within as she cooked for us, swabbed our grazes, stopped our squabbles. What sort of a mother was she, when we were young? Efficient, tender sometimes, but with me, at least, there was always an edge. She spent a lot of time embroidering – for money, but maybe it was a relief to her too, for that was when she withdrew, as if she was not at home to us at all. I thought all mothers did that. She showed her love most by cooking.

The door opens.

'Lunchtime,' says Papa. 'How are you doing?' Or does he mean, '*What* are you doing?' Or even, 'How are you?' They are all the same, in Greek.

'Fine,' Mama says. He nods as if she has survived a battle and I help her off the bed, find her some shoes. 'Not those,' she says. 'My slippers.'

'They're too loose. You'll slip.'

'They're *comfy*.' That's the end of that. The bolshie teenager has never really gone away. But as we go into the kitchen she says sorrowfully, 'I was always challenging my father.'

'Challenging is good.' I think of Katerina at fourteen, the fights that sometimes ended in tears, on both sides. 'You were thinking for yourself. He'd want you to do that.'

'I wasn't kind.'

Leila is out, she is queuing to pay our electricity bill, but she's left us stuffed peppers. I dish these up and as we eat I get a WhatsApp from Katerina. *At Athens. Boarding plane. Send Granny my love xxx*

Mama watches me press buttons in reply. 'A message from Athens, just like that?'

'Amazing, isn't it? She can do it from America too.'

I bring them coffee in Reception and say, 'What was this room like, before?'

In my painting of our house, only Nashita saw menace in the shadows I put round the door. I had no idea, not consciously anyway, that anything like that had happened. But Mama's knowledge of all that loss and death must be printed into me like the face on the Turin Shroud.

'Dark,' Mama says. 'It was Barba Raphael's study. Books everywhere. A lamp on a table. Beautiful cushions. I memorized their patterns.' That's my mother. Going to Hebrew lessons and coming back with her head full of embroidery designs.

'I had no idea you had lived in Askordalos, Mama. Did you hate it? Is that why you wouldn't come with us to see it?'

Papa stares down at his coffee. Mama looks at my phone.

'If we'd had things like that, it would have been so different.'

159

20

Sara/Sophia, June 1944–June 1945

She was lying on a cliff edge, her heart thumping as if it was trying to push her into the void. *The voice of the Lord breaks the cedars*, said Father's voice. Where was he, where were they all? If only he'd stop praying and *do* something.

She heard sobbing and realized it was hers. She was lying on packing cases with horribly hard edges under a scratchy rug that smelt of goat. There was snoring somewhere. Her cheeks were wet, she had been crying in her sleep. Light slipped through cracks in the shutters like spokes of a broken wheel.

It all came back. Endless walking. Burning sun. Andonis abandoning her to a world of rock and wind where she had to pretend to be someone else. And this house. She had never dreamed you could live in such a place. Only one room, with two couches against the walls, on which Stavros and Aspasia were noisily asleep.

How could she *be*, without her parents or Andonis?

ॐ

soldiers are pushing everyone up the street
   no, not everyone, some people are standing watching, like
eleni who is crying
   she says where's sara
   eleni says with andonis

160

she says goldie is under our bed please keep him
safe for me

the soldiers laugh like excited boys, they thump people with
their guns, they poke blind kyria anna who stumbles, she does
not know who they are and father takes her arm, he has his
other arm round mother
   she hops behind, she must not lose them in the crowd
   children drop precious rusks, soldiers brush people along as
if they were crumbs, they pass the turn to the kal

today is shabbat

they shuffle through the narrow curl at the top of the street,
and see trucks lined up in the dark, the soldiers push people at
them, father lifts her in and helps mother then kyria anna who
collapses on the floor, mother stands clutching her bag, grown-
ups are not used to sitting on floors, sit down simcha says
father you'll fall when the truck moves

father scrabbles to get in, a soldier pushes him up and laughs
when he flops on the floor,
   the tail of the truck bangs shut, they are in the dark, the
engine starts, the truck jerks, people standing up fall over
   well done, father whispers, you saved sara, where is she
   she says with andonis and father gasps, she has often
imagined telling him but never like this, then father says he's a
good boy, he will take care of her

෬ා

Every day Mama expected Andonis to bring news of her family.
She learned to feed the hens that appeared soon after she arrived,
and search the rocky hillside for their eggs. She was scared of the

161

scorpions she met under the stones and liked the speckled hen best because it left eggs in easier places.

Aspasia gave her black clothes, much too big. She sewed them small. She wouldn't have believed she could wear such things but what did it matter, who would see? It was only for a short time anyway, till Andonis found her parents.

She learned to recognize different sorts of *horta*, wild greens, bitter greens, herbs. Not *rigani*, said Aspasia, we pick that on the Day of Saint Ioannis.

She weeded tomatoes, peppers, onions, carrots. She fetched water from the well.

We are nearest the church *and* the well, said Aspasia proudly. The full buckets were very heavy. Mama felt sorry for women who lived further away.

⟳

she slides out of the truck, everyone slithers onto white dusty ground, all round are green hills and orange trees but the air smells of engine oil, orange blossom, diarrhoea

people are afraid, embarrassed and afraid

more trucks drive up, more neighbours tumble out, an old man wobbles when soldiers push him and his glasses fall off, they lie on the white ground like two lost eyes reflecting the sun and a soldier crushes them under his boot

soldiers push them through iron gates to a courtyard, barba rafael is here, he whispers where is sara,

she says with andonis, he says that's good

the soldiers herd them into a building, a room with a floor covered in black grass, no, hair, black hair grey hair white hair short tufts long hanks

they push barba rafael on a chair and scissor his head, his hair falls away like snow, blood trickles down his skull

162

mother says i can't, father says don't make a fuss or
they'll hurt you
　she closes her eyes and the blades graze her head
like iron bees

another room, a top floor room, enormous, lit by windows so
high you can't see out
　barba rafael says tell me when the sky goes red, we will say
prayers when the sun is setting
　he makes people sit on the cement floor with paths between
so nobody gets trodden on
　two or three hundred of us, says father and almost a
hundred children
　father finds a place against a wall so they can lean on it, she
sits between him and mother
　rabbi osmos has a bit of wall too, he slumps his head on his
knees, one of his eyes always stares in another direction as if it
wants to be somewhere else, he says the officers know me, it is
a mistake, they'll get me out
　she hears barba rafael ask him to lead the prayers but rabbi
osmos shakes his head and bows his forehead to his knees as if
shutting himself in a tin

twigs of light from the high windows scatter over them, there
are flies everywhere, meaty black flies with silver wings, thickest
in the corners marked for latrines, the smell is so strong you
feel you can see it, but it is so hot the flies don't bother to buzz
　what will goldie do without her, maybe eleni rescued him
and set him free
　there are knobby stones in her back and cramps
in her tummy
　mother says but where's sara, who'll look after sara
　she tells her sara is with eleni, eleni's mother will look

after her and andonis looks after us too doesn't he, when the germans go, andonis will find us and take us to sara

she says mama don't worry there is a garden where everything lost can be found

mother says you're a good girl you always make people feel better

she whispers i didn't know you thought that but mother is breathing deep as if she is asleep

and maybe didn't hear

zips of light from the windows go red and barba rafael stands up, his eyes glitter, his voice flows through the room like water

he says my dear friends this is the hour when we are most aware we depend on a power outside ourselves, when we celebrate the seventh day of creation

two weeks ago we welcomed the bride of the sabbath into our beloved etz hayyim

since then we have lived a terrible time but we are still free to face the setting sun

we have no candles, wine or bread, we are in the wilderness but we have each other

let us pray for strength to see the wilderness as a gift and help each other

may the archangels michael gabriel rafael and ariel guard you under the wings of the shekinah

the chamber is full of murmuring, she thinks of the kal smelling of lavender

of coming out into the courtyard after the service and seeing stars above the wall

the wafers of sky in the windows change from pink to black

∽

It was a world of wind, rock and earth. The wind never stopped buffeting everything, all the time. The earth made Mama's hands itchy as well as dirty but she couldn't keep washing, every drop of water was precious. Apart from picking wildflowers, and cleaning potatoes, she had hardly ever touched real earth.

Three fierce dogs helped Stavros with the sheep on the mountain. In the evening they lay in the yard on the end of rope and snarled when she went past.

They ate cheese, eggs, carobs, wild greens. Sometimes Stavros brought a hare or bird and once a dead snake with grey-pebble eyes. Aspasia made it into soup.

They drank milk from a goat with black-edged ears that slept in a stone hut and in the morning was very anxious to get out. She learned to unwire the gate and stand back. When she tried to milk her, the goat threatened her with its horns. Aspasia tied the goat up and spurted the milk backwards into a can. Like this, she said. Don't spill any. Now you're here, we need more.

᠐᠊᠐

a little boy beside her is looking at the string round her wrist, his eyelids are swollen, his face looks like a mask, his hands are filthy and make her see how dirty her own are

she says do you know cat's cradle, he wags his head no, this shape is fish in a dish, she slips the string over his fingers, sara wouldn't recognize the string it is so black

she widens the boy's hands so the string stays taut

now I take it, look, this is the manger, take these two strings, pull and you get knitting needles, take the X between my thumbs, pull with your little finger and make it into candles, see the flames flicker, now pinch the Xs with your thumb and first finger, there, you've made diamonds

diamonds is home, you can change lots of shapes back into diamonds

165

some shapes are nice but useless, you can't change them into anything else

now pull your fingers up through the middle, pull your hands apart, with your right little finger, that's your right isn't it, pull the left beyond the outside strings

oh dear

his eyes well with tears

let's start again, shall we tell a story with the shapes

he nods

here's soldier's bed, for a brave cretan soldier in the mountains, and here's a shape called two mountains and stream, let's wake the soldier and give him candles

the boy's mother smiles at her

everyone moves slowly, everyone is weak and dizzy, when you move you smell how sweaty you are, but mother pats the cement beside her as if offering the boy's mother her best chair and the woman sits down

she says my boy kostas hasn't said a word since the soldiers took us, usually he chatters all day

it is darker when a light goes out than if you've never seen it shine

൭ഄ

We don't have good earth to grow wheat, said Aspasia. Once we gave cheese and eggs to villages lower down in exchange for things we cannot grow. Now the Germans take everything. But rabbits are silent animals. Easier to hide. With the money from Andonis, I'll buy rabbits.

Mama had not realized Andonis gave them money.

൭ഄ

today is shabbat again and everyone is praying but the little boy kostas holds his hands out for the string

166

are they allowed to play on shabbat

nobody says anything

let's invent a new shape she says, this is flying bird

at home I've got a goldfinch, he has a red face as if he'd
buried his beak in jam and a wishing bone in his breast that
makes him fly

kostas looks round

he is not here, my sister's friend set him free, look this is the
clock, *tick tock tick tock*, her fingers go back and forth, she
says the clock ends the game, she lets the string fall and his
face crumples

want to start again, he nods, she says which shape do you
like best and he suddenly speaks, he says flying bird

his voice sounds like rust, she pictures rust clearing from
his throat

do you like candles she says

his big-lidded eyes fix on the string and she thinks he will
not speak again but he says yes-i-like-candles

she peels string onto his thumbs, look, there is the
flame flickering and he smiles, he waggles his fingers and
speaks again

a-can-dle-of-string

barba rafael whispers well done, you will be a great
teacher one day

she says i'm going to be an artist, he says you are an
artist already

∞

Aspasia took Mama to the church, dipped her fingers in water,
grabbed her hand, pulled up two fingers, poked them at her forehead and chest, and told her to bow to the altar. An old woman
came in with a tiny lamp. This is our cousin Sophia, Aspasia told
her, and the old woman asked where she was from. Rethymno,

Mama lied uncomfortably. When the old woman left, Aspasia said, You do everything wrong. You're not Christian, are you?

They gazed at each other. No, whispered Mama.

Jew?

Yes.

A candle on the sill of the small window threw a mushroomy shadow on the floor.

No one must know, said Aspasia and pointed to a faded wall-painting, a woman with a yellow circle round her head carrying a spindle of wool, and asked who that was. Mama shook her head.

The Panaghia, said Aspasia. Mother of Christ. She's a housewife like us. She feels pain for us as a mother feels pain for her children. She comforted me when Charos came for my son.

Mama did not know who Charos was.

The Angel of Death! He cannot hear our prayers. Nor our laments, our cries. Once, when God sent him to fetch the soul of a young man, he felt sorry for the mother and took an old one instead. That's when God struck him, so he cannot hear.

Mama remembered Andonis saying Aspasia's son had died. Did everyone live with a loss they didn't say? The Angel of Death she knew was the one that struck the sons of the Egyptians. She heard Father's voice, *They put blood on their doors so the Angel of Death would pass them by,* and saw the door of her own house, all the Jewish houses in Kondylaki, hanging open wide and black, furniture piled in the street, and the other doors closed.

Aspasia lit a candle.

Pray. Pray for your family.

Was it wrong to pray in a Christian church?

Pray, said Aspasia again. Pray for their safety, their souls. You eat the same bread and oil, don't you? Don't you have the same God?

The heart of the flame waved back and forth like a soft blue worm.

168

trucks are rattling outside, that loose rattle when the wheels
are still but the engine is going, they hear boots thumping in
the corridor and barba rafael stands up, he is a weak old man
but his eyes are blazing
    let us pray to god, he says, for strength to walk with dignity
conscious of god's love
    the soldiers draw back when the smell hits them, she sees
they are thrilled to be repelled
    barba rafael shepherds the children and mothers as
though they are queens and chants the lord is with me I shall
not be afraid

sun on her skin, first time for nine days
    everything dazzles
    blue sky white ground green hills beyond

barba rafael places a child in a truck and helps the mother in, she
scrambles in too, the grown-ups are used to sitting on floors now
    the back clanks up, it is dark inside, they hear barba rafael
chanting prayers outside, the lord will save you from the
fowler's snare, he will cover you with his feathers, you will find
refuge under his wings
    she looks at father to see if he remembers the wings bit is
her favourite and father smiles

the truck is moving, she looks for a chink in the lorry's side but
there isn't one, she has never been out of chania, she imagines
the sea sparkling, she lays her head on father's knee and holds
the string on her wrist

The first time Mama heard Stavros shout at Aspasia, she was terrified. She had never heard anyone shout inside a house. The only person who ever raised their voice at home, she realized, was herself.

Stavros did not have Aspasia's quick understanding. Aspasia treated him like a child whose wildness she was proud of and gave him the best bits of cheese, the extra egg, the largest helping.

Mama remembered Moumo pressing her to eat. When Stavros chewed, she watched his jaw. Wiry grey fur wagged up and down as he swallowed. She hated his stringy hands, the sound of soup flowing down the inside meat of his neck. Her belly was so empty she felt it sticking to her spine.

☙

heraklion harbour someone says and she sees a little gold
castle against a sea of green, guns on pale boulders pointing at
the sky, and mountains on the horizon
    what do those mountains look like, says barba rafael
    the face of a man looking at the sky, she says
    the ancient cretans said that was where the king of the
gods is buried
    how can a god be buried she said, maybe he is asleep does
god ever sleep

soldiers push more prisoners towards them
    andartes someone says, she looks to see is andonis with
them but he isn't
    where are you from sir says barba rafael, why are you here
    from archanes says a young man proudly, we helped the
english steal the german kommandant, they burned our
village they killed people, they took hundreds of us prisoner,
but we stole their general, they can't change that, the whole
world knows

170

the sun is hot metal on her scalp, the sky roars, father says
english aeroplanes are shooting german ships, bullets smack
the sea, white splashes spring up to meet them, the planes tilt
their wings like birds and one catches fire

there is a gush of flame, the plane bleeds black smoke, spins
like a burning insect and dives into the sea

she feels fire and shadow leaping inside her

༺༻

There were rules for everything. When to wash clothes, when
to light fires. You must not work wool on Wednesday or Friday,
or sow beans on Wednesday, they would not soften when you
cooked them.

And be careful at dusk, said Aspasia, when the *neraides*
come out.

Mama had read fairy tales at school about *neraides*, the nymphs
who send madness. Here they were real, they were everywhere.
Especially round the well.

They won't hurt you unless you tease them, said Aspasia. If you
say a prayer they disappear. But cover your head if you hear their
music at night.

Mama felt like someone living with a wound they dare not look
at. She had never been alone, not even when she hated everyone.
She had pushed people away, everyone except Andonis, but they
were always there. She knew they loved her.

She felt a tearing inside like the laddering rip of black cloth.

༺༻

the sky glows pink, the sea is dark and a ship starts moving
towards them puffing smoke, it is long and low and black and
looks like what kostas might draw if she said draw a ship

171

the soldiers stab their guns in the air to say to get
up, mother almost falls, father holds her, barba rafael
says be strong my friends, blessed be the lord, and
the soldiers shunt them towards the ship, barba rafael
chants the voice of the lord is over the waters, she joins
in the psalm and holds mother's hand, mother's face is
staring and loose
    she tells mother sara will be all right, people are looking
after her, do i really make people feel better, mother hugs her,
she says you always do my pretty you are my ray of light
    mother has never called her pretty before

sailors pull a plank out of the ship as if it is sticking out its
tongue, there is more boat under water than above, they will
be in its stomach like jonah in the whale
    the men from archanes walk in holding their heads high,
scornful as if they don't care where they walk and rabbi osmos
shuffles on someone's arm, he doesn't speak any more
    a soldier jerks his gun at barba rafael as if there is a
hook in its round black mouth and barba rafael is a fish that
must follow
    everyone walks towards the plank, neighbours from all their
streets, kondylaki, portou, everywhere, everyone is strange
now with their lightbulb heads but she knows them
    kostas is asleep, his cheek squished on his mother's shoulder
and the sea swirls green and brown under their feet
    she holds mother tight, they are on an iron deck, how can
iron float, they go down metal steps beneath the surface of the
sea, if there are windows they might see turtles flying through
the water but there are no windows just hot dark smells, oil,
sweat and diarrhoea
    father whispers you are helping your mother, you are a
brave girl, a good daughter

172

they hear an engine start, vibrations all round them, she
squeezes mother's hand
   she imagines huge wheels turning, threshing the sea

છ∾

Mama heard a thin mewing above her and saw a bird with fringed
wings floating in the burning blue. And below it, far away, a fast-
moving cloud of dust.

Sorokos, said Aspasia, and ran to close the door of the chicken
house, shut the goat in its hut, close the door of the house. The
wind began to howl. Grit flew across the yard.

Something evil is happening, Stavros said. Spirits of the air
bring bad things.

Aspasia crossed herself.

The *kalikantzouria*, said Stavros, and spat. Mama knew his
spitting was meant to ward off the Evil Eye. Maybe it did.

What are *kalikantzouria*? she asked.

Don't you have *kalikantzouria* in Rethymno? said Stavros.

I don't think so.

Here, they live in holes in the earth.

They climb *out* of holes, corrected Aspasia. They live deep
underground, in roots of the tree that holds up the world.

All year they chop at those roots, said Stavros. *Chop chop chop.*
But at Christmas they throw down their axes and come *out!* He
bellowed the last word and Mama jumped.

The Christ Child restores the tree, said Aspasia. But
kalikantzouria come out other times too. They attacked Stavros on
the mountain. The dogs chased them away.

What did they look like? Mama asked.

What do you think? Stavros said. Like demons.

Mama began to realize that Aspasia's rules turned on three things:
work, religion and the seasons of the earth. Father's prayers had

173

turned on those things too. *Amidah*, he would order, and make her repeat to herself the silent prayer, *Thou Lord art mighty to sustain us*. In summer, she had to add *by distilling the dew*. In winter, *by making the wind blow and rain fall*. She remembered saying, Why give thanks for rain? I hate rain. Father had laughed.

One day she showed Aspasia her embroidery.

When I was young, Aspasia said, I did this work too. Now my fingers are stiff.

Mama said she could make this into cloth for the shelves. She had sewn it for her dowry but, stuck here, what was the point? As she edged the strips, she felt some tiny connection to the Sara she used to be.

She had never sweated like this. Wearing black made it worse. Walking to the well, she was afraid of meeting the people Andonis mentioned, Kyria Pipina and her idiot son Achillea, the only young man in the village, a large shambly creature with swinging arms and a hanging jaw, who stared at her with a loose animal grin. He had lots of missing teeth, so when he smiled his mouth looked fanged and cavernous. Mama was glad her clothes were so shapeless.

What's a *vrikolax*? she asked Aspasia.

Don't you know? said Aspasia. Someone whose spirit has not crossed to the other world. Maybe they died alone and no one buried them.

Is Achillea a *vrikolax*? Mama asked.

No, said Aspasia. His father was. His spirit walked after he died and he came back to Pipina in the night. That's how Achillea was born.

Are people who come back like that dangerous?

Don't you have them in the city? No, not dangerous. But unlamented blood is a poison that haunts the earth.

174

Aspasia praised, grudgingly, the way she swept the floor.

That comes from sweeping it before Passover, Mama said proudly. We do it specially carefully then. There mustn't be any crumbs in the house at all.

Why? said Aspasia.

Mama didn't know. Everything she had rebelled against or scoffed at now felt precious but unreachable, like a jewel lost in the sea. At Passover, she said, we eat bread that doesn't rise. We mustn't have yeast in the house. Afterwards we buy yeast from Christian neighbours.

All bread rises, said Aspasia. If not, it's no good.

Don't you ever make flat bread? Mama asked.

There was a little pause. Yes, said Aspasia slowly. In Lent, when we start the fast.

We fast too, said Mama. Which day do you bake?

Monday, said Aspasia.

Our day is Thursday, said Mama, when we clean the house, before the holy day.

The Lord's Day is Sunday, said Aspasia.

For us, said Mama stoutly, it's Saturday. We mustn't work or light fires that day.

We must not work on the Lord's Day, said Aspasia. Not from sunset the day before.

Our day of no work begins at sunset too, said Mama, feeling closer and closer to Aspasia, but also more and more homesick.

Moumo, she said – that's my mother, that's what I call her – sends me out to the yard to see if the evening star has risen.

She fell to her hands and knees in tears.

All right, child, said Aspasia gruffly. You cleaned the floor. Don't wet it, now.

The well ran so low the village summoned the priest to beg Prophetes Elias for rain.

The priest arrived on a mule, his black hair scrunched in a knot. His robes smelt of sweat and as Mama passed the mule a thin mist coiled off its urine and swirled around her feet. In church, she copied how Aspasia sipped the wine, and received a crumb of bread. Afterwards she said, We have that too.

What? said Aspasia suspiciously.

Wine and bread.

But yours isn't the body and blood of Christ.

No. It's holy because ... we eat it together. Mama hadn't thought that thought before. Thinking it herself was different from Father telling her.

Through July and August the sun was a fiery lid and the sky dark blue like enamel on bronze, pressing down from the sky. Gradually its weight became softer. How long had she been here? It must nearly be Rosh Hashanah. How would she know, what should she do, what would happen if she didn't? After Rosh Hashanah was the Day of Atonement. She should fast. But how could she ever atone for not being with her family when the Germans came?

One morning, when Stavros was up the mountain, old Trellandonis hobbled into the yard saying the Germans were on the track below and would be here in an hour.

Mama helped Aspasia shove the rabbit cage under the woodpile. The rabbits scuttered about, a whirl of hindquarters and twitchy noses. Mama replaced the wood behind them while Aspasia caught chickens, tied them by their feet like a bunch of herbs and hung them from a nail in the hut. The goat butted and bleated. They tied her up and walled her in with the hens.

Still smells of goat, Mama said.

What can we do? said Aspasia.

They heard cries in the village, two shots, a scream, another shot and the thud of crunching steps. Aspasia dragged the flour sack over the floor, Mama helped shove it under a couch and pile orange-cases, plates and dishes in front. Then soldiers tramped

176

into the yard. Mama had never seen them so close. Two grabbed Aspasia, one thrust his gun at Mama's chest and brought his face to hers.

Nicht help *partisan*, he hissed and passed a finger across his throat.

Others marched into the house. Mama heard crashes, a cackle, squawk and bleat and whispered a prayer, *Keep us O Lord in our danger.* They came out with the hens, bread, onions, lentils and oil. One hefted the goat on his shoulder, her knees broken, her yellow eyes rolling. Her blood left a trail across the yard.

One soldier shook Aspasia.

Animals belong *German* army. *Nicht* hide! *Verboten.*

He pushed Aspasia to the ground. Two kicked her and another slapped Mama's face, pushing his face close to hers.

Marsch, said another, pulling him away. At the gate he turned.

Nicht hide, he yelled and brandished his gun.

Mama's face was stinging, her wrist burning. The soldiers' boots rang on the rocks, stumping away through the village. She helped Aspasia up. Aspasia's cheek was bleeding but she marched indoors as if going into battle. They found cupboard doors torn off and dishes under the bed kicked about, but the orange-cases behind were fine. And behind them, safe, was the flour.

In the back yard was a pool of blood where they felled the goat, but the woodpile hadn't been touched. They pulled out the startled rabbits. Aspasia swayed.

Lie down, Kyria, Mama said. I'll clear up.

I must bake new bread, said Aspasia.

I'll do it, Mama said.

You'll use too much flour, said Aspasia, but Mama said she wouldn't. By the time Stavros appeared she had baked two loaves.

They shot Pipina's loony son, said Stavros. He shouted and Pipina ran up, they shot her too. Then Trellandonis waved his fist and they shot him. If *I'*d been here . . .

They all knew what would have happened if he had.

Tuesday, Stavros said. Unlucky. Constantinopolis fell on a Tuesday.

That night Mama dreamed of Father. Bravo, Sara, he said. May God help you endure the suffering He sends. I thought you didn't love me, she said. But I did, he said. I do.

What? said Aspasia next morning, as if Mama's dream was sticking to her face.

I saw my father, Mama said.

I used to see my son Nikos every night, said Aspasia. You will always have your father, child. Wherever he is.

She put a hand on Mama's arm. You make good bread, she said.

The sun set earlier each day. Aspasia said it was the end of the burnt time, the season for exalting the cross. They would bring basil to the church to be blessed.

Harvest festival, Mama thought. She'd never had to worry about when festivals happened. Surely Andonis would come now and say where her family was. But autumn was approaching and Andonis did not come.

The sun struck new faces of the mountains, picking out different shadows. Mauve petals appeared, pale crocuses flowering without leaves in iron-hard earth. Ioannis the mountain messenger brought more chickens and Aspasia offered him three rabbits in exchange for four hens and a kilo of oil. Ioannis argued. He said it was dangerous work carrying hens, people might kill for them. Then Stavros asked for news and Ioannis said the Germans had shot seventeen people in Kavros village in the valley. But outside Crete, in the world, the Germans were losing.

Mama felt a little pounce of hope. The Germans would leave, she would go home, smells of lavender and cinnamon would drift through the house to greet her.

Then Ioannis told Stavros someone had seen *andartes* carrying his nephew's body down a mountain, after a German troop came through.

Mama stifled a gasp. Ioannis's small eyes flicked towards her and away. He said his friend recognized the boy's nose. Like an eagle, Ioannis said. A very thin boy, covered in blood.

Covered in blood. Covered in blood. The words retreated like a wave and came back louder. Mama wept silently all night. Next day, Aspasia saw her raw face and said, Don't make yourself ill. Ioannis may be mistaken. Wait.

But *dead, dead, dead* now coloured every moment of the day.

Snow arrived. Mama looked at whirling white-spotted wind and mountains white as salt. This was what they used to see, far away, from the bedroom. Now Andonis was dead and she was part of all this whiteness, like a shroud. She felt colder than she had imagined anyone could be. Her mouth sent plumes of ice into the air, her hair froze to icicles, water jewelled itself in frozen dribble on the pail. Stavros brought down the sheep, the dogs slept in the snowy yard. Firewood was as vital now as water had been in summer. Every log was a precious slice of warmth and Stavros guarded them jealously. The world was white outside and black within. The door, main source of light, stayed closed.

On the first day of the new year, Mama stood knee-deep in snow looking out at a dazzling world. She yearned for even the memory of colour. Objects in the yard, the walls and millwheel table, everything looked ghostly. But the white didn't all look the same. Where sunlight did not fall, the faces of the mountains were grey-blue like smoke.

He holds in His hands the depths of the earth and the mightiest mountains, she said aloud in Hebrew. How lightly she had listened to the prayers, how little attention she had paid to words like *mountain*.

This was her life. These mountains, this sky, wind, stones. Water to pull from the well, spirits and demons she couldn't see, and never anything else. Andonis was dead. She would never see her family again. Yet there was still work to do, a self to be.

Silence. Except the wind. And a cry in the distance like the howl of solitude. Or memory, which was also grief. The past swooped towards her with its arms outstretched, like a small child looking for comfort.

On the first day of Lent, Aspasia began keeping the door open in the day and they could see to sweep the floor. Snow was retreating from the yard. The mud was still ice, hatefully crunchy. But thick white lay only on the peaks. Light is coming back to the world, said Aspasia.

One March afternoon, alone in the house, Mama pulled out the blue-striped cotton bag. It had never meant much before. Moumo had wrapped bread in it, or placed it over dishes to protect them from flies. Mama took out Father's Haggadah. This must be the only book in the house, maybe the village, except a falling-to-bits Bible chained in the church. A year ago, Father read from this at dinner. *We remember the escape from Egypt. We think what freedom means.* What would happen if she did not observe Passover? She traced a phrase. *Blessed are you who created the fruit of the earth.* She heard her own voice. Why do we eat *matsah* on this night? *It is the bread of affliction. The bread of going forth.*

In Holy Week, she helped Aspasia dye eggs.

Red for the blood of Christ, said Aspasia. We boil them in onion skins and vinegar, and paint them with oil to make them shine.

We dye eggs red too, Mama said. For Passover. With walnut shells and coffee grounds. We simmer them for twelve hours.

Maybe Moumo was doing that exactly now, wondering where her daughter was. She tried sending her thoughts. *I'm here, I'm dyeing eggs. Where are you?*

On Great Friday, they went to church for the Burial of Christ. The women keened. *He's being betrayed. They're killing Him.* The

180

church hummed with lament. Why all this death, just as the world was turning light? She remembered the bleeding body in the church Andonis showed her and tried not to think of him too, covered in blood. She longed for the hope and comfort of the Seder. *Shulchan Orech*, she murmured, glad she still knew the words. *Set Table*. But what about the bitter leaves, the salt water and the lamb whose blood they sprinkled on their doors? *What is it that passes over?* Father used to say. The Angel of Death, she heard herself reply.

The priest came again, to celebrate the Feast of Archangel Michael, and the whole village crowded into their yard with gifts for the priest, things they had hidden from the Germans. Wine, lentils, cheese. The sky was steel, the mountains glittered, the roasting smell reminded Mama of home.

Children, said the priest. Half our sweet island is free. The Germans have left Heraklion and Rethymno. In Heraklion, *andartes* took down their flag, folded it and gave it to the general. *Take it back*, they said.

What about Chania? Mama burst out. The priest looked annoyed. Girls should keep quiet. We want *all* our island free, Mama said.

Bravo, said old Manolis whose son the Germans shot, thumping the earth with his stick.

Chania is where *all* Germans are now, said the priest. Like rats in a trap. Killing *everyone*.

In June, Aspasia said it would soon be the Festival of Saint Ioannis the *Rigani*-Gatherer, when the sun had done its work and dried the *rigani*, so it could turn back in the sky.

The night before, she said, if a girl looks in water, she will see the man she will marry. Water tells us what we cannot see. It tells the future. Maybe you'll see Andonis.

Mama felt a jitter of hope. Did that mean Aspasia believed Andonis was alive?

You came a year ago. You must be the one to gather *rigani* in the wilderness. Saint Ioannis is prophet of the wilderness.

Next morning Aspasia pointed to the part of the mountain where *rigani* grew best, and Mama set off into a wilderness of stones. White stones, pink stones, grey with blue veins. No trees or landmarks, just different angles of steep. She found *rigani* and began to pick. A lizard crouched beside her. She worked her way to a thorn tree whose shadow blotched the glaring rock. Sheathed in sweat, she looked out from the shade. These millions of pale hot stones, this rocky slope and burning sky, the wind, and the silence behind the wind – they must have a meaning.

They meant, she thought suddenly, that she was alone.

Hours later, in the heavy light before dusk, she carried a sack of *rigani* into the yard.

Aspasia said a wildcat had taken one of Manolis's lambs and Stavros was staying out to guard the sheep. We shall be alone, she said. Get two buckets from the well. One to wash, one for you to look into tonight.

Mama carried them to the well. The water was low, the sides stretched way down to a dark circle. The stone was almost too hot to touch. She knelt. How easy it would be to fall. Wasps clustered beside her, drinking from a small hollow where a few drops had spilt when someone else drew water. They crawled over each other on their little black wire-legs. Were the Germans still in Chania, killing people? Could water really tell a person's future?

She remembered reading her fortune in *malotira* leaves. A year ago, a world ago. The tea leaves did not foretell this. When would she see her family? And was Andonis dead?

182

When she got back, Aspasia was tying *rigani* into bunches. Mama shut the chickens away. Stars came out. The moon rose.

Now, said Aspasia, who seemed excited playing this game, and told her to cover the water in a red cloth.

Kyria Aspasia, Mama said, did you do this when you were a girl and see Kyrios Stavros?

Aspasia smiled and did not answer.

They ate in the front yard. Aspasia lit a small bonfire. Flames danced in black air. When the moon was high Aspasia said, Now you may look. Uncover the pail. Don't tell anyone what you see or the *neraides* will get you. Pour the water away. We should not use it to drink or wash.

Pour it *away*? Mama said indignantly. She had fetched this water, she didn't want to waste it. Can't I give it to the tomatoes?

The yard smelt of *rigani* and wood-smoke. Moonlight caught the curly hook where the metal handle joined the bucket, and turned it into a silver squiggle like letters on a *mezuzah*. She knelt, took off the cloth, peered in and saw her own face.

For a year, she had hardly seen herself. She had given up wondering what she looked like. She saw hollow eyes, sunk cheeks, sharp cheekbones. Then pale rock, full of cracks. Moonlight glowed through the cracks and they started to ripple. Or was she trembling, shaking the water? The rock started to rush past her and she saw Andonis's face, covered in blood. His eyes were closed. It was true then. He had died.

Then she saw the sea. In Chania the sea was part of life, you saw it everywhere. She felt comforted a moment, she hadn't seen sea for a year. But this sea held no welcome, it was flat and dark. No land, nothing. Soft wind scalloped the surface. Dark cloud on the horizon, a livid light below. Whatever had happened, had happened. The moon's trail on the waves was a ladder of bone.

21

Mama's voice trails away. She has been talking all afternoon. Papa's eyes are closed, he knows the story anyway, but I can't take it all in. Her mother, this grandmother I never knew, such a potent dream-figure to me when I was little but impossible to ask about – her name meant *Happiness*? All that happiness, torn from Mama in one night, no idea where they were, what happened. Then, thinking Papa had died too . . .

'I hate to think of you and those soldiers.'

'When they grabbed me, I thought, This is what they did to Moumo and—' She stops. 'I need the toilet.'

I lift her up. She wobbles and I feel how tired her bones are. She stumbles in her slippers, the heels are trodden down, but we muddle through to the toilet.

Dusk is gathering. I put her back to bed.

Monsters Are Rumbling Away Beneath the Earth

22

I wake in the dark. Four o'clock and I can't go back to sleep. This kept happening after David died but I thought I'd got over it. I turn on the mobile, a WhatsApp from Katerina says she has landed and I see an email from Mumbai.

Nashita tells me you are looking for a studio. Ours is free from February, at the top of an old apartment building. No lift, but very light, with cooking facility, a bathroom and couch. It is high up, with a small slice of a view of the sea. You could use it for three months. I'm afraid you would have to pay for electricity and cleaning. Would that suit? I can send photos. Warmest wishes, Sanjiv Narayanan.

That would be wonderful, I write back. A small slice of a view of the sea. I love how he says that. A high-up room in Mumbai for three months? Paradise.

I can't go back to sleep. I do twenty-five star-jumps, throw a jacket round my shoulders and go down the outside stairs. Crete is always beautiful but in this cool dim air, when the mountains are not even pink yet but there's a faint halo over the sea where the sun will rise, it is the most enchanted place on earth.

I make coffee in the kitchen, softly as I can. My parents are asleep the other side of the wall, but the wall is old and thick. I take coffee, pencils and paper out to the dusky air.

A mother telling her daughter about life in the war – other Cretans Cretans my age have had that all their lives. Not us.

I start drawing. Above me some bird tries a questing cheep. I draw patio tables, the twist of a branch. Other birds join in, the songs grow louder. Daylight pools on the sea, silvery snail trails are visible over the flagstones, then the sun pops up like a red balloon, shadows are suddenly sharp and the mountains behind the tree flush into rose.

I think of Aspasia and Mama up there. A mother who lost a child, and a suddenly orphaned teenager. Christian and Jew.

Mama was brought up believing *something*, even if she kicked against it. Maybe we all ride out the difficult times by sheltering in the only place we find, and then are stuck with it. When David came to his first Easter with us – Easter, Mama's great festival, highpoint of her year – did she wonder if he felt as strange as she must have felt then, that terrifying year when Christianity came down over her like a safety net and the Jewish calendar abandoned her, or she abandoned it?

It hits me again that the world she lost should have been mine. Like someone thawing out from a snowy journey, I'm beginning to be aware of what I feel.

I suddenly remember what I was dreaming before I woke. I was with David in a boat and we had a glass fish. One of those round-bellied puffer-fish, modelled in glass. This fish flew up, perched on the deck like a bird, then hurled itself into the sea. Of course, I thought in the dream, a fish always wants to be in the sea. But this fish was glass, it would sink, or break. I saw people swimming and shouted to them to catch it but it flicked past and disappeared. It had rejoined its element but was lost to me, to us.

What if your memories *want* to disappear? We talk about memories, maybe we should talk about forgetting. What will happen if I dredge all Mama's fish up into daylight? She has done her best to keep them on the ocean floor.

She comes to breakfast on Papa's arm and I push across the table the catalogue of my show. She sits there turning pages as if they might bite, stops a moment at her own portrait, then moves on. Thank goodness we didn't put it on the cover. Leila arrives and bursts out laughing. The fuss Mama makes about me painting is a family joke.

'Great pictures, aren't they, Granny? Do you forgive Aunt Rioula for painting them now?'

'Very nice,' says Mama. And that's that.

Leila has brought a bag of young broad beans for our lunch but is due at her children's school, to talk about reports. Papa wants to meet a friend in town so she takes him away with her and I start shelling beans. The white inside the pods is soft as rabbit fur.

'In the mountains, Mama, what was Stavros like? He sounds a difficult customer.'

'He had a temper.' Mama smooths a raffia mat Katerina bought her from New York. 'But he did like ... '

She stops, and sweeps a pile of beans towards herself.

'What, Mama? What did Stavros like?'

She splits open a pod. Her fingers are clumsy but she perseveres. She's suddenly clammed up

'How did you find out Papa wasn't dead after all? How did you get out of there, back to Chania?'

189

23

One afternoon, as Mama was hanging up washing, the church bell began ringing wildly. Then Ioannis came staggering into the yard, leaning on his donkey's neck. Crete is free, he yelled. The fuckers are leaving Chania!

Stavros opened raki, Mama looked at Aspasia, threw her arms round her and burst into tears. She felt Aspasia stroke her hair.

Hush, child.

Later, Aspasia hung a pistol on the wall. I buried it, she explained, when I heard the Germans wanted our weapons.

Mama remembered her father surrendering his holy knife. Maybe he would get it back now, maybe everything the Germans had done would be undone. Even if Andonis was dead she could at last find her family.

Wait, said Aspasia. We don't know what is happening. How will you get there? Wait.

That night Mama lay on her orange-cases and watched the night sky like a black egg rolled in glitter through the open door, while Stavros and his friends sang *mantinades*.

> *Scratch Crete's earth with a pin! Beneath the stones*
> *You'll find our brave young heroes' blood and bones.*

Mama dozed off, dreamed of Andonis, and woke to hear them still at it.

Only the bravest and the best artists in gun and knives
Should set foot on the earth of Crete, or mess with
Cretan lives.

Was her family celebrating too, without her?

They heard no more news, only that the Germans had left Chania and everything was chaos there. In October, Stavros began making the new raki. Smells of grape-sludge spread through the village and Aspasia sent Mama to sweep round the church before the service.

The church walls were creamy against blue sky, with holes where the render had crumbled. Which old woman in black was sweeping here when she first came? If she stayed much longer, that would be her. A lonely old woman in black brushing autumn leaves. She'd been here over a year, she had to go, she would brave the hot sharp stones, the gold vipers that lived under them, the *kalikantzouria*, *neraides* and spirits of the air. She would take her mother's blue-striped bag and find her parents.

Happier now she had decided, she swept on. Then she heard soft slow hoof-thuds and looked up, screwing her eyes against the glare. She saw a donkey approaching, a donkey so old it was white. Beside it limped a man, reed-thin like a tree with no leaves. She saw a long nose. And his eyes ... She clutched the broom, heard the panting breath of a donkey glad to stand still, saw a faded check shirt and at the top familiar curls of black hair.

Sara.

She had always pictured them meeting in private. Out here, the land looked empty but she knew there was always some-one watching.

A smell of warm donkey rose between them. Fiery blue sky

191

raced above. There was a thumping in her ears. She put up her hand and touched his face. His skin was wet and hot. Was he a mirage? Or, oh God, a *vrikolax*? But would a *vrikolax* smell of sweat?

We heard you were dead, she said.

I nearly was, he replied.

She was in his arms. He was hot, his shirt was moist, he was thin, so thin. She pressed her lips to the wet curls on his chest, heard his walloping heart, put her face up and whispered, Where's my family?

He didn't know. He'd been in the mountains too, far away in the south.

I came as soon as I could walk. All I knew is the Germans took them to Heraklion. Someone said they put them on a ship.

She swayed. He held her up. She wanted to stand in his arms for ever, fly with him to Heraklion, lie down with him till the end of time.

Are you a village girl now? he said teasingly and she felt she hadn't laughed for a year.

I'm Sophia! Don't forget. You gave me that name.

There was too much to say. Not touching, as if the air between them were fire, they walked towards the house.

Five days later they stood in a glade of trees on a hill looking down at Chania. The sea stretched silver in the distance, the battered town curled into it like a smile. She hadn't seen trees for over a year, not soft ones like these. Further down they saw collapsed houses, walls dotted with bullet holes, squares filled with rubbish. A cat, dirty white with an orange ear, washed itself in a doorway to nowhere. It was a wasteland she didn't recognize. But Andonis pointed.

This is near where you did lessons. Isn't that the Musselman who lived with Kyrios Rafael?

Mama saw a dark figure bending over rubble. *Tinu*, she called.

He stood up, rake-thin and very gaunt. He looked astonished, then radiant.

Miss Sara, he said, opening his arms, and she ran into them like a rabbit diving into its hole.

Are you all back? she heard him say. She explained she had been hiding in the mountains, alone, and felt him sag. After a moment, he asked if they'd like to stay in the house.

Is Barba Rafael there? Mama asked.

No, Miss. They took all the Jews. All. You must be the only one left in Chania. They came for Kyrios Rafael, they had his name on a list, I wanted to go with him but they pushed me away.

Where did they take them?

Heraklion. Someone said they sent them to South America.

Barba Rafael's gate with its pretty chain was gone. In its place was barbed wire, which Tinu untangled and wound up again behind them. The house still had a roof, but the garden was wilderness. Vast bushes, where once had been rows of ... of whatever vegetables Barba Rafael used to grow. She had taken no interest then. Now she saw good earth, and no stones.

Andonis said he must go to his mother.

You can keep the donkey instead of me. Bargain. I'll be back tomorrow.

Aren't we going to Kondylaki? said Sara.

Someone else is living in your house, Miss, said Tinu. All the Jews' houses. Germans moved into some and people walked in when they left. Others, the Germans gave to men who helped them. Or sold to people who made money on the black market. This is the only Jewish house in town. People pulled the sticks off the doorposts. I found ours tossed away. When they left, I put it back.

But I must see Eleni, said Mama. And – and the Kal.

Why did she say that? She had taken the synagogue for granted,

193

had grumbled about going. Now it seemed the heart of everything she had to get back to.

Your friend went to America. The Germans stripped your synagogue. It's a ruin. Homeless families are squatting in it. I saw a pig in it last week.

A *pig*? Tinu, as a Muslim, would find that as disgusting as she did.

It is as if the Jews had never been, he said. You can live here. We can make you a life.

Andonis limped away and Mama turned to Tinu. I'm going to weed your vegetables. And you need to call me Sophia. That's my name now.

24

I put the beans in a pan for lunch and watch them turn slowly, settling into the water. I can't bear to think of Mama believing her parents were still alive. And coming back as someone else, with a different name, to a town she didn't recognize.

When lunch is half-made, Irene turns up and wants to take Mama to lunch at their hotel. Mama will enjoy the sea air, she can bring her back in the evening.

'She's pretty wobbly,' I whisper while Mama gets ready. 'Will you take her arm, especially down steps?'

'Of course.'

Irene is always kind. When I came here after David died, everyone helped in their way and Irene's way was unfussy practicality. I was moody, unsociable, often in tears. Now I've come back with a catalogue of paintings that are of them but also part of another world. Irene takes all that in her stride, just as she takes Vasilis and his fancy hotel.

'Why don't you come too, Ri? Vasilis would love to see you.'

'Thanks, Irenoula, I'm going to work. Send him my love.'

She drives Mama away and I settle down to draw the bark of the pomegranate tree. It does not matter how slow you are, moving a pencil over paper. All that matters is to grow from not-seeing into a state of seeing, half scrutiny, half meditation.

Papa comes back weary, very short of breath. I sniff smoke on him. And raki. I tell him Mama's out to lunch with Irene, and say

I'll make him a coffee. He settles on the patio with a paper. The headline says, *I am sure they are not dead.*

'Those people are Syrian,' he says. 'They came from Lesbos, looking for their children. Their children fell in the sea.'

When I bring coffee, with a big glass of water, he's lit another cigarette. I make a face, he's only allowed one a day. He squints at me like a cheeky child.

'Don't you remember *anything*, Papa, about how you were wounded in the war?'

'Nothing. I was ill so long. At first it was all just pain. I woke up to an old woman pouring *avgolemono* down me, like watering a plant. She nursed me back to life. I remembered I'd left Sara in Askordalos, but what could I do? I couldn't send a message, what about informers? I had to wait till I was better.'

'And then you came back to Chania?'

He sips his coffee, stares into it, and looks up.

25

He limped into town beside rocks wrapped in barbed wire. Charos had come to every house, every woman he passed wore black. But the sea was the rustling blue it had always been. For four years, no one had looked at the harbour without fear. But the guns had gone. On the spot where soldiers polished the Kommandant's saloon, a boy was leading a thin white mule in a cart. The mosque was intact, but the vaults of the ancient storehouses peered through shattered masonry like ribs of an ox. Café tables were back, someone had placed Greek paper flags on them and these had blown over in the wind, many were bobbing in the sea. Underfoot, everywhere, were splintered planks and metal fragments.

His leg was on fire with pain. Now he knew Sara was safe he let himself feel it. But he smiled, thinking of the nights. At least he was a man.

The alleys of the Ovraiki smelt foul, the sewers must have burst. He was suddenly struck with panic for his mother. He had left her alone with a woman he didn't trust, while the town endured the last fury of humiliated enemies. He hobbled faster and nearly bumped into his mother's neighbour, Kyria Myrto.

We thought Hades had eaten you, she said. Your mother's not well. I took her soup this morning.

Isn't Kyria Pelagia looking after her?

197

She's gone, that one, said Kyria Myrto. Keeping house for a rich man now.

Papa followed Myrto into his mother's yard. At first he thought the house had disappeared, then he saw the vine had gone wild, throwing writhing tendrils over everything in sight. Myrto waded through it calling, Maria! Your son is back.

Papa went in, saw his mother on the couch struggling to sit up, put his arms round her and felt a pang of pain he recognized as love.

Where were you? she screamed in his ear.

He needed work. But so did everyone, and there were thousands of fitter men. While Mama dug up forgotten onions and potatoes in Barba Rafael's garden, bartered them for chickens, and started selling eggs, he cleared streets and buildings, gritting his teeth through the pain, and returned exhausted to his mother. At weekends, he stayed with Tinu and Mama.

His mother complained.

A foreign girl and one of the last Arabs on Crete! A Jew and a black man! Why is she still here when the other Jews left? You're bringing shame on our family. She doesn't belong.

She was born here, Papa said, like me. She has a Greek name now.

She's a serpent, his mother said.

She's a good Cretan girl and she's lost her family. Didn't my father, and you, and my grandfather, bring me up to be a good man?

He couldn't be sharper than that, he felt so bad at having left her alone. As she knew.

But people began to remember he was a carpenter and he found easier work, made a little more money. Everyone's history now was a closed door. Some people had been rewarded by the Germans just enough to not be called collaborators. Others had got rich on the black market and were making even more from the transport and building work everyone needed. Working in their houses, he

198

sometimes recognized things. The glass cabinet, the mahogany table, the carved bed.

One afternoon, limping up Kondylaki in a grey hour when autumn light was ambiguous and faded, he came face to face with Kyria Pelagia. She greeted him grandly as if she had never begged his mother for a roof. She was now housekeeper for Eleni's cousin, who owned Mama's old home.

Kyrios Thodoros is getting married, she said. There is work for you there.

The house, when he went, had a fake-sweet smell like brilliantine. No more lavender and cinnamon. The tree was gone from the yard, the shed he made had a padlock on the door.

One Friday evening, arriving at Tinu's house, he saw Sara planting vegetables, intent on the earth. Twilight fell like smoke on the White Mountains behind. She looked up, saw him and stood up slowly, one hand to her back. In a flash, he knew, and swung her in a careful whirl of joy, pivoting on his good leg. Already she felt different in his arms.

We will marry, he whispered, facing the last scraps of gold and violet cloud. And you must be baptized.

She jolted as if hit by a bullet. No, she whispered. What will Father say?

Had she really not thought about this?

The child must be baptized, he said. And for us to marry, you must too.

26

'Papa. Why didn't you *tell* us she was Jewish and baptized?'

He is suddenly furious. 'What would you like *me* to have done? On the street, they spat as if she had the Evil Eye. *I* can go to town now and have a drink with friends. She can't. She sees neighbours here but she's never gone back to her old neighbourhood. Only once. Once, we went. People shut their doors. You don't know how it was.'

I have never seen him so ferocious. It's like getting an electric shock from a favourite armchair.

'They wanted to forget the Jews were ever here. All right, let her not *be* one. Better for her, better for *you*. Otherwise, we had no future. We'd have been like these people from Syria.' He thumps the paper. 'And no fucking money. Where would we go?'

'All right, Papa.' I get up. 'I'll make lunch.'

Pick your fights. I'll make lunch for him, then go to Irene's. When he's slept off the raki, and I've been away a while, we'll both feel different.

Vasilis's hotel is half an hour's drive, just past the turn to Rodopos, a remote peninsula of dirt roads and rock. I leave the cab on a cliff above and look at chubby clouds in the deep blue cobalt sky. Not yet quite the indigo sky of summer but it could give you a nasty burn. Crete is hotting up like a waking lion.

The sea is all round me. Close in, it is silvery surface-dazzle. Further out, if you half-close your eyes, it is ultramarine, but you'd need the whole paint-box for the details. Sapphire, lapis, emerald, malachite, and dark blue almost to black. Who needs jewels when you've got the Aegean?

Still shaken by Papa's anger, I stare at Vasilis's beautiful little bay, or what was beautiful before he and his pals got at it. Pale rock fringing the curve of the bay. Above that is green foliage broken by the white roof of another hotel and a row of denture-like columns, grinning through the clotted dark of pine trees.

I must start painting. I haven't picked up a brush since I put the last touches to the show. And in that, as Nashita said, I didn't paint the sea. Only through the glass of Nikos's boat.

Far off, to the right, is the rose-blue haze of a headland. In the centre, straight across, a mauve horizon divides sky from sea, blue from blue, and a few misty lumps in the middle invite you to leap off this cliff and land on one of these little islands.

Why does the way an artist looks at landscape give pleasure to other people? This one feels like a promise. I'm the truth, it says. Your new perspective. Now you've seen me, you can be different.

I start walking down. Papa was angry because he felt helpless, wasn't he? Originally, I know, he felt torn between Mama's past and other people. Now he is torn between Mama's wish to forget and me wanting to know. My brothers will want to, too. But if you've lived by covering up, you hate people wanting to know.

The hotel car park is nearly full but no one is on the beach because it is all rock. No one in the sea either, most Greeks don't go in till May and foreigners staying here usually go out for the day. But there are people in the infinity pool, whose blue goes up and over an almost invisible edge, so when you're in, you feel you're swimming in the real sea beyond.

Mama and Irene are on the terrace with a pink tablecloth between them. Behind, little lamps hang along the sea like hopes in a heartbeat. They will come on at twilight and transform this bay to a vast black ballroom, lit by a necklace of jewels.

It is everyone's dream of a posh Greek holiday and costs a lot to keep that way. I am sure Vasilis does not pay all the tax he should. I suspect most of the receipts he hands out look like real ones but aren't, and it was people not paying taxes that got Greece into this crisis. But Vasilis is living his dream and it's a struggle. He has to make it pay.

When he bought this land, he asked what to call his hotel and I offered Asterion, the first king of Crete. Europa's husband, after Zeus finished with her.

Asterion means starry, and some people say it was the Minotaur's real name. They also say the Minotaur was good. There he is still, a benign monster, luminous and alone, dancing unseen at the heart of some universal labyrinth. His death was not the slaying of a fiend but an eternal sacrifice, which allows us to escape our own dark private corridors and get back to the light.

Vasilis loved that. He is good at loving things, his enthusiasms are infectious and make us laugh. Papa painted him a wooden sign with stars round a labyrinth and a merry little Minotaur dancing at the centre. These days there's a bigger sign, lit up at night, but Vasilis goes on telling guests what a self-sacrificing hero the Minotaur really was, and Papa's sign hangs in the bar as a folk antique.

I find Vasilis on the terrace in a white jacket. The black hair and moustache are perfect here. He loves being *patron* and does it very well. He's like his own infinity pool, you can't tell where artificial ends and the real thing begins.

'Golden girl! *Ouzaki* for you?'

'Thanks, Vasilis. How are you, how's trade?'

'Busy, busy. Lots of bookings.' He introduces me to guests. 'Kyrios Panayiotis, from Patras. Kyrios and Kyria Kalligatakis from Rethymno.'

Panayiotis, with a crest of white hair, shirt open to the waist, a froth of white chest hairs and a tan like amber honey, turns his masculinity on me like a blow lamp. I've forgotten what that's like. I'm in a halter-top and he is gazing at my cleavage.

'We saw the catalogue of your show in the bar,' he tells me. 'What are the paintings worth? Why don't you show them in Athens?'

'You should show them in Crete,' says the woman from Rethymno. 'Here in your brother's hotel. Or the art gallery in Heraklion. They have *famous* artists there.'

'They sell like hot cakes in London,' says Vasilis at once. I know he's saying, *My sister's already famous in the west*, but there's a reproach here too. *Why* don't *you show your paintings* here? *And yes, what* are *they worth?*

I suddenly feel bad for him. Nikos and I have always been close, but Vasilis hangs out with different people. Bankers, fixers, businessmen. I put my arm through his. 'Maybe I could do a landscape of your bay? For the lobby.'

His flash of longing is gone in a second but I saw it. Nashita said Crete hadn't finished with me yet. How could it? Crete is endless, changeable as that sea.

'I'm looking for Mama,' I tell him, squeezing his arm.

'On the terrace. I'll send an ouzo after you.'

Irene is delighted to see me. There is a menu to discuss and she advises swordfish, but is busy telling Mama about a hotel owner in Chania who had refugees foisted on him by the government.

'He gave them rooms and food, then the government said stop giving them food, let them find it themselves, and the police tried to throw them out. But they refused to leave. He said they were right. Where would they go? A hundred and forty people. He hasn't been paid a single euro for all that electricity and water. And three meals a day.'

'*Tsk*,' says Mama.

'The government tossed them into his hotel and said Bye Bye!

They didn't send anyone to check on the children, haven't paid his expenses. They said they would, but not in writing. He's lost everything he earned last season. Hundreds of thousands of euros. He's missed three loan payments.'

'Didn't the EU give anything?'

'Yes, ten thousand euros. But it all went to the exhibition centre where those people stayed in their first days on Crete.'

Irene keeps glancing at waiters clearing plates, she is clearly itching to check what's going on.

'Irene, you've a lot to do, I'll take Mama back in a taxi. Don't worry about us, we'll be fine.'

A waiter brings a glass of ouzo on a metal tray that dazzles in the sun. 'From the Kyrios,' he says. I raise it to Vasilis and he smiles.

With Irene gone, Mama presses salad on me. Broad beans, early tomatoes. This is her first outing after her illness, she is doing fine, and proud of her son's hotel. I think of her at sixteen, up in the mountains. An alien world.

'What was winter like in Askordalos?'

'Horrible. Deep snow. Very windy. We couldn't go out. Aspasia said it was the dangerous time. Every month had a dangerous hour when the old moon turned new but Christmas was worst, when the sun was darkest and the *kalikantzouria* came out to do their wickedness. She was right. It was terrible when—'

She stops.

'When what?'

A waiter brings my swordfish. Gulls screech and swoop above our heads.

'Christmas was a bad time.' She prongs a broad bean.

'Were things easier after you were baptized?'

She looks out into the misty horizon. 'Talking to Tinu helped.'

'Why?'

'He was Muslim. He knew what I was feeling.'

27

Mama sat down heavily in the front room. A gusty wind drove rain like handfuls of pebbles against the glass. Tinu closed the shutters, put a cushion behind her back. Mama was surprised how natural it felt living with Tinu. In the old days, he was part of the package of those hated lessons. Now he was her last link with home.

But he too knew what it was like to lose a home. She asked how old he was when he first came to Crete.

A child, he said. They caught me in the fields, took me to the slave market in Cairo, I never saw my family again. But the Turk who bought me was kind and brought me here, to Chania, where I looked after his children. Then the Turks left overnight and I woke up to an empty house. Those were bad times too – fighting, guns, people starving in the street. I was homeless, and the Cretans made us work in the fields. We weren't used to that, we were house slaves. My friends died. Kyrios Rafael found me lying in the road and saved my life.

So you were the last Muslim, said Mama.

No, there were Cretan Muslims then, born here. But in 1922, twenty years before the Jews were taken, they too were dragged from their homes and sent to Turkey.

The lamp lit up his grizzled hair, big shoulders, the oak sheen of his cheek. She remembered him five years ago in candlelight at their Seder and started to cry.

205

I have to be baptized. How can my father forgive me when he returns?

He will understand. Your parents made you who you are. You won't lose that when you make your new life.

It happened early one morning. The priest wore grubby white robes stitched with gold. Andonis had given him oil and two chickens to welcome Mama into Christ's church. She wore a white dress made from a tablecloth, which partly hid her stomach but she was sure the priest knew. Andonis stood beside her, along with a man he worked for who had agreed to be her sponsor in Christ.

A boy swung incense. They had paid for that too. It costs a lot, the priest said, to chrism a Jew. The priest sprinkled water over her and pronounced her name in Christ.

Sophia. She felt the baby move inside. Outside, she felt like she did in Askordalos, alone among strangers, scorpions under every stone.

Three weeks later, same church, same dress, same priest, they were married. Tinu had prepared food afterwards at home. Andonis went into the house to fetch something, stopped on the threshold, and looked at the *mezuzah*.

Sophia, he said.

That's what he had to call her now. They both found it hard to remember.

She met Tinu's eyes and his kind glance nearly made her burst into tears.

Yes, she told Andonis. All right. Take it off. But not today.

That night in bed, Andonis said he would live here all the time now. Next day, Tinu gave her the *mezuzah*. She put it in her father's Haggadah. The door-frame had already been repainted. She could not tell where it had been.

She went to church every week. Local women began inviting her to sit with them. But what Andonis worried about was money. They ate what they grew, but everything was expensive. He was only twenty-two but always in pain. Does this hurt? she asked in bed, running her fingers down him. Or this? All of it, he said.

In spring, Ioannis came from Askordalos and said Stavros had died. The *kalikantzouria* had finally got him and his heart had stopped. Aspasia came to live with them and Mama welcomed her in a sudden rush of love.

I'm Christian now, she said. Aspasia nodded, looking avidly at the rose-brown earth. She was used to stony slopes and started digging straight away. She planted and sold vegetables, and with the money she bought a goat.

Sew embroideries, she said to Mama. We'll sell them to the people getting fat on Crete's suffering.

Aspasia looked after her when she had the baby, and hung blue beads, to keep away the Evil Eye, on the crib Andonis made. They called the baby Vasilis, after Andonis's grandfather. He laughed, screamed, and was expensive. Mama felt astonished and adoring. Andonis heard rumours of compensation for damage the Germans did, and then that the Jews' houses would be given to the Greek state. Also that a wealthy Jew who escaped to Athens had sold all Jewish houses in Chania. But nothing changed, none of those things seemed to happen.

When Vasilis was baptized, Aspasia brought Andonis's mother Maria to the ceremony, the first time Mama met her. Mama quaked inside, but was polite and welcomed Maria, then hated both of them when the baby howled at the cold water and they laughed. That night in bed, when Andonis asked how she felt, she was silent. She remembered what Tinu said before her own baptism. *You won't lose who you are.* Who would her baby grow up to be? He would know nothing of who she was, or had been. A flood of infinite loneliness poured over her. She knew Andonis was

207

worrying. Some mean part of her said *let him* and for a moment she stared frozenly into the dark. Then she turned and burrowed in his arms.

One scorching afternoon, she found Aspasia lying paralyzed under the pomegranate tree. She died without opening her eyes. Mama folded her stringy hands over her chest and stared at the face of this woman who had hidden and saved her. She remembered Aspasia's girlish enjoyment of fortune-telling on the Feast of Saint Ioannis, her determination when the Germans came. Losing Aspasia snapped another strand in her connection to the past.

Andonis's mother came to live with them and they rented out her shack. She seemed to forgive Mama for having been Jewish, she looked after Vasilis, cooked and cleaned, while Tinu sold vegetables and Mama stitched embroideries to sell. Flowers, zig-zags, butterflies and birds. She began to feel she was living two lives. One in which she worked, loved and was loved, and an under-life of loss and rage. Why had her parents sent no message?

I must see Kondylaki, she told Andonis. Can I come next time you get the rent?

They went on a Saturday, the Sabbath, the day she was never allowed to set foot outside the house. She carried Vasilis into crowded afternoon streets and Andonis limped beside her.

She had not seen Kondylaki since that day of gaping doors. Today all doors were closed. Hers was no longer bare wood but glossy black, and no mark where the *mezuzah* had been, though the lion door-knocker was still there.

I used to tremble as I passed, said Andonis, and wonder if you were behind it.

She could not face Thodoros, so they knocked at the door of Yosif's old house. A woman with hennaed hair opened it at once. She must have been watching through the window.

No Jews here, she said, and shut the door. Where were the

neighbours Mama grew up with, people she went to school with, danced the Syrtos with? She felt like her own ghost.

Vasilis squirmed in her arms. His hot little body was the only thing that stopped her falling.

Let's go to the synagogue, she said.

What's synagogue? said Vasilis, sailing in her arms over stones Father had trodden every Friday.

They turned the corner and Mama gasped. The arch was fallen, lintel broken, door gone. A thicket of barbed wire blocked the entrance and a well-dressed foreigner stood in front of it, gazing in. They joined him. The courtyard, where she had decorated the tent for Sukkot, was filled with old wheels, stone rubble, vegetable peel. A dead cat lay in a corner, heaving with maggots.

Pipi, said Vasilis, wrinkling his nose.

Terrible, said the foreigner in Greek. Something in his voice made Mama turn. She looked up into grey eyes. Eyes she had dreamed about, long ago.

Sara. He said it as if reminding her of her name.

Yosif, she said. There was a stunned silence. This is my husband, she said finally. Andonis Manoudakis.

She saw Yosif register that she had *married out.* The two men, who must have passed each other often in the street as boys, shook hands.

We thought you died in Albania, Mama said.

I was in a prison camp in Germany, said Yosif. Carefully, as if Greek was strange in his mouth. When I heard my family had died, I went to America. I thought you were dead too, Sara. How did you escape?

I hid in the mountains. But my family – the Germans took them, I don't know where they are, maybe Germany too. How did your family die?

He looked at her startled, as if he did not know what to say. Then he invited them for coffee in the hotel where he was staying.

Andonis had helped build it, but Mama had never been in a hotel. Nor, since the Germans came, had she drunk coffee. Vasilis gazed curiously at the manager's wife, who had yellow hair and gave him a biscuit with sugar icing. He had never seen anyone with yellow hair, nor tasted sugar icing.

Yosif ordered coffee and smiled his old lop-sided smile. What sort of coffee, everyone? How much sugar?

Heavy-sweet for me, Andonis said. Medium-sweet for ... he gestured at Mama. He was going to say *Sara*, she thought. He doesn't want to let Yosif know I've changed my name.

Hearing Yosif's voice, watching that face she used to know so well, plunged her into a black ocean of pain she had been swimming in already but had been numb to before. She remembered hanging bunches of straw for Sukkot with him in the synagogue courtyard, and the badge Eleni wore to support Cretan soldiers in Albania, how she had wanted to wear one for him.

Yosif gave Andonis an American cigarette. He said he lived in Michigan, he was a town-planner now, he had come to a conference in Athens and wanted to see Crete again, he hadn't realized how much had been destroyed. He went first to Heraklion, to the Jewish Quarter by the sea where he used to stay with his cousin. Long ago, there had been four beautiful synagogues in Heraklion, but by the time he was visiting his cousins the community was only about thirty people and only used one, a lovely medieval building by the sea. But he couldn't find even that one, and all the Jewish houses were in ruins. He'd asked, Isn't this where the Jews lived? A man said, There were never any Jews here. No Jews. This is Crete.

Andonis put his arm round Mama. Many people were glad, he said, that the Jews had gone. She's the only one that escaped.

But you weren't, said Yosif.

As the hotel lobby hummed around them, he said that two years ago, in Detroit, he picked up a local paper and saw that someone called Immanuel Salfatis, from Crete, who escaped from

210

the Germans in the war, had died in an accident. Yosif tracked down Immanuel's widow, who explained that when the Jews were arrested her husband had gone fishing and wasn't in the house when the Germans came. He hid in the mountains, then went to America.

So they only took Amos, said Mama.

No, said Yosif. Last year I was in New York for Yom Kippur and went to a Brooklyn synagogue. In the vestibule, I saw a notice saying one of their community, *Amos* Salfatis, had died of cancer. I found his wife too. She said Amos was the only Jew on Crete to escape. He had scrambled out of a window at the back, climbed along the pipes, he must have passed your bedroom, Sara, and got away. He went to America too. They'd been living in the same country but never knew. Each thought the other was dead.

The yellow-haired woman brought coffee. Mama sipped and felt it surge into her bloodstream as if from another life. Yosif said, Sara, I have to tell you. I'm sorry.

He took a deep breath, looked from one to the other and asked if they had seen film of the death camps in Poland. Andonis pulled Mama closer and said they'd never seen a cinema.

You know, said Yosif, that the Germans sent Jews to them from everywhere. Like Salonica and Corfu?

Mama felt a huge convulsion in her stomach. The air seemed suddenly unbreathable. Is that what happened, she said, to—?

No, Yosif said. They meant to. They put our families on a ship to go there, but it sank. People say they did it on purpose.

Rigid with shock, Mama heard him say, as if from very far away, They drowned. All of them. Your family and mine. No survivors.

They'd been dead all this time. Green bones under the sea. She had no idea how to give that thought a home.

28

I look at Mama's parchmenty face, like a wizened Madonna. Her dark eyes with gold flecks, silver hair looped back from her cheeks, the sea sparkling behind her.

One of Cézanne's friends said the master always began a painting with shadow. He laid down a patch of shadow, overlapped it with another, then another, till all the shadows hinged to each other like screens. That's what Mama has been doing for me. Connecting the dark bits to make a picture of her life.

On the way home in a cab she strokes my hand as if *she* is consoling *me* for having to hear all this. I don't tell her that I knew. That girl in the synagogue told me. She even said the name of the ship. *Tanais*.

It makes sense now, how different Nikos and I are from Vasilis. Vasilis barrels through life without a care, or that's what it looks like from the outside. Nikos and I doubt ourselves, we always wonder where truth is. We are the children Mama had after she knew, really knew, her parents were dead.

I take her to her room. Papa is asleep, she sinks beside him and closes her eyes. I'm sleepy too. It's the first really hot afternoon, the ouzo has gone to my head, or something has. Up in my own room, I scuffle through drawers for something to darken my eyes against the glare and find the envelope Katerina brought from New York. I take it out, put it by the bed, lie down and look at my phone.

No signal. I put a scarf across my eyes, drift into the dark and see David on his bike in a snowdrift.

'Well?' he says in his let's-get-to-the-bottom-of-this voice that sometimes led to enormous relief, sometimes to rows. People said we reminded them of babes in the wood, but even babes in the wood can disagree. David knew how stupidly panicky I get about things like leaking pipes, tax returns, even sitting in a car wash. He knew how to calm me down. But sometimes I didn't want to be. We didn't often have rows, but when we did, he accused me of keeping things away from him.

The deepest things, he'd say, bitterly.

I really don't, I'd say. By now I'd be crying.

You really do, he'd say. You think you don't but you do. It makes me lonely in my mind.

I would boil with injured innocence. How could I hold back something I didn't know? Now, in the dream, that mix of pain and exasperation floods me again.

'So your mum's Jewish,' David says. 'So she wanted to forget it. So? Millions of Jews have had to do that through the centuries. What other option did she have?'

Snow whirls between us. He gets mistier. 'Great you're half-Jewish,' he says, from far away. 'I like that. So was your idol, Amrita. So use it!'

'All very well for you,' I tell him. 'Stop saying "so".'

I'm woken by a *ping*. Sanjiv has WhatsApped photos of his studio in Mumbai. A small room, bare floor, stone shelf with an electric hob, small fridge, white sink. Light from a skylight, and a window looking at distant water, the fawn colour of old rubber bands. Sanjay's face looks nice in the profile circle. Glasses. Serious, but about to smile.

Is 1st February good for you?

Perfect. Thanks. I think of Googling him, but an email comes in from Katerina.

I looked things up for you online. Some journalist says the richer Jews

213

knew what was coming and left Chania early on. Poorer Jews, I guess like Granny's parents, didn't have radios and didn't know. Some archbishop is famous for saving Jews in Athens, so's a bishop who worked with a rabbi in Volos and another who worked with the mayor to save the Jews on Zakynthos. But no one in authority helped on Crete. The rabbi was hopeless, they had no real leader—

The wifi goes off. Waiting for it to return, I open the envelope. Drawings? No, a sheaf of paper, floppy as fine wool, covered in close handwritten Greek. I lift it out and a typed letter in English drops on my chest.

Dear Mrs Gold,

    I was delighted to see, in a newspaper interview, your acknowledgement of Michael Paley's early support for you. He had many accolades for his own work, but was very proud of yours. He told me once, 'I helped her on her way.' When he died in 1998 aged eighty-four, grief prevented me from going through his papers. Now I am in my eighties myself, clearing up before moving to a home, I have found this document. I don't know Greek but it looks like a letter. Michael was in Crete as a young man in the war. He came here and became an American citizen but before I knew him, he went to Crete every summer. I surmise he stayed with your family. After we met, he ceased to go. For twenty years, we lived in the apartment I am now abandoning.

    Michael was revered internationally by the archaeological community, and honoured by the Archaeological Institute of America. I held his hand as he died. But he left a large part of his

214

```
heart — possibly, though it costs me a lot to say
so, the most important part — in Crete.
   With my best wishes,
   Max Freiberg
```

Christ. Out of the blue. I often wondered why Mr Michael stopped coming to Crete but never why he wasn't married. Maybe my brothers did, but not me.

Yes, this is a letter. Dated Battery Park May 1979. Forty years ago.

My dear Andonis,

   The years I've spent in Crete with you and your family have been the happiest of my life. But now I have met someone I wish to spend the rest of my life with, and shall not come again.

   When I left Crete in 1945, I thought you were dead and it was my fault. I took a job in Chicago and tried to forget. But archaeologists cannot shut doors to the past. I attended the opening of Chania's museum and found you alive, with no memory of how you were injured. Now, at last, I want to tell you how that happened.

   Working with Kyriakos, I increasingly felt British agents were making things worse for Crete. British command wanted to tie up German troops on the island so they could not be used elsewhere. The Germans were outraged at Cretan defiance and British support for it. No one had resisted them like the Cretans. But if we hadn't been there, many reprisals and massacres might not have happened.

   What kept me sane was you. Your face, your laughter. Then you told me you were in love with a Jewish girl. I thought I knew Crete, but hadn't known about the Jews.

215

When you brought Sara to the cave, I had no idea of the scale of what she was part of, what was happening to Jews across Europe. I tried not to see her as a rival but I couldn't hide my joy in seeing you.

Soon after that, after the German general was kidnapped, Kyriakos asked me to join an ambush. He had lost a lot of men by now. Robin, whom you all called Kapetanios Kat, agreed to come too. We camped above a ravine where a German patrol would pass next morning. Robin said the Americans had landed in France and were pushing into Germany, so we tuned in to the radio. That was how we heard the Germans had massacred eleven villages in the Amari Valley. Eleven! All the men. Then they looted the houses and burned them. They even burned the animals they didn't take.

We listened in silence, remembering people in the Amari who had helped and hidden us for years. It made us more reckless, I think, when we ambushed the patrol next day. Four of the Germans dropped at once, others ran for cover. Your cousin Georgios raised his head above a rock and was shot at once. Robin stood up to fire and five bullets slashed into him too. When I reached him, his eyes had already closed. Blood was soaking through his shirt. I had known him since I was eighteen, at Cambridge where he broke every heart, including mine.

We killed all the patrol, hid the bodies, and buried Robin and Georgios. Someone had to take a battery to a southern hide-out; I knew you were on a mission to the south so I said I'd go. I walked all night, thinking of Robin, wondering how to tell you your cousin was dead. I reached the drop-off cave at dawn, stashed the battery and lay down outside. I woke to feel you shaking

216

my shoulder. Lord knows where you'd sprung from. You said a patrol was coming up the gorge, we had to hide. Stupid with sleep, I stretched out my arms. You jumped back as if a snake had bitten you. I closed my eyes and pretended to wake gradually. 'Walked all night,' I mumbled. 'Kapetanios Kat has died.' You stood there confused. In a firmer voice, I said we should reconnoitre.

Fatal. In heat like that, it's hard to think straight. If only we'd hidden. But it seemed crucial to know if the Germans knew about the hide-out. We crept across dry scree, the gorge on one side, cliffs on the other. Waves roared on rocks below. We stopped under a thorn tree and scanned the slope. I laid a hand on the tree. You were under my arm.

If it hadn't been for all the feelings stirred up by Robin's death it might have been different. But a raven called, you laughed and turned to me, and before either of us knew what was happening I'd crushed my arms round you. I felt your lips on mine, your slim body against me. Years of love flowed into my fingertips. You pushed me away and raced off at a crazy pace. Your black shirt stood out against the pale mountain, there was a fusillade of shots and you fell behind a boulder.

It happened in a second. Then a terrible silence. That's why we didn't see them, said my mind. They were at the top of the gorge. I blacked out, I think, and came to in a thorn-bush. The heat was scorching. I searched and searched, then looked over the cliff. Far below was a body in a black shirt, face down, smashing sideways onto the rocks, sucked away then flung back, over and over.

29

I stuff the pages back in their envelope. There's more, but that's quite enough for now. So that's how Papa was wounded. I suppose guerrillas found him and carried him to safety.

I revered this man. Mr Michael, my mentor and patron, my great friend – in love, lifelong love, with Papa, and Papa didn't know?

He must have. Mama too. That's why she was prickly when Mr Michael was around. All that time I spent with Papa and Mr Michael in the museum as a child must have felt like defection. No wonder Papa blew up at my questions. He's spent his life covering this up too.

How could I have been so blind? I think suddenly of Amrita's *Two Girls*. Now I'm the one with no eyeballs.

But Mr Michael hid it bloody well. The English are brilliant at concealing things. I remember his face lightening when Papa walked into a room. Otherwise nothing.

What a joke. A bad joke. I owe my career, my husband and daughter, my whole English life, to Mr Michael's passion for Papa. And to his guilt. When he paid for Vasilis's training, for me to go to London, for Nikos's beautiful lute, he was making amends.

It has hit some place of numbness in me. I can hear the pain in his letter, but what does it mean for the rest of us?

I find Papa in the kitchen making coffee in a little one-cup *vriki*, the sugar open beside him.

218

'Mama OK?'

He grunts yes, puts the paper under his arm and stumps off to the patio. In the bedroom, Mama is so still I panic. 'Are you OK? Want some coffee?'

She opens her eyes. 'Can you make *malotira*?'

Mountain tea, herb tea. She probably drank gallons of it in Askordalos. Forget Mr Michael, her story is what matters. Sitting up side by side against her pillow, in the heavy gold light of afternoon, we sip herb tea and I ask the killer question. 'How did you feel, after you knew what happened to your parents?'

30

Sara/Sophia, 1950–1963

She had a second boy, a wriggly baby who wouldn't sleep when she sang because he wanted her to sing again, and the neighbours said *two* sons, bravo. They began to forget Mama had once been Jewish and started dropping in, giving advice on babies. Then Mama had a little girl with curly black hair.

But she began to feel something churning inside her, so big she could only see pieces of it at a time. Something that whispered, *This is not real, this life is not yours. You shouldn't be here at all.* One evening, while she was bathing the baby, Tinu said gently, Why are you crying? That's not bathwater on your cheeks.

The half-laughing, half-anxious way he spoke made her weep more.

I should be happy, she said. Two sons, now this lovely little girl. We have food, Andonis has work. But I've forgotten the blessings Father taught me. I fought him. What happens if you forget *blessings*?

Tinu lifted the baby out in a towel, put her on Mama's lap and emptied the bath outside on the courgettes.

I saw how proud your father was of you. He'd be proud of his grandchildren too. He'd want you to be happy, not cry about not being a perfect daughter long ago.

I have *awful* dreams, she said.

I still dream of my friends who died in the fields, Tinu said. Sometimes God gives us something broken. We who survived, we feel we betrayed the ones that didn't. Your feelings of guilt are really love. And grief, in disguise.

Meanwhile, Andonis was still doing hard-lifting labour and pain was always at him. Even carpentry exhausted him. He was thirty-six but looked like an old man. Then Tinu died, quite suddenly, in one of Crete's little earthquakes. Mama felt the floor of the front room slip like a cart that suddenly started moving, and saw Tinu stagger in the garden. Water sloshed out of the bucket he was carrying, then he and the bucket clattered to earth. The doctor said it was a heart attack.

Shortly after, a terrifying letter came, saying the house belonged to someone in Athens. Was that rumour true, then, had a rich man sold all the Jewish houses? And was someone watching this one, waiting to pounce? Jewish property was impossible to ask about. Andonis said it was all corrupt. He hired a lawyer, who cost a lot of money, and he did extra evening work. He came home in worse pain, but one Saturday he was well enough to walk into town with her to enjoy the cooling air. The boys were out playing football so they took their little daughter and joined the crowds round the Turkish Fountain in Sintrivani Square. As they watched the water glitter in slanting evening light, someone beside Mama said, in a very deep voice, *Andonis?*

A tall foreigner was staring at Andonis as if he'd seen a ghost.

31

So that was how Mr Michael entered our lives.

Mama puts down her empty cup. She's been clutching it as if it gave strength. I put my arm round her. How slippery memories are. They say it's what we've lost that makes us who we are. I wish I remembered Tinu. I had no idea they'd worried about losing our house. I take Mama outside to Papa and mix cinnamon, nutmeg, capers, garlic, sultanas, *rigani* and toasted almonds into mince and rice. Mama is very particular about seasoning, she hates it bland. I stuff it all into bulgy tomatoes. Just as I am sliding them into the oven, the mobile pings, the wifi is back and I have a sheaf of emails.

I read the rest of Katerina's.

. . . so no one helped the Jews on Crete at all. My journalist said – he may be wrong, no idea – the Germans behaved differently with the Jews on Crete because the Cretans gave such trouble! I've seen pics of the German commander, he looks beastly, he was executed for war crimes later. That place in the harbour that sells beads was his HQ. He used to stroll onto the balcony to watch Cretans facing the firing squad. Can you believe?

I tell her about the Salfatis brothers who went to America, and take the tomatoes outside.

There are lights in the bungalow, our American guests are back and Mama is leaning on the table, chatting happily to Papa. She approves the seasoning and has a glass of wine. I help her to bed and return to Papa on the patio. He is staring into the night sky, flicking his keys. Now he is supposed to smoke less, he depends more on his *komboloi*. When he hasn't got them, he twirls keys.

'Another glass, child? Photis made this wine. No chemicals.'

His friend Photis sends him wine from the hills in random bottles. This one, in a large plastic Sprite bottle, is the orangey colour of rose-hips and tastes like the local wine we drank as teenagers. We sip in silence, except the crescendo of a motorbike. Soon the outdoor nightclubs will start and there'll be no quiet at night.

'What was it like,' I ask, 'meeting Mr Michael after the war?'

'I hadn't thought of him for years. He bought you an ice-cream. You sucked your fingers for hours after. We had no money for things like that.'

'My first ice-cream. I remember.'

'Then he asked me to have dinner with him. I felt bad, *we* should have invited *him*. But he solved all our troubles.'

Papa holds his wine up in the moonlight, admiring its tangerine glint.

32

Andonis, 1963–1966

The crowd hummed, waves slapped the harbour wall and Papa gazed into Mr Michael's grey eyes, the skin around them puckered and furrowed. After the first surprise, they all moved in an awkward group towards a café. Papa saw the Englishman notice his limp and politely pretend not to. Then Sara walked the child home and Mr Michael took Papa off for a raki.

I thought you'd died, said Papa. Or went back to England.

Mr Michael said he went to America instead, he was an American citizen now and taught archaeology in Chicago. But, he added slowly, I thought *you* were dead.

He asked how Papa was wounded. Papa said he couldn't remember. Waves lapped in the harbour, bouzouki music filled the evening air and they went on to a fish restaurant, where one dish alone cost more than Papa earned in a week. They moved from raki to wine and Papa found himself pouring out his worries. Someone was after their house, he was sure the lawyer was bribed to act against them, and his leg hurt all the time. He hadn't drunk so much in a long time. It suddenly seemed a joke that he had a wife, three children, a bad leg and a house he might lose.

Old comrades help each other, Mr Michael said. I have an American salary now. He showed Papa a curved piece of clay painted with orange spirals.

Remember my little piece of hope?

Papa didn't.

Why don't we train you to mend ancient pots? You can work sitting down, putting fragments like that together. Archaeology is booming, it brings in tourists, and museums need restorers. You can use your carpentry skills. You'll even get insurance.

And that is what happened. Papa felt he was in one of the fairy tales Tinu told the children. The Archaeological Service took him on as a pot-mender. He was good at the work, he loved it. Finding pieces, matching things up, making things whole.

Meanwhile, Mr Michael hired a lawyer in Athens who worked his way through a labyrinth of claims about Jewish property in Chania. It took years but finally, Papa never knew how many bribes Mr Michael paid, a deal was made. Sara gave up any claim to the house in Kondylaki and the deeds of Barba Rafael's house were put in her name.

Mr Michael also paid for a series of operations on Papa's spine and leg. He still limped afterwards, but there was no pain.

Why is he paying so much to help us? Mama asked.

He says old comrades help each other, said Papa.

33

Papa pours himself another glass. 'Then he built the cottage and we had even more rooms for tourists.'

'Mr Michael used it himself, though.'

'Yes, but he paid. And it was only four months a year.'

How do I square all this with what I remember myself? Mr Michael's confession is in stiff rather old-fashioned Greek, unlike the jokey language I remember him using with Papa in the museum. They were so easy together. When I was about to go off to England, Mr Michael told me he always loosened up when he spoke Greek.

English constrains me, he said. I feel freer in Greek. I'll be interested to see if it works the other way with you.

Well, he never did come and find out, or look me up in London. I see now it was Papa he really cared about. I'm glad, I really am, that he found happiness with someone else. But also that he finally got out of Mama's hair.

In bed, I go on with his letter. I wish David were here to help me know how I feel.

At first, Andonis, I couldn't believe you didn't remember how you were injured. Then I tried to make up for what I did. But I couldn't disguise my feelings about you entirely and Sara – I should call her Sophia now – was always uneasy.

Something else also stood between her and me. Her Jewish ancestors may well have lived in Crete before yours. I'd done the research now: Jews lived in Crete long before Christ. I hated seeing their sole descendant help Crete delete its Jewish past, and her children growing up without knowing their heritage. I saw truth dying into silence, something irreplaceable getting lost before my eyes. I believe she intuited my thoughts about that and resented it.

But I also researched what really happened to her parents, why that boat sank. It had always mystified me. Why should the Germans take the trouble to load Jews onto a boat if they were going to sink it?

I wrote to archives and individuals in Germany and Britain. Meanwhile, along came the dictatorship, which lasted even longer than the Germans. They didn't kill so many people, but the violence came not from outside Greece but from within. I know all countries have these monsters sleeping in their depths, but it was a shock to see that darkness emerge in my beloved Greece. And in the middle of that, I heard from an English navy friend who had wangled his way to records that explained who really sank that boat.

It was a British submarine, HMS Vivid. The captain thought the Tanais was a German ship. Well, she was, by then, but before that the Brits had used her to transport troops. She half-sank at Suda in 1941 under German fire and the British salvaged her, not knowing they would sink her again themselves.

Just off Santorini, in the middle of the night, June 9th 1944, they fired four torpedoes at her, dived to three hundred feet and heard two explosions. Next day they saw oil drums floating on the surface. Some of the German crew survived but everyone in the hold drowned. Italian prisoners, Cretan resistance fighters, and about three hundred Jews. Mostly from Chania.

It was the last thing I expected. I pictured midnight depths off Santorini, and torpedoes gliding through swaying weed. It churned up all the guilt I'd felt when the Germans tortured villagers to find out about British agents. Cretans, I thought, had always been part of someone's empire, always torn. Between Turkey and Europe, Europe and Africa, Germans and British. But in the middle of all that, like the one solid figure in a nest of Russian dolls, were the Jews.

I couldn't make it easy for myself by telling you. I had to take it directly to Sara. I mean Sophia. Telling her was one of the most shaming things I've ever had to do.

It was May 1973. Thirty-two years since the invasion, twenty-nine since her family died. I was cataloguing sherds at the cottage, the water went off and I walked up to the house to see if you had a spare bucketful. It was afternoon, most people were asleep, but Sara was sewing under the pomegranate tree and asked if I needed anything. She always used the formal 'you' when speaking to me. I did the same back, I took my cue from her.

I said I had discovered something about her parents. She looked instantly wary. I said the boat her family died on was not sunk by the Germans but, I was ashamed to say, by the British. They didn't know who was on board.

I felt clumsy, I said I was sorry, I remember hearing cicadas, revving motorbikes and pop music, all the sounds of summer Crete. She said nothing for a while, then muttered, 'What does it matter? They died anyway.'

228

Well, it mattered to me. But my confession made a kind of tragic truce between two people who had always been secret adversaries. She went into the house expecting me to follow, took down a book, opened it at the back, extracted something she raised to her lips, and stared at a page of Hebrew.

I waited in respectful silence. She said it was her father's Haggadah. He wanted her to learn Hebrew, she resisted, now she couldn't read it. She looked at the letters as if they were relics she was not allowed to touch.

I said feebly it was hard to forgive yourself for surviving. I had never forgiven myself for what I did to you. It was only accident it was not your body I saw bumping against those rocks. I was used to guilt. For years it kept rising at me like the Furies out of the ground. You know I was never good with words, Andonis. Not then, and not now. I wanted so much

That's where it stops. Just stops. Maybe he felt he was being too preachy. Or maudlin. A lot of Englishmen don't like expressing emotion.

Wondering what Mama said to him, and what she felt, I think I won't get to sleep. But I do – and wake to hear a cock crow, the sound we woke up to as children. You don't hear it much in Chania now. Tourists don't take kindly to being woken at dawn. But in the crisis, people have gone back to growing their own food and someone here is keeping chickens.

For a moment I am a little girl again, excited about a new day. About everything – Mumbai, new people, new painting. Then I remember Mr Michael and throw off the sheet, go to the window and look into early morning, blue and cool as shadows in yogurt.

I'm the only one who's read that letter and Mr Michael did not send it anyway. What do I tell Papa? I'm the one on the spot now.

229

Papa would like to know how he got shot and how his cousin died. But maybe not about Mr Michael's feelings.

Still, he might simply roar with laughter. It is his last chance to know something vital about himself. He must have known. *And* he used it. Rather successfully, it turns out.

But he's lived his life not bringing it into the open.

But if I don't tell, will I regret it when he's dead? If there's something that hasn't been known and could be, is it an incomplete life, somehow false?

It's the difficult emotions that matter. To say the story of yourself with a whole heart. I can't not offer him the chance to do that.

The cock crows again. Rude, archaic, triumphant. But also the sound of betrayal.

Hundreds of artists have painted the cock that crowed as Peter denied Christ. Nashita and I saved up to visit Rembrandt's house in Amsterdam, where we saw the one that touches me most of all. Peter is making his gesture of denial, someone shoves a candle under his nose and he feels Christ looking at him from behind, forgiving him. That look of compassion is Christ's last gift to Peter as He is led away in chains. Rembrandt puts everything into Peter's lit face, how Peter feels that glance.

Suddenly I feel a rush of excitement. That's where I need to go next, that's what I can explore in Mumbai. How to paint the moment when one person's feelings transform someone else. A look of understanding, from the dark.

The wifi kicks in, bringing another WhatsApp from Sanjiv. *Any idea what you want to see here? I can show you Elephanta Island if you wish. And the Museum of Indian Art.*

Yes please, I text back. *Everything!*

An email from Katerina.

I've found a Salfatis, Mum! Amos's niece. She's old, but she put me

230

in touch with another Chania family here. Not Jewish. A friend of Granny's called Eleni – I'm gonna meet her granddaughter tonight.

I gaze into the pomegranate tree and do all Katerina's exercises, one after the other. I am beginning to enjoy them.

'What happened after Mr Michael came?' I ask Mama, buttoning her blouse. 'I don't remember life without him. Were things easier?'

She sits on the bed suddenly, like a stone tossed in a stream.

'We had a better life. More tourists. More money. And a needle-work shop asked for seven embroideries a month. Mats, napkins, tablecloths. But . . .'

She chokes. Tears spill down her face. I blot them gently with tissue.

About a
Secret Never Told

34

I cut up fruit for the American guests. It is their last day, they are going out with Nikos. We only have coffee and toast ourselves, but Mama spotted early on that foreigners really care about breakfast. Even in early spring, when no fruit is in season but oranges and pomegranates left over from winter, we buy imported fruit to go with fresh yogurt and Cretan honey. It pays off. They love our breakfasts and say so on TripAdvisor.

I add a little saucer of pomegranate seeds like red pearls. Londoners are keen on these now. Californians probably are too.

'How was your trip to the south? Did you swim?'

'Heavenly.' Kelly spoons the seeds on her yogurt. 'Eating this means I'm going to come back, right? Like Persephone.'

'I hope you do.'

The girls eye each other's fruit salads. Doug pours another coffee.

'Awful driving,' Kelly says. 'Jesus, the drops, the corners! But really beautiful.'

'Better beaches,' says Ruby, scraping skin off her yogurt.

Bonny has a new pink T-shirt saying I ♥ KRETA, and is eating with one hand on her *kri kri*. 'We're gonna see the real ones today,' she tells me. Then she sees Papa dragging out of his shed the large metal pieces of a raki still he shares with a friend. It is his job to maintain it. The copper urns, mottled with purple shadow, are taller than Bonnie and have a bizarre alchemical look.

'What's *that*?'

'A liquor-making kit.'

In the old days, everyone made raki freely. Now you need a licence and pay by the day. Papa and his friend book two days in November, everyone brings their own grape-sludge and food. As the distilling bubbles away, they taste the new batch and party in winter coats.

Bonnie goes over to watch Papa lay out pipes, taps and bolts. The urn, condenser and the swan-necked pipe that links them stand beside him on the ground. He up-ends his can of liquid polish on a rag.

'What are you making?' says Bonnie.

'Cretan oo-isky,' says Papa in English, laughing.

'It's like a giant kettle,' I tell her. 'You pour grape-skin sludge in there, and heat it. When it boils, steam rises through that pipe, there and into that other bit. That's where it turns into liquor.'

The mobile pings in my pocket. Katerina has WhatsApped a picture of herself, smiling with a round-faced dark girl. Behind them is a bar and a blue TV screen.

Happy Hour, Brooklyn. Eleni's granddaughter Petra works in IT. Her granny's dead but used to tell stories re Chania before war. Boys. Clothes. Scratchy school uniform. Yuk. So glad I live now.

There they are, 2019 Brooklyn, sharing their grannies' memories from pre-war Chania. I am writing back when Leila calls from the house.

'Quick! She's fallen.'

I race indoors. I should have helped Mama in the bathroom, she gets tetchy and embarrassed but I should have insisted. Now she is face down on the floor, arms and legs spread like an enormous frog. Leila and I heave her up, blood streaming from her face, and support her onto the bed. I sponge her face. I think the blood is from her nose but her eyes are swelling too.

'Can you see me?'

She looks at me and feebly raises her left wrist, which is also

236

swelling. Papa hobbles in, terrified. I ring Bisera the nurse, bandage Mama's wrist and pad her eyes with cotton wool.

By lunchtime, we know she is OK. There are violet bruises round her eyes, she looks like a technicolour panda but she is drinking soup. Papa teases her and she likes that, then he goes off for a siesta. He has moved his things, reluctantly, to an upstairs bedroom.

I put her slippers in a cupboard. Only close-fitting shoes from now on. But from now on till when? What now? Did she mean that about *kaddish*?

'Madam? Hello, Madam?' Kyria Bisera, with her ruff of frizzy hair, is at the door to Reception. I kiss her and take her in to Mama, who smiles weakly. She liked Bisera. Bisera examines her and binds the wrist up better. Nothing broken, nothing to worry about. Mama closes her eyes, Bisera settles into the armchair.

'Thank you for coming,' I whisper.

Bisera smiles. 'Your mother is nice lady.'

In Reception, I put my mobile on the coffee table and start drawing the garden through the glass wall.

Kelly comes in. She really is lovely. Slim, golden, big shiny eyes, a warm smile but very taut, you feel she might twang like a wine glass if you touched her. A Renaissance angel in shorts. I'd love to paint her.

'Hi Ri, I tried to email our boarding passes but the wifi's off?' Her voice goes up at the end, it is a question, not a complaint.

'Sorry, it goes on and off like a yo-yo. I'll print them when it's back. Where are you going next?'

'Italy! Then France and London. Any tips there?' We discuss London a while, then she goes and I turn back to my drawing.

I love drawing in siesta. I can feel everyone's sleep in the air, but I'm alone and working. I get a WhatsApp from Sanjiv about an

237

ancient Indian city he'd like to show me, whose architecture is laid out in the shape of a dancing god. Dreaming of that new world, and someone to show it to me, I change to a softer pencil to capture the shimmer along the tree trunk shed by the sun's reflection from the window.

I have to get that shimmer. It seems to sum up the lure of where I want to go next. Of Mumbai. And a city laid out like a dancing god.

When you draw, you're intensely in the moment but also thinking a few marks ahead, where you'll go next.

The mobile pings again. From Katerina.

Mum! She says there were 2 girls. Granny had a sister.

My brain blanks. My stomach feels as if it has dropped to the ground without me. I stare at the phone. There are three dots. Katerina is typing something else.

My feelings are a whirl of incredulous confusion but my mind, like a lawyer for the prosecution, is already recalling little evasions in Papa's story. And Mama's. Things I didn't realize I had registered, details that didn't quite add up, like that moment in a police drama before the detective identifies the murderer and you see a replay of a scene with the culprit added. One of them stopping what they were going to say, then too obviously saying something else. Papa's eyes flicking sideways when he talked about taking Mama to Hebrew lessons. Did he take the sister too? Mama's mother, her beloved Moumo, lighting two candles on Friday saying 'Two is a good number' and looking down. At two daughters?

Ping. Another message.

Younger sister's name was Elvira. Everyone loved her. She was always drawing. Wanted to be an artist.

I am very still. Also rushing somewhere at helpless speed.

Another three dots. Katerina must have been going home on the subway, mulling over what this girl Petra told her, sending details one at a time.

Eleni last saw Elvira when soldiers were taking her away. Elvira was 12. She told Eleni the soldiers asked where her sister was. She said her sister was dead. That's why they didn't look for her. That's why Granny escaped.

I pick up paper and pencil, put my mobile in my pocket and run out of the gate.

35

I have to get away but I don't know where. After a while I see wild fennel on edges of the road and realize I'm heading west, towards the hills.

Two sisters. Growing up together in that house in Kondylaki. I suddenly get a flash of Amrita's painting *Two Girls*. One in the light, one lost in shadow. But my parents painted her out of their stories. Papa wanted to get Mama out of town, he was sure the Germans would search for her. They had the names of all the Jews, but they didn't search for Mama because Elvira headed them off. She probably saved Mama's life. A child of twelve. Then she must have boarded that ship with her parents.

I feel like a child myself. A child howling in the dark, trying to gauge the scale of what's been hidden from me.

Now I'm among green slopes covered in orange trees. The farmers here pick oranges from November till March, but often leave fruit on the trees. They glow like lanterns beside the new blossom. I can smell the blossom. In Greek, you say hear it, you hear the smell. OK, I'll follow it. I head into the fields. No idea where I'm going.

Soon the grass is high as my chest. It smells rank, as if water is near. Nearly over my head now, full of insects. Further on there are leafy reeds, taller than me. The ground is marshy, and suddenly a lake opens out in front of me.

A mirage. Has to be. There's only one freshwater lake I know of on Crete, but that's miles away, a tourist place with pedal-boats and souvenir shops. This lake has nothing. No one in sight, just open water fringed with reeds.

In front of me is a rickety shack with a tin roof, rusty metal tables and a notice-board. *Snacs. Taberna Limni.*

Lake Taverna. So it is a lake. An unknown lake.

I feel I'm in a time warp, everything here is old and make-do like the Crete of my childhood. I sit on a wobbly chair with hard edges that cut into my bottom. A bony old man appears. Small, close-together eyes peer out from yellow-grey whiskers.

'Good afternoon. Is there *tsipouro?*'

'There is.'

He goes back in. I start drawing, I feel almost frantic to draw. I draw the reeds, the far shore, the bubble-wrap cloud. But from every point in this landscape, the eye is drawn down to the silver tissue of the lake. I think of Nashita's word *withheld*, and will the pencil to conjure everything I see and feel, hold nothing back.

The old man carries out a tray with a mini-carafe of raki, a tiny shot glass, a saucer with a few pieces of rusk and cheese because you should never drink without eating, and a glass of water. He puts it down without speaking.

'What is this place, sir?'

'Don't you know?' He uses the singular *you*, as to a child. In Chania, this would be rude. Here it seems natural. 'Lake Aghias.'

'I only know Lake Kournas.'

'That's another. This lake, God didn't make. Men made it.'

'Why?'

'Irrigation. Now, it is not used. Only by birds.'

The taste of raki is the taste of Crete. Sharp and mineral, like rock. When the first sip hits, I think, the missing piece. The sister. *Everyone loved her. She wanted to be an artist.*

Then of Goya. *No se puede mirar,* Goya wrote on one of his

241

Disasters of War etchings. 'This cannot be looked at.' This child is what my parents could not look at. Papa started the silence about her, didn't he? They must have decided not to tell their children about Mama's family ages ago, but when Mama was in hospital and I challenged Papa, he was on his own. He was the one telling the story, and cut Elvira out. Then they got together and agreed a strategy. Mama told her story without mentioning her either.

That hurts. But hurt is just the tip of the iceberg. A fast-melting iceberg, so many feelings flooding it's going to cascade me into rapids.

I pour another shot of raki.

By the time I've finished the sketch, the little carafe is empty.

Inside the hut is a makeshift bar on a cement floor ridged like grey cream. The old man is sitting at a table with his *komboloi*, staring into space. Just one afternoon, of thousands exactly like it. He is living in aspic. And really old. Wispy, faded, even more ancient than Papa.

'How much do I owe you?'

'Two euros.'

I give him four. 'Don't you have someone here to help you?'

'The Germans killed my son.' He speaks as if it was yesterday, not seventy-five years ago. 'This was where they landed. Here, in Prison Valley.'

'Prison Valley?' Is he being metaphorical? I feel I'm in a country of no explanations, stripped of everything but wind in the reeds. And maybe a bit drunk.

'The prison. Where many patriots died. Isn't that why you've come?' He goes to the door and points. 'There. The place of martyrdom.'

In the green distance, as if his hand has magicked it into being, I see a long white wall. Forty minutes later, after pushing through tall grass, buzzing insects and orange trees, I am under that wall. It is higher than I thought, with watchtowers, and barbed wire along the top. This must be Aghias Prison.

Prisons aren't often in the news here but I know this one is still active because there was a breakout a few years ago when a murderer escaped. I walk along beside the wall but someone shouts at me and a guard appears in rural police uniform.

'What are you doing?'

'Walking. I lost my way.'

'Go back to the road.' He points.

I walk on and then look back. He is staring suspiciously so I veer away from the prison and walk parallel to it round the edge of a wheat-field. When I see the end of the wall, I head towards it again and come out by the prison entrance on a track that leads to a road. Among these gold-green orange trees, this complex of walls and watchtowers, covered in flaking whitewash, is bizarrely sinister. And silent. Nothing moves.

At the entrance, the wall is lower, with flowerbeds in front. Anyone could hop over. Security must happen in the building behind. Behind the iron gates is a yard with pollarded mulberry trees. Their clubbed branches are flailing fists. There are square white pillars either side of the gates and from a stone lintel above hang metal letters, some half-fallen. *Poultry Raising Unit.* And underneath, *Agricultural Prison of Aghias.*

Was this a chicken farm for a while and no one's bothered to take that bit down? Or is the name some sort of camouflage?

This must be where they held the Jews before they sent them to Heraklion. I get out my mobile to take pictures and a guard pops up by the gate. They have been watching.

'No photos! Get away from here.'

I retreat to the road and stand where I imagine Papa stood, gazing at these gates when they were guarded by German troops.

When I get back, Papa has spread his raki equipment over two tables. Indoors, Mama is lying peacefully, eyes closed, and Bisera is doing Sudoku. She has filled in a lot of squares, more than I ever could. On the computer in Reception, I find Kelly's email so

I print her boarding passes and take them to the bungalow. She is packing, blonde hair fountaining over her shoulders.

'Good time on the boat, Kelly?'

'So cool! We loved it, thanks for arranging. We saw the mountain goats, and your brother showed us an airplane wreck on the ocean bed. Ruby and Doug are buying supplies for the journey. How's your mum?'

'Fine, thanks.'

Bonnie runs in. 'We saw the *kri kri*! They were jumping on rocks. I wanted to climb up to them but Nikos said we can't walk on the island.'

Kelly laughs. 'She's always climbing. She's a menace.'

'I do rock climbing back home,' Bonnie says. 'I'm going to be a mountaineer.'

Papa is bent over a piece of copper pipe.

'Can I help?'

'You won't know where things go. Hold that.' He gives me a piece of piping, picks up his pliers and starts screwing a metal joint to the end.

'Guess what? In New York Katerina met the granddaughter of Mama's old friend Eleni.'

Papa drops the pliers. 'Look what you made me do.' He picks them up, and fits the nut to the end of the pipe. I hold it till he's screwed it on.

'Papa, she says there were *two* girls. Did Mama have a younger sister called Elvira?'

We are very still, but a gale is blowing between us. He picks up another piece of pipe and takes his time screwing it on.

'Papa?'

He tips polish on the rag and starts repolishing the urn. The copper glints as he tilts it. He rubs a long time. I watch. And wait. At last he says, 'She was the one I knew first.'

244

36

Andonis, March 1941

His first visit to the house in Kondylaki was a grey day with a smell of wood-smoke on the air. He stood in the yard with Kyrios Mois, looking at timber piled round a tree, and a child came out from behind.

She was a small sallow creature, thin and somehow lop-sided. The skin of her face was drawn tightly over the bridge of her nose, away from enormous grey eyes filled with a hazy dreamy light, giving her a rapt, wide-eyed look of enquiry and wonder. She wore a long brown skirt and a belt she hadn't quite managed to do up. The skirt hung crookedly off her skinny body and her left leg dragged as she walked as if it was something extra, something attached as an afterthought.

Papa felt a sudden strange pain in his throat. All the neighbourhood knew about the little girl run over by a mule cart when she was small but this was the first time he had seen her up close.

My daughter Elvira, said Mois. She's been ill at home, she needs fresh air. This is Andonis, child. He's going to build us a shed.

He said, Hello, Miss. Will you help me build this shed?

She giggled. Of course, she said in a high sweet rush. I've built hundreds of sheds.

Let's get to work then, he said. I'm going to mark the base with string. Is that how you begin too?

245

Usually. She giggled again and held the string while he hammered pegs in the ground.

Doesn't look very big, she said. It's got to hold all Father's tools.

It's the size your dad asked. Maybe it would feel bigger if you stood in it.

She stepped inside the string square, closed her eyes and held her hands out as if imagining sides and a roof.

Making a wish? Papa asked.

She opened her eyes. The same I always wish. To be able to dance.

He glanced at her leg.

I was run over, you see, when I was five. She spoke lightly, to show she didn't mind talking about it.

Is it getting better?

Slowly. If I were a bird, I wouldn't wait, I'd fly. To the White Mountains.

They both looked up. The cloud had lifted, the peaks were clear.

When *I* was five, he said, that's where I lived.

You *lived up there*? She said it as if he'd lived on the moon. I wish *I* did. Sara says *mountains* was my first word. When I was a baby I was crying on the floor, and when she showed me the mountains I stopped. Sara calls them my mountains. But you can have them too. What colour are they up there? Only white?

What funny questions you ask, Papa said, smiling.

That's because I'm going to be an artist. It's important to notice colours.

Some of it's white. But also grey. Sometimes pink. What sort of bird do you want to be?

One that flies high and sings sweet. She spread her arms and hobbled round the yard pretending to be a skylark looking for the shed, trying to land on the roof, not realizing it wasn't built yet.

He now had a devoted new friend. As he worked, Elvira drew pictures of him in her exercise book, which had a flame-patterned

246

cover of red and green zig-zags. She chatted about her parents, her school, and her sister Sara who looked after her and did everything better than she did, except Hebrew. She loved school, she said, but now she didn't want to go back.

You can't make the shed without me!

They laughed. They laughed a lot. But one afternoon, carrying timber through the hall, he looked up the stairs and saw the beautiful older sister. As Sara came downstairs, their eyes met in the unlit hall. Something was decided between them then and there but he went out to the yard and carried on tapping in braces as if he had not just fallen into a world where braces and nails did not matter. Then Sara appeared in the doorway and brought a glass of water. Her figure blocked the light, but she *was* the light, her hair fell round her shoulders, he invited her to stay and help.

We need help, don't we? he said to Elvira.

She looked away and there was a short hot silence. Then Elvira said to Sara, Hold these nails. Sixteen that side, sixteen this.

Sara looked at him and smiled. His heart soared. They already shared something important, affection for this child whose gaiety and lameness touched everyone's heart.

Since when did you know how to put up shelves? Sara said to Elvira.

I'm an expert on sheds. Aren't I, Andonis?

You are, Miss. A world expert.

Elvira giggled, her laughter coming in little hiccups. Sara frowned slightly but as Papa worked he felt her eyes on his body, and when he left that evening he ran up the grass mound of the citadel and whispered her name to the wind.

Sara. *Sara*. A flock of birds wheeled overhead. He saw bright gold flashes on their wings and remembered his grandfather pointing to those birds pecking at thistles in mountain fields. *Karderines*. Thorn-birds. His grandfather said his mother had kept one in a

247

cage, for its sweet singing and for luck. Those birds protect you, his grandfather had said.

The birds flew on towards the sea but two darted into a hawthorn tree and he heard cheeping inside. He thought of little Elvira hobbling round the yard pretending to be a bird. Wouldn't she like a real one? If he gave her a songbird, her sister who was so kind to Elvira herself would see that he was kind too. When it sang, Sara would think of him.

He ran to his shed, whittled sticks for bars and a perch. Narrow, so it couldn't squeeze through. And a close-fitting door, just big enough for his hand. As he worked, he pictured Elvira laughing and Sara's lips shaping *Thank you* in a smile.

He left the cage at the base of the tree and jumped up to catch a branch. Thorns tore his arms and hands, he climbed till he was inside where it was filled with darkness. Handhold, foothold, hand again till he was scratched all over. At the end of one branch, he saw a little brown-green cup between three twigs and wriggled up till he could touch it. The bough swayed. He leaned further. The nest felt soft and tickly, like plunging his hand into cloud. He closed his fingers, felt a frantic beating, found a neck, held it, hauled his arm back, scraped back along the branch and slid down till he stood on earth with a tiny heart pulsing in his hand.

The chick tried to push between his fingers. Ssh, he said. I'll make you a good life. He heard calls, birds flew around his head, he slipped his hand in the cage, opened his hand and fastened the door. A small brown thing like a lop-sided mouse threw itself at the bars. Had he made them too far apart, or would it kill itself trying to get out? He took off his shirt, wrapped it round the cage and slithered down rock the back way into his mother's yard.

His mother and grandfather were eating under the vine.

What kept you, boy? said Grandfather. I've eaten nearly all the lentils.

Why no shirt? said his mother. What have you got there?

248

A *karderini*, said Papa. A goldfinch.

Bird of Christ, said his mother and crossed herself. It has blood on its face from pulling thorns out of His brow.

Not this one. It's just a chick.

They bring good luck, said Grandfather. They protect you against plague.

Great, said Papa. I'm giving it to a little girl. Don't want her to catch plague.

His mother knew who he was talking about. She scraped back her chair and clattered dishes under the tap.

They're good people, Papa said. And he pays well. The Jews are Cretan like us.

The Jews killed Christ, she snapped.

Wasn't Christ Jewish? said Papa. He'd heard Georgios say this. *And* the Virgin Mary?

What rubbish you talk, said his mother.

Papa set the cage on the table and drew away his shirt. The chick was squatting on the cage floor as though tears might roll off its beak any minute. It wobbled to its feet, trying to get as far away as possible.

Grandfather said his mother used to send him out to pick thistle-seed for her goldfinch but it needed water too. Papa filled the lid of a jam jar with water and slid it in the cage, told Grandfather he was in charge of feeding and watering from now on, and went off next day to work at Suda. When he returned three weeks later, the bird was hopping about the cage and Grandfather was bursting with pride. He had sent children out to find seed. He held out a thistle-stalk and the bird darted forward and pecked.

I've tamed it, he said happily and Papa felt sorry he was taking it away. But aren't there two girls in that house? What about the other?

Papa wished he could give Sara a present too, but what? I've given her my heart, he thought. She must know.

Next day Papa picked a cloth from his mother's pile of clean washing and draped it over the cage. To carry through the streets, he explained. I'll bring it back straight away.

My lid too, said his mother sourly. Everything in her kitchen was precious.

Mois met him at the smaller synagogue, where he wanted Papa to fix a door-hinge before Passover. Sara's mother was polishing seats with lavender oil and the smell summoned Sara's presence so vividly that Papa nearly choked. Then he asked if he might present the goldfinch to Elvira. He felt it was obvious the girl he was really after was Sara. But not, it seemed, to the parents.

Certainly, said Kyria Simcha.

Elvira will be delighted, said Mois.

Papa accompanied Mois home, picturing Sara's face as he gave the bird to Elvira. He took out the lid and said the bird would need water. Then he started hanging cupboard doors.

Elvira peeped in.

She's come for her lesson, said Mois. Tomorrow she must ask the Questions.

I have a present for you, Miss, said Papa. He carried the cage outside and took the cloth off. Elvira gasped.

I thought it was a goldfinch, Papa said, but its face isn't red. I climbed a thorn tree and took it from a nest. I made the cage. It eats thistle-seed, you must pick some fresh every day.

He showed her how to open and fasten the door. Put a cloth over the cage at night, he said. Or if it's afraid. It'll feel safer in the dark.

Elvira dropped on one knee, face close to the bars, bad leg out behind. Bird and girl stared at each other. Then she got up awkwardly and flung her arms round Papa. He felt her thin little body tremble.

Thank you! she whispered.

May it bring you good luck, Papa said. And sing as sweet as you deserve. I wish you all a good Passover. He walked back through the streets in a haze of let-down. He had done it, and Sara did not see.

Nor did he see Sara. Not till Easter Sunday afternoon, when he found her with Eleni, asked if she'd seen the bird he gave her little sister and saw her turn her head away. He felt puzzled and shaken. How right Grandfather had been. He should have caught two birds.

There are other things I want to give *you*, he whispered.

Like what? Sara snapped.

What do you think? he flared back. It was as if they had suddenly scratched each other. Some painful but vital electricity was zig-zagging between them. They were both mysteriously enraged. But also, despite Eleni's presence, deeply alone together.

Papa's next chance of seeing her was when he took both girls to a Hebrew lesson. Elvira opened the door as soon as he knocked, she must have been standing behind it waiting. She pulled Papa into the front room to see the bird.

The bird looked less of a mouse now. From its top half, you might think it was a sparrow, but halfway down came bars of gold. Then, bright as paint, the black and white feathers of its rump. Its head was grey streaked with brown as if someone had laid cotton over its crown, and tiny red feathers were growing in on its face.

But Papa did not look closely, he was listening to Sara coming down into the hall. He heard Mois ask if she'd done her homework, and went out to the hall where father and daughter were facing each other. He felt Elvira watching him examine Sara's face. Sara was flushed and mutinous, not looking at anyone.

At the top of the street, afraid Elvira might not be able to scramble up the rocky path, Papa held out his hand. Her fingers were warm and slippery, slightly damp. She clung on when they came out to the grass and he disengaged himself to point out the tree where he found the nest. She asked if Goldie's brothers and

251

sisters were still there. He explained they would have flown and saw a flash of worry. Maybe hers should have flown with them.

Then she spotted his shed, and said it looked like a witch's hut.

It's mine, he laughed. I keep tools there.

She stumbled in among the trees to see but he steered her out, anxious not to lose Sara who was standing, furiously still, with her back to them. Her blue blouse was the same colour as the sky. Her black hair shone streakily gold in the sun.

He led the girls between broken blocks of white stone, yellow daisies and scarlet poppies, to where they could see the sea. The waves were whitey-blue with a purple sheen, like patina on old glass, but Elvira pointed to three ships. One was hiccupping smoke.

That boat's on fire, she said. What's about the *people*?

They'll swim away, he said, remembering men jumping off burning ships at Suda.

What if they can't swim? said Elvira, about to burst into tears.

Other boats will pick them up, said Sara soothingly and Papa realized that calming her little sister was more important to her than nursing her anger.

That's love, he told himself as he led them down to the *plateia*, and love fluttered the heavy leaves of the mulberry trees, love lifted dust across the road in little dun veils.

Elvira, who knew the way from here, pulled him towards a small iron gate. She lifted a chain that ended in a metal dragon's head with a tongue like a flame, and held the gate open grandly as if the garden behind were hers. Sara slipped through without saying a word but Papa bowed politely.

Madam, he said to Elvira.

They all laughed, even Sara, and Papa felt more hopeful.

Elvira kept hold of his hand as they walked under trees heavy with blossom, and introduced him to Tinu, who swept her off the ground in a hug. Later, when the girls came out of their lesson, Elvira wanted to climb the tree to see what was happening in Dove City.

Tinu said no, she would frighten the birds, while Papa exchanged a secret smile with Sara and felt like a king. She liked him again.

The first time he saw the two girls after the bombing, after the Germans had taken over Chania, their mother let him in and called Elvira as if Elvira was the one he had come for. The little crooked figure appeared at the top of the stairs. Elvira descended slowly, carrying the birdcage, and Papa realized she minded him watching her limp. He looked away till she reached the hall, where she set the cage down and flung her arms round him.

You're safe, she sobbed into his chest.

Embarrassed, he unwound her.

Is this the world-famous shed-builder? he said. How's the goldfinch?

Elvira tried to laugh but seemed overwhelmed, and Kyria Simcha invited him to sit in the front room. When Elvira recovered, she said the bird sang beautifully now. She pointed out every feather, white, crimson, black and gold. Then Kyrios Mois came in and, at last, Sara. Papa tried to meet Sara's eyes but Elvira kept coming between, her hair almost brushing his cheek. He saw Sara's face harden and almost exploded with despair. So long since he had seen her and Elvira was in the way. But Mois asked him to take the girls to Hebrew next day and Papa, trying not to be annoyed at Elvira tugging his sleeve, said he'd be glad to. Sara disappeared but Elvira came to the door to see him off.

Yosif left, Eleni right, she said at the door, looking down and up Kondylaki. That's how I learned right from left. Eleni lives there, she pointed. And Yosif here. He's the boy Sara is sewing her dowry for, to marry.

Papa felt suddenly cold. Elvira looked up at him, her little face full of a longing he did not understand. He walked sadly away into the afternoon.

He came for the girls next morning. Both were wearing thick

coats. He was disappointed not to see the shape of Sara's body, but just as well, with German soldiers everywhere. Sara was silent and he did not know how to start talking to her. Elvira smiled brightly.

I can climb trees now, she said. Right up to Dove City. But there are no more doves. The Germans took them.

In Plateia Baphe, they saw two German soldiers walking towards them. The shorter one smiled at Elvira. Sara shrank to Papa's side. Be calm, be natural, he murmured, wishing he could put his arm around her.

Hier. The shorter soldier held an apple to Elvira on his open palm as if offering it to a mule. She widened her eyes and looked at Sara.

Nicht? said the soldier. He looked not much older than Sara. Maybe he really did just want to give a little girl a gift. No – like – apple? he said in broken Greek.

Slowly, Elvira put out her hand. He dropped the apple on her palm. A winter apple, with a shrivelled skin.

Thank you, she said politely.

Please, said the soldier in Greek. He gave a little bow and the two passed on, barely glancing at Sara and Papa.

Sara is so beautiful they daren't look at her, thought Papa with a glow of pride.

Elvira limped to the gate holding her apple as if it was a glass of water she mustn't spill, and they followed her into the garden. After the lesson, when Kyrios Rafael again kept Sara back, Elvira took off her coat and hitched herself into the pomegranate tree. Papa was worried but Tinu smiled. They followed her upward progress through the waving branches.

Can you see me? she called.

Some of you, Papa called back. But you have a very pretty dress. You'll get it dirty.

She slid down. I'm getting better, aren't I? I'm going to be all right, aren't I. *Aren't* I?

It was the first time he heard any edge in her voice. She dusted her dress, which was grey with little red spots.

I put this on specially for you, she said.

Beautiful, he said, but something in his voice disappointed her. She put on her coat in silence and on the way back she went ahead, leaving him alone with Sara.

That night he met Sara in a ruined house. He put his hands round her waist and gazed at her face in moonlight. She let him kiss her, he cradled her, his cheek against her head. Drunk with the closeness of her, and because he really did care about Elvira, he whispered, Tell me, how was Elvira hurt?

The silence was like a knife. Too sad to talk about? he asked.

It was my fault.

I don't believe it.

In tearful whispers, she described standing in the harbour aged ten, holding Elvira's hand while Father bought cabbages from a mule cart. Another cart arrived just as a ship blew its horn, the new mule reared and galloped away, cucumbers rolled everywhere and somehow Elvira's hand wasn't in hers any more and Elvira was on the ground all over blood. Her father said the words of Prophet Elijah, *Let this child's soul come into her again*, and carried her home. Sara followed, crying so much she could hardly see. Their father sat with Elvira for months and said Prophet Elijah sat with him. That was when Father started teaching Elvira Hebrew. Girls didn't usually learn Hebrew grammar, he tried to teach them both but Elvira was the one who learned. Soon it was Elvira, not Sara, asking the Questions in the Seder.

You felt shut out.

I suppose so, Sara said, surprised, as if this hadn't occurred to her. Yes, I did.

Next time he managed to come down from the mountains to see them was much later, maybe a year. He missed Sara but Elvira

255

surged up to him like a puppy. She hugged him, pressing against his chest. He felt her tremble and wished it was Sara.

Sara's just left, she said. We've been telling the future in *malotira* leaves. They say the Germans will go and you'll be with us all … the … time! Would you like a piece of matsah? I was saving it, but you can have it. It's the bread of affliction. And freedom.

Who's this? he said, teasing. I don't know this person. You're a new young lady. I've never tasted *matsah*, Madam, but we're all eating the bread of affliction, aren't we? I'll take freedom, please.

She giggled and put a crumb of biscuit in his hand. We are going to eat the bread of freedom, she said fiercely. Freedom or death.

You talk like the *andartes*, Papa said.

That's what boys at school say. And I'm *so* good at climbing trees now. Better than any boy!

A young lady like you, climbing trees?

Elvira giggled and told him it was nearly Shavuot, May was when the mountain in the Holy Land blossomed with flowers because the Jews received the Torah, and that's when they used to eat *bougatsa* and fruit.

She licked her cracked lips. Not now, she said. The Germans take all the fruit.

Maybe she could hardly remember life without Germans. Three years, a long time for a little girl. Was she eleven? Twelve? He took a quick look. Her breasts were little lemons.

Another visit. He was in the yard with Mois and Elvira, wondering where Sara was, while they talked of finding food in the mountains. *Horta*, snails, hedgehogs.

The prickles come off when you bake them, he said, laughing. And twelve big snails are a really good meal.

Everyone laughed at the face Elvira made. You're a city girl, he said. In villages, they boil snails four times to get rid of slime and then they're lovely. Snail, *rigani* and olive oil, mmm ...

Sit still, Elvira commanded, drawing him, looking him up and down in a birdlike glance. I can dance the Syrtos now, she said. I'm going to dance at the end of term.

Bravo, said Papa. Can you fly too?

Elvira laughed. I'll do that when I'm thirteen, when my wings grow. She asked if Andonis could hang the goldfinch in the window so he could see the sky all the time.

Papa could hardly breathe at the thought of seeing the girls' bedroom. Suddenly they heard a clatter of gunfire somewhere in town and Sara ran into the yard looking frightened, saw Papa, and stopped as if struck by a rock.

He came up to her in one swift movement.

Don't worry about the guns. They're not coming here.

They stared at each other while Mois gathered up string, hammer and nails and they all trooped upstairs to a room off the landing. Papa saw a carved wooden bed covered in a white sheet, with another sheet folded neatly at the end. He imagined Sara taking off her clothes and climbing in. The cage was on the windowsill. The bird fluttered, upset by so many people.

Looks good, said Papa. Red face, gold wings – have you been at him with your paint-box?

Elvira giggled and pointed out a spot at the top of the window. Papa stood on a chair to reach it, rested a foot on the headboard of the bed, and screwed a hook in the ceiling.

Elvira handed the cage up. Hang it low, she said, so I can get it down myself.

When Papa stepped to the floor, he felt Sara close behind.

See if you can reach it, he told Elvira, helping her up on the chair till her eyes were level with the bird. It stared back, pale beak glistening like a child's new tooth, while Papa felt heat from Sara's body on his back and legs.

Mois helped Elvira off the chair and kept his hand on her shoulder as they went downstairs. Behind them, Papa pressed Sara to his heart. All right? he breathed.

I'm so frightened for you in the mountains, she whispered.

I think of you all the time, he said. You keep me safe.

He kissed her but she pulled away and followed the others down. He saw Elvira look back at them when she reached the bottom stair.

That was the last time he saw Elvira. Next time he went to Kondylaki, she was gone. Eleni said Elvira had pushed the cage under the bed so the soldiers wouldn't see it and asked her to look after the bird, but the soldiers would see it when they took the bed, and carry it away. Papa got them into the house and raced up to the girls' bedroom. The sheet was thrown back as Elvira had left it. He looked under the bed.

Not here.

Yes it is, said Eleni. There, at the back. That's the cloth she covers him with.

Papa drew the cage out, squeezed it into the food bag and piled the rusks on top. When they got out of the house, Eleni wanted to take the bird.

No, said Papa. I gave it to her, I'll give it back.

258

37

'Oh Papa.'

The gold of afternoon is deepening. The hot comforting familiar smells of dried grass, fennel and thyme mingle with the cleaning fluid Papa is using on the urn.

'I loved that child,' he says. I put my arm round him, my head on his shoulder. We sit without speaking.

'Why didn't you tell me about her?' I finally ask. 'She was with you all the time. Why did you leave her out of the story?'

Papa stares at the urn. His friend Photis is coming tonight to fetch the raki equipment and take him off to supper. He'll be glad to get away.

'Your mum can't talk about her.' He rubs at an invisible speck. 'Never been able to.'

'What did Elvira look like?'

'An owl.' He smiles fondly. 'Eyes too big for her face. Her mouth was big too, but she had a sweet, sweet smile. Later, when I came back from the mountains and she was a bit older, she was – straighter. Not beautiful like Sara but a girl, not a child.'

'Did she mind you liking her sister?'

'She was only a little girl.'

'Little girls have big feelings.'

'We joked a lot. She loved laughing. She had a – I don't know – an angel about her. It lifted your heart. But when I met your mum, I told you, I fell in love.'

'How did Elvira feel about that?'

'She was nothing to do with it.' He up-ends the liquid polish can on his rag.

'How did they get on?'

'Adored each other. Slept in the same bed.'

I can't believe that Mama, talking about her life back then, never said she shared a bed with her sister. Her lame sister.

Papa goes on polishing the taps. 'Sara looked after Elvira. I used to see them walking to school in the rubble. Sara held Elvira's hand. But, well, Sara never said, but I thought she minded her dad being so proud of Elvira's Hebrew. When she told me how Elvira was run over, I understood how she felt.'

'How who felt?'

'Sara. She thought her father blamed her.'

'Why did you give that bird to Elvira?'

'I felt sorry for her. I knew she'd like it, but what I really wanted was for Sara to hear it sing and think how good I was, to give it to her sister. Stupid! It didn't work. Georgios said it wouldn't. But he also said to blind it to make it sing. You make a wire red-hot, he said, and stick it in its eyes. I told him fuck off, it was for a little girl. At first, after I gave it to Elvira, Sara wouldn't speak to me. Then she forgave me and we started meeting. Elvira didn't know.'

'Bet she did.'

'She was too young to understand.'

'Papa!'

I think he knew Elvira adored him. Tough, really, in love with the older girl, to have the little one's devotion. He did love Elvira. But not how she, even at age nine, wanted. Mr Michael's letter has made me see Papa in a new light. He was deliberately blind to Mr Michael's feelings, didn't let himself know he knew, and maybe that happened with Elvira too. Papa loves to be loved. But except with Mama, he doesn't really want its consequences. Maybe he enticed little Elvira, as well as Mr Michael, into more love than he could handle. Maybe the war was to blame too. In a war, you have to hide as much as you can. Animals, children, guns, food. Your identity, your name, your religion. And your feelings.

'Papa, you left that bird out of your story too. *That's* why you went into the house when the Germans were looting it. What did you do with it?'

'Took it to the mountains. Sara wanted to keep it for Elvira, but then she ignored it. Mr Michael asked why was I lugging it along, I said it belonged to Sara's sister but Sara didn't care about it and I should set it free. Mr Michael said Sara was in shock, she'd want it later. He was right. She kept it alive that year. When we left, Stavros tried to stop us taking it, the bugger. Wanted to keep it.'

'It's the cage in your bedroom.' A dog barks in the distance. 'That's why you called this place Rooms Karderini.'

I remember what Mama said Aspasia told her, how unlamented blood is a poison that haunts the earth. Through all Crete's tragedies, all the Turkish and German massacres, at least the Christian Cretans were able to mourn their dead. No one's done that for Elvira.

And yet Elvira's bird gave its name to our home, and Mama keeps its cage in her bedroom. She may not have been able to talk about Elvira but Elvira has been with her, and with us, all along.

Whatever you find unforgiveable, that's what you've got to forgive.

38

Outside, the garden is beginning to quiver in evening light. Inside Mama's bedroom, the twilight is like breathed-on metal. Mama is standing up, doddery and rebellious, white hair fanning around her shoulders, leaning on Bisera's arm. We are in the next phase of looking after. A commode in the bathroom, a three-wheeled walker in the bedroom. While I was out, Nikos and Vasilis came round and arranged with Bisera that she will do nightshifts. Papa will sleep upstairs like me, until we move a bed into Reception. Nikos will take Bisera home now, and bring her back at eleven. I'll share the cost with Vasilis. Bisera is expensive but what's money for if you can't look after your mother?

Bisera is short, but sturdy as a tree. Her nose curves out to a bell-like flourish, her firm mouth has a deep runnel on the upper lip, and she moves as you imagine Michelangelo's Sibyl might, sturdy and unflappable. I like her. It's not easy being foreign in Crete on good pay when many Cretans have no work. She'll earn much more here than in Bulgaria. There are hundreds of second-home owners, Greek, European and English, and the huge American base. They'll all need looking after, sometime or other.

Bisera makes me feel Mama will be safe. I take a photo of them together on my phone and they smile. Mama too feels safe with Bisera.

'I will coming eleven o'clock,' Bisera says. Mama nods. I hear Nikos in Reception and escort Bisera outside.

'How's your garden? Will you go back to Bulgaria soon?'

'Is good. At Christmas, I seeing my mum.' She gives me a vivid smile.

'She's well, your mum?'

'Is good. With my sister.'

'That's nice.'

Papa is packing up his raki still and Nikos kisses me. 'All good?'

'Fine.' What else can I say till we have an evening to ourselves? 'The guests loved your boat.'

'Good people,' he says. 'We had a great time.'

In the bedroom, Mama asks me to brush her hair. The brush is on the chest of drawers beside the birdcage and when I pick it up I have a good look at the cage. It's pretty crude, only about nine inches square. I hate to think of anything living in it, least of all a goldfinch. Dark reddish wood. The bars a little crooked, like twigs of a broom. I put it in Mama's portrait for the shape and lines, and enjoyed doing the shadow stripes of grey, cream and brown.

Mama must dust it every week. What is it like, dusting a cage full of such absence?

'What are you waiting for?' says Mama and I start on her mass of hair. It is like combing snow. Long, soft, insubstantial. The scalp beneath is the colour of a dried sea-urchin, pale brownish-pink.

'Something amazing has happened,' I say as I comb. 'Katerina met the granddaughter of your old friend Eleni in New York.'

Mama jumps as if I've pronged her with a fork. 'Is Eleni alive?'

'No. Didn't do as well as you. But her granddaughter,' I feel like a heart surgeon making a first incision, 'told Katerina something I had no idea of. She said you had a younger sister. Elvira.'

Silence. Mama is still as a mountain.

'Papa told me ...'

She flings up a hand to stop me. 'I will not talk about this.'

'Mama.' I sit beside her, take her hand in both mine. She pulls away. We are back at my teenage years but now she is the one rebelling. In that tent of silver hair, she looks like a sulky witch. I tell myself this to stop myself crying, I can't bear that Mama has lived with this all her life, all my life, and never said.

'Can you say something about Elvira?'

Nothing. This moment feels like the creepy music before a murder in a film. I put my arm round her. She is stiff as a sword.

'Mama?'

Silence. I stand up, finish the last tangles, coil up her hair and pin it. My hands are trembling. 'Come and sit in the kitchen while I make supper.' The walker is folded up in the corner. I open it and push down the seat. 'Want to have a go at this?'

'No.'

I support her to the kitchen, pour her a tumbler of Photis's orange wine, cut up cucumber and cheese, sprinkle them with *rigani* and put them in front of her to nibble while she drinks.

'*Kephtedes* tonight, Mama. Papa's eating with Photis.'

I choose a head of garlic and peel the white papery skin. Mama watches, pokes at a cube of cucumber, sips her wine.

'Eleni's granddaughter said your sister was always drawing. She wanted to be an artist.'

I don't look at her, I get the mince out, slap it on a plate, chop garlic and onion, mint and *rigani*, break an egg, knead everything into the mince and watch it spurt red through my fingers.

'Don't forget cumin,' she says.

Damn her. I shake in cumin, salt and pepper, wrap the lot in a cloth, put it in the fridge and start peeling potatoes. Finally, so slowly that each syllable sounds like a separate event, Mama says, 'She was five years younger than me.'

I go on peeling potatoes. God knows what she is thinking. Eventually I say, lightly as I can, 'She wanted to be an artist?'

I tip the potatoes into a pan, squeeze lemon over them, shake in oil and salt and remember Mama sitting for her portrait. She didn't want to sit. But she knew how to. She'd done it before.

'Yes. She drew everything, everyone. She was ill for a year when she was small, and my father gave her a book on birds. That's when she began drawing, she copied the bird pictures, she was fascinated by birds, she slept with her arms in the position of wings. Every year for my birthday she painted me a picture of a different bird. But she drew other things too. She never stopped drawing.'

'And you both came here for lessons?' I slide the potatoes into the oven.

'We used to walk here round the harbour and watch the boats. We'd never been on a boat. Elvira longed to. She said she wanted to see the fishy world beneath. Once we saw a turtle swimming, very close. Holding up its face for air, then diving under again.'

I can see the moon through the window. There's only one lamp on, over the stove. I light a candle, I don't want electric light.

'Your father gave her a songbird,' she suddenly says. 'A goldfinch. I couldn't believe he was giving her a present, not me.'

Of all things to remember.

'Goldie,' she says in a soft sad voice that makes me want to bang my head against the wall and howl. 'She called it Goldie.'

39

The week before Passover, they beat the winter rugs and folded them away. Then they swept all the floors, and helped their mother get ready for the festival. Finally, in the middle of the kitchen, Elvira held out her arms like a dancer.

Pesach is a war dance, she said solemnly, in the voice patriotic speakers at the end of term introduce the Syrtos Chaniotikos. She pointed at Moumo. And you're our *kapetanios*.

They all fell about laughing. Elvira was brilliant at making people laugh.

But later that day, standing at the open window washing the Pesach china when Elvira was about to practise the Seder Questions with Father, Mama saw Andonis in the yard give Elvira a box. No, a cage, with a little bird inside.

A bird. Elvira would be overjoyed. But then Mama saw Elvira fling her arms round Andonis and was furious. It wasn't fair Elvira was free to show how much she liked him.

Then Andonis left. Didn't even glance in the kitchen. Too proud to call out, Mama heard the front door close and felt desolate, then enraged. He was Elvira's friend first, but she'd been sure he liked her best. She stayed at the kitchen window and saw Father, too, give Elvira a present.

My grandmother's silver sugar bowl, she heard him say. When

I was a child, I was called to the front room when she drank tea and she gave me a spoonful. Like you, I loved sweet things. It is the right size for your bird to drink from, child. You can polish it.

Elvira filled a saucer at the yard tap. Mama longed to rush out, yank the cage open and shake it so the bird flew away. She watched Elvira put the dish in the cage and fasten the door.

Little fairy fingers, she heard Father say.

Mama took a deep angry breath and went outside. There were heavy purple clouds in the sky, lighting the yard in a strange mustardy glow. Elvira was shaking with excitement.

Look, Sara, she said. A bird, a real live bird. Andonis climbed a tree and got it from a nest.

Normally, Mama loved making Elvira happy herself but now she wanted to hit her. She stalked back into the kitchen where Moumo was cutting up chicken. Elvira followed. It turned out Moumo also knew about the wretched bird.

Want to pull the wishbone? said Moumo, sensing tension.

A wishing bone? said Elvira. Does my goldfinch have a wishing bone too?

Put your little finger in here, said Moumo. Wish, and pull. If you get the flat end, put it under your pillow at night and your wish will come true.

Moumo smiled the smile that meant this was not true but she enjoyed pretending it was.

Wish, said Mama roughly, hooking her own little finger into the power place, at the bottom. She wished for Yosif to come back, closed her eyes, heard a snap and found herself holding the piece with the flat end.

Better luck next time, she said to Elvira's disappointed little face.

Afterwards she wondered, Will my wish not come true because I made sure I won? Or because I was mean?

After supper, Father held up the lamp so they could hunt for crumbs. They peered in corners, swept and burned the crumbs. There was a burst of thunder. The storm had finally arrived.

Bed, Elvira, said Moumo. Join your bird, little one.

Why should I share my bedroom with a *bird*? Mama hissed as Elvira climbed the stairs.

Sara, please, said Father in a low voice. This is the eve of Pesach. We are about to celebrate the story that made us who we are. Look after your afflicted sister. She loves you, she yearns to be like you. But she knows, and you know, she can't.

Silence rolled up the stairs like dark flame.

Tonight, said Father, Elvira was given something that made her very happy. And I have something for *you*, my dear. I polished it for you.

What? Mama asked, knowing she was being rude, feeling guilty, not knowing how to back down.

A necklace, Father said. It belonged to my grandmother, Sultana Riketta.

He put an ivory box in her hands. Inside were exquisite silver flowers, curling round a moonstone. Moumo smiled, she knew about this too. Father's lamp shed a shell of light round the three of them and Mama suddenly felt folded in love.

Wear it tomorrow night, Father said. You resemble Sultana Riketta, my dear. She was a very beautiful woman. She lives again in you.

Mama went upstairs. What did silly old Andonis matter? She undressed in the dark, but knew by Elvira's breathing she was not asleep.

What did Father give you? Elvira whispered. He said he polished it. He gave me a silver saucer but didn't polish that. What is it?

Show you in the morning, Mama said, and turned on her side.

Another thunderclap burst above them. Elvira burrowed against her, resting her cheek on top of Mama's spine as she always did when she was afraid. Glad of that, despite everything, Mama fell asleep to rain drumming on the roof.

Next evening, she looked in the mirror and felt astonishingly, ridiculously, beautiful. Silver flowers circled her throat and flowed down over the two small bones in front where the moonstone nestled. It seemed to promise a magic power she suddenly felt she really had. She wished Andonis could see her. *And* Yosif.

Barba Rafael and Tinu were guests. It was an honour for Barba Rafael to attend their Seder. In lessons, she always tried not to look at him. Now, when they sat at table, the candlelight painted his face into luminous slabs like mother of pearl. She had decorated the table with spring flowers, and a circle of daisies round the *sini*, the gleaming brass tray that held the foods that were not for eating but remembering. But she also felt everyone gazing at her necklace as if the enchantment of Passover was concentrated entirely in that.

Barba Rafael recited the Haggadah, Father carried the *sini* over everyone's head to show how important the story was, Elvira asked the Questions and they hunted for the hidden piece of *matsah*. All the time, in the flickering candlelight, Mama felt herself glowing. She knew Moumo felt proud of having such a beautiful daughter, as she was proud of the delicious spices and meat. Everything tasted wonderful, though there wasn't much of it.

It's like eating stars, said Elvira, and everyone laughed.

The gold haze of the candles made the faces seem nearer than they really were. Everything beyond the shutters was forgotten.

Beautiful, said Barba Rafael, looking at Mama's necklace.

It belonged to my grandmother, Father said. Elvira turned quickly to Tinu.

I've got a bird, she said. A real live bird. May I fetch my bird to show Tinu? When we've finished, said Moumo.

At the end of the meal, Elvira scraped back her chair. Father rose too, to open the front door for Elijah.

269

Elijah guides our wandering through life, he said. When we open our door for him, we are opening our hearts.

He was looking only at Elvira – didn't he want *her* heart to open too? Mama heard Elvira climb laboriously upstairs while Papa opened the front door and the candle flames wagged in the draught. She imagined Andonis walking in, seeing her in her necklace and gazing at her. She felt like a flame herself.

The grown-ups started talking about the Germans.

They are in Salonica, said Moumo. If they get to Athens, what will happen here?

They won't, Father said. The British and Greek armies will stop them.

They heard Elvira clop downstairs into the hall – and then pause. When she came in, she carried the birdcage to Tinu without speaking.

This will bring you luck, he said. It is a *karderini*. It will keep you safe.

But its face isn't red.

It's young, Miss. Like you. The red face will come in time.

Barba Rafael lifted the cage to look and Mama saw how thin his arm was. She always thought of him as strong but he was old. And weak. Her necklace seemed to give new powers. She saw with new eyes, felt scraped and excited. Anything could happen.

The little bird fluttered.

Please be careful, Elvira said. He doesn't know you.

Does he know *you*? Mama heard herself say, as if a wedge of darkness had flown out of her to hurt Elvira. But Elvira was bubbling over with something else.

I saw Elijah, she said. He was in the rain, he had white hair and a white beard and a shepherd's crook. A black bird sat on his shoulder. I said, will you come in, sir? But he wouldn't.

Everyone let out a breath like an unlaughed laugh.

Elijah the Wanderer appears in many guises, said Barba

Rafael. This is the night of passing over. Maybe he'll come in next year.

Elvira smiled and caught Mama's eye. Mama smiled back. Suddenly she felt like Kind Sara again, who warmed Elvira's feet and waited when she was tired. But later, in bed, Kind Sara disappeared.

Prophet Elijah wasn't really there, she told Elvira. You know that, don't you?

He was, said Elvira. He truly was. At first there was only rain and night, then he was there, his eyes burned. I said, will you take us under your protection, sir? But he wouldn't.

She sounded frightened, she must have heard the talk about Germans. Mama turned and put an arm round her. Drifting into sleep, she saw Elvira standing in the dark facing Elijah the Wanderer with a raven on his shoulder. Then the bird raised its wings and there was nothing but night and the empty street.

40

I refill Mama's glass, make little balls of mince, place them on a baking sheet and shove them in the oven. 'That was your last Passover before the Germans came?'

'It was.'

The moon has moved, I can't see it any more. The rafters, sooty crosses and crockery, the life Mama has made here, are all around us. But a terrible pain is in the room with us too. I feel we are down on the nursery floor somehow, the ground zero of her soul.

'Why did you call your mother Moumo?'

'That's what I called her when I was a baby. I went on calling her that.'

'Did Elvira call her that too?'

'No! I wouldn't let her. She just said *Mother*. I think. I can't remember.'

'She had an accident, didn't she?'

Mama bends her head.

'Papa said you blamed yourself.'

She is silent a moment, then says in a husky voice, 'I kept hearing her say, *You let go my hand*. I don't think she ever did, even Father said it was an act of God. But I *felt* them saying it.'

'You were saying it to yourself.'

'When she began walking again, it was awful. *Clunkety clunk* . . . Every step she took, I felt guilty.'

'But she got better?'

'Yes. That last spring, at school, she danced the Syrtos with the rest of us.'

My throat is seizing up. 'When was the last time you saw her?'

'A Friday afternoon. Very hot.'

Mama looks down at her knuckles. I'd like to draw the little creases round each finger joint, the tension folds in the skin. The soft-raised veins, glimmering in the light of that one candle. Her hands, gripping each other like a prayer.

'We sat in the bedroom window, leaning our backs against the shutters. It was a thick windowsill. A ... a recess. I was sewing, she was drawing me. I remember her saying she couldn't get the folds of my embroidery right. She always wanted it to be *right*.'

'Perfectionist.'

'Yes. But I was thinking about going to Andonis's shed that night. The first time.'

In her watery old eyes, I glimpse the ghost of teenage pride in her unusual beauty.

'I was scared. Excited. We wouldn't be out longer than usual, I wasn't afraid of the curfew, but my parents. Elvira was always asleep when I got back, she never told them I went out, we never talked about it. But I thought, that night, she sort of knew *something*.'

41

Sara/Sophia, May 1944

The goldfinch twittered above their heads. Rays of sun caught swirling dust like flakes of silk and turned the floorboards gold. When Elvira was little, they played a game that those floorboards could talk, telling each other stories of when they were trees.

I've been drawing flowers in my new sketchbook, said Elvira. Flowers are *com-pli-cat-ed*. She sang the word.

How about drawing yourself in a mirror? Mama asked.

I did that in the old book, said Elvira.

Can I see? Nope, said Elvira, teasing but not. It's hidden. Where you'll never find it.

Mama knew what she was saying. That she had a secret too.

This moment felt like all the other moments, all their lives, when they had sat here looking out at the yard and the mountains, but in the last few years a rift had grown between them. First, when Elvira went on about Andonis. Then, when Mama met him herself and felt he belonged to her. Then, worse, when Andonis gave Elvira that bird. And now, now when she and Andonis were close. Whatever happened in that shed tonight would seal it for ever.

Mama shifted on the windowsill. She felt strongly her body with its warmth. Her heavy breasts, her thighs, her heart, beating under the soft blouse. But suddenly she was desperate to be close to Elvira again, close as she used to be.

Let's play Cat's Cradle, she said.

I've got string, said Elvira eagerly. I kept it when Andonis hung the cage.

Mama tied the string in a circle, drew it taut between Elvira's hands, and flipped it over.

That's *Diamond*, Elvira said. What's next?

Fish in a Dish. Keep your hands apart, don't let it slack.

They passed the string to and fro. *The Manger. Knitting Needles. Soldier's Bed.*

The sun dipped lower in the sky.

There's always another pattern hiding in the one you've got, said Elvira, picking *Candles* from Mama's fingers, changing it to *Falling Snow*. Only you can't see it. Like the broken *matsah* in the Seder, the bit we have to hunt for. Barba Rafael says each of us searches, all our life, for the hidden part of ourselves. The *matsah* on the plate is incomplete. Like me without you.

Mama picked string off Elvira's fingers and felt hot tears in her eyes. I'm sorry I'm so horrid sometimes, she said.

Aren't we sisters? said Elvira lightly, untangling the string. We can say *anything*. She smiled teasingly. Look out, here comes *The Scorpion*. She held him up, tail poised.

Mama separated the central strings and flicked them onto her fingers. *The Clock*, she said, holding it up. *The Clock* calls time. Look, it's nearly sunset! We must be with Moumo when she lights the candles.

In the kitchen, they watched Moumo wave a hand over the flames. Moumo hoarded candle stubs for this moment. *Zakhor*, to remember, she murmured. *Shamor*, to protect. The two flames danced. Mama remembered Elvira when she was little saying, Come on, Sara, I'll be Remember, you be Protect!

The shadows lengthened, the clock ticked, the ceiling creaked in the heat. Mama felt little flickers on her spine about the night to come. Father returned from synagogue and blessed the food.

275

He shall cover you with His wings. You shall be safe under His feathers. No evil shall happen, no plague come near your tent.

Mama could follow that, it was one of the prayers she knew by heart. It was all right for Elvira to be so good at Hebrew. She had Andonis, she had the night.

Supper was rusks and a very small omelette. Elvira pushed the morsel of omelette on her plate. She had wound the string they'd played with round her wrist. She'd had to wind it several times, her wrist was so thin. One bone, no flesh at all, and the skin glistening a little, damp with sweat. She said her tummy ached, she couldn't eat, being hungry made her not want food.

Mama was so keyed up she hardly felt hungry either but she knew it had been hard to find eggs and forced herself to finish.

Eat, Moumo said to Elvira. You must stay strong.

I will tomorrow, Elvira said.

42

I open the oven and pull out the potatoes.

'Then I left,' Mama says with a crack in her voice. 'After supper. I said I was going to Eleni's. If I'd known . . .'

'What else could you have done? Not knowing saved you.'

Her story hangs in the dark air. She eats the meatballs with no comments on cumin. With her bruised eye sockets, she looks like an exhausted clown.

'Bed, Mama?'

The commode and washing are difficult for us both. Her body is soft and floppy, very heavy. Afterwards I swing her legs up to the bed and sit with an arm round her as darkness dissolves the forms of things in her room. These are the shapes and shadows she has seen all her life. Forms she has lived with for decades, closed her eyes to at night, opened her eyes to in the morning. With all this knowledge of a lost world, lost sister, festering behind.

'How did you feel in the White Mountains, where Elvira always wanted to go?'

'I thought, I must remember what this looks like, so I can tell her.'

'Oh, Mama.'

As if death fell asleep and dreamed of life.

43

Sara/Sophia, June 1944–1956

One day in Askordalos, moving a stone to look for eggs, she saw Elvira's frightened face as if it was lying in wait for her underneath. That's when the dark rip began inside her. Some irrevocable, absolutely central, inward fracture. She remembered, in the middle of the bombing, telling Elvira not to draw her. They were both terrified, but she was secretly terrified for Andonis too. Was he alive or dead?

She'd been so cruel. Her tears splashed that stone, darkening it.

Her only connection to Elvira was the goldfinch. When she picked seed, she thought of Elvira doing it. When she watched him peck, those little sharp stabs, that tiny throat making its tiny swallows, she felt a tremor of hope.

Goldie, she said. Goldie. He didn't look up then, but one day he hopped casually on her knuckle. She felt as if Elvira were lightly touching her from wherever she was now.

Stavros was proud of Goldie and hung the cage over the front door. The bird sang in the morning but drooped when sun fell on it in the afternoon. Mama carried the cage indoors. She was learning what Goldie needed, she tried to see this alien world through his eyes. When the Germans approached she thrust the cage under the couch. That's what they saved from the soldiers. Rabbits, flour, and a goldfinch.

278

The night after, she dreamed Father was sitting in the yard.

Bravo, my dear. Keep your love for your sister alive.

I thought you only loved Elvira, she said.

You are our firstborn, said her father. I cherish your spirit of challenge.

I wish you'd told me that, she said as he faded.

At Christmas, the year's darkest hour, Goldie stopped eating and drooped like a dying plant. Stavros said *kalikantzouria* were attacking him. Mama pictured little black demons poking Goldie with sticks. If he died, Elvira was dead, they were all dead, she would never see any of them again.

Aspasia brought out a tiny bottle.

Water blessed by the priest, she said, at the Baptism of Christ.

She sprinkled Goldie with it. Blessings were Father's panacea too, and Mama felt a little comforted.

Pray, ordered Aspasia. Pray to the Panaghia, to heal the Bird of Christ. We saved him from the Germans, we won't lose him to Charos.

Mama thought of Father moving his finger on the page to help her translate a psalm. She murmured a prayer.

What words are those? said Aspasia suspiciously, as if they might contaminate the holy water.

Keep us O Lord in our danger. I said it when the Germans knocked you to the ground.

What language is it? said Aspasia.

Holy language, Mama said indignantly. God's language.

When you say it in Greek it sounds like a real prayer.

Next morning Goldie finished off a thistle-head. At noon, he opened his beak and sang. His eyes were bright again, his feathers smooth.

You're a magician, Kyria Aspasia, Mama said.

No, child, said Aspasia. It's the holy water.

One night Mama remembered a moment in the bombing when Elvira limped out of the room and went upstairs alone, with the house shaking, and brought down the cage. To lighten our darkness, she said in a lull. Good girl, said Father. Elvira's face flushed and she glanced at Mama. Triumphing over me, Mama thought then. Now she thought, how petty I was! She saw a frightened little girl looking at her sister, sharing the trying-to-endure.

God help me, she sobbed into the goaty blanket. God forgive me my sins. At so many moments she had hardened her heart, exactly what the Torah said you mustn't do. Those moments now slurped back at her like flotsam thrown by waves. She remembered a phrase in the Day of Atonement. I *turned away my head*, she told herself.

She saw herself slipping into bed beside Elvira, fired by Andonis's kisses. Elvira fast asleep, curled in the shell of her breath. She would give anything to know she had put an arm round Elvira then. But she knew she had not.

When they met Tinu in Chania, the first thing he did was pick up the birdcage.

Miss Elvira's little bird. Where is she?

Mama burst into tears and shook her head.

As she settled into living with Tinu, she kept wondering why her parents sent no message. Had they forgotten they had any daughter but Elvira? She pictured herself giving Goldie back. And Elvira's face saying thank you, thank you.

The night before she was baptized, she thought, Elvira knew all the Hebrew prayers. She knew the meanings of the festivals. She remembered what Father taught. I didn't. I can't. When I see her again, we'll be divided. And yet, as she worked in the garden with Tinu, she kept imagining it was the garden of lost and found, where everything you had lost would reappear. She imagined Elvira walking in under the trees. The eager smile. The open arms.

Instead, her boys came. And then a little girl she longed to call Elvira. It almost felt, for a second, as if Elvira really had come back. But Kyria Maria said the child would never get married with a foreign name.

You changed your name to a Greek one, she said. Your children should have Greek names too.

Then Yosif told them what really happened to her family. That night she dreamed of Charos, deaf Charos who could not hear prayers, plunging Elvira in wild blue waves. She heard Elvira call *Sara! Sara!* Next day she picked up the cage and gave it to Andonis.

Set it free, she said. No point keeping it now.

They gathered under the pomegranate tree. The leaves rustled, the cage sat on the table and the bird fluttered, not used to so many people at once. The gold in its wings made little hooks of light. She remembered Elvira sending it flying round the bedroom. Andonis opened the door and the little scarlet face peered out.

Nikos was sobbing. Why? he kept saying. Why must we lose it?

Arianna, aged one, wailed in sympathy. *Ri*, she howled. Ri was her shot at the long word, *karderini*. She called herself Ri too, which was confusing. It wasn't always clear when she meant the goldfinch and when she meant herself.

Ri will still be here, Tinu said. He'll join the other goldfinches. He'll start a family.

When did I catch him? said Andonis. Twelve years ago. He could be a grandfather. He will be, now. We'll see his children in this tree.

With a little bounce, the bird was out, standing motionless on the table.

Ri! howled Arianna again, *Ri! Ri!* She lifted her arms. The movement lifted the bird into the air, into the tree. Nikos cried harder. Tinu put an arm round him but his own cheeks were streaming too. Mama remembered Andonis asking Tinu if he'd

281

build another dovecote so they could keep pigeons. Don't ask, Tinu answered. Let Dove City rest in peace.

I can't see him, wept Nikos. Mama gripped his little hand but she could hardly see for tears herself.

He's exploring his new home, said Tinu.

How will he eat? wailed Nikos.

We'll leave the cage open, said Tinu, with seed beside it. But he'll smell out the right food.

How can birds smell? said Nikos, anguished. They haven't any noses.

They have beaks, Andonis said.

They have noses in their beaks, said Vasilis, and Nikos giggled through his tears.

The cage became a doll's house for Arianna, who soon forgot about the bird. Her lumpy little doll went through terrible adventures, dreamed up by Nikos, but always got back safe to the cage. One day, when Andonis was drinking coffee, he saw Arianna feeding her doll tufts of bread, and asked what dish the bread was in.

It's black, he teased. Your doll will get ill.

The little girl wobbled over, trailing crumbs. He tipped the bread into his own saucer and gave her that instead.

This is beautiful, he said, holding up a small black dish. Old silver, very fine. Where's it from?

Mama turned it over in her hands. The silver saucer. The bird drank from it. How had she not remembered? Father ate sugar from it as a boy, Elvira filled it with water for years. So had she.

I must have carried it through everything, she said slowly.

You should polish it, Andonis said, but Mama ran her fingers over lines of leaves and flowers. Elvira touched these, she thought, and left the saucer in its tarnish. She placed it on her chest of drawers. When Arianna lost interest in the doll, she put the cage there too.

Mama went on embroidering, she made things comfortable

for the tourists and her family, but at night she descended into a darkness where Moumo, Father and Elvira floated like unshriven souls. The dead release their demons, she said to herself. She was living her life for Elvira. But which life? The nice one full of family, or the cave of guilt beneath?

New life and bitterness go together, she heard Elvira say. *Maror*, that was the word. Bitter leaves. The one Hebrew word that stayed when so many were lost.

44

Mama lies back on the pillow. I feel tension go out of her, she is giving so much, she has been so ill, she is so old.

'Why didn't you tell us about Elvira?' I say softly. 'Didn't you want her to go on living in our hearts?'

Mama has always had such power over me. That's why I had to get away when I was young. Sometimes I felt it stopped me doing things. Just now it is making me so sorry for her I can hardly breathe.

'I wanted to forget.'

'But you kept her things. Weren't you losing her a second time, not telling us?'

She says nothing. I kiss her, hold my cheek against hers, turn out the light, and go out to the silvery dark of the patio. I must wait for Nikos to bring the nurse. And for Papa.

There is light in the bungalow. Kelly and Doug must be packing. The moon is high in the sky like a frozen tear and bats sweep through the air in enviably smooth curved lines. I fix on one, imagining it a pencil tip, drawing on the night, and try to dig out my earliest memories. The goldfinch? Playing with the cage? No. Nothing. My memories are as elusive as those bats.

How close to truth are my visions of Elvira? She seems to me bright and out of reach, like gold falling through water. David would be devastated by her story. He adored being the father of a little girl. He was sweet with Katerina, always interested in her ideas.

I wish I'd known about Elvira when I was growing up. What she drew, how she drew, what painters she liked. She seems to have grown back to life in me, like seed from an ancient tomb. My name should be Elvira.

Well, in a way, it is. Ri was my baby name for myself, I've always known that. Now I know I called Elvira's bird that too. And also, that little bird gave its name to our home.

What you seek is what you are. I became what Elvira wanted to be. But in a lifetime of trying to see better, I never saw what was under my nose. Elvira has been with us all the time, in little moments of daily existence, whenever Mama dusted her bedroom or picked up a hairpin. She was in the singing bird on Papa's painted sign, *Rooms Karderini*. Maybe even the other sign he painted, for Vasilis. *Asterion Hotel.* The Minotaur, shimmering and dancing alone in the labyrinth. But at the heart of this labyrinth is a little girl.

A car pulls up by the gate and a shadowy figure comes through, teeters and nearly falls. I run to help. Papa says, 'Don't fuss me,' and stumps down to the front door.

'Your things are upstairs, Papa.'

'I am *not* sleeping up there.'

'It's only one night.'

'I'll sleep on the sofa in Reception.'

'It's too narrow. You'll roll off.'

He sways and I take his arm. He is shaky. He too has been through so much. I have never given that the weight it deserved.

'It won't help Mama,' I say gently, 'if you fall too. What if *you* had to go to hospital?'

Another car stops. Nikos comes down the slope with Bisera

and sees the problem at once. 'Come on, Papa, I'll take you up. Tomorrow, when the Americans leave, we'll move a bed from the bungalow into Reception.'

He takes Papa up the outside staircase and I escort Bisera in to Mama, who is fast asleep.

'Thank you, Kyria Bisera,' I whisper. 'Glad you're here. My mum really likes you.'

'She is nice lady. She is being well.'

'Thanks. Have a good night.'

'He fell asleep straight away,' Nikos tells me afterwards, laughing. 'He really had a skinful.'

'Fancy a drink yourself?'

'Love to, but we've got ants in the kitchen. They're swarming, I must help Loukia. I'm working early tomorrow.' He looks in my face. 'You OK?'

'Fine.' He hugs me and goes. The tourist season has started. I stand on the patio watching the red lights of his car, then walk up to my room.

Mama's guilt at surviving must be shot through with sisterly envy that would have shaken down fine if Elvira had lived. Maybe Mama was afraid the wrong sister did live. Then I appeared. And all the complicated things she felt about Elvira, this little girl who was *always drawing*, got burned into me like pokerwork. Maybe Mama felt I was Elvira's ghost. A revenant, a *vrikolax*, a drop of that unlamented blood which haunts the world.

I flick back, trying to see my childhood from this awful angle. Yes, there were times I did feel unrecognized, as if Mama was talking to someone else. I thought that was how all children felt. But also I clung to Papa. Then to painting, which Mama so didn't want me to do. Like Elvira who began drawing when she was ill, I turned to art when things outside hurt. Especially, now I come to think of it, any coldness from Mama.

But I did what Mama did, made my home inside a different shell. She did it in another faith, and by taking another name. I did it in a foreign language, and a foreign country. You don't realize you're copying your mother till you do. I'll have to learn to paint from a different self.

I can see Mama adored Elvira. But she was also jealous of the disabled child who enchanted everyone. Maybe she worries that even I, now I know about her, will love Elvira more.

That's another place where the labyrinth leads – Mama's shame, at her jealousy.

A homemade birdcage and a tarnished saucer are the only things she has left, from a family wiped off the map. They were gifts from her father and husband, but not to her – to Elvira. She has never believed that what she has is truly hers.

But I am.

45

The windowsill is wet from rain in the night. Farmers will like that, we need every drop we can get before the blast of summer. I do Katerina's exercises gazing into the pomegranate tree. In the dawn, its leaves are beginning to glow. They are shiny and dense, they will not let through one single heartbroken ray.

The sky is the shade of untreated wool with seed-pearls of mist. I hear a questioning cheep from a bird like a coin falling on a metal tray. Night scents are sinking back into dry earth. The mass of cloud above the sea has a red neon edge. Another bird calls with the underwater clucky sound of a marimba. Then an outcry of jackdaws, chinks of a stone skidding on ice. Morning is moving through the garden, pure and heavy as gold.

I think of Mama's memories sieving through her brain as she sleeps. And Papa, sleeping himself into a hangover next door.

The wifi wakes up and loads me with messages.

From my college, arranging teaching in the autumn. I love teaching but can't think about this now.

From Marcus. *Your mum's portrait going to a collector in America. Greek Embassy bought White Mountains. And congrats, St Ives bought Glass-Bottomed Boat.*

The money's useful. Great that people like the paintings and want to live with them. But I feel distant from them. My painting will have to catch up with – well, however I am learning to see now.

And from Katerina. *Gutted over Granny's sister, Mum, but have to stop thinking about this now. Yassim and I work till midnight every night on our project. He's great to work with. I've got a grant for equipment to film at Lemon Tree. Dora's asked us to teach film-making workshops there. Tell me what Granny says. Xxx*

Daughters need to live their own lives. She'll be pleased I'm doing the star-jumps.

I look in on Papa, deep asleep, making gentle animal whiffles. Horizontal, he looks even more worn, like a felled and dried-up tree.

Leila is off today, so while Bisera gets Mama up I make an early breakfast for the guests and take it out. Doug and Kelly are hefting suitcases onto the patio. The girls drag rucksacks to the table looking sulky and uncomfortable, jackets tied round their waists.

'Give that back.' The older one pushes Bonnie.

'Ruby!' says Kelly. Ruby looks angry and Bonnie triumphant.

Doug comes indoors with me and we wait for the wifi, for the credit card machine.

'We've had a great time,' he begins, then stares at Mama emerging from the bedroom on Bisera's arm like risen Aphrodite. It is a *grande dame* entrance, out of the dark, with the authority of a woman who has been a beauty all her life and still has that poise. Her dark almond-shaped eyes. Her snowy swept-up hair. She makes a perfectly ordinary blue cotton frock look stately. Her face is foxed ivory. Leonardo should have painted her, not me.

'It was lovely here, ma'am,' says Doug. 'We'll come back. Maybe hike, next time.'

'In summer, is swimming,' says Mama in English. She does not know *hike* but recognizes *come back*. She is delighted her hospitality has given pleasure.

Doug strides outside to pick up the bags, Bisera helps Mama to the patio, settles her on a chair, then goes off to find her bus.

Papa appears on the outside steps. He beams at the guests and hobbles down. No sign of a hangover. He didn't survive guerrilla life for nothing.

Kelly hugs Mama.

'Hope you get better, Sophia! It's been wonderful. Lovely to meet you, Ri, we'll look out for your paintings.'

'*Kalo taxidi*,' says Mama, and Ruby picks up her rucksack. But Bonnie has vanished. A rucksack and pink jacket lie abandoned on the ground.

'Where's that child got to?' says Doug.

In disdainful silence, Ruby points to branches waggling in the pomegranate tree. Bonnie wasn't going to depart without having a go.

'Bonnie,' Doug calls. 'Come down, hon. We've got to leave.' We hear a splintering sound. The leaves are so dense you can't see in. 'What are you *doing*?'

Silence, then a wild rustling. Kelly smiles at us. 'They say you've succeeded as a parent if you give your kids roots and wings.' She raises her voice. 'Bonnie! Come down, please. We'll miss the plane.'

Bonnie slithers to the ground clasping something to her chest.

'There's an old tree house in there. I found this in it.' She puts her trophy on a table and starts tearing at crumbly oilcloth.

'Gently,' says Kelly. 'It's stuck to something.'

'It's a book,' Bonnie says.

'Not a regular book,' says Ruby. 'A kid's schoolbook.'

Kelly looks over their shoulders. 'You should give that to Sophia.'

Bonnie picks up the book and hugs it to her chest. Everyone is silent. Then, like a promise she could break but won't, Bonnie walks over to Mama and plonks it in front of her. It does look like a school exercise book. Under the leaf-mould and cobwebs are flame-like zig-zags, red and green.

Papa takes a sudden breath. Cautiously, Mama brushes off dead leaves and a few ants.

'This book,' she says painfully in English, 'belong my sister.'

'Bonnie,' says Kelly, 'let Sophia keep it, please. It was her sister's. You're very clever to find it. She's really grateful.'

Bonnie looks on the verge of tears. Mama simply holds out her arms. After a second, Bonnie leans in to be kissed.

'Thank you,' Mama says in English. Her voice shakes and Kelly puts a hand on her shoulder.

'That's OK.' Bonnie is dying to look inside. 'Why was it there?'

Mama looks at me for help.

'We're amazed, Bonnie,' I say. 'This is an extraordinary moment for us. We can't thank you enough. Can I email you when we've looked at it? Send some pics?' Bonnie is beginning to look proud of her discovery. 'You see, doves used to live in that tree. When my mum's sister was little, she liked climbing trees too. She must have hidden this in it.'

In her teacher's garden. Where her sister, who hated coming here anyway and would never climb a tree, would never find it.

'What was her name?' says Bonnie. 'Why didn't she tell you it was there?'

'Elvira. She must have forgotten.'

A car honks. A butter-yellow taxi crunches into the yard. Doug scoops up Bonnie's rucksack.

'C'mon, girls. Gotta catch that plane.'

Kelly has realized how shocked we are. She hugs Mama close, then me. Bonnie opens the car door clutching her goat.

'Can't you pack that thing?' says Doug. 'Don't want to lose it on the journey.'

'He wants to come on the plane,' says Bonnie. 'He wants to see where he's going.' She bursts into tears.

Kelly smiles at us. 'She doesn't want to leave. None of us do. Good luck.'

'Thank you,' Mama says.

The taxi goes. We are left with our own stunned silence. I get a cloth from the kitchen. The notebook rests on our white plastic table. It has probably only ever touched wood or stone before. Did plastic even exist, in 1940s Crete? Mama stares as if it holds the Ark of the Covenant.

'She never let anyone else turn the pages. Just showed one at a time.'

Papa lifts the front cover. On the first page is a crayon drawing of a girl sitting in a recessed window, her back against a folded shutter. She looks like Katerina at fourteen, except for a high-buttoned blouse Katerina would have hated. She has long black hair and is holding embroidery.

'That's you,' Papa says gently to Mama. 'As I first saw you.'

A charcoal sketch of a woman under a high ceiling, beside a window with a lamp behind. She is chopping peppers, face in profile, coil of hair at her nape.

'Moumo,' whispers Mama. I hug her shoulders, put my cheek against her hair.

Here she is again. Kyria Simcha, my unknown granny, lighting two candles. In smudgy *chiaroscuro*, the artist has tried to suggest on her face a glow from below.

'*Shamor*, to protect,' says Mama. '*Zakhor*, to remember.'

A double page, covered in goldfinches. One pecks a rather wobbly thistle, another flies over a wooden bed. Then more sketches, scribbled out.

'She used to complain she was no good.'

'But she was. Very.' Every line is alive. The work is polished and raw at the same time, full of energy.

Now an old man's head. Bushy white eyebrows, bright blue eyes. 'Barba Rafael.'

A dark room in watercolour, books round the walls, red rugs and cushions. I recognize the door as the door to our kitchen. This must be Reception when it was Barba Rafael's study.

Now the head and shoulders of an African man, holding a dove.

'Tinu,' says Mama. 'Don't you remember?'

'No.' My throat is silted up.

A watercolour of fruit trees. In one corner, the sketch of a chain ending in a dragon's head. Then the girl again, laughing, and a man with tight receding curls, deep-set eyes, wrinkly lines around the mouth. All very carefully drawn, the pencil pressing hard.

'Father,' says Mama with a catch in her voice. 'And me.'

Turning pages as if afraid what she might find, she stops at a sketch of a bird's wing. The feathers are carefully crayoned in yellow and black. Somehow the contrast is rather shocking. Then a swimming turtle, lovely and confident, head and shell lifting out of the water. The legs paddle beneath, the head turns towards us with a broad smile and a wink. Elvira had wit too. Now the goldfinch cage on a window-ledge. Beyond, below, rather small, is the girl again, standing under an olive tree with a blade-thin boy. Elvira found the foreshortening difficult, she has rubbed bits out and done them again. I want to reach through the decades and say, Bravo, how about trying it like this?

On the next page, girl and boy are together in a street, drawn from above. Elvira must have been looking out of the front window. The two figures stare at each other, his hand on her cheek. She holds it there, gazing in his eyes.

'She knew,' whispers Mama. 'And never said.'

Below, Elvira has written in neat cursive Greek, *Sara has the life I'll never have.*

Mama makes a little moaning sound like a wounded dog. Papa puts his hand on her shoulder.

'Why?' she says in a small lost voice.

'Well . . .' Papa hesitates. 'You had everything. You were beautiful as an angel. She was crippled, wasn't pretty, couldn't dance . . .'

'She was *jealous* of me?'

'Of course.'

'But *I* was jealous of *her*. Father adored her. She was brilliant at Hebrew, he was so proud of that. And her art . . .'

293

'Didn't he praise your sewing? Wasn't your mother proud of you? She praised you all the time.'

'*You* loved Elvira too,' says Mama. 'Yes, you did! I used to worry you liked her more than me. You were always laughing with her.'

'I loved her *because she was your sister*! I longed for her to be really my sister.'

She gives a sob that is also a laugh. 'And you gave her the gold-finch. So – so *special.*'

'I told you, I did it to impress *you*. I thought you'd like me because I was kind to her. I was an idiot.' He turns a page rather quickly.

'Oh – the necklace Father gave me. I wonder where it is now.'

We gaze at an ethereal teenager, almost embarrassed at being so beautiful, smiling into the artist's eyes. Round her throat is a neck-lace of filigree flowers. The sheer love in the drawing, the touch of the pencil, overwhelms us. Underneath, Elvira has written, *Sara is fourteen today. She is the best older sister in the world.*

'She adored you,' says Papa.

'I didn't love her enough. Not as she deserved.'

'You did. She thought you were wonderful. You were.'

Mama turns more pages, touching the paper as if touching the psalms. Sketches of that thin boy, sawing, hammering, sorting nails. Little try-outs of his hands, arms, neck. And over and over, his face. Now smiling at the artist, now serious, intent on his work. Full face, three-quarters, profile. The back of his head. His ears, eyes and mouth.

I look at Papa. Muscle-shadows flinch round his mouth. I think of cloud-skeins in early autumn, when you shiver in what you thought was summer. It occurs to me Papa has no inner picture of himself. He just is. He doesn't think about others seeing him. That's how he protects himself from his effect on other people. These sketches must be a real shock.

Mama turns to a new sequence, red and black. Lots of black, lots of scribbles.

'What's this?'

'Planes bombing Chania,' says Papa. 'Look, the churches, the mosques, the harbour. That's how I saw the planes from Perivolia. Circling, smashing the city.'

'But *she* can't have seen them. We were indoors.'

'She must have looked out of the window.'

'She couldn't have seen *this*.'

'She imagined it,' I put in. 'She was an artist.'

More planes, giant black birds with fiery tails dropping eggs on mashed houses. Bricks and broken glass fountaining in all directions.

'But look.' Papa points to the corner where the goldfinch, very small, is flapping his wings. Feathers bright as egg yolk, beak open, challenging the aeroplane birds. 'He's fighting back.'

More whippy-tailed birds, but now with kind eyes. They swirl round the page and the little goldfinch flies with them, a flame on wings. Whatever they are, fire birds, birds of paradise, birds of jealousy, they have made friends, they are having fun.

'That goldfinch kept her going, Papa. In that awful time, it was a wonderful gift.'

I turn a few more pages, just to get a sense of what we'll find when we really look. Rows of military buckles. A store-room of jars. Wildflowers in a glass. She has focused on glints in the water, the spaces of the glass. She really was going to be an artist. A bronze door-knocker in the shape of a lion's head, and a column of German soldiers, seen from above marching up a street that is recognizably Kondylaki. Elvira has solved the perspective fine, but what a shock to see those uniforms and grim faces in that street. And a little girl was sitting up there, daring to draw them.

One more page. 'Thank God,' Mama whispers.

Elvira has drawn herself. Head and shoulders, short

feathery hair, huge eyes. A taut, bony face, smiling. All lit up and ready to laugh.

Surely, if Mama had known what to wish for, it would have been for this.

And We Have Been Here
Before But We Go On

46

I sit beside Mama, turning the pages. We all feel dazed. A gift has come from the underworld and we don't know how to talk about it. After a while I leave them alone with it, wash up breakfast, make coffee. Nikos comes to help move a bed from the bungalow for Papa. He's in a hurry, I fill him in as best I can and he promises to come tonight. I ring Irene and ask her to come too, with Vasilis. In siesta, when everyone is asleep, I take pictures of all the pages on my phone. The sketchbook must never be lost again. It should be in a museum.

That evening they all come, stare at the sketchbook and crowd around Mama. Everyone wants to touch her, hold her. She has tears in her eyes but her face looks soft as I've never seen it. The past has been private to her alone. Sacred, but untouchable. Now, with pictures in front of us, her lost world can be seen and talked about.

Next day, Leila climbs into the tree to photograph the nest boxes. She says they are a bit crumbly but intact, except where Bonnie splintered them.

'Tinu was a good carpenter,' Papa says, peering at Leila's screen.

Summer is on its way, we have a lot of bookings. We have curtained off a corner of Reception for Papa, who limps round the patio every morning, chats to increasing numbers of guests, advises in broken English on car rentals, sunburn, where to buy honey, how to get sea-urchin spines out of your foot. He also sneaks extra cigarettes with guests partial to a late-night raki.

But we have reached the point he has always refused to think about, when they can't hack it on their own, even with Leila coming in. Nikos and Loukia give up their house and move in, but it is full season, they are hardly here except at night. I sleep on the roof and help Leila with changing sheets, cleaning rooms, buying fruit and yogurt, and fifteen breakfasts every morning.

All this time, Mama is growing stronger, as if Elvira has given her new life. The sketchbook lives by her bed, I hear her discussing it with Bisera. Finally Papa moves back to the bedroom and we say goodbye to Bisera. I hug her. 'You were wonderful, Kyria. I'm sure we'll be calling on you again.'

She smiles. 'Is good, your mamma, the book she finds. From sister.'

One afternoon when Mama is resting, there is only one Swedish couple on the patio reading guidebooks and Papa is in Reception, I say, 'Papa, someone gave me a letter for you from Mr Michael. He wrote it, but never sent it. It was found among his things when he died.'

I bring it out. The blades of the fan rattle over our heads. He looks balefully at the handwritten Greek. 'What does it say?'

'He talks of being with you in the mountains. He saw your cousin Georgios die. Georgios stood up to shoot but the Germans shot first.'

'Can you read that bit to me?'

Afterwards, he says simply, *'Aman.'*

'Mr Michael also says it was his fault *you* got shot.'

'Why?'

I look at his white hair, millions of wrinkles, purple broken veins around his nose.

'It was in the south. He was asleep outside a cave. You woke him up and said there were enemies around. Then, he says, you ran down a hill and they shot you.'

'Nonsense. Why would I do that?'

'Did you ever think he fancied you?'

'Of course not. You don't know what you're talking about. Don't read me any more.'

'Mr Michael gave me my lute,' says Nikos that evening, slumped in the kitchen after a long day at sea.

'Didn't you ever think ...'

'So what? He was a good man.'

The town gets hotter, fuller, noisier. These summer months are an endurance test. One couple rents a car and crashes it. Others lose their bank cards and, briefly, their children. There are sprained ankles, broken arms. The *meltemi* arrives, the wild north-westerly wind we all dread. Some years it blows strong in the afternoon but dies down at night. This year it blows six days and nights without a break, whistling through town, stripping the fruit trees, tormenting shepherds on the uplands, farmers in the fields, and our tourists. No beach, no dining by the harbour. You can't go out, awnings blow away in an instant.

Then it drops, but the heat is over 40. Even at midnight, cups in the cupboards are as hot as if they have been in a dishwasher. We don't have air conditioning, only fans, they are always on and electricity bills shoot up.

But after the *meltemi*, the afternoons are all still, and all mine. I enjoy working through the surreal siesta. So far, I've only drawn, and the paints have stayed in the bottom drawer. But one morning I get up on the chair and reach to the top of the wardrobe. Pushed far back, as I left them, are a folding stool, a bottle of turps and a portable easel. They are thick with dust and I wipe them down. The fabric on the stool is stiff but OK. I check my brushes, find the bundle of charcoal. At noon, after the breakfasts and washing, I pack everything into a rucksack and take it to the bus stop.

301

In Asterion Hotel, Irene takes me to their ground-floor bedroom. I am surprised and touched by it. Vasilis puts on such a show in public, but the room they live in is a small bare cell. The window doesn't look at the sea, the only things on the wall are a crucifix twined with plastic flowers and a tourist poster of Knossos. So this is where they sleep, ready to leap out and help guests at any moment. Their one luxury is air conditioning.

'I'll give you a key, *agape mou*,' Irene says. 'Lie here if you want to rest. Keep your things here. They'll be quite safe.' She unlocks a little dressing-room, a cupboard really, with metal shelves full of boxes, an ironing-board and a small table with a laptop and a plate covered in lacy cloth. She lifts the cloth to show *kourabiedes*, almond biscuits coated with sugar. 'In case you're hungry. I know you love them.'

'Irene! Thank you. No one is ever hungry when you're around. But will you mind the smell? Oil paint takes ages to dry, and maybe I'll work here a bit too. You can't work in the sun all the time.'

'We're so exhausted when we get to bed, we won't notice any smell.'

She gives me the key and goes. I take a biscuit and carry everything out of that lovely cool into the furnace of afternoon. Instantly there's a mist of sweat on my face and sweat pouring between my breasts. I walk up the coast, the sea dazzling away beside me, to find the right place.

Maybe here, these pine trees near the cliff edge, surrounded by scents of resin and the buzz of cicadas, where the swing of the bay on the left balances the headland on the right. Where whatever it is I want to say, about Crete, about Mama, about all of us, might possibly come through. If I'm lucky. I set up the easel, making sure the legs are even.

When I start a new work, I have to feel open and unknowing, so what the painting needs will come to me freely. Picasso said it was like jumping off into space. For me, it's like being a door. You wait, and hope something will enter.

The canvas floats in front of me, daunting but familiar. A pure, clean, beginning-again. I get out the charcoal. Pencil has been with me all this time but pencil shows through oil paint. Charcoal, the burnt stuff, stuff you can smudge, will take me into colour.

I don't usually draw on canvas anyway. Sometimes I draw with a thin brush in turps solution and a little pigment. But I haven't touched a brush since Nashita said that word *withheld*. Not since I've discovered I'm a different person from the one I knew to be. And that our lives have been lived over a black hole. Not since I've learned what this sparkling sea conceals.

I draw a swift line on the left. The curve of the bay. I love the feel of charcoal. The soft friction of it on primed canvas. Why haven't I been using charcoal all along?

Now I have to find the central space from which everything will radiate. A space to trust, an area of stillness that lets me realize the rest. Where I can – well, the way I put it to myself is, where I can tell the truth. Whatever that is. Once I've got that, I can play with form, light, colour, shadow, the whole circus, and go forward.

But the heart of it mustn't come too easy. A line on the right, for the looping hug of the headland. Too far in, it doesn't have the vigour I want. I smudge it out, draw another. Now the cross line of the horizon between. Below that, three small islands.

Gradually the shapes open up to me. In the right-hand top corner, I add a few lines for the shaggy branch above me. The pine tree's contribution.

I take the top off Cobalt Blue. The smell joins the hot wafts of pine needle and brings a sense of return. This is who I am. This is how to let the mud settle, so I can see.

The bit of sea near the shore is a jigsaw puzzle, crystal blue with a curious light-giving quality, slabbed with giraffe-like blotches of deep turquoise, each blotch a different shape. Crazy blue paving,

303

edged in luminous jade. Beyond that are gently rocking peacock eyes, deep calm emerald, each with its own black under-triangle.

A friend of mine once said he didn't feel a colour was real unless there was black in it. That's always true in Crete. As I mix colours, and feel the rhythm of the brush on canvas, I begin to feel black everywhere, like spilled ink. Below the silky vitality of blue, glowing like the skin of some fabulous animal, are these eternal dabs of black. Below the dazzle is the heart.

By seven, when the long shadows come, it has settled. Working in the sun all day, like the Impressionists, you become part of the place and it becomes part of you. One Monet study of a beach has sand in its paint, blown on the wet surface of the canvas as he worked. I feel these colours have blown into me, along with the heat.

In the hotel bedroom, I hear someone in the shower, so I go off into the little boxy side-room, open the easel there and set the painting on it. We look at each other a minute. Then I leave it for the night and lock the door.

Vasilis comes out of the shower with a towel round him, rubbing his hair. Smudges of black come off on the top towel. Something in that, or maybe seeing his enormous naked shoulders and pelt of wiry chest hair, white now but still curly as a sheepdog, makes me ask, 'Vasilaki, when we were growing up, how did you feel about Mr Michael? Did you ever think—'

'Of course! That's why we wouldn't play cricket with him.'

'You played football with him.'

'That's different.'

'Why?'

'Cricket's an English game.'

What a lot I could have seen, and didn't. At work, I look for the strangeness in what I know, and try to paint that. But I haven't done that in life, have I? Nor in my family.

Now I am obsessed. At noon, after helping with breakfast, rooms and guests' problems, I take the bus, crowded with Cretans going about their lives and foreigners with beach gear and rucksacks. In the hotel, I pick up the easel, stool and paints, take a couple of biscuits, and set up under the pine tree.

Gradually, the streaky muscle of each wave, the shape-shifting lines of the currents, violet, emerald, indigo, feel more and more sinister as well as beautiful. This sea drowned Mama's family, the family I never knew. I look at blue and see black.

The bay is dotted with swimmers and sunbathers. Sometimes a motorboat or yacht. I leave them all out. But looking at it just before it's finished, when I get it back to indoor light, I know what it needs. Next day I add three very small, very distant figures on the headland.

Finally, I rest my hand on the bark of the tree and look at it in situ one last time. I hardly have anything to do with it now. It's not a question of what I've made but what it is.

The hotel bedroom is empty. This hour, just before evening, is busiest of all. People wake from siesta and want coffee, or drinks for twenty-five on the terrace. I prop the painting on the easel.

Portrait of a Summer Sea. Not a big canvas, thirty by twenty inches. Just an empty bay. But something in it feels immensely sad. Rembrandt said a painting is complete when it has shadows of a god. The colours here vibrate but every ripple has a grin of dark. Even the cloudless sky has black in it. Cretan black, the black of knives, the black of loss. Like the song Nikos sings. *Heavy as iron are the black clothes I wear for people I loved.*

I've painted a memorial.

I feel a pang at parting with it, but I did it for Vasilis and maybe it wouldn't have worked if I hadn't. I move the easel into the bedroom and leave it there.

Early next morning, I find a text from Irene. *What HAVE you done, paidi mou??? We got to bed at 3, Vasilis saw it and burst into tears. He adores it. Thank you, thank you xxxxx*

Then from Vasilis. *Thanks, Rioula mou. Beautiful. But you haven't signed it.*

Forgot, I text back. *I'll come tonight.*

I have a drink with them that evening. The strings of lights loop beside us on their terrace, the black sea rustles behind. I bring a brush and tube of citron, rest the painting flat on the table and initial it, very small, bottom right. *AG.* The letters float over a dark bit of sea.

'Will you come to the Memorial Service next week,' I ask Vasilis, 'in the synagogue?'

'*Synagogue?* Where? Why?'

'It's the anniversary of the day that ship went down. They hold it every year.'

'We can't get away,' he says at once. Irene looks at the painting and says nothing.

Mama won't come either. Wouldn't she like to see the synagogue, meet the people? She shakes her head, and Papa stays with her. So on a warm June evening, against a sky as clear and pale as primroses, Nikos and Loukia come with me through that door in the wall.

We step down into the little cobbled courtyard. To my surprise, it is full of people. The girl here said people who come to their weekly service are from many different faiths, but it still is a real Jewish service. Throughout the year, Jewish expatriates who live on Crete come often, and Jewish tourists drop in. For big festivals, people come from Europe and America. But tonight is different. Most of these people are local. Nikos and Loukia smile at people they recognize. Twilight falls, and we go into the building. People at the door hand skullcaps to the men and give us all a service booklet in English, Greek and Hebrew. *Askava*, it says. *For the Jewish Community of Crete.*

We find seats on a bench. The place is packed, lit by an extraordinary chandelier I didn't notice last time, a horizontal rim of iron whose inner struts are a six-point star. At each point hangs a lamp of white glass, blazing down on huge ostrich eggs the colour of raw wool. The bulbs shed a little mantle of extra light on the top of each egg, just the bit you'd slice off if you were going to eat it.

The doors stay open, cats wander in and out, latecomers crowd by the door. Suddenly the glossy black moustache of Vasilis appears among them. And beside him, the top of Irene's head. 'She made him come,' whispers Loukia.

I have been in synagogues before but Nikos and Loukia haven't. They watch what other people do. We don't need to do much, just follow Hebrew prayers in Greek. *Shield us from the stroke of the enemy. From pestilence, sword, affliction, evil, famine, sorrow, destruction and plague.*

Then everyone begins to speak, like a forest rustling in sudden wind, reading out names in the back of the booklet. The names of everybody taken from their homes here, imprisoned, then drowned. We hear *Trevezas, Mois, silver-worker. Trevezas, Simcha, housewife. Trevezas, Sara, student. Trevezas, Elvira, student.*

Nikos takes my hand. It now seems mad we never knew Mama's name. One of those things that happens in a family, the secret you don't realize you are keeping. Let out of the bag by a heart event.

'They must take her name off that list,' Nikos whispers. Over heads of the crowd I see tears running down Vasilis's face.

Then silence. The rustling anguished silence of a hundred people. Finally they recite *kaddish*. The Hebrew speakers say it properly, the rest of us follow the translation in silence. One way or another, Mama has been having it said for her all this time.

The packed crowd loosens. People start lighting tea-lights, one for every name. We join in, placing them round the synagogue,

307

in the courtyard, the olive tree, the *mikveh* and back garden, on the rabbis' graves. Nearly three hundred candles, alight and alive in the dark.

Back home, Papa is on the patio, cigarette in one hand, *komboloi* in the other, chatting to a Danish couple. Indoors, Mama is watching TV. She looks up nervously as we come in with our eyes full of the night.

'It was beautiful, Sophia,' says Loukia. 'It's a wonderful place. You'd love it.' She shows Mama the booklet, the service. Mama lingers over the Hebrew prayers. And then the names. It is a hot evening, I go to the kitchen to get chilled water from the fridge and when I come out Mama is crying. They are hugging her.

'Maybe we'll go there one day, Mama?'

'Maybe.'

I wash the glasses and leave them upside down on the draining-board.

In July, Katerina comes from New York with her Lebanese colleague Yassim, who turns out to be her boyfriend too. They are going to run film-making workshops with the Syrians at the Lemon Tree in Greek and Arabic. Yassim gets out of the cab after Katerina, a tall dark boy with faun eyes and a shy smile. They walk down to the patio and I remember bringing David here for the first time, long ago.

I wish you were here to be happy for her, I tell him in my head.

Yassim turns out to be Palestinian. His grandparents fled to Lebanon in 1946, he went to the American University in Beirut where many of my Greek friends went, he feels like family already. Katerina is proud of him, maybe of us too. But watchful.

'You look good, Mum,' she says when we hug. 'Fitter. Are you doing the exercises?'

'Of course.'

Mama does not light candles but Papa brings out his tangerine-coloured wine and everyone laughs. Yassim does not even blink at the taste and they look at the sketchbook, they hear Elvira's story. Mama is used to telling it now. Katerina's rage at being lied to has vanished. Yassim looks at Elvira's drawings of the goldfinch, the bombs, the soldiers marching down Kondylaki Street. He looks up shyly and says something in Arabic.

'What's that?'

'*Singing in a cage is possible, and so is happiness,*' he says in English.

Katerina translates for Granny.

'Our national poet,' Yassim says. 'It is a poem about a canary – and our own occupation.'

When she understands, Mama takes his hand. Arabic is now part of our family.

47

In September I go back to London, teach my one-term-a-year art course, live off fruit from the Afghan grocers and organize an Indian visa, tickets, vaccinations. I find people to rent the house while I am in Mumbai and agree a date with Sanjiv. 31st January, as soon as I finish marking exams. The day Britain will leave the EU.

I also spend a long time putting this house in Katerina's name. It's been my home for thirty-five years, but the era of trusting Britain to look after incomers, as David's family always did, seems to have gone. Katerina was born and grew up here, she has a British passport.

As the nights draw in, I go to Muswell Hill synagogue, trying to work out what I feel about my new heritage, but don't feel any connection. I loved Seder with David's family, but there I was a guest. Maybe I will feel more Jewish in Crete. Next time I'm there, I'll go to a service in the synagogue where my granny used to polish the benches with lavender oil.

I don't paint, yet, but I print out my photos of Elvira's sketchbook and pin them round the studio. I want her talent to ring out to everyone. Maybe we can put on an exhibition of her drawings, this child who might have become an artist for Greece to be proud of. I look so closely at the rooms she drew that her house feels almost more real to me than mine. It is much older. It has high ceilings with heavy wood beams, as if Cretan forests are marching in to guard the inhabitants, although the hall roof I remember seeing, among those racks of Indian clothes, was vaulted stone like the cloister of a church.

I scrutinize her father's anxious face. And Kyria Simcha, so like Mama but with some flavour of Katerina and me. Her brows are black feathers, downy at the inner ends. And, most of all, Elvira's wide mouth, owl eyes and hollow cheeks. I suppose everyone was very thin then, they were living through near-famine as well as an occupation. But her bones are like sandalwood fretwork. I'd like to paint her but that feels almost taboo. To find a way forward I start researching Indian miniatures. Didn't they inspire Amrita? The portraits have tiny background landscapes, little backdrops to the sitters' lives. I'd put in Elvira's gold-feathered bird. And the mountains she loved but never climbed.

The miniatures are ivory. I'd use Cretan olive wood. A very fine brush, almost a single hair. I'd want her face to glow. And her parents too. Faces of the dead, alive.

I WhatsApp Nashita. *Anyone doing this kind of work in India now? Using miniature portraits to make contemporary art?*

In Rajasthan they are, she replies. *One guy, grandson of a famous master in the Rajasthani miniature tradition, has painted his way into very interesting new work. He has a patron here. You can meet him. I'll set it up.*

I also keep thinking about that glance you feel, but do not see. The gift of someone looking at you from the dark, with understanding. I have no idea how this fits into what has happened, or where I want my work to go now, but I'm interested in exploring how one person is transformed by another, or brings goodness to someone else. No more withholding.

I love Elvira's winking turtle too. Maybe the gaiety and energy of her work will release Mama from darkness she has carried all her life.

*

311

Two days to go. Nearly packed. This evening I'll do the online check-in. In the studio, in fading winter light, I wrap some brushes in newspaper and notice idly, as you do, that two men in Rome have caught pneumonia in some far-off Chinese province. I take Elvira's drawings off the wall and pack them. I'm shivering, it's late January, I'm in two thick jumpers.

David's photo, should I take that? Do I really want to leave the safety of this room, his room once, for unknown Mumbai? But this house, this country are no longer mine.

The phone buzzes in the back pocket of my jeans.

'Ri! Papa's in intensive care! He has emphysema. They say it's severe. He nearly died. I know you are due to go to India but—'

'I'll come, Nikos. Now. How's Mama?'

'Terrified. Loukia's with her, I'm at the hospital. Fifth floor, this time.'

Oh man, writes Nashita. *I'd set up a welcome party, all the great and good of the art scene here. But of course you must go to your dad. oy veh. Shall I ask them for a month's time?*

I am so sorry, writes Sanjiv. *Of course defer a month. I hope your father recovers.*

Two days later I'm staring at Papa through a glass door with Nikos's arm round me. Papa is asleep on his back, white tape round his head, a jointed silver arm reaching out from a computer to clamp a plastic valve on his nose. From a bag behind, liquid trickles into a vein in his elbow. His arms are bare. The shaggy hairs on them are whitey-grey. When I was little, they were black and I loved rubbing my cheek against them. His eyelids twitch occasionally but stay closed. With that beaky nose, he looks like a cormorant peering up out of a cage.

I burst into tears. He doesn't know we're here. 'Where are his *komboloi*?'

312

'I've got them! Don't worry, Ri, if this treatment works, he can live with the disease. They can't repair the damage to his air sacs, but can stop it getting worse with breathing exercises. And no more fucking cigarettes.'

We wait a week to see if it does work. The air is very cold, the clouds are heavy and low with rough edges like unworked silver. The harbour water is wild, slopping the walkway, spraying over the headland. At home I draw, study Elvira's sketches and read a book on Indian painting. I put off my ticket to India a second time.

We have one guest in the bungalow, Klaus, a German doctor on sabbatical to write a book about his grandfather who was a soldier here in the war. Klaus has a wrinkly kind brown face. He is learning Greek and has been drinking lemon raki with Papa, chatting about the occupation. With Papa away, he practises his Greek on me. Under the gaze of the Knossos bull, he shows me photos on his phone of the German War Cemetery.

'Very well kept,' he says in careful Greek. 'Look at the beautiful views. Many graves. And flowers. Beautiful.' He scrolls through pictures of grey stone slabs set in a gentle slope above the sea. The names are in large whitey-gold capitals.

'*Gefreiter Walter Stutz,*' I read out. '*26.12.20 to 20.5.1941. Ein Unbekennter Deutscher Soldat.* Is that "an unknown soldier"?'

'Yes,' he says after a moment.

'Twenty-one. *Gefreiter?*'

'Private.'

That boy could be one of the men Papa killed. Seems incredible now.

Klaus studies Greek newspapers carefully. One day, he asks about a word I've never seen. 'How do you translate that, please?'

'*Koroniós?* I don't know that word. Seems to be the name of a disease.'

By next morning we all know. *Koroniós* is slaughtering our neighbours in Italy.

Papa comes out of intensive care into a ward, and we take Mama to see him. His white stubble is frosted lichen round the plastic line under his nose, but his eyes twinkle.

'What are *you* doing here?' he teases. 'When will they let me home? You can't run that place without me. What about Klaus?'

'We're getting on fine,' says Nikos. 'Klaus doesn't drink so much without you. He says he writes better in the mornings.'

'But he misses your stories,' I say. 'You'd better get well quick.'

Sanjiv's studio is waiting in Mumbai. Once Papa is home, I can go. As Nikos drives us back, I ask Mama, 'Shall we take you to see the synagogue?'

She looks out of the window at burly silver clouds and the shifting skin of the sea. She shakes her head.

'Can I ring them, then? Invite that girl over? She'd love to see Elvira's sketches. They are serious people, Mama, nice people. They're making friends for the synagogue in the town. Last autumn, they invited the ambassadors of Germany and Austria to a memorial. They came, they were both women, they were warm and genuine, they made wonderful speeches of . . . well, apology. It's a place of real feeling. Catholics and Orthodox also go to services there. You'd fit right in. Please let's ask her over for coffee.'

'Maybe.'

'When? I'm going to Mumbai soon.'

'When?'

'Next week. Mama, I hate to say this but, but when you do die, which won't be for ages, do you want a funeral in the church or in the synagogue?'

We are passing the fortification walls, angled against the sea.

'The church,' she says finally. 'But . . .'

'Yes?'

'Can they say *kaddish* for me at the synagogue?'

Two days later, we bring Papa home. A moist west wind is blowing and the White Mountains sparkle. In fields round the hospital are lacy fronds of fennel and asphodel. Papa has a plastic tube under his nose attached to a machine in a bag he carries over his shoulder.

'It runs on battery,' he says proudly. 'It lasts twelve hours. You plug it in anywhere.'

We get him into Reception. He will sleep here again a while, in a curtained-off corner of Reception, so he does not disturb Mama. The hospital advised night care so I've left a message for Bisera. I plug in his oxygen line. Klaus shakes Papa's hand and says in growly Greek, 'Welcome home.'

'We'll have a *tsipouro* tonight, my friend,' says Papa slowly. He is expert at speaking to foreigners learning Greek. 'You can tell me where your grandpa is now.' He laughs, he can laugh fine with a tube under his nose. All he needs now is a cigarette and a raki.

'I am going home to Berlin,' says Klaus. 'Someone is ill in Salonica. *Koroniós* has come to Greece.'

Leila holds the machine for him to put in his PIN while the rest of us stare. He planned to stay three months. Has he cancelled his long-yearned-for writing holiday on Crete just because someone is sick miles away in Salonica?

'Three people in Greece have it now. I must go home.'

That night, TV says the government has cancelled carnival. They may close restaurants and schools. The tourist season may not happen.

'How would tourists get here anyway?' said Vasilis gloomily when he calls. 'Queue two metres apart to check in? Sunbathe two metres apart on the beach? What sort of holiday is that? It will be even worse than five years ago, when they closed the banks.'

Irene is growing courgettes in his infinity pool.

48

Early morning. I am starting a new painting, straight to colour, of the tree that kept Elvira's secret. The dense branches, oscillating gently in a dawn breeze, feel like the shaggy pelt of some huge green animal shaking itself in slow motion.

It is covered in cornet-like buds with crimson tips like sharp red pencils. A few have already unfolded and the flowers are out. Scarlet, flaring, almost blowsy, which shows you should never judge by first impressions because the pomegranate is a healing plant. The Minoans loved painting it. I remember a pot with a pomegranate Papa pieced together. And twenty years ago, the Millennium Festival of Medicine took it as its logo.

We could do with a healing plant. This is April, the wild explosive Cretan spring you can't ignore, but also 2020 and a pandemic is rampaging across the world.

We never thought, in our generation, to see what my parents saw, what those squatters saw in the ruins at Knossos – how quickly life can fall apart. People are saying we'll never live normally again. This is a very clever virus. It came from a cave and spread across the globe at the speed of human breath. When I rang Bisera a second time, someone else answered. She has died. Someone she was looking after had come to Crete from Italy and hadn't said.

She was probably sending money to her mother in Bulgaria. Whoever has her phone has wiped the contacts, but when we get out of lockdown I'll track down her mother and see if there's any money due. No one knows where she was buried, and putting flowers on graves is not one of the six legal reasons to leave home, but I'd like to see where she lived, the orange and lemon trees she loved.

For now, we can go only two kilometres from home. To shop, I download an SMS form, fill it in and keep it on my phone with my ID. We're very lucky to have land. Nikos, Loukia and I are planting vegetables, turning the garden back to what it was in the hard times, when Barba Rafael lived here before the war, and when our parents were struggling after it.

I should have loved, really loved, to go to Mumbai. It was something precious to me and I've lost it. But billions of people across the planet are losing worse things every second. I worry about Katerina among the mass graves of New York. She is with Yassim, they are being careful, but when will I hug her again? On Facetime, on the screen behind her head, I see a window and an empty parking lot. When the wifi works, we do Zoom. We are lucky we can be together in this new way. But is this new way for ever, like the destruction of Minoan Crete? No Zoom for survivors of that world. Nor for my mum in the war.

At least now I know where I belong. Crisis clarifies. Lockdown makes you see new things. I do love England, London especially, and I'm grateful for my life there, but this is my home, my bedrock. Some evenings, Nikos plays his lute and Papa even swaps *manti-nades* with him, though he still has that plastic line under his nose and is short of breath. His face looks so translucent, I feel he can't last long, but one night he sings cheekily to Nikos,

'When you get coronavirus, you can't smell or taste a thing,

'But you can drink, you smoke, you look at the girls and sing.

'Photis sang it to me down the phone,' he says when we laugh.

Nikos sings the old songs, but also a Greek internet hit about lockdown, a YouTube sensation by eight Cretan musicians raising money for hospital workers. They put it together from their separate homes and it went viral.

Who would expect in springtime
to see no doors open for a thirsty stranger?
Who would expect in springtime
to see no children pick flowers in the field?

The way Nikos plays it, the sound of the strings, run of the notes, the rhythms – all of it says Crete Crete Crete and brings tears to our eyes.

At six every evening, like everyone in Greece, we turn on the TV to see two quiet men sitting several metres apart, a soft-spoken professor of infectious diseases who reminds me of Mama's doctor in hospital, and a civil defence minister. They tell us calmly what is happening and we do what they say. The hashtag is *Menoume spiti*, westayhome.

We have a very low death rate, very few deaths. I'm sad Bisera was among them.

But the British news I get on my phone sounds angry and confused. There, the government's watchwords to the public are commands. *Stay home. Stay alert.* What use is *stay alert*? They have the highest death rate in Europe.

Here, politics can be violent but we are always communal and have never believed we were immune. We live in earthquake country, we know anything can get you. Enemies, empires, spirits of the air. Maybe the Evil Eye and certainly the *meltemi*. We know we need protection. God's word at your door, a smoke cross at Easter, a sword of healing in the mosque. Keep a goldfinch against plague, break a pomegranate on your doorstep at New Year. Use a face mask. Do as the doctor says.

The light is growing stronger. So are the shadows, can't have one

318

without the other. This is where the new work has to come from. The labyrinth of your own backyard.

These leaves are a thousand shades of green, each flecked with its own streak of light. I am using emerald and violet but also sulphur, lemon, primrose, ivory. The sun is touching every leaf, as life touches all of us, in different ways. I'll put the White Mountains behind the tree. Somewhere in the leaves, I'll put a goldfinch with a tiny scarlet face.

I owe you the truth in painting, said Cézanne, and I will tell it to you.

In the evening, while Papa is on the patio with his *komboloi*, drawing out his one raki of the day, I put cumin in the mince while Mama watches, ready to pounce if I get the spices wrong.

'I'm going to paint three small portraits, Mama. Your parents and Elvira. Like little ikons. I'll use her drawings. OK with you?'

She looks wary.

'We could hang them here, on the kitchen wall. Wouldn't it be nice to have them around? Their faces?'

'Could you do that?'

'I can try.'

ACKNOWLEDGEMENTS

This book is dedicated to the memory of Nikos Stavroulakis, who rescued Etz Hayyim Synagogue in Chania, rededicated it as a working synagogue and established a research centre there. I am deeply indebted to everyone I met at and through the synagogue, over the last thirteen years, for information and for their friendship. I have tried to make my fictional account of the Cretan Jews' last years as accurate as possible according to research conducted and collected there, and also by local historians drawing on oral memory and newspaper archives, by the Maritime Museum of Chania and by the Historical Museum of Crete in Heraklion.

Sara's story, and my account of the arrest, is loosely based on two true stories. First, Victoria Fermon, who escaped to the mountains with a non-Jewish boyfriend. Unfortunately he died of pneumonia and she came back alone to a broken life. I am very grateful to Chania photographer Manoussos Daskalogiannis for sharing memories of her when he was a boy. She spent her last years in his mother's house. Secondly, the story of Sara and Ioudita Kounio, two young sisters who drowned on the *Tanais*, told by Nikos Stavroulakis in *The Jews of Crete II 1900–1944*, published in 2002 by Etz Hayyim Synagogue with a photo of them and eyewitness account of the arrest by a non-Jewish schoolfriend. My characters Amos and Immanuel are based on two cousins whose descendants both visited Etz Hayyim, separately, within the same week.

A few other Cretan Jews survived. Cretans who helped them have been honoured three times by Yad Vashem's title of Righteous Among the Nations. The title was awarded first in December 1972 to the Petrakis family, Manolis and Antigoni Petraki from Hania. Manolis, already dead by 1972, saved the life of Iossif Konen, one of the few Hania survivors. In January 1999 the title was awarded to the Xirouhakis and Paitakis families from Kastelli Kissamos, and in October 2018 to Athina Varvataki, a young woman who saved the life of the poet Iosiff Ventura, then a toddler. All were private citizens.

Until May 1944, German command merely gave orders intended to cripple Jewish daily life. The deportation, a month after the kidnapping of German commander General Kreipe, seems to have been almost an afterthought to the huge earlier deportations from Salonica and Athens. A photo from spring 1944 discovered by Manolis Manousakas, a Chania optician who collects historical photographs, shows Rabbi Osmos with German officers at the German consul's funeral. This suggests that even two months before the arrest, he felt secure with them, and that most people in the Jewish community were unaware of impending danger.

But at the synagogue I also met Kostas Papadopoulos, born in 1942, who survived because his mother *was* aware. I based my character Kyria Sezana, whom we never actually meet, on her story.

While studying art history in Berlin, she apparently witnessed Kristallnacht and returned immediately to Heraklion. She married a non-Jew, and when the Germans came they hid in a village. The baby, Kostas, was born in hiding in 1942. They all survived. Continuing his mother's art history tradition, Kostas later ran an upmarket antique shop in Heraklion. Living there writing my first book, I used to look longingly in the window, never dreaming I would one day meet the proprietor and hear his history.

I left out one detail from what we know happened after the arrest. The Jews were imprisoned a second time, in Heraklion, in a bastion of the old city wall where the Germans held Cretan prisoners in 1943, before sending them to Mauthausen concentration camp. In June 1944, they held the Cretan Jews there a few days before embarking them on the *Tanais*.

Heartfelt thanks to the place and people at the heart of the story, above all Nikos Stavroulakis for his gift of friendship, his stories, memories and erudition. Even his cookbooks are works of art and history.

Also warm thanks to people taking forward his vision for the synagogue and research archive, above all historian Anja Zückmantel, Etz Hayyim's Administrative Director, who has advised and helped me with so much: I cannot thank her enough. Also to former President of the Etz Hayyim Board Marianna Vinther, and to the Trustees of Etz Hayyim and members of the Havurah, the community around the synagogue, both Cretan and international. Especially Nicholas de Lange who officiates as rabbi there, brought me back to west Crete after many years focusing on the Heraklion area, and has given such generous encouragement as well as helpful comments.

Many thanks also to Cheli Duran, for sharing with me a vivid fragment of an unpublished diary by Heraklion artist Thomas Fanourakis, who was drafted to Chania for clearance work in 1941, after the Germans arrived.

Further back, thanks to archaeologists from the British School at Athens, especially Peter Warren and Gerald Cadogan, who by inviting me to Crete and into the trenches opened up for me and my family a lifelong relationship with Crete. Many thanks to the people I worked with on excavations at Knossos, who told stories of the occupation and taught me dances, songs and *mantinades*, especially Nikos Daskalakis and his family.

Thanks to Cretan musicians Nikos Stratakis, Antonis and Nikos Xylouris, Andreas Manolarakis, Antonis Martsakis, Giorgos Stratakis, Dimitris Spyridakis and Costas Saridakis for their lockdown hit song 'Who would expect in springtime', sung to raise funds to buy nursing supplies for Thoracic Diseases Hospital SOTIRIA; and to a recent *mantinada* quoted in an article by Yannis Samatas (sponsored by Aerakis Seistron Music) on www.explorecrete.com/cretan-music/mantinades.html, a lovely reminder of how endlessly fertile the *mantinada* tradition is.

Outside Crete, warm thanks to painters and artists from whom I have learned over the years, and who commented on passages when I asked if they rang true – Phyllida Barlow, Helen Ganly, Catherine Goodman, Nicola Lane, Gieve Patel and Fabian Peake. Also to Syrian artist Issam Kourbaj, from whom I learn so much when we work together, Nancy Adajania and Ranjit Hoskote, and art historians, critics and writers in Mumbai. Also to artist Jeff Clarke for his 2020 exhibition *Chiaroscuro* (Carey Blyth Gallery, Oxford), reprising work he did when we were both working at Knossos and he was drawing Cretan shadows as well as Minoan finds.

Many warm thanks to Kerin Hope for decades of advice, knowledge, stories, comments and support, and to Rupert and Elizabeth Nabarro for years of generous hospitality in their flat over Chania harbour, the most beautiful place anyone could ever write in. Thanks also for reading and comments to Daphne Astor, Gwen Burnyeat, Jane Davies, Elaine Feinstein, Andrei Gomez-Suarez, Eva Hoffman, Aamer Hussein, Angelika Klammer, Benjamin Wood and my agent Robert Kirby who has seen this so patiently through so many drafts.

Many thanks also my inspired editor James Gurbutt, Olivia Hutchings and copy-editor Tamsin Shelton and all at Corsair for making this such a beautiful book.. And finally, though not at all least, to Gwen and Andrei in lockdown.

The lines from George Seferis, 'Thrush', written in 1946, are my own translation.

Many thanks to Not-for-Profit Corporation Etz Hayyim for permission to use the sketch of a tree by Nikos Stavroulakis and to Marianne Vinther for finding it among his papers.